Lynne Graham was born in Northern Ireland and has been a keen romance reader since her teens. She is very happily married, to an understanding husband who has learned to cook since she started to write! Her five children keep her on her toes. She has a very large dog, which knocks everything over, a very small terrier, which barks a lot, and two cats. When time allows, Lynne is a keen gardener.

Michelle Smart's love affair with books started when she was a baby and would cuddle them in her cot. A voracious reader of all genres, she found her love of romance established when she stumbled across her first Mills & Boon book at the age of twelve. She's been reading them—and writing them—ever since. Michelle lives in Northamptonshire, England, with her husband and two young Smarties.

THE ITALIAN'S BRIDE WORTH BILLIONS

LYNNE GRAHAM

RULES OF THEIR ROYAL WEDDING NIGHT

MICHELLE SMART

MILLS & BOON

First published in Great Britain 2022
by Mills & Boon, an imprint of HarperCollins*Publishers* Ltd,
1 London Bridge Street, London, SE1 9GF

www.harpercollins.co.uk

HarperCollins*Publishers*
1st Floor, Watermarque Building,
Ringsend Road, Dublin 4, Ireland

The Italian's Bride Worth Billions © 2022 Lynne Graham

Rules of Their Royal Wedding Night © 2022 Michelle Smart

ISBN: 978-0-263-30109-0

12/22

THE ITALIAN'S
BRIDE WORTH
BILLIONS

LYNNE GRAHAM

MILLS & BOON

As always and with much love
for the daughter who is the port in my every creative storm.

CHAPTER ONE

GIANNI RENZETTI SWALLOWED a curse when he was informed that his father, Federico, awaited him in his office. He knew what that was about, wished he didn't. But that was life and Gianni always met adversity head-on. As the phenomenally successful and youngest ever CEO of Renzetti Inc, he was determined to stand by his convictions.

His PA couldn't quite meet his eyes when she relayed the news about his father's arrival and the faintest trace of colour edged Gianni's hard-edged cheekbones, throwing into prominence the striking bone structure and stunning dark good looks that usually granted him a second and even a third glance from women. Of course, his PA would have seen the photos in the newspaper and, momentarily, Gianni was embarrassed rather than powered by the anger that had exploded in him the instant he saw that grubby article.

Here he was, evidently, labelled for life by a moment of sexual idiocy. His wide sensual mouth compressed. Yet his strongest conviction *was* that his private life— for that read sex life—was an entirely confidential matter. Unfortunately, on this particular occasion, the lines had become blurred. Gianni had been set up and he had, regrettably, succumbed to temptation in a private room at a nightclub. That had resulted in attempted blackmail and the involvement of the police followed by a very sleazy spread of photos in a downmarket tabloid. When the extortion attempt failed, the story had been sold instead.

A resigned blankness in his dazzling dark eyes, Gianni entered his office. He had always had a toxic relationship with his father. His late mother had excluded his father from her will and left her vast wealth in trust for her son and Gianni was well aware of his father's resentment on that score. What relationship the two men had had, however, had nosedived the instant that Gianni stepped into his father's shoes at Renzetti Inc. Federico Renzetti had made several poor business decisions and the board of directors, which included his father's two older brothers, had voted him out, preferring his son, who already ran a highly profitable company of his own. Although at the time Federico had insisted that he was keen to retire, his bitterness had only seemed to increase when his son had lifted the family company into the *Fortune 500* category.

'Federico.' Gianni greeted his only surviving parent with the name and formality the older man preferred and extended a stiff hand.

The older man, tall but a little portly in shape from good living, surveyed his son with tight-mouthed censure. 'I'm only here to tell you that when the board of directors vote you out at the end of the month, neither I nor your uncles will be supporting you,' he spelt out.

Gianni froze, taken aback by that declaration of intent. He had not been aware that there was any risk of him being voted out. In his experience the directors always put profit first. But evidently, the jungle drums in the family had been busily beating behind his back. A cold chill ran down his spine. Gianni cared about few things beyond work because he was the overachiever he had been raised to be. He ate, breathed, and slept business and he not only thrived as CEO of the family company, but also deeply valued his position of responsibility.

'This sordid episode has brought the company's reputation into disrepute,' Federico Renzetti ground out thinly. 'It cannot be overlooked.'

'It has brought *me* into disrepute,' Gianni contradicted steadily. 'I made a foolish misjudgement, and I won't even try to defend myself.'

'You had sex with a woman in a nightclub!' his father slashed back at him in disgust. 'With a camera on you!'

'Naturally, I was not aware of the hidden camera,' Gianni said drily. 'But neither was I willing to give way to blackmail.'

'You were in the wrong. You should've paid that scheming slut off to protect the company name!'

'Too late now,' Gianni responded, seeing no reason to argue and prolong the meeting. He saw in his father's eyes that the older man was reaping a certain amount of enjoyment from his downfall and as always that cut him deep. It made him wonder, as he so often had growing up, what he had done to deserve that lack of affection.

'You have always refused to listen to me and take my advice!' the older man denounced bitterly. 'If you kept a mistress, it would be discreet. There would be no surprises, no scandals.'

Gianni gritted his teeth because he had always believed that a mistress would be as suffocating an addition to his life as a wife. *One* exclusive woman to satisfy his every desire? Gianni enjoyed freedom and variety but even a mistress would be entitled to expect a fair degree of fidelity. Why would he sign up for that option when most of the young women he met were content to settle for a casual encounter? Furthermore, that kind of detached lifestyle reminded him too strongly of his father and he refused to make such a choice, particularly as the son of a mother who had felt humiliated by her husband's mistresses.

'Better still had you married by now and settled down!' Federico Renzetti continued grimly.

'Why on earth would I want to get married at twenty-eight?' Gianni demanded with incredulity.

'I was a married man at twenty-three.'

'Back in the day,' Gianni scoffed, resisting a cutting urge to remark that his mother had been the richest heiress in Europe and too good a prospect for his impoverished father to pass up. 'Few adults want to settle down that young now.'

'Had you been married, even engaged, the board would have seen some sign of hope and better behaviour on the horizon for you. But you just won't grow up!' Federico told him in furious condemnation. 'What have you got against settling down?'

'Like my mother and you were so happy *settling down*,' Gianni breathed with emphatic distaste.

The older man paled at that unwelcome reminder and stepped back. 'I am sorry that you were so aware of our difficulties.'

Discomfiture filled Gianni, for he had not intended to get that personal with his parent and he rarely referred to the mother, who had died when he was thirteen. His memories of her were too private and painful. A charged silence fell for several uneasy seconds.

'Look.' Federico spread his hands in hesitant appeal. 'You could still turn this whole ghastly situation around by just choosing the *right* woman to marry. However, do you even know any decent women? You're unlikely to meet them at the raunchy private clubs and wild parties you frequent,' Federico declared with frustration. 'She would be mature and respectable, and she would have an unblemished reputation.'

'Bearing in mind the headlines I attracted over the weekend, I would imagine that a *decent* woman would be the very last one willing to marry me at the moment,' Gianni countered ruefully.

'Don't talk nonsense,' his father advised him impatiently. 'You're richer than Croesus. Even the most moral woman would be tempted by all that you have to offer...although, to be frank, she might not be tempted by your conduct.'

'And I'm not tempted by the idea of a gold-digging wife,' Gianni responded with finality. 'Let's not discuss the impossible. I can't credit that a wedding ring on my finger would silence the board's concerns.'

'We're all old men on the board, Gianni. We equate settling down with growing up, with maturity and stability,' his father fielded drily. 'Surely even you could contemplate the picket fence if it delivers the results you want?'

Gianni gritted his teeth and said nothing. He knew party girls, bored socialites and aspiring models. But then he wasn't seriously considering his father's advice, was he? No, he wasn't. He had made a misstep and he would learn by it, even if that meant learning the hard way. He wasn't about to entangle himself in a miserable marriage to satisfy other people's moral scruples. No, not for anything, he swore vehemently.

Her fingers crumpling the letter of refusal from the bank, Josephine Hamilton stared out of the attic window towards Belvedere, the palatial mansion adjacent to her own family home. It belonged to the Renzetti family and Gianni Renzetti was the biggest landowner and employer in the area. Technically, he was also their next-door neighbour. He owned almost every scrap of ground around them and what remained was the size of a postage stamp.

Dating back to Tudor times, Ladymead, the Hamilton family home, was dilapidated. While the Hamilton family fortunes had waned, the Renzettis' fortunes had steadily risen. Over a century ago, someone on the maternal side of Gianni's family tree had bought land from the Ladymead estate to build their lavish Edwardian property. Piece by piece over the years, Gianni's ancestors had bought almost all of Ladymead's original land. Only the walled garden, the outbuildings and the strip along the lakeshore still belonged to them, she reflected sadly, wondering if Gianni would now step in like the predator he essentially was to scoop up what was left of her home once debt forced them to sell. Ladymead would sell at a knockdown price, she conceded unhappily.

Slowly descending the rickety and narrow servant staircase, idly wondering when there had last been a servant in her dusty home, she suppressed her overwhelming sense of failure before straightening her shoulders and composing her face. She had to be strong for the sake of her nearest and dearest.

Jo settled the bank's letter on the kitchen table in front of her grandmother and her two great-aunts, Sybil and Beatrix, better known as Trixie. It was a Hamilton family meeting.

'Another refusal,' her grandmother, Liz, registered in dismay, her creased and kindly face troubled beneath her halo of white hair.

'But I lit a candle for success!' Her witchy great-aunt, Trixie, exclaimed in furious disappointment, her earrings and bracelets clattering noisily, her long greying hair flying round her face as she shook her head. '*Why* didn't it work?'

The third and youngest sister, Sybil, rolled her blue eyes and lifted her false eyelashes high in true femme-fatale style. 'It didn't work because we're a bad financial bet for a loan,' she said with the innate practicality that was as much a part of her as her glamorous image. 'So, what now?'

One hand toying anxiously with the end of the long braid of her blonde hair, Jo winced, her dark blue eyes strained in her delicate pointed face. She swallowed hard. 'I've made an appointment to see Gianni and ask if he's willing to loan us the money. I've tried all the banks. He's our last hope.'

'Not sure you'll be safe seeing him alone,' Sybil quipped, referring to the shocking newspaper article that everyone local had read and devoured.

Jo ignored that crack. 'I'm seeing him this evening when he's at home for the weekend. I thought it was best to keep it casual.'

'I bet you're wishing now that you'd said yes to dinner when he asked you out again last Christmas.' Sybil sighed. 'After all, it was the *second* time he'd asked you and you rejected him. I shouldn't think those rejections will dispose him to generosity.'

'I think he would have been more shocked if I'd said yes,' Jo countered, keen to kill that subject.

Jo knew herself well and she had always refused to allow herself to be tempted by the man she suspected was probably her equivalent of Kryptonite. Gianni was the original bad boy and she had been determined not to become another notch on his heavily marked bedpost. He tempted her when no other man had contrived to do so and she was painfully conscious that she was vulnerable with him. But she had also known Gianni since she was a child and she valued even their casual friendship too much to risk losing that unique link.

'In some cultures, they believe that if you save a life, that person's life belongs to you,' Trixie mused absently. 'Gianni hasn't got much return from the effort he put in that day.'

Sybil's eyes flared. 'It didn't happen that way, even if nobody is prepared to acknowledge it. Jo saved *him* from drowning, not the other way round!' she argued.

Jo wrinkled her nose. 'I was nine years old and he was thirteen,' she reminded her great-aunts gently. 'We were both stupid and we both survived. That's all that really matters.'

Sybil parted her lips to argue and then glimpsed her eldest sister's taut face and closed her mouth again. Liz Hamilton's son, Abraham, had drowned himself in the lake and nobody liked to discuss that thorny subject around his mother.

Uncomfortably flushed by that reminder of the uneasy link she had formed with Gianni and the secret they had suppressed when they were both too young to do otherwise, Jo rose from the table. She had first met Gianni the year before that incident. Her grandmother had gone to visit his mother, who had endured a long struggle with cancer. Federico Renzetti had been less to everyone's taste than his charming, friendly wife, Isabella, who had borne her illness with such stoicism. Gianni's father had been a cold, distant man with no desire to mix in any way with the locals.

Liz Hamilton had brought roses, which Isabella had adored. High tea with all the trimmings had been served in a sunlit drawing room. Jo had been bored listening to the adult conversation and then Gianni had come in, a tall, rangy twelve-year-old with a shock of glossy blue-black hair and olive skin. Jo had seen the love in his eyes when he'd looked at his frail mother, a love that had been fully reciprocated as his mother had drawn him forward to introduce him, her pride in him patent.

He had been very polite and hadn't grimaced when Isabella had asked him to take Jo outside to entertain her. He had asked her some awkward questions to fill the silence between them, such as why she lived with her grandparents. And she had told him that her mother was dead and that she didn't remember her and that nobody knew who her father was. Gianni had been disconcerted by such honesty, but she had been too naïve to dissemble.

She had told him that she would rather see the library than the garden and he had shown her a shelf with English books and in no time at all she had been curled up in an armchair reading a children's book that had once been his.

'What age are you?' he had finally asked her.

'Eight,' she had told him proudly.

'You're absolutely tiny,' he had remarked.

'I'm not. You're just very tall. My goodness, you can read English as well as Italian,' she had gathered, impressed to death by such an accomplishment.

'If I speak English, I can read it,' Gianni had pointed out. 'My grandmother was English. My mother wanted me to be bilingual. That's why I go to an English school.'

He had attended an elite boarding school, rubbing shoulders with the rich, the titled and the royal. In spite of his mother's illness, he was rarely at Belvedere, and it was the following year before Jo saw him again and in circumstances she would have preferred to forget.

'That poor boy,' she recalled her grandmother saying to her sisters. 'His mother has died and he never got to spend any time with her. He's only home from school and it's too late... She's gone. Isabella said his father was extremely strict about his schooling and wouldn't let him take time out to be with her during her last weeks.'

Jo had been sitting in a tree in the front garden when she saw Gianni in the distance striding down to the lake. Aware that he was grieving, she had not even thought of trying to approach him. She wouldn't have known what to say in such circumstances and it wasn't as though they were friends. There was too big an age gap for that. She had watched as he'd walked into the lake and she had leapt down from the tree, wondering if he knew that there was a very steep drop several yards out, wondering why he wasn't wearing swimwear.

And as he had walked, she had remembered a conversation between her great-aunts that she had overheard, a conversation about her uncle Abraham's death the year before.

'She saw him do it!' Trixie had sobbed. 'How could he do that to his mother? She saw him drown from her bedroom window. She watched him walk into the water and keep on walking until he vanished below the surface. She started running and she was screaming.

'But she was too late. It was all over by the time we got down there.'

At the time, Jo hadn't understood that her uncle had taken his own life, distraught at having lost his family's money in dodgy investments. But she had understood that he had drowned and worry about Gianni had made her break the rule that she was never ever to go near the lake without an adult with her. She had run faster than she had ever run in her life and then she had raced straight into the water to reach Gianni. An accomplished swimmer, she had had no fear.

She had shouted at him just as he'd dipped below the surface but assumed he hadn't heard her. In an effort to help him she had moved in deeper, starting to swim just as her feet had got tangled in the weeds below the surface. As panic had taken hold of her, she'd forgotten everything she had ever learned about how to handle herself in water. She'd struggled, flailing her arms wildly as she'd tried to free her legs and she'd only sunk deeper and faster into the murky depths.

That was all she remembered until she'd surfaced again, spluttering and gasping on the shore. Gianni's eyes had been wild and desperate above hers, a fierce burning gold as he'd turned her over and urged her to breathe.

So, who had saved whom? she still wondered. It had

never been discussed because she had never told anyone the truth of what she had suspected: that Gianni, devastated by his mother's death, had gone into the lake with no plan to come out of it again alive. Certainly, she would have drowned had he not grabbed her and dragged her out of the water to get her breathing again. Ever since then she had given the lake a wide berth, reluctant to revisit those memories.

She had no appetite for her evening meal and her grandmother scolded her, telling her that she was already thin enough. To keep the older woman happy, she agreed to have some soup but, in reality, when Jo was apprehensive all appetite deserted her.

'I suppose you'll offer Gianni the lakeshore land in return,' Liz Hamilton assumed quietly. 'You might as well. Nobody here has fished the lake since your uncle died.'

'I have to offer him something. Our roof won't go through another winter,' Jo pointed out ruefully.

'The roof on my shop needs attention as well,' Trixie piped up.

'The roof of the house is more important,' Sybil countered. 'And then there's the rewiring. That's next on the list before we get disconnected for failing safety standards.'

'Yes, one thing does lead to another.' Liz sighed heavily. 'The wiring stymied Jo's plans to open a bed and breakfast here. Everything demands money and we don't have any. We only bring in enough cash to pay the weekly bills.'

Her shoulders down-curving, Jo pushed her soup plate away. Sometimes it all got on top of her: the sheer weight of responsibility, the robbing Peter to pay Paul outlook she had to maintain, the need to stretch every penny until it squeaked. Essentially the family had coped until her uncle had lost the family savings and then her grandfather, who had had a good business head on his shoulders, had died. Jo had planned to use her business degree to find a job but supporting Ladymead and her family had had to come first. And she had had some good ideas to bring in an income from the unused buildings in the rear courtyard. Unfortunately, any changes or improvements required to *make* money also *cost* money.

Trixie now had a little shop selling crystals, candles and handicrafts. She was also much in demand for tarot readings locally. Sybil's heart was in the small animal shelter she ran in the barn, but she also sold the organic vegetables grown in the walled garden via their one surviving employee, Maurice, who was as old as the hills, lived in the courtyard and refused to retire.

Duffy flew in and landed on the chair in front of Jo and began to sing the song from a popular musical about money making the world go around.

'You said money, the *fatal* word, and he heard it,' Sybil reproved her big sister.

'It's better than the biblical quotes, although he's amazingly soulful when he starts reciting Shakespeare's sonnets,' Trixie said fondly.

'He's a very well-educated parrot,' Liz Hamilton murmured with quiet pride.

Jo left them to it and went to freshen up, Fairy, a graceful greyhound, gliding upstairs with her. Their Scottie, McTavish, who hated everyone but Jo, was out chasing rabbits, which was just as well when she was planning to visit Belvedere. He had a particular vicious dislike of Gianni, and his housekeeper had had to phone her twice recently to come and retrieve the little animal when McTavish had lain in hopeful wait for Gianni.

She smoothed down her faded blue sundress and sighed, loosening her long hair from its untidy fraying braid and deciding simply to brush it to save time. Gianni was such a stickler for punctuality. She couldn't afford to get off on the wrong foot with him, could she?

Fairy by her side, she climbed into the pickup truck that was the only vehicle left at Ladymead, its usage on a strict schedule to allow all of them a chance to take advantage of the freedom it brought. Gianni had a huge garage full of cars of all descriptions, most of them of the fast, sports variety. Her smile dimmed as she recalled their most significant meeting in recent times.

It had been very awkward. Gianni had attended Ralph's funeral, lingering long enough to offer her his personal condolences on her 'loss'. Ralph Scott had died in a military helicopter crash. He had been a friend, but just about everyone, with the exception of her family, had believed that Jo and Ralph were unofficially engaged. In reality, the engagement had been a story put around by Ralph to save face when he'd discovered that his former fiancée, Jane, was cheating on him with his best friend. Jo had been shocked when Ralph died but she had grieved only over the loss of a dear friend, not over the loss of a man she loved. She would have liked to explain that to Gianni but with so many people standing nearby she hadn't had the opportunity.

Even so, Gianni had tried to offer her comfort in his own unique way, declaring that loving someone only got you hurt, and when she'd queried that statement, he had admitted that he had had his heart broken when he was younger and had learned a useful lesson from the experience. She had been stunned that he should have told her something that personal even though she hadn't agreed with his outlook. Ever since she had wondered who the woman was and what had happened between them.

Suppressing those untimely and inappropriate reflections, Jo parked at the front of the house, crunching over the gravel in her grass-stained canvas sandals to the imposing front entrance. The door opened, Gianni's plump housekeeper, Abigail, bestowing a smile on her before ushering her in.

'Mr Renzetti is in the orangery. It's lovely there at this time of year with the terrace doors wide and the evening sunshine flooding in,' she said, showing Jo through the big echoing hall out to the leafy splendour of the orangery. 'How have you been? I ran into your grandmother yesterday and she said you'd been terribly busy.'

'There's never enough hours in my day,' Jo admitted rather breathlessly as she heard footsteps crossing the tiled floor, strong, sure, like the man himself.

'Jojo,' Gianni purred. 'What are you collecting for this evening?'

He had told her once that Josephine was too much of a mouthful and that Jo made her sound like a boy and he had begun calling her Jojo even though she frowned every time he utilised it.

'C-collecting?' She stammered out the word, colour rising in her cheeks as she stared at him.

At the worst possible moment, she was remembering that grainy image of him in a suit in that room with that half-naked woman. Her tummy flipped, butterflies breaking free. Her grandmother had told her that Gianni was their neighbour and acquaintance and that it was disrespectful to have that rag of a newspaper in their home when he had been extorted and unaware of the camera. She had been ashamed of herself for devouring every dirty detail. And she was even more ashamed to feel the prickling of her nipples as they tightened and the heat rising between her thighs. But at the end of the day, she was a woman like any other and her body betrayed her in his presence because he *was* that irresistible.

Standing only bare feet away from him, she was shockingly aware of how incredibly handsome he was, how tall, how well built. His beautifully tailored dark pinstriped suit fitted him perfectly and it was designer fashionable, cut to enhance his broad chest and lean muscular thighs. Unaffected by Jo's self-consciousness, Fairy located a rug, turned three times and settled down happily for a snooze.

'For charity. When you visit you're always collecting for something but you don't usually go for the formality of making an appointment,' Gianni clarified lazily, studying her with veiled eyes, the stirring sexual pulse at his groin all too familiar and fiercely resisted.

Josephine Hamilton was exquisite. There was no other word. The pretty child had grown into an incredibly beautiful woman with a mane of golden hair, sapphire-blue eyes, a delicate little nose and a luscious pink mouth. She was a slender five feet four or so with the grace of a ballet dancer and sometimes when he saw her, she could still take his breath away. A member of the church choir, she had been among the carol singers that had called at Belvedere the previous Christmas, her lovely face the only one he'd noticed in the crowd, her jewelled eyes shining, golden hair rumpled and, for once, she had been smiling at him.

Gianni laughed at her blank look. 'You were collecting for the homeless last time you were here, and you did very well out of my dinner guests. Your speech could have wrung water from a stone.'

Jo coloured again. 'Yes, they were very generous, but I wouldn't have called in had I known that you were entertaining.'

'Come and sit down,' he suggested as his house-keeper bustled in with a tray of coffee and cakes.

'Nothing for me,' Jo said tightly, both nervous and embarrassed as she sank down into a basketwork cushioned chair.

'You usually eat like a horse,' Gianni remarked in surprise. 'What's wrong? You seem very tense.'

Jo stiffened. 'You're treating me like a welcome visitor and that doesn't feel right when I've come to ask you for a loan,' she confided uncomfortably.

It was so Jojo to just blurt it out like that and he was wryly amused. 'I'm not a bank,' he said quietly.

'The banks said no.'

Gianni concealed his amusement with difficulty. 'You really shouldn't be telling me that in advance.'

Jo lifted her chin. 'I'm not stupid. I know you would check that out.'

'What do you need the loan for? *The money pit?*'

Jojo compressed her lips, offended by that label being attached to her home. 'The roof is in a bad way and the wiring is causing problems. I want to set up a bed and breakfast and the regulations are extremely strict.'

Gianni schooled his shrewd gaze. His father had

been obsessed with acquiring Ladymead and ridding the neighbourhood of the eccentric Hamiltons and the folksy business operations they had cobbled together to stay afloat. Officially, Gianni had owned Belvedere since he was thirteen and the presence of a Tudor dump on the other side of the screening wall his parent had erected bothered him not at all.

'Of course, I'm not expecting you to help out of the goodness of your heart.'

'Well, you know I have none of that,' Gianni inserted drily.

'You didn't report McTavish for biting you,' Jo reminded him in disagreement.

'You'd never have forgiven me.'

'I know you don't like long-winded speeches, so I'll get straight to the point. We're willing to sell the lakeshore land to you.'

Gianni gritted his teeth and groaned. How did he tell her that when the Hamiltons eventually went bust he would buy Ladymead on the cheap, close the shops and install tenants? It was an historic building, as he had reminded his father, and it couldn't be demolished. But what exasperated him the most was Jo's admission that she was planning a bed and breakfast operation.

'How on earth could you cope with guests in the house? You're already run ragged trying to keep the place going,' Gianni demanded impatiently. 'You would have to renovate the entire house and you would need staff. Trixie would need to stop worshipping at her shrine to nature in the back garden. Sybil would have to stop taking in every stray animal that comes along. Your grandmother, who isn't getting any younger, would never get out of the kitchen. It's not a viable proposition.'

'I didn't ask for *your* opinion,' Jo told him tartly.

Gianni sprang up restively. 'Too bad…you're getting it. It's a totally impractical ambition.'

'And you just expect me to accept your judgement on that score, do you?' Jo slung back at him angrily.

'I do,' Gianni delivered succinctly. 'I know you have a business degree, but you've not used it or been out in the world. You don't have the experience to—'

'If being out in the world means shagging some trollop in a questionable club and making sleazy headlines, then I don't think I want to be *out* in the world as you put it!' Her face flushed, her hands knotted into fists, her sapphire eyes alight with fury, Jo stared him down in challenge.

CHAPTER TWO

GIANNI FROZE, UNPREPARED FOR that level of anger and vitriol from her lips because Josephine Hamilton was known far and wide as a very kind woman with endless compassion, a woman who never put a foot wrong. And she had just hit a spectacular own goal. His lean, darkly handsome features were taut but his glittering dark-as-night eyes took on an arrested expression as he stared back at her rigid figure because all of a sudden, he was seeing possibilities he had never dreamt he might consider. She had a backbone of steel and an astonishing streak of honesty, regardless of the circumstances, and he respected those traits.

In that same timeless moment, Jo turned pale as death, overpowered with regret for those fiery, merciless words. Such an attack had been beneath her and a low blow when it came to such a sensitive subject. Particularly when he had welcomed her warmly into his home. Since when had she stood in judgement over others?

'Gianni...' she said stiltedly. 'I am really sorry. That was cruel, unkind, and derogatory. I don't know what came over me...or maybe I do. The past few weeks...all the bank visits and getting shot down in flames, trying to pretend everything was normal for my grandmother to keep her calm. I'm afraid the stress got to me and that I took it out on you. But that's not an excuse.'

'No, it's not,' Gianni agreed very quietly. 'And a highly inadvisable approach for someone in need of a loan. But because you were honest, I will be equally frank. Repossession or bankruptcy was always on the cards for you and Ladymead because you lack the income to support living in such a house. I planned to pick up Ladymead when you were forced to leave it. It's not a burning ambition for me as it was for my father, but there is no advantage to me in helping you or your family to remain there.'

'I kind of guessed that,' she muttered unevenly, still pale as milk and trembling a little from the shock of losing her temper to such an extent and the struggle it was not to tell him things that he wouldn't want to hear.

Such as the fact that he was worth so much more than those sleazy headlines. He had succumbed to the temptation of some slutty scam artist, but he could do so much better and would be so much happier if only he would put value on something less ephemeral than a cheap sexual thrill. It infuriated her that he was so short-sighted, so set against falling in love, so determined to reduce relationships between men and women to the lowest common denominator. And it shamed her that, when she had first seen that photo, she had been jealous that it wasn't *her* with him. Naturally, an alternative imaginary version of her, a woman sexually confident enough to tease him in a raunchy corset. And how weird and unforgivable was that when she had thrown his miscalculation in his teeth like a challenge?

How much worse was it that instead of concentrating on his refusal to loan her family money, she was knee deep and wallowing in a personal reaction to Gianni that had no place between them?

'I'll leave now,' she muttered, calling Fairy from her slumber, eager to be gone and yet devastated that he had refused to help her family. Somehow, inexplicably, even though she had known that a positive answer would have gone against his essentially predatory nature, she had still contrived to hope for a different response.

'Join me for dinner at La Vie en Rose tomorrow evening. I'll pick you up at eight,' Gianni told her, rather than *asked* her. 'I may have a solution for you that also benefits me but I want a day to think the concept over. And, no, don't shoot yourself in the foot by voicing another knee-jerk refusal to my invitation!'

Flustered by that unexpected assurance and the invitation, Jo snatched in a ragged breath and nodded her head. Dinner with Gianni? No, don't think about that, she urged herself irritably. Think about what kind of solution to her family's financial problems could possibly offer benefit to a filthy rich Renzetti, blessed in every way. Her mind was a complete blank. But of course he wasn't blessed in *every* way, she reminded herself ruefully. Being rich didn't protect Gianni from having problems, not least the scandal that he had unleashed with his uninhibited sexual appetite.

He owned the very exclusive French restaurant in the village. Nobody in Jo's family had ever dined there because it was Michelin-starred and extremely expensive. Well, no doubt if she could get over her nervous tummy, she would at least enjoy a rare treat, she told herself soothingly as she packed Fairy back into the pickup truck.

Gianni strode through to the drawing room and poured himself a brandy while watching Jojo drive off in her battered, noisy vehicle. He had not seriously considered the possibility of taking his father's advice and getting married until he found himself involuntarily picturing Jojo in the role. Jojo was a perfect fit for his blueprint. She had impeccable credentials. Charitable work, church work, loyal to her family, former fiancée of a decorated soldier. Her reputation was so clean it shone like a halo next to his own.

Gianni had few illusions about himself. He knew that he was brilliant in business. He also knew that he was ruthless, occasionally callous, selfish and quick-tempered, not to mention sporadically impulsive. And right at this very moment, a foolish and fleeting sexual impulse was threatening to destroy his career and everything he had worked so hard to achieve. Nothing less than that threat would have induced him to consider marriage to *any* woman.

Jojo, however, was in a class of her own. For a start, Gianni found her very attractive and she had all the allure of being the only woman who had ever said no to him. He had wanted her for several years and had resolutely suppressed that desire. On two occasions when the desire had overpowered his scruples, he had invited her out to dinner. Ironically, he had felt weirdly relieved when she had turned him down. After all, prior to his current crisis, what could he have offered her? She would have wanted meaningful, and he would have wanted a one-night stand. He was well aware of his limitations. Keeping his distance had been the kindest thing he could do for both of them.

Marriage held little attraction for him. His parents had been miserable together even before cancer first afflicted his mother. They had had separate bedrooms and his father had kept a mistress and nothing could have hidden the truth that his parents had barely a thought in common. Even raising their only child had been a cause of disagreement between them, his father insisting that his mother was too soft with him, his mother refusing to forgive his father for sending Gianni to boarding school. Nobody was more aware than Gianni that marriage could be a stony road paved with obstacles and bitterness. Yet he was equally aware that his seemingly cold father had grieved deeply after his wife's death and he had never understood that conundrum. Jojo was of a different ilk, Gianni reasoned. There was nothing cold, hard or bitter about her. She would, undoubtedly, endeavour to improve him but he decided that he could live with that just as he was likely to have to live with generous doses of the crazy parrot, the nutty family and the homicidal McTavish. In return, she would take care of his homes, act as his hostess and nag him into attending church more often. But in spite of the drawbacks he foresaw, he also believed she was a catch and a top-quality one.

Unaware of the sterling talents being awarded to her, Jo returned to her family and explained only that Gianni would give her an answer over dinner the following evening.

'He's trying to get his pound of flesh,' Sybil opined

darkly. 'He's finally getting you out to dinner. Make sure you don't end up on the dessert menu, Jo!'

'It's a business proposition. He probably wants to check everything out first,' her grandmother reproved her sister. 'He would have to consult his solicitor and estate manager as well.'

'Have you seen the way Gianni Renzetti looks at Jo?' Sybil scoffed. 'Like she's a juicy rabbit and he's a fox!'

'Are you trying to put Jo off dining with him?' Trixie asked, glancing at her great-niece's burning cheeks. 'I'm quite sure he will be able to restrain himself for one meal.'

'What on earth are you going to wear?' Sybil pressed.

'The dress I wore to Ralph's regimental dinner.'

'Oh, yes, that's very pretty on you, and I'll do your make-up and hair,' Sybil announced with pleasure.

'So although you don't think he can be trusted, you're happy to doll her up like a human sacrifice?' Trixie sniffed disapprovingly.

'Will you stop worrying? I can look after myself,' Jo declared with quiet confidence, and she left her relatives to do a stint in Trixie's shop so that her great-aunt could enjoy a longer tea break.

That same confidence had dwindled a good deal by the time Gianni drew up at Ladymead in a very snazzy sportscar. Jo had gone for a more natural look than Sybil favoured, reluctant to appear as though she had made a huge effort to impress him. In any case it would be a wasted effort, she reflected, considering the beauties Gianni was regularly seen with. Even at her best, she could not compete with a supermodel.

Watching her climb ineptly into the low-slung car, her full skirt flipping up, Gianni, treated to a glimpse of slender thigh and very shapely legs, was entranced, arousal humming through him in a persistent pulse that would not be stilled. The subtle light scent of something flowery assailed him.

'Have you eaten here before?' he asked as he parked the car.

'No. It's a little pricey for us,' Jo said lightly. 'I heard that there's a waiting list for a table.'

'It's proved immensely popular. Wait,' he urged as she moved to open the passenger door.

He opened the door for her and reached down a lean brown hand to help her out of the car, his hand dropping lightly to her waist to guide her onto the pavement, her spine prickling with a powerful awareness of his touch and proximity.

'Is this the treatment all your women receive?' Jo joked as she smoothed down her skirts and preceded him into the restaurant.

'No. You're in a class of your own.'

Aside from hovering staff, there wasn't a single other diner. Jo lifted a brow and settled down into the private booth. The lights were low, a candle burned and fresh flowers adorned the table. 'Gosh, this feels like a *real* date,' she quipped.

'It must be. You put lip gloss on,' Gianni fielded silkily.

'You should feel short-changed. Sybil tried to get me into false lashes and something she called a smoky eye,' she revealed, dark blue eyes wide with amusement.

'You don't need them. I like the restrained, natural look.'

Says the man seduced by a corset and a thong, Jo

thought wryly, but at least she didn't make the mistake of saying it out loud.

'Why's it so quiet in here?'

'The restaurant was fully booked but I wanted privacy for what I have to say to you,' Gianni explained levelly. 'Next week the diners we displaced will enjoy their meal at my expense.'

As the wine arrived, along with a selection of tiny tasters and plates, Jo swallowed hard and pinched her thigh to keep herself alert. She knew that she had to stay on top form to deal with Gianni.

'What on earth do you need privacy for?' she asked bluntly, rebelling against the insidious intimacy of their setting.

'Will you listen to my proposition without interrupting me?'

'I'll try.' Jo lifted her wine glass, suddenly all of a quiver with nerves.

'The consequences of the scandal I caused mean that I require a wife,' Gianni told her wryly. 'I need to be seen to be settling down to retain my position as CEO of Renzetti Inc, otherwise I've been warned that I'll be voted out at the end of the month. You strike me as perfect wife material.'

Jo gulped but she couldn't find her voice to interrupt. She was stunned by that assurance and flattered as well, although the part of her that felt gratified was feeling that way very much against her will. Her attention clung to the mesmeric tawny golden glow of his black-fringed eyes in the candlelight, the shadows cast below his slanting cheekbones and the lush pink of his full lower lip.

'I won't *loan* you the money you need, *cara*. I'm telling you that upfront,' Gianni spelt out with perfect diction as he helpfully divided up the tasters on the platter and served her. 'What would be the point of giving you a loan that you couldn't afford to repay?'

She drank down her wine to ease her dry throat and inside her chest her heart thumped at a fast drumbeat. He was giving it all to her, piece by piece, breaking the situation down into what he probably saw as manageable chunks. Didn't he realise that labelling her as 'perfect wife material' simply blew a giant hole in her concentration? The idea of marrying Gianni Renzetti struck her as so incredible that she was wondering if she had somehow misunderstood him at some point during that speech.

'You're in so much debt that even the sale of the lakeshore land wouldn't turn the situation around,' Gianni told her succinctly. 'I suspect that your bank must be close to considering foreclosure.'

Jo only just contrived to suppress a shudder, but their bank had given her the same impression when she had had the temerity to ask for a new loan. Her family's financial situation was dire. Insufficient money coming in and too many bills had sent the overdraft climbing the previous winter and she heaved a sigh.

'I feel like such a failure,' she muttered tightly.

'You're not a failure. Previous generations of your family neglected the property. That house has been in decline for many years and a full-scale restoration is probably required now. Are you struggling to hang onto the house for your grandmother's benefit?'

Jo grimaced and shook her head. 'No. I'm more selfish. Ladymead has been in the family for hundreds of years. I don't want to be the one to lose it. I know once it's gone, it's gone for ever. I also know that even though it's in poor condition I love every historic nook and cranny in that building,' she confessed ruefully. 'My earliest memories are of Grandad taking me round Ladymead and sharing his recollections of *his* childhood.'

Gianni studied her lovely face in the low light, the plush peach curve of her lower lip as she worried at it with the edge of her teeth, and an almost blinding surge of lust tightened every muscle in his long lean body. He topped up her wine and rested back in his seat, suppressing that arousal with all his strength.

'My next question has to be are you *willing* to marry me to keep Ladymead in your family?' he asked levelly. 'If you marry me I will finance the restoration of the house. I will cover every necessary expense and ensure your family's security and comfort.'

Jo blinked rapidly and began to eat in haste, needing that simple act to ground herself again. What Gianni was offering was the fulfilment of her wildest dreams. She would be able to stop worrying and give up trying to work every hour of the day while trying to dream up new ways to make or save money. In addition, her family would be safe and secure and freed from the same anxiety.

'Gianni…you haven't thought this through.'

'On the contrary, I've thought very deeply about it.'

'Why me?' she demanded helplessly. 'I mean, there must be so many women who would be eager to marry you.'

'I need your respectability and you need my money, but you're not a gold-digger. That is an important distinction for me,' he admitted as the main course was brought to their table.

'What sort of marriage are you talking about?' Jo enquired uncertainly.

Gianni frowned, shapely ebony brows rising enquiringly as if she had asked an unexpected question. 'A normal marriage.'

'Normal?' Jo questioned, her incredulity obvious, her eyes wide. 'Like share-a-bed, have-children normal?'

'What else?'

Jo flushed. 'We could *fake* it…being married, I mean, and just do the surface show for the sake of appearances. Surely that would gain you just as much?'

'I don't do fake, *cara*,' Gianni murmured softly. 'I'm not keen to try celibacy and the alternative is to play away and take the chance of being exposed as an adulterer. In the current moral climate in which I work I'm not prepared to run that risk…'

Jo cut into her tender steak with determination. 'I understand…' she conceded reluctantly. 'I was only trying to suggest a more workable version of what you proposed.'

'A promise to keep my hands off you would—inevitably—be broken,' Gianni told her frankly. 'I've been attracted to you for a long time. I have to be truthful on that score. I wouldn't be asking you to marry me if I didn't find you attractive. *Dio mio*, I assume that if we have reached the stage of discussing sex, you're thinking about it…'

'Of course, I'm thinking about it,' Jo protested in a guilty, stifled undertone. 'My family means everything to me, and we've all been working really hard to keep things afloat and yet, we're still sliding down the slippery slope of debt at speed. Then you come along like some knight on a white charger...'

Gianni raised a lean brown hand at that point to silence her. 'No. I'll never be your knight on a white charger. I haven't been in a relationship for a long time and I've no doubt that I'll be challenging to live with. But I assure you that I will look after you and your family to the best of my ability.'

It was like a lifebelt being thrown to Jo just when she felt as though she were on the very brink of drowning. She had had a mad crush on Gianni when she was a teenager but half the girls at school had been equally keen to see Gianni Renzetti as a pin-up. That glimpses of him were rare had merely added to his mystique. Seen around the village only at weekends and holidays, Gianni, clad in designer jeans and driving a flash car, had been the perfect adolescent fantasy figure.

'You're staring...' Gianni breathed. 'What's going through your mind?'

'You don't want to know.' Jo shook her head as though to clear it and frowned at him as she pushed away her plate, ashamed that she could be allowing teenaged fantasies to influence her when all such nonsense was long since dead and buried. 'I just can't believe that you're asking me to marry you.'

'Get with the programme, *cara*,' he urged, and that faint hint of impatience only gave his slight accent a smoky edge, an effect which was underscored by the gentle stroke of his forefinger across the back of her hand. 'We're way beyond that stage. We're negotiating.'

'Are we?' Jo sighed. 'You have unlimited confidence, Gianni.'

'And secretly, you like that about me. If we set the

parameters now there'll be no room for misunderstandings,' he asserted with remarkable optimism.

'I haven't said that I accept yet,' Jo protested in dismay. 'I need tomorrow to think about stuff. But misunderstandings will occur whatever we discuss beforehand. Perhaps what we really need is a time-limited agreement.'

His ebony brows drew together in a gathering frown as the dessert trolley arrived. 'What sort of limit?'

Jo turned aside to order her dessert. 'Six months?' she suggested.

'Why bother getting married in the first place?' Gianni asked drily. 'It's nowhere near long enough and it wouldn't fool anyone into believing I was settling down.'

'A year?'

In response, Gianni simply frowned and shook his head in immediate dismissal.

He said that he disliked sweet things and had ordered coffee, which she knew for a fact he drank with a ridiculous amount of sugar in it. As in other fields, Gianni could be wildly unpredictable. Hadn't she simply assumed that he would leap at the offer of a six-month marital stretch?

'What if there's a child to be considered?' Gianni asked.

'That's why it might be wiser to leave the possibility of children out of the arrangement,' Jo proposed, stifling a pang of disappointment at that prospect even if it was the more sensible option.

Gianni dealt her a frowning look of reproof. 'If we're planning to play house, we should do it properly. I don't only partially commit to a new project. If we're doing this, I want the whole shebang.'

Jo swallowed slowly and nodded. *The whole she-bang.* A normal marriage, Gianni as a husband, Gianni in the same bed most nights. She burned as a surge of fantasy-induced heat washed through the most sensitive places in her body. There was no use pretending to herself that she wasn't curious about what *that* would be like. Her skin warmed. She couldn't imagine being in bed with Gianni but she had had one or two totally wanton fantasies about him over the years. And yet tonight was the very first time he had truly touched her. She didn't count that time he had saved her from drowning in the lake as a child.

Gianni wasn't a touchy-feely type of guy and he was circumspect about not touching a woman unnecessarily. That was why every physical touch he had utilised since picking her up for dinner had very clearly underlined the change he now saw in their relationship. A tiny little shiver snaked through her taut frame. She liked that change, that revealing shift away from casual friendship. But he wasn't 'courting' her, wasn't offering her a wedding ring on the usual terms, she reminded herself irritably. He had utilised the word *normal*, but two people who were not in love opting to marry was *not* normal, in her view, particularly when one of them was endeavouring to bury a scandal by putting on a public front of embracing respectability.

'Let's go,' Gianni intoned a few minutes later when she had finished dessert. 'Unless you want coffee as well.'

'No, I don't drink coffee this late,' Jo muttered, torn in two by the conflicting reactions assailing her.

Without Gianni, her family would forfeit Ladymead and any security, for once the debts were settled, there would be little, if anything, left to support another life elsewhere. With Gianni on board, those debts and the worry caused by them would disappear.

But what would it cost her personally to marry a man she didn't love? A man who was very unlikely ever to love her? That was the big question…

CHAPTER THREE

'WHAT ARE YOU agonising about?' Gianni prompted as he ignited the car engine.

'I'm not agonising about anything,' Jo lied.

In reality, Jo was glancing back with a near wince at the couple of colourless forgettable romances she had had over the years. She didn't even count Ralph, who had asked her to marry him purely as a face-saving move. He had never been more than a friend. Sadly, she had only ever met one man who inspired anything more than liking in her and that felt like a personal failure. She had told herself off for being too choosy, too critical, particularly when she had always been conscious that she wanted a long-term relationship and children in her future.

And yet here she was, twenty-four years old and still a virgin and the only man she had ever really, *really* fancied was Gianni Renzetti. What did that say about her? That she was an unrealistic dreamer? Gianni had always seemed totally unobtainable. But now he had shocked her with a proposition she could never have foreseen, and the sensible side of her brain was in conflict with the idealistic side.

'About marrying me?' Gianni guided the powerful

car smoothly into the rough, potholed lane that led to her family home and slowed down to a snail's pace. 'If the marriage didn't work out, if we were miserable a few years down the road, we could separate, and it wouldn't be the end of the world. Unfortunately, you don't like risks, *cara*, and I accept that you must see me as a high-risk venture.'

'Where do you get the idea that I don't like risks?' Jo demanded curtly, annoyed by the confidence with which he spoke.

'You choose the safe, sensible path most of the time. You did your business degree and you brought it home and let your family bury you alive in *their* problems. You don't seem to have a single streak of ruthlessness. If you had, you would have walked away and made your own life.'

'My family and my home *are* my life. I had a poor start as a baby but my family loved me enough to overlook those beginnings and they gave me a very happy childhood,' Jo argued vehemently.

Jo was troubled just thinking about what she might have been like without the family who had raised her and given her so much love. She didn't remember her mother and knew little about her but she knew that her mother had wanted to share her child with her family. And truly, there was nothing Jo wouldn't do for that same family, who had given her so much, and she knew that she owed every ounce of her strength and self-respect to the way she had been brought up.

Gianni parked the car. 'You can keep your family close if you marry me,' he murmured in silken addition.

Jo shot him a furious glance. 'I *know*! Is there anything you won't use to get your own way?'

'Probably extraordinarily little,' Gianni breathed, his wide mobile mouth taking on a cynical twist. 'You should probably ask me about the scandal.'

In receipt of that unexpected piece of advice, Jo turned red with mortification and, reaching for the door handle, opened the door to clamber out in haste. 'It's none of my business.'

Gianni sprang out of the driver's seat and stalked round the low-slung bonnet of the car like a man bracing himself. 'I asked you to marry me. You have a right to know the facts. The woman concerned was a model, not someone I knew whom I could trust. We dined together in a private room at the club. I had no suspicion that I was being set up as, to be frank, I had utilised a private room in that way before. Sex without even leaving the building…it was convenient for both me and the women concerned.'

Jo's face felt so hot it felt as though it were on fire. Heaven forbid, she thought helplessly, that any man would ever view the sharing of her body as a mere convenience.

'I left myself open to extortion. That kind of behaviour in my position was reckless. I didn't think. I didn't pause to consider what I was doing or where I was. I just took what was on offer for all the usual dumb male reasons.'

'Oh, dear,' Jo mumbled uncomfortably.

An involuntary laugh of appreciation escaped Gianni. 'I was a complete idiot,' he admitted, closing long fingers round her narrow wrist to ease her closer.

'No arguments from this corner.' Her mouth ran dry as she looked up at him in the moonlight.

He looked breathtakingly handsome, a powerful intensity etched in his lean, hard features and in the narrowed set of his stunning dark golden eyes. He ran a finger slowly across her cheekbone and her gaze widened, her breathing fracturing as he eased her back against the bonnet of the car. 'I want to kiss you.'

'Go ahead,' she heard herself mumble without hesitation because having got this close to Gianni she had no intention of denying herself that experience. Unsteady on her feet, nervous as a cat on hot bricks, she trembled when he brought her into full contact with his lean, powerful body. His arms closed round her, lifting her up to him as he circled her closed lips with his, plucking at the lower with his teeth, sending a shard of sharp craving arrowing down into her belly. His mouth travelled everywhere but where she wanted, teasing and dancing across her cheek before grazing down the soft slope of her neck and making her shudder in reaction and arch into his heat and strength.

'Don't do that. I'm on an incredibly short fuse,' Gianni growled, one hand suddenly splaying across the rounded curve of her bottom and pressing her into the cradle of his thighs, acquainting her with the hot, hard thrust of the erection shaped by the fine material of his tailored trousers.

Her tummy flipped, warmth and moisture gathering between her thighs as he finally found her mouth and took it with raw hunger.

The power of that smouldering kiss shot through her like an electric shock and her arms wrapped around him, hanging onto him to ensure she stayed upright, fingertips curling into the black hair at his nape. Her body was going haywire, her temperature soaring. His tongue stroked hers and the fierce pulse of desire clenched tight at the heart of her. In turmoil under that racing onslaught of sensation, Jo pulled back.

Gianni closed his hand over hers to prevent her from moving away. 'Are you going to take me indoors to speak to your family? Or are you planning to run away?'

Some inner strength powered Jo into raising her head high even though she was still quaking inside herself from the force of the reaction she was containing. 'Neither. I will deal with my family alone when I've reached a decision.'

'Then give me a decision over breakfast tomorrow at Belvedere. Eight. If we're going to do this, we need to move quickly,' Gianni murmured softly.

Jo had forgotten about the time constraints, and she ground her teeth together. She wanted to hold him at a distance because of the way he had made her feel in his arms and breakfast was only a matter of hours away, not long enough in which to recover her equilibrium and make the most major decision of her life to date.

'Eight?' she gasped.

'I'm pushing the time back for your benefit. I usually eat at six.'

'Even on a Sunday?'

'At least you won't miss church,' Gianni pointed out, sliding back into his car with the feral grace of a prowling panther.

Jo discovered that she was still holding her breath as she walked into the house, feeling as though she had gone through several rounds with a top prizefighter, exhausted and yet excited, challenged and yet exhilarated, dazed yet with her mind still racing. Her heart was still pounding inside her, her legs felt weak and wobbly.

Sybil cornered her in the hall. *'Well?'*

Jo smothered a fake yawn. 'We're meeting at eight for breakfast before we make a final decision.'

'We?'

Jo leant closer. 'Can you keep a secret?' She had to tell someone, and she knew that she could trust Sybil. 'He's asked me to marry him and in return he will take care of everything here.'

'I suppose you practically bit his hand off for an offer that good…' Sybil laughed at Jo's shock at that frank estimation. 'You've always wanted him, Jo. This is not exactly coming out of left field, is it? He does need to rehab his image…but are you willing to risk getting hurt?'

Shifting from surprise to acceptance at her great-aunt's shrewd reading of her predicament, Jo smiled. 'Yes. Probably because I don't think I can resist his proposal. If I said no, I'd always wonder if I'd made a mistake and I'm not sure I could bear seeing him marry someone else when it could have been me.'

'Do what's right for *you*,' Sybil urged, giving her an affectionate hug. 'I won't offer you any advice, but do appreciate that I can get a proper job and so can Trixie and we can find somewhere to live. We're far from helpless. I only worry about your grandmother.'

Jo went to bed and lay awake. Her whole body was buzzing with nervous energy.

Gianni couldn't sleep either. He was thinking about getting married and torn between lust and panic at what having a wife would be like. Jojo had standards, *serious* standards. There would be no grey areas with Jojo, no looking the other way. He didn't want to be the kind of husband his father had been: lying and cheating behind his wife's back. He needed to be honest with Jo, however, frank about the reality that he couldn't offer her love. He understood Jo well enough to know that she wouldn't be happy to hear that truth. They would *both* have to make compromises, he acknowledged.

On the lighter side, Jo would turn Belvedere into a home, something it had not been since the death of his mother, he mused thoughtfully. Furthermore, it was boredom with the women he met that had plunged him into that shabby encounter at the nightclub. Jo was not boring. She made intelligent conversation and could be very amusing and there was something about her, something he couldn't define, that turned him on so hard and fast it should have been scary. But it was exciting and it had been a very long time since anything outside business had truly excited Gianni.

Jo got up early and put on a light skirt and casual white top, pushing her bare feet into sandals. She decided to walk over to Belvedere and left Fairy behind slumbering in the kitchen. McTavish caught up with her on her walk and she told him to go home repeatedly while he capered around her in mad excitement at the pheasant he had scared into flight.

'You're not allowed at Gianni's house. You disgraced yourself,' she reminded him and she left him whining on the front doorstep of the mansion.

Abigail led her through the hall. 'Mr Renzetti fancied something less formal than the dining room, so he had us set up a table on the terrace. I don't know what's got into him,' she whispered. 'He's never eaten breakfast here *outdoors*.'

'It's a beautiful morning,' Jo said soothingly.

She strolled out through the leafy orangery to the terrace and there it was, a table set with all the formality of an Edwardian dining room in the open air. Of course, the housekeeper knew no other way of doing things because Gianni's mother had preferred the pomp and ceremony and Gianni had probably never even bothered to say that he wasn't quite as enamoured about that kind of superficial show. That was assuming that Gianni had even noticed and she was not sure he would or why he had made such a choice. He had about as much interest in how his home ran as she had in high finance.

'Jojo...' Gianni sprang upright, a lean, powerful figure dressed in chinos and a dark green tee. Even casually clad, he looked amazing, his black cropped hair gleaming in the sunshine, heavily lashed dark golden eyes intent as he smiled at her.

'I don't think I've seen you out of a suit since you were a teenager,' Jo commented, butterflies flying free in her tummy. She was trying not to reel from the charisma of that smile and the knowledge that if she went ahead, she would always be stressing just a little about the worry of having such a very good-looking husband.

'I work at home on Sundays.'

'That'll have to stop. I'm a firm believer in Sunday being a day of rest,' Jo murmured quietly.

Gianni's stunning eyes flashed pure gold and stared into hers with the piercing potency of a laser scalpel. 'Does that *mean*...?'

Abigail bustled about fetching plates, pouring tea and coffee, setting out toast and a basket of *pains au chocolat* that would usually have made Jo's hand reach straight out because they were a favourite of hers.

Jo angled up her delicate chin, sapphire-blue eyes schooled to a tranquil expression, her calm only a surface show when deep down inside she was quaking at the far-reaching effects of the decision she had made. 'I suppose it must. However, there would be conditions.'

His strong jawline clenched. 'Not a fan of that word, *cara*. I don't like limits and conditions outside the business world.'

The housekeeper finally retreated and left them alone. Jo began sipping her tea with the same air of composure. Only the realisation that her hand was trembling made her set down the cup with a slightly jarring snap of china meeting china. She didn't want Gianni to guess how shaken she was by her own daring choice. She had to be strong with Gianni. If she weren't, he was one of those fiery passionate personalities who would walk all over her. He *had* to respect that she would have demands to make too.

'The first condition is that I won't be sharing a bed with you until *I* feel comfortable with that idea.'

'Even though we'll be married?'

'We haven't even dated. I know you as a neighbour, a casual acquaintance. I will be happy to share a bed with you when we're in a proper relationship as a couple, but not before that,' Jo extended.

The minute Gianni had registered that she was agreeing to marry him he had planned to ask her to stay that very night with him. An annoyance that came from the strangest sense of hurt rejection rippled through his lean, powerful frame and he suppressed the reaction, knowing that he only wanted Jo to be with him when *she* felt right about the idea. Anything less was inconceivable to him. 'So, I will also be on trial as a husband?'

'That's not how I see it. I view it as a reasonable request.'

'I can understand your feelings,' Gianni responded.

Jo succumbed to a crispy soft *pain au chocolat* and tore off a piece of flaky pastry. She felt naïve for not having foreseen that that condition of hers would be challenging for him to accept.

Gianni raked long brown fingers through his luxuriant black hair and paced to the edge of the terrace, tension in the lines of his powerful physique, his broad shoulders squared, his long legs braced apart. Just as suddenly he swung back to her. 'And you think that this would get our marriage off to a good start?' he queried in a calm tone, making it clear that it was a genuine question, not a scornful one.

Jo nodded, relief flowing through her in a heady wave that made her feel slightly dizzy. 'I do.'

'Then so it will be. I accept your terms,' Gianni conceded levelly. 'I don't do relationships with women, *cara*. You have to tell me what you want and need and, as you have just seen, I'm not always fast on the uptake.'

'But you *did* have a relationship while you were at university,' Jo reminded him.

Gianni froze in front of her, eyes narrowing, spectacular cheekbones taut, his stubborn mouth compressing. 'I only told you *that* because I was trying to express sympathy for your loss. It was unwise of me and I would like you to forget that confidence. It is not a topic I care to revisit.'

Jo turned pale at that chilling little speech. It definitely wasn't the optimum moment to tell him that

Ralph Scott had not been her fiancé or the love of her life, since evidently Gianni regretted telling her even as little as he had about his past relationship. She felt snubbed and hurt and embarrassed all at the same time.

'Maybe I should go home…' she began awkwardly, just as a warning growl sounded from the depths of the shrubbery closest to Gianni. It was a welcome interruption and she was instantly upright to stalk over there and say angrily. 'McTavish…go home, *right now*!'

'I was expecting him,' Gianni confessed. 'He follows you everywhere.'

He returned to the table and lifted a steel dome on the trolley to reveal a massive meaty bone. He picked it up with a wince of distaste and as the terrier erupted from the shrubbery he dropped it on the grass. McTavish screeched to a halt and sniffed the bone with the enthusiasm of a dog whose every Christmas had come at once. He lost all interest in Gianni and concentrated on trying to drag the giant bone away.

'My goodness…' Jo whispered.

'He'd much rather chew on that than my leg,' Gianni said drily. 'Sit down, *cara*. I have something to give you.'

Her smooth brow pleating, Jo dropped back down into her seat.

Gianni extended his hand, palm upright. An extraordinarily elaborate jewelled ring lay in the centre of it. 'Your engagement ring. If you don't like it, I'll get you something more contemporary. It's from my mother's collection of medieval jewellery and the sapphires and diamonds are of the highest quality. It once belonged to an Italian *duchessa*, but if you want more information on its background, you'll have to look up my mother's catalogues for yourself.'

An engagement ring? No, she hadn't been expecting that, but she supposed that it tied in with his desire for them to look and behave like a normal couple. She stared down at the rich blue sapphires and the glittering diamonds in wonder. 'It's absolutely gorgeous,' she muttered weakly, still in shock at the gesture.

More relaxed now, Gianni strode round the table and lifted it from her again to slide it onto her finger. 'It'll need resizing, I'm sure... *Dio mio*, you have tiny fingers.' As the ring settled into place as though it had been made for her, Gianni smiled down at her. 'Now, isn't that a good omen? While you eat your breakfast you can tell me about your other conditions.'

Jo was reluctant to speak up after the reaction her first condition had drawn from him. 'Er...well, maybe this is not the right time.'

'It is the *only* time,' Gianni sliced in smoothly.

Jo swallowed hard. 'Well...er, fidelity.'

Gianni tossed her a withering glance. 'Don't even say it. I'm not going to cheat on you. My father had other women throughout his marriage. I will not be following in his footsteps. What else?'

'You have to make an effort not to work all the time.'

'Monday through Friday, I will make no promises, but weekends and holidays I will be entirely yours,' Gianni asserted with characteristic certainty.

Jo chanced a sip of tea and a sliver of her pastry but she was strung too high on nerves to swallow easily. Her mind had fallen on that 'entirely yours' phrase like a vulture and refused to move beyond that level.

Gianni sank down on the seat beside hers and

reached for a piece of pastry and held it up to her mouth with amusement. 'You have to eat, Jojo…you barely ate last night and this morning you're starving yourself again. You need your strength,' he told her softly. 'How else can you hope to hold me at bay on our honeymoon? I've got skills at seduction like you wouldn't believe.'

Jo almost choked on that piece of pastry as a laugh escaped her, unexpected happiness bubbling up through her. 'Promises, promises.'

'I can't give you love but I do know what women want and I believe I can make you happy,' Gianni concluded.

And that little bubble of happiness simply burst right there and then. Her incredible ring cast a fiery rainbow across the table as the light caught it. Not this woman, Gianni, Jo reflected ruefully. You don't have a clue what *this* woman you're marrying wants. And that was hardly surprising when she barely knew herself.

She wouldn't be putting him on trial as a husband, no, she *wasn't*, she reasoned unhappily. She was protecting herself, refusing to give way to his apparent belief that any woman would just fall into bed with him the minute he asked. Jo, he's a gorgeous, young billionaire, she conceded grudgingly, of course he has lofty expectations that whatever he wants, he will receive. Only marriage should be different, shouldn't it? Equal partners and all that. Gianni would have to make an effort. Was it humanly possible that he had *never* had to make an effort to persuade a woman into bed before?

Gianni did not savour the chilly welcome of a cold shower instead of a warm companion in his bed that night. He was still in shock at Jo's conditions. He hadn't been prepared for Jo to dream up something that Machiavellian. No sex. And yet she wanted him. He knew that. He had felt that desire in her just the same as his own.

Why would any adult woman make sex such a stumbling block? Sex was sex…a mere bodily function, an exercise of simple pleasure, Gianni reasoned in bewilderment. Was it some religious thing with her? He was utterly mystified by her attitude. Around him, women usually couldn't wait to shed their clothes. Now he was marrying one who was making a hard limit of the one thing he was almost convinced he couldn't live without…and if that was a little glimpse of his future as a respectably married man, he was not impressed by the view.

CHAPTER FOUR

'IT *IS* THE most gorgeous dress,' Liz Hamilton said softly with pride as she surveyed her granddaughter in her full bridal regalia.

Jo examined her reflection with a rare streak of satisfaction at her appearance. Her gown was quintessentially feminine and the instant it had appeared on the laptop screen set before her, it had stolen her heart. Pearls encrusted the lace corset bodice while the long, narrow skirt descended into fluffy ruffles that showed only a hint of her lace-covered high heels. Long lace gloves completed the look. A lightweight but superbly elegant pearl tiara anchored her upswept hair, courtesy of the pearl set Gianni had removed from his safe and offered her.

But then, Gianni had everything at his fingertips. She had been unaware, prior to their wedding plans, that Gianni utilised his personal wealth in promising investments. He co-owned an internationally famous wedding company, just as he co-owned many of the local businesses—almost everything from the nearest supermarket to the blacksmith's forge had a Renzetti stake in it. Gianni kept horses and ensuring the necessary services were available made sense. Jo had always wondered why their village seemed to be more populated and prosperous than others nearby and only now did she understand that Renzetti gold powered their presence and success.

The day after she had agreed to marry Gianni the wedding planner from London had arrived to organise everything, from her gown right down to the colour of the napkins at the reception to be held at Belvedere in the ballroom. Professional caterers had been hired. Expense was not an issue with *anything*! And that was such a total shock from Jo's point of view because she had never lived in a world in which cost was immaterial. Money had always been in short supply at Ladymead and giving up that mindset was a challenge for her. Initially, Gianni's lifestyle and spending habits had struck her pious soul as wasteful. Sybil, however, had talked her round with common sense, asking her if she was seriously expecting Gianni to live any way other than with the fabulous opulence that was all he had known since birth. And, of course, that had changed her attitude because she could not imagine Gianni without his spectacular car collection, his stable of thoroughbreds, his discreet security detail or his designer suits.

One surprise had, however, awaited her when she went to her family's lawyer to check through the prenuptial contract she was to sign before the wedding. There in bold print she had read that the renovation that her family home required, and which Gianni was financing, meant that Gianni had stipulated that their marriage had to last a minimum of five years. That had been unexpected but also just a little gratifying. She had wondered whether or not she should tackle him about that clause.

Did that clause mean that Gianni was ensuring that they stayed together for at least five years for his own personal reasons? Or was it merely the act of a shrewd businessman, who knew that fixing Ladymead's many deficiencies would cost a fortune and wanted to ensure that he received the fullest possible benefit from his convenient marriage?

Whichever reason had motivated Gianni, Jo had decided not to question it. After all, what difference did it make to her when she had decided to marry him for the sake of her family home and her relatives? And in five years' time, she told herself staunchly, even if Gianni chose to divorce her, she would still only be twenty-nine years old, an age at which she could more easily move on and make another life for herself, other than that of being a Renzetti wife.

'It's not the dress, it's *you* in the dress who is gorgeous,' Sybil insisted fondly as she escorted her great-niece out to the wedding car where her grandmother now awaited her.

'Let's hope Gianni thinks so too,' Jo quipped nervously, because it was his reaction to her appearance that mattered most to her.

And why was that? she asked herself in exasperation. Her thoughts and her emotional involvement in her wedding day were utterly inappropriate for a woman making a marriage of convenience. She wasn't about to marry some man whom she loved, she reminded herself. She liked Gianni. She found him physically attractive. But that was all, absolutely *all*, she assured herself firmly. Getting too attached to Gianni Renzetti would be sheer insanity in such a relationship, one based on practicality more than anything else.

You *are* a gold-digger, a little voice whispered deep inside her and she tensed even more. It didn't matter that Gianni didn't see her that way at present—who could tell what future changes would occur in their relationship? After all, she was marrying him for his wealth and what that wealth could do for her family and Ladymead.

'I can feel you trembling beside me,' her grandmother said worriedly, grasping Jo's cold hand. 'What on earth is the matter?'

Jo turned with a soothing smile she thought worthy of an award and replied, 'I suppose I'm just realising what a big step marriage is.'

'All that matters at the end of the day is that you love each other, and, the way Gianni looks at you, I have no doubt concerning his feelings,' the older woman responded calmly.

Neither Trixie nor her grandmother had doubted that Jo and Gianni's sudden plan to get married related to anything less than a passionate romance. Of course, both her grandmother and her great-aunt were a little naïve in that line, Jo conceded guiltily. Sybil was infinitely more worldly-wise than either.

Mercifully, Gianni had put on a good show when he had been invited over to supper one evening and that hospitality had been returned by a lavish dinner for her family at Belvedere on another night. Yes, Gianni was a smooth act when it came to such familial stuff. He had taken a video of Duffy singing his *Cabaret* phrases. He had brought another bone for McTavish. He had even let Trixie perform a tarot reading for them both, although at one stage of that rather melodramatic show from her great-aunt Jo had realised that Gianni was trying awfully hard not to laugh out loud. That had been when

Trixie had forecast that he would be the father of twins within the year...

The village church loomed in front of the wedding car. It had been a very short drive as the church was built at the edge of village and on the Belvedere estate, funded by the original Renzetti, who had built the house. It was a picturesque Edwardian building surrounded in well-tended lawn and seasonal summer flowers. Jo slid out of the car, careful not to soil her dainty shoes, ruffles or gloves. She rested her hand on her grandmother's arm.

'You knocked it right out of the park this time,' Gianni's best man murmured, staring down the aisle. 'She's lovely.'

Gianni turned his darkly handsome profile and saw his bride. The entire outfit somehow contrived to be the sexiest wedding gown he had ever seen. He wondered if it was the gloves, or the fact that almost every inch of her creamy skin was covered, or that the inescapably elegant line of her slender figure was revealed. He shouldn't be thinking in those terms, he reminded himself grimly, not without a wedding night ahead. Of course, she could still change her mind...

That single glimpse of Gianni as he turned, the very image of stunning dark good looks, perfectly groomed in formal attire, made Jo's mouth run even drier. Her breasts tightened, an uncomfortable ache stirring between her thighs in a way that only made her more apprehensive than ever of what their marriage would mean. She didn't want Gianni to know how much he attracted her and certainly that nobody else had ever had the same effect on her. No way was she planning to make herself into another one of the little toys he took so briefly into his bed. She was worth more than that, way more!

Sunshine cascaded through the stained-glass windows high above the altar, creating a myriad tiny rainbows to dance over the interior. The elderly priest of their parish began the service and the formal vows. Gianni had requested a short service while Jo would have preferred the longer one, but she had kept quiet on that score, reminding herself that they were a fake bridal couple in most ways and only pretending to love and care for each other. In such a ceremony, only the formalities had to be observed.

Gianni threaded the ring on her finger, his heart beating very fast. Her gossamer-fine lace gloves ended at the knuckle, anchored only by the thumb. She repeated the gesture for him. He glanced at the gleaming ring on his hand with a compressed mouth and a stormy look in his dark eyes, recalling his father's satisfaction when he had announced his plans, wondering why his parent should be so pleased that he should enter an institution that had brought the older man no personal happiness that his son had ever seen.

Jo had to almost trot to stay level with her new husband as he sped them back down the aisle, reluctantly pausing for formal photos while those waiting outside with their phones were immediately approached by security to request that the image be deleted. Gianni hurried her on into the waiting limousine.

'You look very beautiful,' Gianni murmured once

they were alone. 'And for some reason I find those gloves outrageously sexy, *cara*.'

Jo went pink. 'You always know the right thing to say,' she told him, knowing that there was no way on earth she could ever tell him that her heart had stuttered inside her chest when she'd first seen him awaiting her at the altar.

She refused to give Gianni the impression that she reacted to him like some infatuated teenager…even if it was true. She reckoned most women had frivolous thoughts on their wedding days but she was very conscious that she had no excuse to behave the same way. Attraction was one thing, anything more out of the question. She wasn't planning to fall down that rabbit hole for Gianni in a marriage that she assumed would last no more than five years. She wasn't queuing up to get a broken heart, because she wasn't that stupid. That confirmed in her head, she relaxed a little.

'You don't like weddings, do you?' she remarked as they emerged from the limo outside Belvedere, a line of catering staff, headed by a smiling Abigail, already awaiting them.

'Not much. I don't think I believe in that happily ever after stuff,' he quipped. 'Too much cheating and too many divorces in my social circle.'

'You mix with the wrong people,' Jo countered. 'My grandparents were married for over fifty years.'

'They had fewer choices and temptations than the people I know,' Gianni traded, unconvinced.

And there was no time for any further personal chat because they were plunged straight into greeting guests. Some very beautiful women in fabulous dresses and jewellery were attending but equally, from the snatches of dialogue she heard around Gianni, it was almost a business occasion for an equal number of men.

Sybil strolled in with Federico Renzetti, his hand resting at her spine, and Jo resisted the urge to give her glamorous great-aunt a warning look to keep her flirtations out of the family circle. That ship had already sailed, after all. Some years earlier, Federico had invited Sybil out to dinner and she had gone, only to say that once was enough because all Gianni's father had been able to talk about was his late wife, whom he had remained obsessed with.

'And, as I remember it, Isabella treated him like dirt beneath her feet!' Sybil had commented at the time. 'Maybe that old "treat them mean, keep them keen" saying works better than you think.'

They took their seats in the ballroom at a traditional top table.

'I don't feel married yet,' Gianni murmured silkily.

'Wait until I start nagging,' Jo advised with a wide smile as she sipped her champagne, relieved that the most formal part of the day was over.

'My father's chatting up Sybil,' Gianni groaned.

'Don't worry about it. He had his chance with her and he blew it years ago.'

'Is that so?' Gianni did not hide his surprise. 'What happened?'

'Apparently, he could only talk about how much he missed your mother.'

Gianni tensed. 'I doubt that. He didn't treat her very well while she was alive.'

Aware she was treading on sensitive ground, Jo shrugged. 'I'm only repeating what Sybil told my grandmother back then. Who knows?'

'He was a terrible husband,' Gianni informed her.

Jo nodded. 'But don't forget, there's two sides to every story.'

'And what's that supposed to mean?'

Jo raised a finely arched brow, her sapphire eyes questioning his sharp tone. 'Only what I said. I know they weren't a happy couple, but you have to be fair. Your mother was ill for a good deal of their marriage and that must have imposed immense strain on them both.'

'It's none of your business.' In reality, Gianni was shaken that he himself had never grasped that obvious truth about his parents' relationship.

Jo dealt him a pained glance and turned her head away, her profile taut. He had a terrible relationship with his father, and she wasn't surprised because both men avoided discussing anything that might have improved it. She had watched Gianni greet his father almost like a stranger when he'd first arrived, and it had disturbed her. In her opinion, life was too short to cherish that kind of bias but, even so, she resolved never to mention his parents again. Unfortunately, Gianni's views were set in stone and he saw his mother as a misunderstood saint and his father as a dreadful man. He had never, she registered ruefully, really moved an inch on that issue since his mother's death when he was thirteen.

'I apologise. I was rude and you made a good point,' Gianni murmured half under his breath.

'I'm too outspoken sometimes,' Jo said lightly. 'We tend to speak the truth and shame the devil in my family.'

'While the Renzetti men barely speak at all,' Gianni completed wryly.

'That could be a point of contention between us,' Jo admitted quietly. 'I like to talk things out.'

Gianni grasped her tiny fingers and sighed. 'Why do you always foresee problems? Why aren't you more optimistic?'

'I suppose I'm just too practical. I'll work on it,' Jo promised, her plump pink lips parting in a wide smile.

Desire flashed through Gianni with the efficiency of a lightning strike. He gritted his teeth in annoyance because that level of susceptibility made him feel as though he had been plunged back into adolescence. Every time he looked at his bride, he wanted her. Of course, it was only because his libido was on a hair trigger because he hadn't had sex in so long, he reasoned with assurance. That was the *sole* reason. The scandal in the tabloid newspaper had appeared many weeks after the actual incident had taken place. In that interim period, shocked by the manner in which he had been targeted and set up for blackmail, Gianni had concentrated on the police investigation and had slept alone.

A famous singer entertained their guests during the meal. The wedding cake was cut and then Gianni swung Jo out onto the dance floor. He drew her close. The tangy aroma of his cologne mingled with his underlying scent of masculinity and warmth and she breathed in deep, with colour flaring in her cheeks. Was it pheromones or some such thing? she wondered. Because he smelt amazing to her...so amazing that she wanted to bury her nose in his jacket and just stay there.

'You're very quiet,' he complained above her head.

'Just relaxing,' Jo proffered, hoping her flush died

off before they left the floor because she loathed the fact that she still blushed like a schoolgirl, having assumed that would be something she left behind after she passed her teen years.

With every movement on the floor the contact between their bodies seemed to increase, the shift of his lean hips fluid against hers, the strength and breadth of his chest pressing on her breasts. Sexual heat stole into her like a thief in the night, lighting up a glow in all her sensitive areas. She made excuses for herself. Aside from that single kiss, they had never been so close before. But he was aroused as well. That awareness made her feel less awkward and even made her hide a smile against his shoulder. It was strange, she reflected, how something that had made her uncomfortable with other men somehow enthralled her when it was Gianni in the starring role.

And possibly more than a little naïve, she admonished herself for, aside from his veneration of his mother's memory, Gianni seemed to have little interest in women beyond sexual satisfaction. She had sort of guessed that about him when he had changed girlfriends at head-turning speed as a teenager and teenaged beauties with broken hearts had littered the neighbourhood. Back then gossip had always kept her up to date with Gianni's extra-curricular activities, but that handy conduit of information had died once he went to university. Once again, she found herself wondering who that first and only love of his had been. As far as the gossip columns were concerned, he had dated no woman for long, so the likelihood was that he had fallen in love as a student.

Questioning her own intense curiosity, Jo suppressed

it. What did the whys and wherefores of Gianni's one and only love matter to her? It was none of her business, and cultivating an interest in such things would only lead to friction in their relationship, but he was too reserved a guy to share confidences.

Later that afternoon, she went upstairs to change because they were leaving soon to fly out to Italy. Sybil was smiling and unusually cheerful.

'Federico flirting up a storm?' Jo teased. 'It's always nice to be appreciated.'

'I've got goss about his marriage,' Sybil revealed. 'I think he only told me because he wants me to eat out with him again but this lady's not for turning.'

'I'm not sure I should listen to it,' Jo confided ruefully. 'Gianni is still so sensitive about his unhappy childhood, not that he would even admit that it *was* unhappy.'

'He's got to have the odd flaw or two. His parents' marriage was a disaster,' Sybil opined. 'The year before Federico met Isabella, the love of Isabella's life, the man she *planned* to marry, died in a plane crash. Her father threatened to leave his fortune to another relative if she didn't find a husband and that's why she married Federico. He didn't find that out until years afterwards. She closed the bedroom door after Gianni was conceived and it never opened again. She just used him!'

Jo wriggled out of her wedding gown and laid it carefully on the bed. 'I hate taking it off.'

'Gianni should be playing maid here, not me!' Sybil quipped. 'No comment about what I just told you? I think that if Gianni knew those facts, he wouldn't be so hard on his father.'

'His father should tell his son himself,' Jo said prosaically. 'I'm not going to get involved. Are you planning to see Federico again?'

'I haven't decided yet. He hasn't stayed at Belvedere since Gianni took official ownership a few years back. It's wicked that Isabella even took this house from Federico. She put so much money into fixing it up after their marriage that she demanded he sign it over to her.'

It was news to Jo that the Renzettis had ever been that short of cash and she simply sighed, thinking that Federico had known how to forge a path into Sybil's heavily guarded heart. Just as she rescued stray animals, Sybil liked to rescue people. 'You feel sorry for him,' she said softly.

'How could I not? Isabella fooled us all into thinking she was so vulnerable and poorly treated, but her husband also suffered. His wife didn't love him, she only loved her son and Federico's only child doesn't even *like* him!' Sybil proclaimed with spirit.

'Perhaps he should put more effort into talking to his son.' And that was Jo's last word on the subject, for it seemed that her great-aunt saw a softer side to Federico Renzetti than others did for, even as a child, Jo had found the older man cold and silent. Evidently, Sybil had the power to turn him into a positive chatterbox. She herself barely knew the man and had no opinion to offer.

Sheathed in a midnight-blue sundress, her feet in high-heeled sandals, Jo accompanied her aunt down the huge wide staircase that ornamented Belvedere's marble front hall where a few clusters of guests, who had left the ballroom, stood around talking and drinking. Lounging in a chair at the back of the hall with his father, Gianni sprang immediately upright, a smile lightening his taut, dark expression, and strode forward.

At the foot of the stairs, a woman intercepted Jo.

'What have you got that I haven't got?' the woman demanded imperiously and very loudly, her champagne glass wavering in her hand. 'That's what I want to know!'

'Sorry, I—' Jo moved to sidestep the clearly inebriated woman.

'It's a simple question, answer it,' the woman slurred, heads swivelling all around them. 'I got one night with Gianni and then I sat wasting my time and waiting for a phone call that never came.'

'This isn't the time or the place for this, my dear,' Sybil interposed. 'Let's return to the ballroom.'

'No, I want the bride to answer me!' the blonde ranted even louder, her expression one of desperation, her face tear-stained as she closed her hand over Jo's wrist to prevent her from walking away from her. 'Hell, you're beautiful, anyone can see that, but what special quality do you have?'

'Milly, how lovely to see you again,' Gianni interrupted smooth as glass as he signalled someone. 'Jojo's special quality is that I love her. '

Milly looked at him as though he had stuck a knife in her heart, her eyes overflowing, tears trailing down her quivering cheeks just as one of Gianni's security men approached, clearly intending to remove her from the house.

'No, it's all right, Milly,' Jo said gently as the hand fell from her wrist and the other woman's head lowered in defeat and embarrassment. 'Let's go somewhere quiet where you can sit down and relax while we find your friends.'

As the security man hovered and Gianni froze, bewildered by his bride's unexpected intervention, Jo walked the weeping woman across the hall into the nearest room, knowing that Sybil would ensure that Milly's companions were located to take care of her.

'You'll have to try to be kinder,' Sybil warned Gianni on her way past him again. 'Jo has a huge heart.'

Gianni had said he loved her with such panache even though they both knew it was a lie, Jo reflected as she left the distraught woman with her friend, who had made many apologies for her, dismissed as unnecessary by Jo. People got drunk, upset, sometimes forgot themselves and said stuff they shouldn't. That was life even at a luxury bridal occasion at Belvedere. But the other woman's pain had wounded Jo. She couldn't help wondering how many other women her bridegroom had hurt over the years and supposed that there would be quite a few with disappointed hopes. Well, she wasn't going to be one of them, she promised herself. No way was she going to fall for him!

Impervious to Sybil's advice, Gianni only waited until the limousine door had closed on them to say, 'What on earth possessed you to take that woman aside after she had insulted you?'

'She didn't insult me. She was drunk, hurt, bitter, jealous. *Your* doing,' Jo murmured with succinct bite. 'That's the other side of the coin to your lifestyle.'

Gianni slung her an incredulous appraisal. 'We're *not* discussing this.'

'Of course not.' Jo had expected exactly that response, but she hoped she had made him think about the damage that could result from his enjoyment of his freedom and a wide variety of women.

'You should have stood back and allowed my security men to handle her in a more appropriate manner,' Gianni imparted curtly.

Jo said nothing. She inclined her head, dug a fat book out of her new capacious leather bag in her favourite shade of electric blue and read all the way to the airport.

Gianni breathed in deep and slow, mastering his temper. *His* lifestyle? His former lifestyle had been destroyed the minute he put that wedding ring on her finger and he did not appreciate having his past sins thrown in his teeth the same day. In any case, it was not as though he planned to emulate his father and keep a mistress, an act that had broken his mother's heart. Even if he didn't love Jojo, he would be a good husband. At least she hadn't preached at him about his sexually adventurous past. Evidently her sympathies were with the woman. But he hadn't wronged anyone! He hadn't seduced Milly or done anything questionable with her either! For a long few minutes, Gianni quietly simmered.

Eventually, he registered that for once in his life, he had been naïve to believe that he could marry Jo Hamilton without experiencing moments of frustration. In comparison to him she had led a very clean, God-fearing life. They had lived at opposite ends of the worldly spectrum and naturally cherished very different views. Yet, he still respected Jojo more than any woman he had ever met. He liked her brand of refreshing honesty, her quick intelligence *and* her strong streak of compassion. Another bride might have thrown a scene about her perfect day being ruined by a former lover of the groom, might, indeed, have taken her resentment out on him. Jojo had done neither. No, she had empathised with the other woman. Unbelievable, he thought wryly, and yet it had happened...

Jo had never travelled in a private jet before, indeed had only enjoyed a handful of trips abroad, all relating to school organised trips. Now she was seated in an opulent cabin furnished like a very superior office with comfortable cream leather seating, even recliners. Magazines had been brought to her and a menu of refreshments tendered by an efficient steward. Like so many of the rich trappings of Gianni's life, it felt like another world to Jo.

'We're heading for my mother's family home on Isola di Cristoforo,' Gianni explained as they left the jet in Italy only to board a helicopter. 'It's an old property and the island enjoys a rich history with several ancient ruins. I thought you would enjoy it.'

'Is that a crack about the money pit that is now your responsibility?' Jo joked, because temporary repairs to secure Ladymead were already taking place. Her relatives were now discussing whether or not they would move out during the extensive renovations because Gianni had offered them a village house for the duration of the work to be done.

'Not at all. I merely thought it would give you an interest for a honeymoon that's not really a honeymoon,' Gianni remarked.

Jo reddened and wished she had kept quiet, because of course theirs wouldn't be the traditional honeymoon that most couples enjoyed.

She craned her neck but only saw a dizzying view

of mature trees as the helicopter descended. When she emerged, she glimpsed stone walls through the tree trunks.

'It's a medieval castle,' Gianni told her with amusement. 'My mother's father owned the island and my mother told me that he revelled in his fortress on the hill as a symbol of his power. I'm a rare visitor and most of the island is a nature reserve now and open to the public. I never knew him. All my grandparents were gone by the time I was four years old. I envy your close ties with your grandmother.'

'That's because Gran's really been my mother,' Jo explained as they arrived at giant double doors standing open in the sunshine in readiness for their arrival. 'But I'm probably closest to Sybil. My great-aunts were still quite young when Gran got married and the sisters have always lived together.'

'My father thought it was a rum set-up in your household—three sisters and one man.'

Jo shrugged. 'It worked for all of them. The house was large enough. Grandpa was a bit like a father to Sybil and Trixie, although Trixie was already a teenager. Families stayed together in those days. Grandpa married Gran knowing her sisters came with her.'

'People still mention him. Your grandfather was well liked.'

An older woman with greying hair greeted them in Italian in the medieval hall with its stone walls hung with imposing family portraits. Gianni took charge of showing Jo upstairs, opening an oak door on an elegant room furnished with a scarlet-draped four-poster bed. Flowers were scattered across the quilt and beautiful ivory blooms were massed in several vases throughout the large room.

Jo's sapphire blue eyes widened. 'My goodness. It's lovely.'

'It's been set up for our wedding night. I'm sleeping next door,' Gianni informed her as her luggage was brought in. 'I understand that dinner will be served in an hour on the terrace.'

Jo went pink. Gianni stalked towards her, spectacularly lithe, lean and darkly handsome, his stunning dark golden eyes welded to her hot face. 'But when our marriage becomes normal, I will demand that you put on that beautiful dress and those gloves again just for me one evening,' he imparted silkily.

Her blue eyes flew wide, and her generous lips curved. 'It's a deal,' she almost whispered, relieved by his attitude.

'We've got everything going for us, *cara*. You married me in the wake of that scandal and I appreciate that,' he admitted in a driven undertone as if such an admission did not come easily to him.

'And I appreciate you being…understanding,' Jo selected awkwardly.

'Kissing still on the menu?' Gianni surveyed her with dark eyes glittering below a lush canopy of black lashes and her heart skipped a beat.

'Of course,' she muttered tightly, barely able to get air into her lungs.

His arms closed round her and her heart began to pound as if she were running a race. He tipped her face up, covered her mouth with his and teased her sensitive lips with the tip of his tongue, igniting a fierce desire in her for more. But she couldn't have more…she knew that. Gianni needed a challenge with a reward. He knew that himself. He was already practically training Mc-Tavish into begging at his feet out of sheer greed. And not in this lifetime did she plan to find herself begging at Gianni's feet as so many others of her sex had done before. His fingers strummed down her spine and a wanton shiver ran through her entire body, her breasts peaking, her thighs pressing together. Out of the question, she reminded herself angrily.

She pulled back from him and smiled soothingly. 'Sorry, but I'm desperate for a shower before dinner.'

Gianni's gorgeous eyes flashed like the shimmer of pure gold in sunlight, much as if she had thrown him a challenge. 'I'll see you downstairs, then, *cara*.'

He was so smooth, so practised, it was impossible to shift him out of automatic charming mode, she mused ruefully as she freshened up. But she needed much more from him than that polished surface show.

The next morning, Jo stirred drowsily, voices filtering out from somewhere bringing her eyes open.

As she woke up, she recalled the beautiful meal she had shared with Gianni the night before and the guilty enchantment of the wedding day that was already behind her. Her spirits were buoyant after a long and very necessary deep sleep in an incredibly comfortable bed. She went into the bathroom and washed before tugging on a light robe to head downstairs. She didn't have to get fully dressed first thing, did she? Gianni was always so laid-back. She didn't need to dot every i and cross every t for his benefit.

It was only when she reached the stone stairs that she realised that there were two male voices speaking very loudly in Italian towards the rear of the castle. Indeed, they weren't speaking, they were shouting in what sounded like a bitter argument. What on earth was happening? she wondered as she followed the voices to source.

Jo was astonished to cross the threshold of the room Gianni used as an office and find herself in the midst of a heated dispute between Gianni and his father.

As the two men focused on her, both fell ominously silent.

'What on earth's going on?' she exclaimed.

Federico Renzetti turned his censorious gaze on her with disdain. 'Perhaps that's something *you* could clarify for our benefit.'

CHAPTER FIVE

'*ME?*' Jo ECHOED in disbelief, wondering what on earth *she* could possibly have to do with their argument.

Gianni looked at Jo as he had never looked at her in his life before: with furious distaste and condemnation.

'This is my fault, *all* my fault,' Federico muttered in a pained declaration as he shot a guilty glance in his son's direction. 'I persuaded you to get married and, like you, I too would have believed that you had made a very safe and sensible choice of wife.'

Jo was not slow on the uptake and that statement was an attack on her integrity. 'I don't know what you are talking about,' she told her father-in-law. 'But I think it's time that I did.'

Gianni strode across to his desk and punched a hand down on the crumpled newspaper lying there. His dark golden gaze was lit up like the hot, stormy heart of a bonfire.

Jo raised a brow. 'Words, Gianni...*words*,' she urged.

In a violent movement he swept up the newspaper and thrust it at her, drama accompanying his very gesture. 'Read it and weep!' he advised. 'You've been exposed as the fake you truly are!'

Although shaken by his attitude, Jo remained outwardly composed. She grasped the newspaper and registered that it was the same sleazy publication that had published the article on Gianni's worst mistake. It was a misunderstanding, Jo told herself, a ghastly, embarrassing misunderstanding. What else could it be? She didn't have any enemies that she knew about and had nothing in her past that she wished to conceal. Her knees loosened when she recognised the photo of Ralph's one-time fiancée, Jane Yerry. Not a pleasant girl. Jo had gone to school with the attractive brunette, who had been a terrible bully. But what on earth could Jane have to say about her? Her phone was vibrating madly in the pocket of her robe and it was a challenge to ignore it while two angry men stared at her as if they were expecting her to spontaneously combust or breakdown.

Instead, Jo backed down into an armchair on wobbly knees to address her attention to the newspaper. As she read, she was instantly infuriated by Jane's vile claim that Ralph had cheated on her with Jo and that Jo was the reason why Jane's engagement had been broken off. In one corner there was also a photo of Gianni and Jo emerging from the village church after their wedding, the only part of the day when camera phones had been less restricted.

'This is a load of bilge,' she spelt out unhappily, because she was affronted to find herself the target of such lies in print even though she was conscious that just about all the people who knew her and the other parties concerned were also aware of the *true* story.

My goodness, she reflected wretchedly, why the heck would Jane make up such outrageous lies? Her brow furrowing, she contemplated that puzzle. Jane had never been a fan of Jo's longstanding friendship with Ralph and Jo had been careful to stay in the background once she had recognised that reality.

Sadly, that broken engagement had, in the end, turned out very badly for Jane Yerry. Ralph had turned his back after discovering her in bed with his best friend, Peter, but Peter had been shamed into walking away from Jane as well. Jane's parents had been outraged by their daughter's conduct and by the cost of cancelling a large wedding at the very last minute. Jo's ongoing friendship with Ralph afterwards and the rumours that they were actually together as a couple would have annoyed Jane. Evidently hearing talk about Jo's marriage to one of the richest men in the country had ignited Jane's bitterness and she had made a crazy attempt to rescue her own reputation at the cost of Jo's. Even so, while Jo would not have counted Jane a friend, she would not have believed her to be an enemy either.

'I'm at a loss to understand why Jane would make such claims to a newspaper,' Jo confided quietly. 'But I think she'll find she's made a major mistake because most people will be annoyed with her for trying to shift the blame for her broken engagement onto me.'

Both men studied her with varying degrees of disbelief.

'And that's all you have to say on this subject?' Federico Renzetti pressed almost delicately.

'I do not even know who these people are!' Gianni told Jo.

'Why would you?' Jo responded, her tone even softer. 'And why would you even care about this nonsense?'

'Nonsense?' Gianni fired at her wrathfully. 'My bride's reputation has been trashed!'

His father measured the flash of Jo's steady sapphire gaze and said, 'You must understand. Gianni *married* you to rehabilitate his image. Being plunged back into another scandal is not what he expected or even prepared for.'

'Possibly *you* don't understand that I don't intend to shoulder any responsibility for someone telling bold and wicked lies about me,' Jo cut in curtly, her apparent composure lurching because she had not been ready for the older man to instantly throw the reason for their marriage in her face. It struck her that her father-in-law had judged her guilty the instant he'd learned of the tabloid piece even if he was being less obvious about the fact than Gianni was. But no, it wasn't possible that Gianni could believe such a character assassination, she reasoned. Gianni *knew* her. He knew her nature, her moral outlook. He could not possibly credit that she could have slept with Ralph behind Jane's back...*could he*?

'Obviously, you're going to say that it's all lies...and yet you did step into that woman's shoes after he ended things with her,' Gianni reminded her very drily. 'Even if I didn't know you or much about anyone involved, you wouldn't be the first woman to lie to me.'

Losing colour, Jo jerked shakily upright. 'I'm not having this conversation with you in your father's presence. I'm going upstairs to get dressed.'

'I'm returning to London immediately,' the older man declared with a hint of awkwardness and regret that ironically made her like him a tiny bit better. Most particularly, when her bridegroom was still regarding her much as if she had suddenly sprouted hooves and horns. What was the matter with Gianni? What had happened to his quick and clever brain?

As Gianni alerted the pilot to return his father to the airport, he was reeling in shock. Federico had arrived at the castle barely thirty minutes earlier and yet Gianni, famous for his fast reactions, was *still* reeling in shock and disgust. He could not explain to his own satisfaction why he felt so shattered by what that newspaper story had told him. Jo's coolness under fire had merely made him more suspicious, giving him an unwelcome view of his bride as a practised dissembler. Why had he been so convinced that Jo was the exact opposite of most of the other women he had known?

Why the hell, when he had previously been such a cynic, *had* he decided that Josephine Hamilton was in an entirely different category from the liars, swindlers and gold-diggers who littered his own past?

After all, liars and adulterers came in all shapes and sizes. Gianni had seen enough men and women behaving badly over the years to know that. Unluckily for her, Gianni had a particular aversion to the disloyal, dishonest, and unfaithful, having seen his own father in that guise from childhood. And he could not deny that the idea of Jo sneaking around behind backs to sleep with a man engaged to another woman filled him with rampant revulsion.

But why was he *so* angry?

It was her past, it was before they had even got together *and* the guy was dead and buried, the saner side of his mind argued. But it didn't change his mood one iota. He was furious with Jo for ripping apart his good-living image of her and he was furious with himself for being savagely disappointed in her. He had genuinely believed that she was above such behaviour and incredibly honest, only nasty reality had washed a film of grime over that conviction.

Even so, in his heart, Gianni did know *why* he was

so enraged. He had believed in Jo, admired her character, even begun to like her. And although it was most unlike him, he had somehow managed to place Jo on a very tall pedestal. Regrettably, she had fallen off it with a resounding crash and it had happened so fast that his mind was still spinning with a sense of incredulity. Initially, he had had a ferocious argument with Federico and had been ready to defend Jo until his dying breath…and then he had read that article and tied it in with what he already knew. And the awareness that he could still be so gullible as to place that amount of faith in a woman's honour and decency hugely embarrassed him.

Worst of all, however, he told himself bitterly, the reason he had married her had become redundant for there was no way her grubby affair with a man promised to another woman could clean up his image. That meant that he had also taken on the money pit on false pretences. Federico had warned him that he was insane to take on Ladymead without setting a strict budget, but then his father had never enjoyed the kind of wealth that his son had inherited. And something about Jo had made Gianni, usually the shrewd businessman when it came to cost, want to be as generous as proved necessary. He tossed back a second brandy without savouring the vintage.

Upstairs in her bedroom, Jo was all fingers and thumbs as she fought her way into linen shorts and a tee. Gianni was acting crazy, she reflected in consternation. He hadn't asked her any questions; he had simply assumed that that horrible story was the truth. Did she strike him as that kind of woman? Or was that distrust innate in him with women? She was shaken by the way he had looked at her and acted. She hadn't recognised him in that angry mood, all warmth and familiarity stripped from him, and all that did was make her wonder if she had *ever* had a clue as to what really went on inside Gianni.

But how dared he behave like that?

A little voice at the back of her brain reminded her that she had chosen not to tell him that her true relationship with Ralph had been platonic. On some foolish level, had she preferred to let Gianni believe that she had had, at least, *one* serious relationship? Jo paled at that glimpse inside herself where she suddenly recognised her insecurity. She was insecure with Gianni because he was infinitely more experienced and sophisticated than she would ever be.

Nobody knew better than Jo that she had led a sheltered life, surrounded by outdated rules and protected by her family. Circumstances had confined her at Ladymead, depriving her of the independent choices and freedom that many young adults took for granted. Even as a student she had lived at home because it was so much cheaper to do so. And although she would not have brandished the fact, she suspected that she was naturally rather unadventurous in her habits. Marrying Gianni was far and away the most dangerous step and the biggest risk she had ever taken.

In point of fact, she acknowledged with piercing dismay, she and Gianni were a bad match with almost nothing in common. What did that leave her to work with when they had a dispute? He was burning up like a Roman torch and she was striving to stay calm and collected even though her tummy was lurching with nausea.

Jo went back into Gianni's study. He was standing at the doors open onto the terrace with his back turned to her. 'We need to sort this misunderstanding out,' she told him bravely.

Gianni swung round to face her, his lean, strong face grim. 'I'm not stupid, *cara*. This is no misunderstanding.'

Frustration currented through Jo, putting her even more on edge. 'I didn't have an affair with Ralph and if you'd ever met Ralph, you would know that. Jane's lying. She's the one who had the affair that made Ralph break off their engagement.'

'Isn't it strange how you never mentioned any of this before?' Gianni sliced in, his wide mouth flattening, his narrowed dark eyes hard and unyielding. 'You never acknowledged that Ralph even *had* a previous engagement, and it wasn't referred to at the funeral either—'

'Why would it have been mentioned?' It was Jo's turn to interrupt, an edge of panic gaining inside her because she knew he wasn't listening to her. 'Ralph dumping Jane and *her* infidelity kept the gossipmongers busy for months and he was horribly embarrassed and hurt by the whole business. Nobody was likely to mention that broken engagement.'

'I don't want to hear about Ralph or your grubby affair with him and I'm not interested either in hearing your counter-accusations against this Yerry woman,' Gianni incised chillingly. 'In one sense what you chose to get up to prior to our marriage is nothing to do with me, but in another it's very much *my* business. I married you to clean up my image. I believed that you had a spotless reputation. That's the only reason I married you.'

Pale as milk at that cutting clarification, Jo lifted her head high and tilted her chin. 'I'm sorry if you don't feel that you got value for money,' she murmured flatly.

'That's not what I said, but it does express something of what I feel now,' Gianni confessed in a raw undertone, volatile dark golden eyes full of condemnation. 'I certainly wasn't expecting a twenty-two-carat virgin, but I *was* expecting a wife without a mess like this behind her and the subsequent mortification of her being exposed to derision in the media.'

Even though she hadn't done anything wrong, Jo felt shamed, as though she were responsible for Jane's deceitful attempt to rewrite history at Jo's expense. Her cheeks flamed and she swallowed hard. He was talking down to her—how dared he? But on another level, she knew that she was still traumatised from becoming the target of such a character assassination. Her phone had kept on buzzing while she was getting dressed. She had a dozen missed calls from various people and she had texted Sybil, promising to call her back later. Ralph's parents had also attempted to contact her and she would have to speak to them as well. They were quite an age and anything that disparaged their late son's character would have deeply distressed them.

'This is a storm in a teacup,' Jo declared, trying another tack with Gianni in an attempt to dial down the tension.

'It means a hell of a lot more than that to me!' Gianni fired back at her, his seething dissatisfaction blazing in dark golden eyes, semi-concealed by dense black lashes. 'I had complete faith in you and you've blown it.'

'I've done nothing, Gianni,' Jo countered steadily, holding her ground. 'Jane Yerry is lying. I didn't have an affair behind her back with her fiancé. I was *never* intimate with Ralph.'

'And how likely am I to credit that in this day and age?' Gianni derided.

'Ralph and I were only friends…at least on my side,' Jo adjusted, sticking scrupulously to the absolute truth for fear of causing further misapprehensions. 'We weren't engaged. Our supposed engagement was only a rumour, which I think he encouraged.'

'No more!' Gianni slashed a lean, powerful hand through the air, contriving somehow to express anger, disbelief and boredom all in that single gesture. 'I refuse to listen to another word of this nonsense!'

'You don't believe me,' Jo registered in consternation, blaming herself for not sooner correcting his impression that she had once been engaged to Ralph.

Gianni dipped his chin. 'I don't,' he confirmed without remorse.

'Where does that leave us, then?' she asked numbly.

Gianni lifted and dropped a broad shoulder in dismissal before striding out of the room without another word. When she heard his bedroom door close upstairs, she shivered, wondering how she was supposed to disprove Jane's contentions when she was so far away from home. A chorus of family disagreement would soon have disabused Gianni of his suspicions, but she was shaken by his inability to simply accept that she was telling the truth.

A little while later, she heard Gianni's steps on the

stone stairs and hunger drove her from her room. The table below the thick canopy of vines at the front of the castle was set for lunch and she sat back in her sunglasses scanning the magnificent view of the mountainous island. Directly ahead stretched a shaded drive through an avenue of stately palm trees that led down to an empty golden strand washed by the tide. Just as she finally noticed that there was only one place set at the table, she heard the whine of the helicopter and turned to watch it fly out across the sea until it became a vanishing speck. She breathed in slow and deep and planned an exploration of the nature reserve.

Later, as she wandered along deserted winding trails, she tried not to think that her marriage had crashed and burned on the very first day. Negative thoughts were not her friend. Gianni had an explosive temperament. He needed time to think and calm down. She had known that when she married him. She had suspected that the burning passion that powered everything he did from his work ethic to his libido could also be a problem. So, she would have to fix him…somehow. Teach him to talk? Put him in a cell so that he couldn't walk away? Lock every outside door?

For the first twelve hours of his desertion, Jo was sanguine. She wandered round the island, explored the Roman ruins and she swam and lazed on the beach in the sun. The second day she was on edge, even after a long swim in the sea. And by lunchtime she was burning with a strong and rare anger.

She phoned Gianni.

He answered her call in the middle of another call and her lips compressed at the suspicion that her bridegroom had walked out on his new marriage and basically buried himself in the convenience of work. She wondered how often Gianni had buried life's problems in the world of business and straightened her slight shoulders to brace herself.

'Jojo…' he breathed tautly.

Jo didn't give him the chance to regroup. 'I'm only calling to ask you to arrange transport for me to go home—'

'Home?' he cut in, audibly taken aback by that decision. 'To Ladymead?'

'Where else? Sitting alone in luxury on a deserted island is not my idea of fun. You've gone.'

'I'm coming back.'

'When?' Jo enquired briskly. 'I have no intention of sitting here like faithful Penelope waiting on Odysseus.'

Torn between admiration that she had read Homer's *Odyssey* and shocked surprise that she was calling his bluff, Gianni murmured quietly, his accent more noticeable than usual, 'This evening…this has got out of hand.'

'And before you return,' Jo replied, 'you accept certain facts, which anyone in my family could confirm for you. I didn't have an affair with Ralph two years ago. I liked him as a friend and I felt considerable sympathy for him when he found his fiancée and his best friend in the same bed. I suspect Ralph would have liked a closer connection with me after that discovery, but I wasn't interested. His parents were aware that we were only friends and they have been hurt and offended by that newspaper article because, of course, they know the truth. They're having a lawyer's letter sent to Jane and a retraction is to be printed in the newspaper.'

There was a short, dragging silence.

'I'm sorry.'

'You have to say it in person or I don't listen,' Jo told him gently.

CHAPTER SIX

EARLY EVENING, AND THE sun was sinking in a peach-coloured sky, but summer sunshine still bathed the colourful terraced gardens in a shimmering veil of heat.

As the whine of a helicopter approaching the island sounded, Jo left her seat on the shaded roof terrace and darted over to the telescope that Gianni's late grandfather had installed to survey the island from his hilltop eyrie. Breathless, she watched the helicopter land on the pad. Seconds later, a tall male sprang out to stride along the path through the trees and her heart started to beat very, very fast.

It was Gianni, sleek and spectacular in a cream lightweight suit teamed with an open-neck dark shirt. Light glimmered over his tousled black hair, accentuating the slant of his high cheekbones, the proud jut of his nose, the mobile slash of his passionate mouth and the hard, clean, angular line of his jaw. Her breath rattled in her dry throat and then she questioned what she was doing...*spying* on him? *Waiting* for him? Disturbed by that suspicion and annoyed with herself, Jo grabbed up her book and descended the winding stone staircase to the foot of the tower before strolling, flushed and a little out of breath, out onto the loggia, surprised to see that Sofia, the housekeeper, already had the table set for two.

Gianni came to an abrupt halt on the path and flipped off his sunglasses, dark golden eyes flashing over her before his lashes lowered to conceal his expression. For the first time ever in her experience of Gianni, he looked a little hesitant.

'I was wrong. I screwed up,' he bit out in a taut undertone as though he could not bear to wait any longer to offload those necessary words. 'I'm deeply sorry.'

'I need you to explain *why* though,' Jo muttered uneasily. 'Why you were so quick to assume?'

Gianni raked long brown fingers through his hair in a gesture of frustration. 'I'm not good with words, Jojo...not when it comes to emotional stuff.'

Jo almost winced. 'I know but—'

'I suspected that buying you something would be the wrong thing to do, so I passed on the flowers,' he murmured flatly, sliding a hand into his pocket as he sidestepped her question. 'But then, as you will see, I succumbed all the same.'

Gritting her teeth in confusion at that declaration and discomfort because she didn't want Gianni thinking that he could buy his way out of trouble, Jo flipped open the jewellery box with its famous logo to reveal a delicate platinum necklace. She lifted it out to examine the diamond and sapphire studded pendant, which was in the shape of a bouquet of flowers. Gianni intervened to click open the bouquet to let her see the words engraved within.

'I'm sorry,' it said, with the addition of his name and the date.

'In case I didn't get the right words out fast enough,' he breathed tautly.

The backs of her eyes prickled horribly with a surge of tears and she blinked rapidly. 'It's very pretty. I appreciate the thought behind it,' she told him quietly. 'But, you know, you didn't need to buy me anything.'

His hand closed over hers. 'I hurt you. I do very much regret that.'

Sofia bustled out with a tray of drinks and Jo tugged her hand free. Her stiff knees began to give way to the strain of standing so unnaturally still and straight and she sank down into a padded chair, grateful to have a glass to curl her restive fingers around.

'Let me put this on for you…' Gianni lifted the necklace from the box and stepped behind her to loop the pendant round her neck and fasten it. She felt his fingertips brush her nape and a shiver of awareness shimmied down her tense spine.

'Thank you,' she said unevenly as Sofia lit the candles on the table, determined, it seemed, to make the most of what she deemed to be a romantic occasion for the *odd* couple, Jo reflected in chagrin. After all, the bride and groom had occupied separate beds on their wedding night, enjoyed a huge row the next day and that had been followed by the departure of the bridegroom.

As the older woman moved back into the building, Jo lifted her head, her blue eyes very serious. 'Why did you just assume that I was guilty?'

Gianni tensed. 'I had a blazing row with Federico when he arrived and first voiced his allegations. In the beginning, I didn't want to credit what he was telling me. I was furious with him for attacking your reputation…and then he gave me the newspaper. Unfortunately, the few facts I knew seemed to fit. I was appalled,' he admitted tautly.

Her smooth brow furrowed. 'But I don't understand why. Although I didn't do what I was accused of doing, you're not *that* narrow-minded and you yourself—'

Gianni lifted soothing hands to silence her. 'I know, but I've always seen you as being special, as being a cut above me in your behaviour. Why do you think I never tried too hard to persuade you to join me for dinner?' he asked her with gleaming dark eyes. 'I suspected that I would upset you and I was determined not to do it.'

As Sofia set a variety of tiny savoury tarts before them as a starter, Jo stared at Gianni, his words still echoing inside her head. *Special? A cut above?*

'Look,' Gianni murmured very softly. 'I am not a gentleman and many of the women I have been with have only been ladies in the strictest sense of the word. They had few boundaries and no illusions. Their only desire was to have a good time. I know my limitations, *cara*. I knew that you and I would want different things.'

'Only until you decided that I was exactly what you needed to rehabilitate your image,' Jo reminded him as she lifted a tiny tart with determination. 'Therefore, I'm a plaster saint and you're a sinner, so you pretty much kept your distance. Actually, I'm a little more human than that, and rather more flexible and flawed.'

Luxuriant lashes dipped low over his golden gaze. 'Not as flawed as I am,' he admitted on the back of a rueful sigh. 'My whole outlook on life is pessimistic. That's why I jumped so fast to my conclusion that I had been mistaken in your character.'

Jo countered, 'You lost your head. You erupted like a volcano.'

'That my father was present put my temper on a hair trigger. It was bad enough that I should be forced to view you in such a light, even worse that he should have instigated that exposure.'

'You felt humiliated by his witnessing that scene,' Jo whispered. 'But he was upset on your behalf. I think he was trying to protect you in some clumsy way just by being there.'

'My father has never tried to protect me from anything. Eat up,' Gianni urged, sneaking another tiny tart onto her plate. 'Sofia said you've been skipping meals and you're too slender to do that.'

'I don't get very hungry when it's this warm. You contacted Sofia before your arrival,' Jo guessed then.

'I knew you wouldn't mention that I was returning.' Gianni dealt her a shrewd look. 'You didn't quite trust that I *would* return.'

Jo shrugged a slim shoulder. 'Do you blame me?'

But Jo was still struggling to come to terms with what he had already told her, shaken by what he had admitted about his view of her prior to his proposal. A woman he had seen as prim and proper and above suspicion, squeaky clean in mind and body. What did it say about her that it cut her to the bone to recognise that he had never seen her as a normal sexy, adult woman? Was it any wonder that he had really only been teasing her when he'd invited her out to dinner? She wasn't his type, had *never* been his type of woman.

'You walked out on me,' she extended tightly. 'I find that hard to forgive.'

As Sofia's daughter delivered the main course, Gianni gritted his teeth. 'I was afraid of what I might say if I stayed any longer. I felt…out of control. I thought it was wiser to leave until I had got a grip on my temper again.'

'But leaving me here…*alone*,' Jo persisted. 'That was unacceptable. I was ready to go home but I didn't know how to get off this blasted island!'

'It didn't occur to me that I was leaving you stranded.' Gianni grimaced. 'I have to learn to start thinking for two, rather than one.'

'You only need to start thinking for two if this marriage survives the first week,' Jo murmured wryly. 'And so far, we're not ripping up any record books here. When you tell me that you see me as some prim and proper prude with whom you have nothing in common—'

'Aside from a very strong attraction,' Gianni cut in. 'I'm trying to be honest, *cara*, but you finding fault with that honesty isn't any encouragement to continue in that vein.'

Jo paled. 'I didn't mean—'

'Yes, you did. You're still angry with me, which is perfectly understandable. Do you remember the first time I asked you out?'

'Vaguely,' Jo lied in a face-saving excuse because, even though six years had passed, she still vividly remembered that day. 'It seemed very random. One day I saw you at that music festival and the next—'

Gianni groaned and pushed his plate away. He leant back in his seat. 'It wasn't even slightly random. I saw you dancing at the festival with your friends.'

Jo lowered her lashes and continued to savour her tender steak. It had been *totally* random because Gianni had had a gorgeous girlfriend with him, a famous fashion model with titian curls and incredibly long porcelain limbs, who had complained throughout his attempted introduction that she was burning in the sun.

Gianni, in comparison, was recalling Jo at eighteen, sheathed in worn denim shorts and a floaty blouse, her blonde fall of sun-streaked hair bouncing at her slender spine as she danced. At the time, she had been the sexiest sight he had ever seen, the very picture of glowing health with her curvy hips shifting to the beat of the music and every inch of her unenhanced and natural. He hadn't been able to take his eyes off her and the following morning he had shown up at Ladymead, drawn by a powerful need to see her again.

Sheer lust, he labelled in retrospect. Her grandmother had directed him out to the barn where Jo had been helping Sybil to feed her rescue animals. As he'd spoken, she had stared at him as if he had taken leave of his wits and then those beautiful sapphire-blue eyes had glimmered with warmth and pleasure. He had been so sure that she was about to say yes and his conscience had twanged accordingly, because although she had finished school, he had been very much aware of her youth and inexperience in comparison to his own. And then she had said no, sorry, and a crazy mix of anger and relief had swept through him.

'I've never wanted a woman as much as I wanted you that day,' he confessed grudgingly. 'But you weren't ready for someone like me.'

'No,' she agreed reluctantly. 'Panic made me turn you down. I didn't think I could handle you either.'

As she connected with glittering dark golden eyes fringed with a lush canopy of black lashes, her heartbeat stuttered and made it hard for her to breathe. *'I've never wanted a woman as much as I wanted you that day.'* Could that possibly be true? Even with that beautiful redhead vying for his attention? Had she underestimated her own powers of attraction to that extent? Apparently, she had.

'You made the right move,' Gianni told her disconcertingly. 'I wasn't looking for anything serious.'

'You were only twenty-two…why would you have been?'

'I had just come out of a long relationship, and I was enjoying my freedom that summer,' Gianni explained flatly, his lean, strong face shuttering.

Well, that was Gianni, Jo reflected helplessly. He shot her up to the sky one moment and dropped her down to below ground level the next. Sex appeal was something, but it wasn't worth quite as much if a woman knew from the outset that she wanted more. Gianni had got badly burned in that long relationship he had no wish to discuss. Was that why he only seemed to indulge in superficial affairs? Or was that too neat an explanation? After all, Gianni had always seemed to revel in his freedom. But she couldn't forget him saying that loving anyone just got you hurt.

'And the second time I asked you out, you were wearing a stupid hat with bunny ears and singing Christmas carols,' he reminded her.

'You do pick the worst moments,' Jo teased, her cheeks warming at the recollection. 'I was shocked.'

'You looked like an angel when you came inside to persuade my guests to contribute to your charity. I was hooked all over again.'

'So hooked that you forgot that your latest lover was

sitting at the same table?' Jo scoffed with wide, wondering eyes. 'I knew you were together because I'd read it in the gossip columns.'

'Which just goes to show that you can't rely on gossip. She was with another man.'

'I got it wrong. I thought you were shameless.' Jo lifted her spoon to taste the lemon sorbet that had been brought to the table for dessert. It was delicious and refreshing.

'I am.' Gianni watched her licking the spoon, the pink tip of her tongue skimming over the metal, and every muscle in his long, lean body went rigid. She could wind him up like a clockwork toy, he acknowledged reluctantly.

He questioned that she even understood how the sex embargo had affected him. He already suspected that sex wasn't that important to her. She didn't understand how much he wanted her, and he didn't understand how she could be impervious to the electric tension between them. But even so, he knew that he wasn't about to quibble over her terms.

'*Every* member of your family phoned me while I was away,' Gianni told her over coffee.

Jo leant back in her seat and stared at him in horrified disbelief.

Helpless amusement slanted Gianni's expressive mouth. 'First, your grandmother to assure me that there wasn't a word of truth in that nasty woman's story.'

Jo cringed. 'And then?'

'Sybil breathing fire on your behalf. Enraged by my father's interference and stupidity and even madder than your grandmother about that article. Trixie was much more low-key and full of advice about the current full moon…and us needing to take advantage of it.' Brimming laughter dancing in his golden eyes as her gaze evaded his, Gianni grinned. 'I didn't like to tell her that there wasn't much chance of that…'

Jo's creamy skin had flamed pink. 'I'm sorry. I have embarrassing relatives. When did they phone you?'

'This morning. They love you very much and they are very loyal. If anything, I'm envious,' Gianni admitted.

'Where were you staying?' Jo finally asked. 'In a hotel?'

'No. An apartment in Rome. I've also been thinking…if you're in agreement, we will move on from here tomorrow and spend our week elsewhere,' Gianni continued. 'Coming to an isolated island wasn't the best idea. It may have worked for a normal honeymoon couple but a couple like us requires a little more outside stimulation.'

Jo nodded, although she was discomfited by the reminder that they were not a normal newly married couple. But then she couldn't have it every way, could she? And then she looked at him with a warmer gaze and accepted that she had forgiven him. He had apologised and for the very first time he had made the effort to explain himself. He was changing. He was *trying*. Didn't that mean that she could try to loosen up a little as well?

After eating, they walked down to the beach. Jo kicked off her sandals, lifted her long skirt and skipped along the edge of the surf. Like a child, Gianni thought as he watched her, relishing her lack of self-consciousness with him and her zest for life, not to mention her ability to forgive and forget one of his worst ever errors of judgement. Moonlight glimmered over her lovely face and his gaze centred on the luscious pout of her pink lips, laughter falling from her as the tide forced her to run back up onto the beach.

He closed long fingers round a slender wrist and tugged her to him. For an instant, she remained static and then she shifted closer, lips parting in invitation, eyes luminous. Gianni caught her to him with possessive hands that curved to her hips.

For a timeless moment, Jo was still with anticipation and a growing sense of security. Gianni brought his mouth down on hers with a ravaging sweetness that dialled up the urgency already thrumming through her taut length. Her bra felt too tight for her breasts, the soft peaks firming to hard points and, breathless, she pulled back from him.

'Let's go back,' she muttered unevenly.

Gianni drew in a slow, deep breath and said nothing as they strolled back up the hill. He would not put her under any kind of pressure.

'Maybe we should consider taking advantage of that full moon Trixie mentioned,' Jo mumbled in a rush, terrified that she would lose her nerve as they entered the castle.

Without even glancing in Gianni's direction, Jo clattered upstairs to the bedroom they could have shared that first night. It was too late now for her to wish that they had. Had they consummated their marriage then he might well have appreciated that she could never have had an affair with Ralph behind anyone's back.

Undressing, she lifted the filmy nightdress Sybil had given her, tossed it on the bathroom chair and stepped straight into the shower.

Grains of sand sprinkled the floor of the shower basin, and she suppressed an anxious sigh as insecurity threatened to overwhelm her. How could she possibly hope to meet Gianni's expectations? She wasn't the experienced woman he would assume she was. So, she had to be honest, enthusiastic, and quick to learn. That made her feel rather as if she were about to attend an evening class in an unfamiliar subject. Grimacing, she towelled herself dry and donned the nightie, which was rather more glam than her usual shorts and tee.

Running a brush through hair tangled by the sea breeze, she left the bedroom, only to freeze on the threshold at the sight of Gianni already sprawled across her bed, only a towel linked round his lean hips. Being Gianni, he looked even more enthralling half naked. His skin was the colour of bronze. She had not realised how muscular he was.

'What can I say? I'm keen,' he confided insouciantly as he watched the colour climb in her cheeks.

'Evidently,' Jo agreed, forcing her stiff legs forward and seating herself awkwardly on the edge of the bed.

'Why are you so serious?' Gianni chided, rising up on his knees to send his passionate mouth travelling very briefly over hers.

'Because this is serious for me,' Jo admitted as he closed his hands to her hips and pulled her up onto the mattress beside him. 'I haven't got naked with a guy before.'

His mobile black brows lifted. 'You can't mean that you're a virgin?'

Jo shrugged a stiff shoulder, her face burning. 'I didn't plan it this way. It just happened.'

'How did it just happen?' Gianni queried in surprise. 'You were at university. You must have had boyfriends?'

'A few, but nobody who made me want more from them. I just didn't meet the right guy and I wasn't interested in having sex purely for the sake of it.'

Gianni sighed. 'If only I had been as discriminating. I lost my virginity at fifteen to a girl a couple of years older. It was meaningless. I don't deserve to be your first lover—'

'Oh, shall I go out and look for a more deserving man?' Jo cut in playfully.

Gianni laughed. 'If I thought you meant that—'

'Well, if you make me discuss this any more I will,' she threatened.

'I've never been with a virgin before,' he confessed.

'Don't you think it's fortunate that at least *one* of us knows the score?'

Amusement lightened the darkness in his frowning gaze and he tumbled her into the pillows, smiling down at her with sudden warmth. 'You always surprise me, Jojo. I never know what you're likely to do or say next.'

He kissed her until the blood was drumming in her veins and her heart was racing. His tongue twinned with hers and skimmed the sensitive interior of her mouth. A knot of excitement unlocked deep in her pelvis and her hips rose to his in an uncontrollable wave. He was teaching her what wanting more entailed, and she was grateful that she had waited because she was convinced that, whatever else, Gianni would not give her a mediocre experience.

He reached beneath her to peel off the nightdress

and as it caught there was a slight ripping sound that made him suppress a curse. 'I'll buy you another one,' he promised. 'Although you won't be wearing it much.'

'Forget it,' Jo told him, running her fingers through his black tousled hair as she sat up, determined not to be uncomfortable with her nakedness.

Gianni moulded a hand to a small pouting breast and pressed her flat again, an intent look narrowing his dark golden eyes. He let his mouth roam across her breasts and caught a pert pink nipple between his lips, pausing to suckle and savour the responsive bud, smiling as tiny sounds of appreciation escaped her parted lips. Tugging at the other swollen peak, he shifted his attention there, revelling in every sound he could wrench from her. He toyed and teased while her movements grew ever more frantic until the tiny little shudders racking her slender body strengthened and finally coalesced into a gasping cry of surprise and pleasure.

Rocked by that climax, Jo stared up at him, her eyes sliding shut as he claimed her mouth in a hungry, driving kiss, and the tightness at the heart of her increased. She wanted more, she registered, she wanted more so much that her fingernails dug into the smooth skin of his back. For the first time, impatience was claiming her and she knew why he was taking his time and that it was for her benefit, rather than his own, but she was still tempted to urge him on.

Gianni traced a line with his mouth from her breasts down over her stomach and lower. When she froze, he kept going, ignoring the fingers flexing taut in his hair.

'I want you, *cara*. I want every bit of you that you are willing to share,' he growled.

Jo swallowed hard and rested back. He stroked the

fluted pink lips between her thighs and she shifted, struggling not to jerk, a little quiver of powerful awareness running through her. He lowered his head and flicked his tongue across her clitoris and in seconds, as that electric sensation engulfed her to send a glittering arrow of heat into her pelvis, she was lost. The ache between her legs built and built, tightening muscles she had not known she had and increasing a sensitivity that heightened by his every caress. He slid a finger into her hot, wet sheath and then another, scissoring them to ready her for him and she quivered as the excitement surged up and overflowed, sending her careening into another climax.

Gianni slid over her and she felt him hot and hard against her warm, damp entrance. She trembled, struggling not to tense, eyes wide at the sensations that gripped her as he slowly sank into her. And then came a pinch of discomfort followed by a sharp flash of pain that took her by surprise and made her cry out. Instantly he stopped.

'No, don't stop!' she gasped. 'Finish it!'

Her teeth gritted as he pushed deeper into her untried body and then she felt him, hard and urgent inside her, and she recognised the strain etched into his darkly handsome face as he fought to stay in control. The discomfort ebbed and he circled his lean hips and withdrew before burying himself in her again with a masculine groan of pleasure. A wave of equally enjoyable response travelled through Jo and she relaxed, her body sensually adapting to his rhythm.

'You feel so good,' Gianni confided in a ragged undertone.

Jo arched up to receive his next powerful thrust, excitement generating afresh, sparking in her tummy and blazing up to consume her as he increased his tempo. She lifted her hips up as he ground his body down into hers, setting off a chain reaction as the intensity of sensation clenched her every muscle tight. Hungry need gripped her as he slammed into her, control no longer his driving ambition, and ripples of delight rolled through her in an intoxicating wave.

Caught up in that wild exhilaration, she flew higher and higher, rejoicing in every very physical moment of that flight. Her body was humming and stretching and reaching, and then suddenly she was there where she most wanted to be, and a dizzying explosion of emotion and reaction engulfed her. Ecstasy flooded her, followed by convulsive spasms of intense sensation. In a world of her own, she was only dimly aware of Gianni's harsh groan of release and the jerk of his powerful body against her own.

'I've never had sex without a condom before,' Gianni murmured breathlessly into her tumbled hair. 'It felt wickedly erotic and forbidden.'

'Oh...' Jo responded and even finding her voice took effort when she was still drowning in the hazy aftermath of bliss. She felt weightless and drowsy.

'No, you're not allowed to go to sleep,' Gianni censured. 'You need to get in a bath to soak away your aches and pains.'

'I can't feel anything.'

'But you will tomorrow,' he assured her, springing out of the bed to stalk into the bathroom.

Still in a reverie, Jo lay listening to the water run. Gianni had exceeded her expectations and she didn't think it would be wise to tell him that. A sunny smile softened her mouth. No, she definitely wasn't about to tell him that.

A pair of hands slid beneath her and her eyes flew wide. 'What are you doing?' she exclaimed as she found herself in his arms.

Gianni slid her down gently into the warm water in the bath and she sat up and hugged her knees, feeling awkward and shy, which struck her as ridiculous in the circumstances. 'Do you do this for all the women you've been with?'

'Only wives,' Gianni declared deadpan. 'And you really *do* feel like my wife now, *cara*.'

He strode naked into the shower and she watched the bronzed silhouette of his lean, strong body through the water streaming down the glass, blinking rapidly as if that could somehow help to clear her foggy thoughts. She was happy, she thought in wonder, frowning at that unexpected development. Gianni's wife, a role she had never thought to fill and yet, here she was…

As she slid back into bed still feeling very sleepy, she turned her head on the pillow as Gianni joined her, her curiosity stirring. 'Can I ask what happened in that long relationship you had at university?'

'I prefer not to tell you. Talking about it only stirs up bad memories,' he told her bluntly, his lean, darkly handsome features taut and cool as ice.

Jo lost colour and flipped over to sleep with her back turned to him. He was under no obligation to tell her his every secret. Marriage didn't mean he had to bare his chest and tell all, she reminded herself. But even so, she reasoned, she had been forced to confide in him about Ralph and about her virginity and she felt as though she had no secrets left. Some reciprocal confidence and clarification from Gianni would have been welcome. She couldn't help but feel hurt by his lack of trust in her.

By the next morning, that shadow of anxious concern had faded. Jo winced when she got out of bed, the ache of soreness at the heart of her a surprise and a reminder of what they had shared. But she had no regrets, most particularly not when Gianni casually wrapped a towel round her as she emerged from the shower and then closed his arms round her. The effortless way he touched her and drew her close spoke volumes in the wake of his former reserve. Intimacy had brought down barriers that had made both of them stiff and uncomfortable. She smiled as he told her that, after breakfast, they were flying to the south of France. Without a doubt, there was a new ease between them. In time, she told herself firmly, as they forged stronger ties, Gianni's ability to trust her enough to talk to her would improve.

That afternoon, they arrived at the Provençal farmhouse, an idyllic old property built of stone with a weathered terracotta roof and a host of well-maintained ancillary buildings. It was surrounded by wheat and lavender fields and lush orchards of fruit trees. In the distance the snow-capped peaks of the mountains were visible.

A tiny man called Antoine greeted Gianni with great familiarity in French and Gianni had to interrupt his eager flood of conversation to introduce Jo.

'Antoine lives on site. He's a former chef and a fantastic cook. I used to come here every summer as a child with my mother. Sometimes, I was left here with a nanny while she returned to London for treatment,' he confided when he had taken her up to a big traditional bedroom. The bed linen was white, the windows were wide and a fat sheaf of purple-blue lavender in a vase scented the hot, still air. 'After she died, I didn't want to return because the memories of her here were too painful.'

'I'm surprised you brought us back,' Jo admitted.

'Enough time has passed now and it's a beautiful, tranquil place. We can relax here but we can also easily go out as well,' Gianni pointed out calmly. 'It feels good to be back under this roof.'

'I'm glad,' she told him gently.

Antoine served them a superb late lunch that included a tapenade starter and a sea bass and asparagus salad. The meal finished with home-made ice cream and fresh cherries. Replete and laughing at Antoine's suggestion that they might also enjoy some cake with their coffee, they sat chatting in the shade.

The next morning, Gianni took her into Villeneuve to explore the Saint-André gardens and the art exhibition in the abbot's palace. It was a peaceful place to wander, and Jo took countless photos for her grandmother's benefit. Liz Hamilton was the gardening enthusiast at Ladymead, and Jo knew that she would enjoy seeing the roses in full bloom, the beautiful pergola walk and the colourful mosaic of parterres and flowerbeds. The views from the terraces out over Avignon, the Alpilles and Mont Ventoux were spectacular. An evening meal in a tiny exclusive restaurant completed the day.

Before they climbed back into the car, Gianni cupped his hands to her cheeks to keep her still and kissed her passionately. It was as though an electrical charge raced through her veins and the feel of his aroused body against hers only made her push closer to increase the connection.

'My word!' she exclaimed in the aftermath, rocked on her feet by how hot that single kiss had proved to be. The dull throb of desire between her thighs was instantaneous.

A grin slashed Gianni's mouth. 'You have the same effect on me.'

'I've recovered,' she confided shyly.

'Is that a fact, Signora Renzetti?' he teased.

Gianni's phone was buzzing when they entered the house.

'Go on up to bed and I'll follow you up,' he urged. 'I have to take this call.'

Her curiosity sparked and she glanced at his shuttered expression before going upstairs. She fell asleep long before Gianni joined her.

'Who was that on the phone last night? You were absolutely ages,' she complained when she wakened the next morning.

'It was Fiona, a close friend from my student days.'

'An ex?' Jo questioned.

Gianni compressed his lips. 'A connection,' he rephrased. 'She didn't receive our wedding invite, so the news that I was married came as a shock. I should've made the effort to phone her to tell her personally.'

Jo was annoyed that he had spent so long talking to another woman the night before. And what was the difference between an ex and a *'connection'*? Why was he being so secretive when it came to voicing simple facts? Furthermore, if the other woman weren't an ex, why would she be shocked by news of his marriage? And how was she supposed to feel when this was the *third* incident relating to another woman since their wedding, the third incident in the space of four days?

First there had been the hurt, jealous drunk at their wedding, then his fierce reluctance to discuss his past relationships. And now Fiona, the woman he had had to talk to in private. So, who was Fiona? A 'connection' or *the* actual ex-girlfriend who had hurt him when he was at university? Was it possible he was still in touch with his first serious love? Stranger things happened, she acknowledged. In silence, Jo quietly fumed and fretted. How many other blasted women were likely to come out of the woodwork? She would have been less suspicious of Gianni had she not been aware of his womanising reputation prior to their marriage. As she saw it, that meant that Gianni required careful observation and handling, but she assured herself that she was too intelligent to openly parade her misgivings and make them a stumbling block in their relationship.

He stroked long caressing fingers down a slender thigh and Jo shifted and stretched like a sleepy cat. 'You missed a treat last night,' she told him out of sheer badness.

'I'm here now,' he pointed out.

'Too late!' Jo laughed as she slid out of bed with the dexterity of an eel escaping a net. 'Antoine promised to show me how to make croissants if I got up early enough.'

CHAPTER SEVEN

GIANNI WATCHED JO vanish into the bathroom in a movement as sleek and fast as the flow of quicksilver and suppressed a curse.

He hadn't expected Jo to have a mercurial side, but she did. Yet she held his attention like a magnet. In addition, she enjoyed a depth of charm that could only impress him whether it was chattering to Antoine in her inept schoolgirl French or meticulously noting down the names of the roses she had captured in photos for her grandmother's benefit. She was gracious, kind, and thoughtful. In fact, his bride was a much more complex creature than he had initially assumed: disarmingly honest and chatty while at the same time contriving to be ridiculously mysterious. It disturbed Gianni that he very rarely guessed what was going on inside Jo's head before she spoke.

Gianni had gone when Jo returned to the bedroom to pull on shorts and a T-shirt ready for her baking lesson. Her generous mouth down curved and she scolded herself for that secret sense of disappointment. She refused to feel any more for Gianni than he felt for her. To get more deeply involved with him would only lead to her being hurt. He had spelt out the boundaries of their relationship and love didn't come into it.

He had work to catch up on, had mentioned that necessity the evening before. She was conscious that within days he would be facing the board meeting where he might still find himself voted out as CEO of Renzetti Inc. What would it do to their relationship if it turned out that their marriage had failed to change anything for the better? Then, she would be surplus to requirements, she reflected worriedly.

Gianni spent the morning working on his laptop and Jo strove to copy Antoine's slick skills in the kitchen with varying results. Gianni drank his espresso and accepted without comment a horribly misshapen croissant made by his wife's own fair hand. Later, having lost himself in work, he glanced out of the window and saw her weeding the shrubbery in the garden while Antoine cut the grass on the mower. He grinned. He could not think of a single woman he had ever been with who would have let him work undisturbed while quietly occupying herself with weeds.

He strolled out to talk to her. 'I'm finished for the day. Let's go out.'

'Give me another ten minutes and I'll have finished this,' she urged, wiping the perspiration from her brow. 'I hate leaving a job half done.'

'You look incredibly sexy,' he breathed in a husky undertone.

Jo studied him in wonderment. She was hot and dirty and sweaty. 'You can't be serious.'

'You really don't see yourself the way I do,' Gianni whispered, scanning the swell of her firm breasts above the camisole top, her tiny waist, and the length of her shapely bare legs. The damp sheen across her cheekbones merely enhanced her bright sapphire eyes. There was even a smudge of flour on her face from her baking activities earlier that day. 'Earthy and sexy...'

'I'll wash off the earth in the shower,' she declared.

'But not the sexiness,' he quipped with a slow-burning smile.

That magnetic smile did something to her. It lit her up inside like a torch and she had never been more conscious of her body as she climbed the stairs. *He* did that to her, let her connect to the sensual side of her nature, the one she was only just learning about. She looked at him and she wanted him. It was that simple. It had *always* been that simple, she acknowledged belatedly. Without her ever admitting the fact even to herself, for years Gianni had figured as her perfect male fantasy figure. And with Gianni as her ideal, was it any wonder that she had never deemed another man worthy of serious interest? That awareness embarrassed her.

Even though she had never seriously believed that she would ever be with Gianni, even though she knew that their lifestyles were incompatible, she had cherished that secret fantasy of the bad-boy billionaire who could charge her up with the most wicked hunger with one electrifyingly casual smile. It shook her that she could have been so unaware of what went on inside her own head. Sybil had guessed. *'You've always wanted him,'* her great-aunt had said bluntly when Jo had told her about Gianni's proposal. Sybil had had no doubt whatsoever that Jo would marry Gianni.

She hadn't married Gianni solely for her family's

benefit or for Ladymead, Jo appreciated guiltily. She had fallen back on convenient excuses to protect her pride. She had wanted him for herself. She had had a photo of Gianni on a polo horse on the inside of the door of her school locker. He had sent it to her when his team won a big match. But she hadn't let the rest of the sixth form see it because she hadn't been willing to share it or him.

As she stripped off her grimy clothes she looked at herself in the bathroom mirror and wasn't surprised that she looked hot and flushed. The lies she had told herself to save face!

She stepped into the shower. As she emerged from the glass cubicle again, a muffled squeal was wrenched from her when she realised that she was no longer alone.

Gianni held out a towel and wrapped it round her. 'You hadn't locked the door. I thought it was all right to join you,' he murmured soothingly.

'You're not the only one of us who needs to remember that we're a couple,' Jo admitted with pink cheeks as she lifted another towel to dry her hair. 'And couples share…stuff.'

'Like beds,' Gianni agreed with dark eyes alight with merriment.

'You came in here with an ulterior motive,' Jo registered.

'Guilty as charged,' Gianni responded equably. 'The thought of my very beautiful wife in the shower naked and alone was too much for me.'

Jo flipped back her damp hair and rested her fingertip against his full lower lip, noting the shadow of stubble that had appeared there since morning. 'How many times have you said that to a woman?'

'You're the only wife I've ever had,' Gianni told her with strong satisfaction as he eased her closer, brushing away the towel so that it dropped to the floor.

Every line of his lean, powerful physique was pressed to her naked body. She felt the urgent thrust of his erection. She slid her hand down his chest and allowed her fingers to trace the hard, ready length of him and he shuddered against her in response. She found his responsiveness to that slight advance incredibly hot.

With a stifled groan of surrender, Gianni lifted her up fully into his arms and carried her into the bedroom to tumble her down on the bed.

'I should have dried my hair!' Jo exclaimed.

Gianni laughed out loud. 'Forget your hair, *cara*. Recognise your priorities here,' he urged.

Jo flung her head back and surveyed him appreciatively. 'Are you saying that you expect to be my priority?'

Gianni's stunning dark golden eyes gleamed as he peeled off his tee shirt, revealing his strong shoulders and the solid wall of his muscular chest. 'What do you think?' he traded as he toed off his shoes and began to unzip his trousers.

'I think that, yes, you *expect* to be my first and only priority,' Jo murmured with amusement. 'But I know that you don't appreciate anything that comes to you too easily. You like a challenge. It intrigues you.'

Gianni discarded his boxers and came down on the bed, reaching for her in almost the same movement, his hungry urgency providing another lift to her confidence.

'I want you so much,' he breathed raggedly.

'I like that,' Jo told him truthfully. 'I like to be needed.'

'Right now, I need you like I need air to breathe,' Gianni growled.

He nipped along the fullness of her lower lip, teasing her into opening her mouth before taking rampant advantage by sliding his tongue against hers and making her shiver with reaction, her whole body suddenly so sensitive it was ridiculous.

He pushed her knees back and she felt him brush against her damp heat. Hooking her legs over his shoulders, he rose over her. Disconcerted, she gazed up at him in feverish anticipation, locked to the smouldering gold of his eyes. He sank into her hard and fast, filling the emptiness, stretching her to fullness until she didn't know where he began and she ended. The pleasure came in an intense surge that made her inner muscles clench.

'You feel divine,' Gianni groaned, snaking his hips to pull out of her clinging flesh only to surge in again with even greater vitality. And so it began, a passionate assault on her senses as he plunged into her again and again and she bucked and arched beneath him as the excitement between them built. A frantic ferocious need climbed inside her. Her hands raked through his hair, over his shoulders and down his back. Her heart was racing, her skin damp with perspiration and then she reached a climax in a great rush of sensation that triggered an intoxicating explosion of reaction. Gianni jerked and shuddered with an uninhibited shout of satisfaction and then they both slumped, drained by the pleasure still rippling through their connected bodies.

'Was I too rough?' he whispered into her hair.

'No, I liked it…like that,' she framed unevenly, still

trying to catch her breath. 'But I'm glad Antoine is still out on the mower because he would have heard us if he'd been indoors.'

Gianni burst out laughing as he released her from his weight and rolled over, only to curve her round to face him again. 'Only you would think of that,' he said appreciatively. 'I think we expended so much energy that we've almost dried your hair.'

'It'll be like a haystack after that,' Jo forecast without much concern because she knew she would be getting back in the shower to wash it again. 'Gran used to say I had hair like my mother and it had a will and a life of its own.'

'You never talk about your mother.'

'I have no memory of her at all. I have photos of her, but I only know her through what others have told me about her,' Jo confided. 'It's all second-hand and some of it is likely just conjecture.'

'Tell me about her,' Gianni urged.

'She was quite independent. She married a man who was a lot older when she was twenty and it was against my grandparents' wishes. Unfortunately, the marriage didn't last and she wouldn't come home to the family after the divorce. I kind of understand that,' Jo admitted wryly. 'Her brother, Abraham, was the star on the home front because he was an up-and-coming businessman and Grandpa's big hope for the future. He was always being held up to her as the act to follow. There wasn't really room for her to be herself there and she had an office job in London, lots of friends and a good social life.'

'When did she get pregnant with you?'

'A few years after the divorce. My grandparents didn't know until after I was born and she brought me back for a visit. They offered to keep me during the week so that she could work and she agreed, saying she would spend weekends with us at Ladymead. Six months later, she died in a train crash on her way to visit.'

'It's tragic that both your grandmother's children died before her. It's possible that I could have enquiries made to see if we could establish who your father is… if you were interested?'

Jo gave him a rueful smile. 'Thanks, but no, thanks. I have all the family I need. Sybil thinks my father may possibly have been a married man and a colleague of my mother's. I think I'll let sleeping dogs lie. I can live with not knowing.'

Gianni pulled her closer and curved an arm round her. 'I felt I should offer.'

'It's a kind idea but I'm happy as I am,' she told him truthfully, loving the easy affection with which he held her close even though she reckoned it was virtually meaningless to a man who had already decided she only had a shelf life of five years' duration. A minimum of five years for her as wife could also mean Gianni's maximum, she reasoned, wondering why she hadn't seen that possibility before.

'Hi, this is Jo,' the voice declared brightly. 'I'm sorry I can't come to the phone right now. Please leave a message and I'll get back to you later…'

Gianni almost threw his phone at the wall in frustration. How many times had he listened to Jo's voicemail? He had told her what the time difference was and she had still tried to call him back when he was asleep! He had barely spoken to his wife in two long weeks. He had asked her to accompany him to New York for the all-important board meeting that would decide his future. Jo, however, had cited the many workers starting repairs at Ladymead and her need to help her family to move out into their temporary home in the village and he had grudgingly given way.

He strode down the gilded corridor in the penthouse that his mother had once furnished like the Palace of Versailles. Glimmers of that theatrical magnificence still lingered in the elaborate walls and ceilings, but Fiona had made a clean sweep of all the fussy furniture and had installed modern pieces.

Gianni was in a rage. Fresh from the board meeting that had lacerated his hopes and expectations, he was in very bad form. While his position as CEO of Renzetti Inc had been confirmed, the board had insisted on reviewing his status in three months' time. Gianni, who had made multimillion-dollar profits for the business, was *on probation*. Nobody had employed that provocative term but that deferred decision had still gone down with Gianni like a lead balloon. He had wanted certainty and certainty wasn't on offer. Consequently, it seemed to him that he had got married for nothing. Certainly, his marriage hadn't paid off!

What was even worse in his opinion was that no sooner had they returned home than Jo seemed to have become perpetually unavailable. Her driving motivation seemed to be finding a million things to do other than simply being *his* wife. And he wanted Jo around more. He wanted her with him. Why shouldn't he feel like that when they were a couple?

He had brought forward his flight home. It infuriated him not to be able to speak to Jo. He had wanted to tell her about the board meeting, had known that she would instantly make him feel better about that contentious decision. Unlike him, she had a way with words. But Jo, it seemed, had little room for him in her busy itinerary. They were still in the first month of their marriage but Jo was more interested in her family's needs, not to mention organising the co-ordination of the complex repairs on Ladymead and the housing of her pets. He had little doubt that she was also still loyally meeting her duties at the church and for her various charities! Only Gianni seemed to have drawn the short straw.

That same morning, Jo screened a yawn as she endeavoured to keep the joiners and the roofers from each other's throats as they quarrelled about who had arrived first and who therefore had the right to clear everyone else out and start work unimpeded. Jo was already stressed by the fact that her grandmother had tripped over a rug and hurt her ankle and Sybil had had to take the older woman to the local A & E for treatment. Trixie was fairly useless in a crisis, prone to panic attacks and absolutely hopeless at handling grumpy men. While Jo suggested staggered access to the foreman as a means of keeping the peace between the various work teams, she pushed back the hard hat, which was hot on such a warm day, and longed for the fresh air and the chance to shed her fluorescent high-vis jacket. The council health and safety representative had insisted that everyone who crossed the threshold of the house had to wear protective gear even though the real work hadn't started yet.

Jo checked her watch as the workmen reached agreement and she left them to it because she had to help prepare the church hall for the summer jumble sale. Her grandmother had volunteered and Jo felt duty-bound to cover for her absence. She wondered where Gianni was and what he was doing. Most of all, she wanted to know how that board meeting had gone and he hadn't called her yet.

Shedding her safety gear with relief in the front garden, she headed back to Belvedere where Duffy, on his perch in the orangery, greeted her with a biblical quote. "'In the world you will have tribulation…'"

'Thanks, Duffy. Just the cheery word I needed,' Jo jibed.

The house her family would be using until Ladymead was liveable again was too small for a parrot with a giant noisy personality and Gianni had agreed that the bird could stay with them.

'Have you time for lunch, Jo?' Abigail asked as she passed back through the hall.

'Give me five minutes. I'm all dusty and I need to change first,' Jo confided as she hurried up the stairs.

At the top of the staircase, she felt suddenly dizzy and grabbed onto the balustrade to stay upright. She had broken out in a cold sweat as well. Breathing in slow and deep, she wondered if she had been racing around too much in the heat, although she hadn't had much choice about that after her grandmother's fall. Trixie had been in hysterics and she had had to rush over there. And she still hadn't remembered to thank Gianni for having a gate cut in the wall between Ladymead and Belvedere, so that she could easily move between the properties without taking a car out onto the road.

She grabbed the first cool dress that met her eyes in her dressing room, an old favourite that still had plenty of wear in it even if Gianni had suggested that she should now be dumping her older clothes and utilising the designer garments she had worn on their short honeymoon. A dreamy look momentarily crept across Jo's face. Those few short days in Provence had been magical. She had never felt closer to another human being than she had felt to Gianni, but she didn't kid herself that it had been the same way for him. Gianni had buckets of charm and she was quite sure that most women responded to him as she had. He was very passionate, but she didn't count sex as an advantage. Gianni liked sex and he found her attractive. She refused to believe that that made her anything special in his eyes. So, here she was, talking herself down again, trying not to get too emotional about stuff.

Unfortunately, without even trying, Gianni could hurt her feelings as well. Out of sight seemed to be out of mind when Gianni was involved. He had only phoned her a couple of times since he had departed and her chatty texts had gone unanswered apart from the very first when he had texted back,

What are you telling me this stuff for? Do I care about scaffolders who have gone missing?

She hadn't felt that that was much of a joke, but then he was in the midst of work at a tense time and she had clearly irritated him, so she had simply ignored that response and had kept on texting, striving not to be too thin-skinned and to keep up a cheerful front.

Downstairs, Abigail had a salad waiting for her in the dining room. Jo ate with appetite. She had risen soon after first light when Trixie had phoned about her grandmother's accident and she had missed out on breakfast when she'd gone to help. Thanking the house-keeper, she left the house and walked to the church through the grounds, enjoying that pleasant amble along the shaded walk below the trees.

Gianni's helicopter landed on the helipad at Belvedere. He was tired and unshaven and he would have enjoyed a shower, but he was even more determined to run Jo to earth…and ground her, possibly *for ever*. He strode into the grand house to be greeted by Abigail.

'Where's Jo?' he asked lightly.

'I'm afraid I don't know. She was here for lunch but, to be honest, she doesn't spend much time here. She's probably next door organising the tradesmen. Mrs Renzetti is a tireless worker,' she said admiringly.

Gianni's lips compressed. 'She is,' he agreed as he turned on his heel and headed back out again.

He strode through the arched gate he had had constructed and walked into the Ladymead front garden. He didn't stop to admire his foresight. In fact, just about then, he thought it had been crazy of him to facilitate her visits to her family and make her more accessible to others. When was she planning to make time for *him*? He had texted her to tell her that he was coming home. He had expected either a response or to find her waiting for him. To receive neither had only angered him more.

He found Sybil in the barn feeding her motley collection of animals.

'Oh, she's at the church for the jumble sale,' she told him brightly.

McTavish whimpered behind a metal mesh gate, penned in and clearly hating it.

'Why's he locked up?' Gianni enquired in surprise.

'He couldn't be trusted with the tradesmen.'

'Let him out,' Gianni urged.

'Are you sure? I thought he hated you too.'

'No, we're making progress,' Gianni insisted as he opened the gate and McTavish emerged, visibly thought about attacking him and then stilled with a bewildered expression on his face. 'Come on, we'll go find your mistress.'

A jumble sale. His wife was helping with a jumble sale. He had vaguely assumed Jo did only hands-off stuff like fixing flowers in the church and of course she sang solos in the choir on special occasions. It was infuriating to credit that even a jumble sale was more important than he was on Jo's terms.

He strode into the garage and climbed into his sports car. He was about to reclaim his wife. McTavish barked at him. 'Forgot about you.' Gianni sighed, opening the passenger door, trying not to wince as the Scottie sprang into the car and sat down, flexing his claws on the pristine leather upholstery.

He drove round to the church by the road. He had no doubt that Jo had walked, ignoring the fact that he had a brand-new four-by-four sitting ready for her use. She shunned personal gifts if she could get away with it, yet she accepted that he cover the heavy expenditure of the repairs to Ladymead. Annoyance snaked through Gianni and his dark golden eyes flashed with ire.

He strode into the church hall, which was a hive of industry. Women were rushing about setting up stalls and unpacking bags and boxes. He saw Jo and then he saw nobody else. He was so intent on reaching her that he almost tripped over the priest and was then forced to pause and make gracious small talk when he was anything but in the mood for it. He watched Jo over the elderly man's shoulder. What on earth was she wearing? Some sort of shapeless cotton shroud the colour of grass? Or the colour of grass stains? He couldn't decide. But even that ugly garment couldn't stifle her luminosity, the gold of her hair and the jewelled perfection of her eyes against her pale skin. A hunger as unstoppable as his temper lanced through Gianni and he thoroughly resented that surge of lust.

Jo looked up from the box she was unpacking and saw Gianni and everything, literally *everything* just fell away from her as if someone had waved a magic wand. He stalked through the crowd looking very much like a Greek god, an exquisitely tailored black pinstripe suit sheathing broad shoulders, lean hips and long powerful legs. A red shirt and silver-grey tie bucked the conventional vibe he had utilised for the board meeting. The cut male lines of his perfect features were breathtakingly spectacular even with a heavy cloud of stubble darkening his skin. Jo stared and a helpless stab of yearning was followed by a far more earthy inner clench that made her flush and press her thighs together. For a split second, she couldn't believe she was married to him or that the same man could possibly have declared that she was a cut above him. He was her perfect ten and he was *home*. Only a split second from rushing forward to grab him and rush him back to Belvedere, she encountered his eyes and she froze.

His dark golden eyes were scorching hot, his lean, darkly handsome face taut and hard. She frowned because he was clearly angry. What the heck had happened to put him in such a mood? My word, was her first thought, had the board of directors ousted him from his position?

Gianni leant over the stall to say, 'Why aren't you at home?'

Jo blinked. 'Oh, my goodness,' she whispered. 'Why did nobody tell me that I'd been spirited back in time to the nineteen fifties?'

CHAPTER EIGHT

GIANNI'S SHIMMERING EYES flamed like torches in receipt of that comeback. 'I texted you to tell you that I was on my way back—'

Jo dug her phone out of her pocket, her palm damp. 'No, you didn't,' she began and then she realised that her phone was as dead as a dodo because it had run out of charge. 'Oh, dear.'

'Is that all you've got to say?'

'Let's go outside to have this conversation,' Jo urged, moving out from behind the stall. 'I don't want anyone overhearing us and I can only give you five minutes.'

'*Five minutes?*' Gianni seethed, only half under his breath.

'I have to take care of the stall. There's no one else to do it.' Jo lengthened her steps to walk outside as fast as possible. The back of the church hall housed the bins and the occasional smoker, but it was at that moment quiet and empty. 'I'm sorry I didn't get your text. I forgot to charge my phone.'

'If I can't even reach you on the phone,' Gianni shot at her, 'what sort of marriage is this?'

'Obviously not a marriage that meets your expectations,' Jo conceded with stiff reluctance, wounded by that question. 'You're doing that not-listening thing that you do when you get angry. Take a deep breath, count to ten, whatever works for you.'

At that advice, Gianni's gaze flared with incredulity. A moment later, he stepped hastily out of the way as an elderly woman trod past him to plunge a bag into a bin, exchanged a cheery word with Jo about the queue forming at the front of the hall, and went back indoors.

'Your phone battery is past it. If you were actually *using* the new phone I gave you…'

'Gianni…the phone you gave me has diamonds all over it,' she reminded him in a pained whisper. 'It's very extravagant.'

Gianni shrugged a broad shoulder in dismissal. 'You reject everything I give you. The phone, the car, the clothes, but when it comes to Ladymead, you take it *all*.'

'Stop scoring points. It's not like that, you know it's not,' Jo begged. 'Please, just tell me how the board meeting went.'

Gianni stepped back, shoulders squaring, mouth taut, bright narrowed eyes grim. 'I'm still CEO but they're planning to review the situation again in three months.'

'Oh, no, I know that must make you feel like you're still on trial!' Jo exclaimed in dismay and immediate sympathy, moving closer to stroke his arm in a consoling gesture. 'I'm so sorry, Gianni.'

'I feel like I'm getting absolutely nothing out of our marriage,' Gianni spelt out in a harsh undertone as she stepped back from him again. 'You're never there for me.'

Jo stared at him in a panic. 'Don't say that!'

'Why not? It's the truth.' Gianni was not in the mood to give any quarter. 'You could have been in New York *with* me. Instead, you put your family and Ladymead, even your blasted pets before me! You're my wife. I should take precedence.'

'I think that sounds very old-fashioned,' Jo protested even as guilt and regret burned through her like a stream of lava because she had not realised that he resented her choices quite so much, had indeed assumed that he would be far too much in demand to miss her. For her, however, the days of his absence had run one into another in a mad blur as every day had thrown up new complications at Ladymead or fresh family challenges. 'I'll start using the new phone.'

'Too little, too late,' Gianni breathed in a tone of finality. 'A month into our marriage, I can't accept that it's extraordinary that I should expect more of your time.'

That criticism hit Jo hard. At that moment, it seemed to her that everyone in her life was expecting more from her and that, one way or another, she was short-changing or disappointing all of them. Sharp anxiety engulfed her. The days weren't long enough to cover all that she had to do, and now Gianni was home with every right to expect her attention and some cruel fate had ensured she was unavailable.

'Perhaps not. Gianni… I have to go inside now and finish setting up the stall,' she muttered apologetically, her sapphire eyes clinging to his lean, strong features in vain search of some understanding of her predicament. 'I'll be home in a couple of hours.'

'As you wish…' Gianni turned on his heel.

'We'll continue this back home,' Jo pointed out. 'Let's hope I don't lose my temper as well.'

'I haven't lost my temper,' Gianni countered with

quiet dignified assurance, for he had been careful about containing it. 'Nor have I said one word that I regret.'

Jo went back into the hall and finished unpacking. The scrum of shoppers kept her from thinking too much about the argument. She felt crushed by Gianni's dissatisfaction though. He deemed her a complete failure in the wife stakes. Clearly, he had wanted her with him in New York. She had got that decision badly wrong. Furthermore, she should be using the new phone and the new car and wearing the clothes. He was spending a fortune on her family home and she wasn't quibbling about that, so why was she refusing to utilise his generous gifts? That was petty and thoughtless of her. He saw it as a form of rejection and she had offended him.

"'Give every man thy ear, but few thy voice,'" Duffy warned as Gianni walked through the orangery and strode outside, drinking in the fresh air after the hours of travel and strife. The parrot's Shakespeare quote only made Gianni groan.

Jo would never have agreed to marry him had he not promised to repair Ladymead. That was the crux of the problem, he reasoned tautly. Strip all the other stuff away and what was he left with?

'She married me for my money,' he reminded himself, thinking that his expectations had been too high, if not out of order.

Just inside the doorway, Duffy trilled in delight and began singing his song about money making the world go around, pacing to the beat along his perch.

'But she wasn't a gold-digger.' Gianni sighed, accepting that essential truth that was an obstacle that stretched like a mountain range between them.

Even so, if Jo didn't have time for him or their marriage, he had a very practical solution to the problem. He needed to hire a project manager to free his wife from the onerous duties of overseeing the work being done on the money pit. That was simple, straightforward, a first step in the right direction, he told himself ruefully. He would organise that transfer of labour immediately and free Jo from the responsibility. In addition, he would organise a break for them on the yacht because they had had a very brief honeymoon, and marriage, he was beginning to appreciate, required a lot more effort and time input than any casual affair.

Jo walked back to Belvedere with McTavish and Fairy at her heels. She was deeply troubled. Gianni had treated her unfairly. He had not looked at his own behaviour. He had kept every one of his secrets, locking her out, keeping her at a distance and refusing to give her his trust. Yet she had told him everything about herself without reservation. He had allowed his father to insult her with his allegations about Ralph only the day after their wedding and he had not had enough faith in her to defend her. That had hurt and damaged her ability to trust him.

And whether he liked it or not, Jo had a responsibility towards her family. Gianni didn't really have a family beyond a father he barely spoke to and her as his new wife, so how could he understand her position? Jo had gladly taken charge for Sybil at Ladymead after her grandmother's fall and had stepped in at the jumble sale because her family would have done the same thing for her. Such things happened and had to be dealt with sensibly.

'I'll bring you tea. Mr Renzetti is on the terrace,' Abigail told her cheerfully.

'"Though she be but little, she is fierce,"' quoted Duffy randomly as she petted him as much as he would allow, which wasn't much. He had never been a touchy-feely bird although he was happy to sit on a family member's shoulder if invited.

'Whatever,' she muttered, bracing herself and walking out onto the terrace.

'Finally, you're here,' Gianni purred with more than a hint of sarcasm as he lounged back against the wall that separated the terrace from the lawn that stretched right to the edge of the natural woodland.

Gianni had changed since she had last seen him at the church hall. He had shaved and exchanged his suit for designer jeans and a casual shirt the rich green of a pistachio nut. He looked stunning. That shade brought out the bronze of his skin and the darkness of his hair. And his sun-kissed skin accentuated the smouldering dark gold of his gorgeous eyes. Her husband, only he really truly wasn't hers, Jo reflected unhappily. He was a husband on temporary loan and that time element of a five-year maximum could well relate to his lack of trust in her and in other women.

She was to stay his wife for a minimum of five years but was that not really a clue that five years was the longest Gianni could see their marriage lasting? Or even wanted it to last? Certainly, that time limit was not something that Jo could manage to forget. Sadly, she couldn't argue about that limit either, she acknowledged, not when she had agreed to that contract, her only thought being the saving of her family home. Unfortunately, once that five-year period had been mentioned, she had only been able to view their marriage as a very transitory affair, which Gianni could already see ending. And that aspect, when she had been doing nothing to avoid a pregnancy, could not give Jo any peace of mind.

Abigail bustled out with a tray of tea. Gianni waved away the offer of tea as a refreshment in favour of the whiskey glass in his hand, but Jo was thirsty and she poured herself a cup.

'I have some things to say,' Jo announced then, her lovely face pale, her eyes shadowed with tiredness, her expression unusually serious. 'Sybil intended to look after the work at Ladymead, but my grandmother had a fall and Sybil had to cry off to take her to A & E for treatment. She's okay. It's only a sprain. But that's why I was over there this morning. The jumble sale was something my grandmother had volunteered to do and I took care of it for her this afternoon.'

'Jo…' Gianni murmured tautly.

Jo set down her cup and saucer and stood tall. 'No, let me speak first. You didn't once *tell* me that you wanted me to accompany you to New York. My family moved out of their home this week and they needed my help. There's a big gap in trust between us, Gianni.'

Gianni angled his dark head back, eyes glinting in the sunshine as he frowned. 'I disagree.'

'If that's true, why can't you tell me who the love of your life was at university?' she asked levelly. 'Why can't you talk freely about Fiona? Those are simple questions that people in a relationship would normally ask and have answered. That you refuse tells me that you don't trust me…and that makes it hard for me to trust you as well. You are, after all, the man who stood back and let his father accuse me and question me about false allegations made against me.'

'Federico wants a private meeting with you to apologise for his behaviour,' Gianni interposed. 'He phoned me about it over a week ago. He knows he was in the wrong and that he shouldn't have interfered. We'd have heard about that tabloid article soon enough through your family.'

'None of that changes the fact that *you* didn't have faith in me.'

His smouldering gaze narrowed, his strong bone structure clenching hard at that blunt reminder. 'I thought we had already laid *that* business to rest.'

Colour flamed over her cheekbones. 'Forgiving you doesn't mean I forget how you acted,' Jo pointed out defensively, her voice rising involuntarily. 'Or how you're acting now. As if I've let you down…as if I have no right to be loyal to my own family! As if sometimes life doesn't force you to roll with the punches because you have to do the right thing. My loyalties were torn between you and them! Why can't you understand that?'

Gianni set down his glass and reached for her, his hands dropping down on her shoulders. 'Jo—'

Jo broke angrily free of his hold. 'No! Right now, I'm going for a nap to make up for my very early morning start today and then I'm going to see my grandmother, where I will stay for dinner. I'll see you later. Maybe by the time I return you'll have started trying to see things from my side and not just your own!'

Slammed by that criticism, Gianni made no attempt to hold her back and he watched her stalk back into the house, proving that she was as close to losing her temper and screaming at him as he had ever seen her.

Bemused by that raging comeback from peaceful Jo, of all people, Gianni groaned out loud. Should he follow her? Or wait, let her have a break and allow the dust to settle? The truth was that he didn't honestly know what to do because he had never been in a relationship long enough to have arguments, unless he counted his time with Fliss, and Fliss had never once argued with him about anything. So, that somewhat unreal experience was of no help whatsoever.

He had been in a bad mood when he flew home, he conceded grudgingly. It galled him to admit that he had been unreasonable, possibly even selfish. But he had been. He had missed her in New York. He had wanted her by his side. Only he hadn't been prepared to admit that to himself. Getting mentally attached to Jo had never been part of his plan. How naïve had he been to believe that he could marry a woman without making the smallest adjustment to his new lifestyle?

All his adult life, Gianni had believed that he had to have complete control over his emotions to protect himself and, until Jo had appeared in the church on their wedding day, he had fully believed that he had achieved that feat. But little by little, Jo had infiltrated his life on every level. Sexual attraction was no longer Jo's main appeal. He expelled his breath slowly, wondering why he had such a powerful need for her presence, her company, her validation.

Jo raced upstairs, walked to the master bedroom and stripped off her dress, which she now loathed. She had seen how Gianni looked at that dress and she knew it hadn't passed muster. It could go to a charity shop. From now on she would wear her new wardrobe. She slid into the comfortable bed with a sigh. She would have made more effort if she had known that Gianni was coming home that afternoon. There she had been wearing a comfortable but shapeless dress and wearing no make-up. She winced.

Gianni was accustomed to the company of beautiful, well-groomed women, many of whom would be willing to invite him into bed regardless of the wedding ring on his finger. Why did she care? What difference would it have made? Had she looked more alluring, would he have scooped her up in his arms and kissed her breathless? Jo rolled her eyes. No, he had been too annoyed with her. She muffled a yawn and, tucking her cheek into the pillow, closed her heavy eyes. Why, oh, why was she so extraordinarily tired?

Gianni studied Jo intently while she slept. Once again, she hadn't been looking after herself, he decided worriedly. She had blue shadows beneath her eyes and there was a hint of frailty to her fine bone structure. Abigail had admitted that Jo didn't eat very much and usually ate on the run, always rushing from point A to point B to cover her various obligations. And he had made her feel bad. A trip in the yacht would do her the world of good.

Jo felt much better when she awakened and stepped straight into the shower to freshen up. She donned a flowing blue sundress with a designer label and slipped on a toning cardigan to cover the cooler evening temperature. Keys clutched in her hand, she climbed into the brand-new four-by-four Gianni had gifted her to drive it for the first time and turned it down the manicured drive slowly before, gathering confidence, she headed for the village and her family's temporary home.

One step in the door of the low-ceilinged house, she learned that Gianni had already visited and had brought flowers to her grandmother. He had also, apparently, reiterated his suggestion that her relatives simply move in with them at Belvedere for the duration of the work being done at Ladymead. Her grandmother had politely refused, once again voicing her conviction that newlyweds needed their own space.

Liz Hamilton looked reasonably well after her ordeal, her bandaged foot resting on a stool. But she looked exhausted and every year of her age. Jo's heart clenched tight. Since her sister was out of action, Trixie had cooked and dinner was a vegetarian feast.

'Gianni is worried about you,' Sybil remarked. 'He thinks you look very tired.'

'I'm fine. We've all been run off our feet with the move this week,' Jo protested. 'He fusses.'

'And so he should. He's your husband,' her grandmother said staunchly. 'It's his job to look out for you.'

'Is everything good with you?' Sybil asked, her keen gaze probing Jo's strained smile.

'Everything's marvellous,' Jo swore.

After telling that lie, Jo couldn't face going inside Belvedere when she got home. That would mean dealing with the fallout from her bitter exchange with Gianni. It was a pleasant light evening and she decided to walk down to the lake instead of going directly indoors.

The lake path was shaded by trees, and she was glad of her cardigan because it was cool. The waning light left long stretches of the lake in darkness and it was a little eerie. In daylight it was beautiful though, a tranquil expanse of water surrounded by trees and leafy water plants. A duck fluttered up out of the undergrowth at her approach and she flinched and gasped. Her invasion caused a noisy exodus of birds and a bunch of them surged across the path and into the water. She sat down on the bench her grandfather had installed for his fishing.

The faint thud of steps on the grassy path made her look up as a long, tall shadow blocked her view of the lake. 'Gianni?' she wheezed in surprise.

'I saw you walk down in this direction and wondered where you were going. You never come down here,' he murmured with a frown. 'Yet when you think about it, this is virtually where we started. Not the best of memories but the experience created a bizarre link between us, didn't it?'

Her stomach hollowed as she remembered him walking into the lake that day and she looked up at him with wide, troubled eyes.

'You never betrayed me. You never told my secret,' Gianni mused reflectively. 'It makes me wonder why I've been so reluctant to trust you.'

'I didn't really understand what I'd seen you do until I was a bit older. I just thought you were being foolish.'

'I *was* foolish…and out of my mind with grief,' Gianni sliced in heavily. 'My mother provided the only warmth and softness in my life and I couldn't face the future without her. I was angry and bitter that I didn't get to be with her at the end. When I walked into the lake, I didn't want to come out of it again. I was very intense, an all-or-nothing teenager.'

'Yes,' Jo agreed ruefully. 'After you rescued me, you looked at me like you hated me because I'd stopped you in your tracks.'

'I would have drowned if it had not been for you. What on earth possessed you to go into the lake to try to reach me?'

Jo tensed, for she had often asked herself that same question. 'It was instinctive. I felt so desperately sorry for you because you'd lost your mum. I was a good swimmer, only unfortunately I didn't have time to think about what I was doing. I only knew that you walking into the lake like that was very dangerous and I wanted to stop you.'

'So, you got into the water yourself and almost drowned before I contrived to fish you out.' Gianni groaned as he crouched down fluidly in front of her, his stunning dark golden eyes alight with emotion. 'Jo, you have too much heart…it was a crazy but very brave thing for a little girl to do.'

'I wasn't expecting the weeds and I got all tangled up and then I panicked,' Jo recalled hoarsely.

'You made such a commotion in the water that I realised I wasn't alone and struck out to see what was happening. I saw you sinking below the surface, that red jacket you were wearing ballooning up round you.'

'You saved my life,' she whispered.

'But you saved mine as well,' Gianni pointed out levelly, closing a lean hand over her knotted fingers. 'It must've been fate… How else can you explain us being together now?'

Jo lifted her head, faint amusement dancing in her eyes. 'Careful, Gianni…you almost sound romantic.'

'Why did you never tell anyone about what you saw me do that day?' he asked wryly.

'I didn't want to get you into trouble. I mean, I knew what you did was stupid, but I found your father scary back then and I assumed you'd be punished even though you'd lost your mother.' Jo sighed. 'It was just easier all round to let everybody believe that you'd seen me in the water and gone in to rescue me.'

'The last thing I wanted that day was to be christened a hero when I didn't deserve the accolades.'

'But you did deserve them because you *did* save me,' Jo contended gently. 'We kind of saved each other.'

'Yet, right now, it feels like I've blown everything apart with you,' he breathed tautly. 'That's not what I intended when I married you. I did want to make a go of this.'

'We both do,' she conceded gently as he vaulted upright and pulled her up with him. 'So, *talk*...fill in all the blanks for me.'

'It was first love,' Gianni explained flatly as he walked her back in the direction of the house. 'I don't know if Felicity—Fliss—was the love of my life exactly, because I was only nineteen and in my second year at uni when I met her and her sister. Fliss and Fiona were identical twins. She was studying art history. I fell madly in love with her. We hung around in a group.'

'Most of us do at university,' she chipped in, disconcerted to learn that the Fiona he was still in touch with was his ex-girlfriend's identical twin sister. 'I bet you were really popular because you're clever, rich and sporty.'

'I did have a lot of friends,' he conceded.

'What was Fliss like?'

'She was tall with long dark curly hair, obsessed with art, always dragging me off to exhibitions. I faked my interest. I'm not particularly into art,' he confided. 'She liked to cook, she liked to feel that she was looking after me. She thought I worked too hard, but then I had Federico at home, questioning even a hint of a lower grade in any subject.'

Jo breathed in deep, afraid to interrupt him. 'How long were you together?'

'Two years. But only a couple of months after we met, Fliss started finding bruises in random places. She went to the doctor. Blood tests were done. Leukaemia was diagnosed,' Gianni continued in a curt undertone. 'She went straight into chemotherapy. The doctors were hoping for a remission, but the treatment didn't make her any better, although the sessions probably extended her life. She got weaker and sicker, and in the end she died.'

Jo was utterly appalled by what he was telling her in that flat, unemotional voice. Only a few years after his mother had passed away after her long struggle with cancer, Gianni had found himself in love with a very sick girl.

'I was devastated,' Gianni admitted gruffly. 'Fiona helped to get me through it. She was very close to Fliss and was with us from the beginning. I wanted them to move into my apartment with me, but Fliss didn't want that. They didn't have any other family. Their uncle had raised them and he died shortly before they started university.'

'I'm so sorry, Gianni. I can understand why you didn't want to talk about her now,' Jo said uncomfortably because her throat was thick with tears. She was thinking about Gianni, whose childhood had been staged against the daunting backdrop of his mother's illness, falling in love with a girl who had also become ill and ultimately died. She realised now why he had told her at Ralph's funeral that falling in love only got you hurt, because the only two people he had loved in life had died and left him behind. Her heart broke for him and her eyes stung and she had to breathe in deep to stay in control.

'Fiona is still in your life, though,' she remarked carefully.

'She's like the sister I never had,' Gianni said warmly. 'I set her up in business after we finished university and she's gone from strength to strength, one of the best investments I've ever made. She renovates and decorates houses with real flair. She's made quite a name for herself abroad.'

'I look forward to meeting her some time,' Jo replied.

'Are you satisfied now that I've told you everything?' Gianni enquired as he walked her upstairs.

'It wasn't a matter of needing to know so much as a need to know that you trusted me enough to tell me,' Jo explained tautly. 'Don't make a secret of things just because you would prefer to avoid talking about them.'

In their bedroom, Gianni slowly turned her round to face him. His dark golden eyes were very serious and his hands flexed on her slim shoulders. 'Stay in touch with me when I'm away. Send me your silly texts telling me what Duffy said or how McTavish got frightened off by a fox. I like hearing from you. That connection is important to me, *cara*.'

'I do not send silly texts,' Jo declared with amusement.

'You do and they lighten my day.'

'Then what about the text about the missing scaffolders that irritated the hell out of you?' she dared.

Gianni groaned. 'Once again, my apologies. Federico and my uncles were with me complaining about profit margins in this new company we've acquired.' He fell silent, recognising that she was smiling and that he was forgiven.

In relief, Gianni bent his dark head and brushed his lips very gently across hers before sliding his tongue against hers in a hungry exploratory foray. 'What do you think of early nights?'

Her slender body quivering against the hard muscularity of his, Jo struggled to catch her breath. 'One would be very welcome right now,' she muttered unevenly.

Gianni scooped her up into his arms and tumbled her down on the bed. 'I like this dress but it's coming off,' he warned her. 'We're going away for a week on the yacht tomorrow and sailing round the Greek islands.'

'But I can't leave—'

'Yes, you can, it's all organised,' he overruled as he stood back and peeled off his shirt. 'Sybil will take over supervising at Ladymead. Trixie's shop is closed at present, so she'll be able to keep your grandmother company until her ankle heals.'

Involuntarily deprived of speech, Jo stared up at him.

'I discussed it all with your family while you were sleeping. I want you all to myself,' Gianni admitted with a slashing smile. 'The honeymoon part two.'

Jo sat up to lift her dress over her head and discard it before coiling back against the pillows like an embryo temptress with a glint in her bright eyes. All of a sudden the world felt as though it was full of infinite possibilities. 'I may pack my wedding dress and those lace gloves. I seem to remember making you a promise.'

Gianni flat-out grinned, lean muscles flexing as he came down on the bed and shifted over her, sliding between her slender thighs. Smouldering dark golden eyes glittering, he was all sensual heat as he strung a line of kisses across her collarbone and arrowed off into the sensitive skin of her neck to press his mouth there, making her hips arch up and a little gasp escape her.

Jo laced her fingers into his tousled black hair. 'I want you,' she said for the first time ever. 'I missed you.'

'I'm not sure you had time. According to Sybil you've been racing around like the Energizer bunny.'

Jo tugged his head up. 'Very funny. I kept busy because you weren't here,' she told him.

Gianni gave her a smile that was pure invitation and shifted lazily against her, the sensual spell he could cast holding her fast as her heart rate climbed. 'I'm here now…ready, waiting and very willing…'

CHAPTER NINE

JO BOUNCED HER sandalled feet to the annoying pop song playing in her head. She had heard it in a restaurant on Corfu and still couldn't get it out of her head.

Ten days had passed since they had left for a tour of the Greek islands. A dreamy smile tilted her lips. Island-hopping round the Greek islands had been enormous fun. There had been picnics in secluded bays and once on a rugged hillside where a herd of goats had tried to steal Gianni's lunch. Just thinking about it, she laughed again. They had visited Little Venice on Mykonos and ended their day there dining by the shore where Gianni had given her another ring, a diamond hoop that had shone brighter than the stars above them. A magical trip to the volcanic island of Santorini had followed and they had walked hand in hand up the steep streets, taking advantage of the most spectacular sea views. The nights were hot and very passionate, she recalled abstractedly, emerging from her reverie to wonder why she was sitting on the edge of the bath when she had already showered.

And then reality stole back and she paled and remembered that she was anxiously awaiting the result of the pregnancy test she had done. She hadn't thought it was possible to fall pregnant so quickly but then her period had failed to arrive while they were abroad and she had begun to worry. After all, now that she was finally thinking about that momentous decision to try to get pregnant from the very start of their marriage, she was guiltily regretting it. She hadn't really thought through the consequences of an early pregnancy when their marriage was still very much in the honeymoon phase. It would alter so much between them.

She had no doubt that Gianni would be pleased that she had conceived because he had made that same decision with her. Sadly, neither of them had devoted much time and thought to that life-changing choice. How much did Gianni know about pregnant women? That they got big? That they shouldn't drink alcohol? That they had to take extra care of themselves and got tired more easily? Wouldn't he find all those restrictions a drag? Mightn't he find her larger body a bit of a passion-killer?

Finally, Jo checked her watch and reached for the wand. Well, she was pregnant, no doubt about that. A bubble of happy satisfaction broke through her insecurities. Gianni's baby, she thought dreamily, *their* baby. Maybe a little boy, maybe a little girl, she didn't much care which, only that her child be healthy. It had happened. She wouldn't be surprised to learn that Trixie had cast some crazy fertility spell on them at the full moon. There was nothing the Hamilton women loved more than a baby in the family. *I'm going to be someone's mum,* she thought dizzily, absolutely blown away by the idea.

She would tell Gianni when she was ready to tell him. Just at that moment she wanted to hug her precious secret to herself for a little while. In the meantime, she would see her doctor, have herself all checked out and present Gianni with the complete package. Why? She suspected that her pregnancy would make Gianni inclined to fuss over her every move and she wanted to be in a position of superior medical knowledge.

Jo went downstairs for breakfast in a pensive mood. She was surprised to find Gianni, superbly sleek and sophisticated in a tailored navy suit and an unusually conventional white shirt, still seated at the table reading the *Financial Times*. 'I thought you had an early flight,' she remarked.

'The meeting was moved back and I rescheduled. I'm leaving in five minutes,' he warned her briskly, all switched into business mode, which made her want to smile.

Madre di Dio, that beauty of hers could light up the room, Gianni conceded, shaken by the thought, particularly when it came directly after his decision to leave her peacefully sleeping earlier when, in truth, he had wanted her company. Their relationship had shifted from a business deal to a level of complexity that stunned him. He told himself he didn't need to think about it, that the closer they got, the better and more successful their marriage would be. But there was no denying that what they had was very far removed from what he had originally envisaged. As a rule, he skipped late travelling and stayed in London overnight, but Belvedere had developed an allure that had nothing to do with bricks and mortar and Gianni knew that he wouldn't be spending the night anywhere but with his wife.

Jo helped herself to tea and toast and then wondered if she should be eating more protein and, when Abigail came in to check on them, surprised the older woman by asking for scrambled egg.

'*Madonna mia,*' Gianni swore in sudden impatience. 'I meant to tell you last night but I forgot. Fiona arrived last night.'

Jo tensed. 'Fiona?' she queried. 'I didn't realise she was coming here so soon—'

'She wouldn't have been if this were purely social. I hired her services,' Gianni told her, his satisfaction over that decision patent. 'She'll take care of everything at Ladymead for us. It's win-win for everyone. She'll put Ladymead in some glossy-magazine spread when it's all finished and it'll be great PR for her and attract more business.'

Jo was so stunned by that quickly delivered speech that her jaw literally dropped.

Gianni slanted his charismatic grin, even white teeth visible, dark golden eyes glittering with amusement. 'I've finally found out what it takes to silence you... one little surprise—'

Jo relocated her tongue. 'I would hardly call Fiona a *little* surprise,' she murmured stiffly. 'Have you already arranged this with her?'

Gianni smiled even wider. 'I'm very efficient,' he told her smoothly. 'Our estate manager informed me earlier that she picked up the keys for the gate lodge yesterday, so she'll already have moved in.'

'She's going to be living in the gate lodge?' Jo gasped in astonishment.

'With the job she's going to be doing for us, she needs to have somewhere to stay nearby. Why not the lodge? Until we have a head gardener hired, the property is sitting vacant. I would have offered her a room here but we need our privacy,' Gianni advanced cheer-fully. 'It wouldn't kill you to say thank you at this point.'

An expectant silence spread from his side of the table.

'Thank you?' Jo repeated loudly, still reeling in shock from his announcements. 'Are you kidding me?'

Gianni raised a brow as he set his espresso cup down. 'Why would I be kidding you, *cara*? Fiona is the answer to all our prayers. You'll get to be a lady of leisure and I'll get to see a lot more of you. Sybil will be able to return to her rescue animals with a clean conscience. It will suit everyone.'

'But you didn't consult me!' Jo exclaimed rawly. 'You didn't even *discuss* it with me!'

'I organised it for you that day you were at the jumble sale and I meant to raise the subject with you but I forgot about it again,' Gianni told her with a distracted air as he checked his watch and sprang upright. 'Sorry, time for me to depart.'

His long stride got him as far as the threshold of the dining room when he turned back to her. 'I arranged for you to meet Fiona for coffee at eleven today at that new place in the village…what do you call it?'

With difficulty, Jo snatched in oxygen to breathe. 'As You Like It?'

'I thought it would be less formal for a first meeting and that you might not want to invite her here until you get to know her better,' Gianni advanced, in the same helpful *I'm only thinking of you* tone.

Jo was keeping a very tight hold on her temper. She wanted to scream at him but she wouldn't let herself when he was about to leave. 'Didn't it cross your mind that Sybil and I might *want* to take care of Ladymead ourselves?'

Gianni shrugged a broad shoulder. 'Well, it's too late now. Fiona turned down another job to come here at short notice. She's doing us a favour. Why are you making such heavy weather of this? I assumed you'd be grateful for Fiona's help.'

As he moved on into the hall, Jo flew upright and followed him, her cheeks flushed, her eyes bright. 'Ladymead is my home and you went beyond your remit when you organised Fiona without consulting me or my family about it,' she told him frankly.

'First of all, *this* is your home now.' Gianni frowned, taken aback by her attitude when his only thought had been to release her from the burden of overseeing repairs in a dirty, dusty environment. 'You don't get to be consulted unless you're an expert...and you're not an expert in any field relating to that building, aside from its history. I make the major decisions about Ladymead because I'm paying for the work being done,' he framed with succinct bite. 'And I'll have to pay more if any mistakes are made, particularly the kind of mistakes that might fall foul of the rules to protect a listed building and would have to be rectified before the authorities will certify the work.'

And with that unsympathetic and cutting statement delivered, Gianni swung on his heel without another word and strode off for the helipad.

Jo's hands knotted into fists. He *forgot* to tell her about hiring Fiona? Chance would be a fine thing! Gianni wasn't that innocent. He had been determined to release her from the demands of Ladymead while the repairs were being carried out. Maybe he thought she was going to sit at Belvedere all day sewing a fine seam or however that stupid phrase went! What did he think that she was planning to do with herself all day? Ever since she'd left uni, she had been running Ladymead, taking care of the accounts, keeping everyone happy, dealing with every little problem.

But maybe that phase of her life was over now that she had Gianni, Belvedere and his other homes to consider, she reflected uncertainly. Was that possible? Did she need to do a rethink about her life too? How dared he speak to her like that though! Yes, she knew very well that he was financing all the work, but he hadn't had to throw it in her face like that, had he? She could have said in much the same vein, 'Yes, I know you're paying for it. Isn't that why I married you?'

Ironically, Gianni would have hit the roof at that taunt. It wasn't something he ever mentioned. He had pretty much bought her with Ladymead, but he didn't like to be reminded of that hard fact. It seemed that he now wanted her to be the woman of leisure he assumed would suit his needs best, always available, always on call, as easy as his past undemanding lovers, there for him the instant he snapped his fingers. Her even white teeth gritted and she said a very unladylike word under her breath.

And now she was stuck with Fiona, whether she liked it or not! Fiona, who was like his sister, she reminded herself grimly. Well, he had accepted her family and she had to accept his, even if Fiona was only an honorary member. She tackled her scrambled egg and fresh toast with a murmur of thanks and a lack of appetite she concealed. Being at odds with Gianni stressed her out. Had she been unreasonable? She called Sybil for a second opinion and Sybil's annoyance at being summarily replaced without warning reassured her as to her own wounded feelings.

'Gianni thought he was doing me a favour. He seemed to be expecting us all to be delighted,' Jo proffered apologetically.

'And a woman you've never met being installed in a house at the foot of your driveway? What on earth was he thinking?' her great-aunt fumed on her niece's behalf.

'The truth is that he doesn't think a lot about things from my point of view.' Jo sighed, deciding not to mention the prearranged coffee date, news of which would probably send Sybil into orbit. Talk about Gianni being high-handed! Taking over? Moving her around on his own mental chessboard as if she had no will or wishes of her own and no other life. He was utterly ignoring the truth that she liked to be busy and active as much as he did.

'He needs to learn to communicate…and fast.'

'Agreed. It's quite challenging.'

'His father is too, although if you give Federico a good dressing-down, he does eventually get the message,' Sybil informed her tellingly.

'I thought I had you to thank for that apology of his,' Jo admitted with sudden amusement. 'He was very embarrassed. He's getting rather more human than he used to be. Are you seeing him socially? I don't like to ask if you're *dating*.'

'Good heavens, no!' Sybil gasped. 'He's trying but he's not there yet, particularly with that stupid stunt he pulled with you and Gianni when he crashed your honeymoon! He'll have to up his game a lot before I give him another chance.'

But Federico Renzetti obviously went for strong women, Jo reflected thoughtfully as she went upstairs to go through her wardrobe, trying to pick an outfit that would do for a visit to her doctor and, afterwards, the coffee date with Fiona. Dress up, she decided, unable to imagine Gianni having such high regard for a woman who wasn't elegant, at the very least. She donned a lightweight pair of trousers and a matching top in a light summery print.

Her doctor confirmed her pregnancy and wished her well, sending her off with a prescription for vitamins and a lot of useful advice. Jo walked into the coffee shop and ordered tea, instead of her usual coffee, and took a seat at a table in the window.

A woman pulled up outside in a sports car. She was eye-catching with her mane of black curls tumbling down to her slim shoulders, perfect long tanned legs displayed in a short white skirt and a clinging white sleeveless top that hugged her curves. She strolled into the coffee shop, snapped her fingers at the startled barista and ordered an espresso. Every eye was on her because she looked like a celebrity. Her sunglasses were on top of her head, her sheer confidence showed, and she was, not to put too fine a point on it, gorgeous. She had big sparkling dark eyes, a glowing complexion and luscious red-tinted lips.

'You're Jo. I saw the wedding photo online. I'm Fiona Myles. You must have some courage taking on Gianni,' she remarked with a mocking smile as she approached Jo's table.

'You think so?' Jo laughed, thinking that that wasn't the nicest way to greet a new acquaintance.

'I *know* so,' Fiona replied seriously. 'He doesn't wear monogamy well.'

Jo shrugged, not knowing quite how to answer that leading comment. 'That hasn't been my experience.'

'Initially I was simply so shocked that Gianni had got *married*,' Fiona admitted in a tone of disbelief.

'You're not alone,' Jo said lightly.

As the obedient barista delivered Fiona's coffee to the table, she smiled and thanked her. 'I can't wait to see Ladymead. I adore old houses,' she declared.

'Would you like an official tour tomorrow morning...about ten?' Jo asked cheerfully.

'That would be good. I want to get started asap,' Fiona told her. 'Gianni has never been patient. In fact, in all the years that I've known him, I've realised that when he wants something done, he wants it done yesterday. Some people don't understand that about him.'

And once again, Jo ignored the challenge, the underwritten hint that Fiona knew Gianni far better than Jo ever could. 'Are you comfortable in the gate lodge?'

'Very,' Fiona assured her as she hefted a fat file onto the table and thrust it across to Jo. 'My most recent commissions. Now, tell me about the repairs that are ongoing.'

Jo was happy to do so while warning that her grandmother and her sisters were planning to move back in as soon as the electric was back on.

'I'll advise them to stay where they are,' Fiona responded. 'It's not a good idea to try living on a work site and it could even be dangerous.'

'I agree,' Jo said. 'But my relatives are stubborn.'

Jo leafed through the file, noting that Fiona had done a lot of renovation work and interior design but that none of her projects had related to historical buildings. She chewed at her lower lip and deliberately admired the image of an opulent bedroom to be polite. In truth she thought it contrived to be both flashy and bland. Fiona's style was in no way suited to Ladymead's ancient quirky charm and eccentric layout. But she said nothing. Gianni's sister, she reminded herself firmly, determined to make the best of their association and handle the brunette with tact. She was disconcerted, though, by Fiona's very personal remarks about Gianni. That attitude didn't quite strike the right familial note to Jo's ears. In fact, Fiona's stance put Jo more in mind of a woman hostile to Gianni's marriage and his wife, a woman who was possessive of him because, for whatever reason, she had long considered him hers. Or possibly her late sister's?

'I'll see you tomorrow, then.' Fiona waved and departed.

Jo's phone rang as she was walking back into Belvedere.

'How did you get on with Fiona?' Gianni asked.

'I didn't expect to hear from you this morning again, not after the tone of your departure,' Jo confided in a tone of censure.

'I'm sorry. I'm too used to everyone agreeing with me and if they don't I tend to steamroller over them,' Gianni admitted tautly. 'I shouldn't have said that about the money.'

'Why not? You didn't say one word that wasn't the truth, even if I didn't like what you said,' Jo conceded, striving to match his honesty. 'Fiona? The jury's still out on that one. She made a couple of snarky comments, one being that you're not monogamous. But I suspect that she wouldn't have warmed up to any woman you married, so I'll give her a pass on this occasion. Perhaps she was looking at me and resenting me and the position I was in because she lost her sister and wishes *she* were your wife. I want to be fair.'

'She shouldn't have said that to you.' Gianni warmed her heart by conceding that point. 'Fiona doesn't have many female friends. She's more a man's woman.'

'Didn't need you to tell me that, Gianni.' Jo chuckled, reckoning the short skirt and clingy sex-bomb top had told her that loud and clear. 'But if she's good at her job I'll do my best to get on with her.'

'You're being generous. I'll be late back tonight,' he warned her. 'But I'd still like to see you.'

'Oh, by the way, before I forget again,' Jo added, 'thank you for that gate through to Ladymead. It makes it so much easier to visit.'

'You see, I do get most things right,' Gianni drawled rather smugly, and she didn't pick him up on it.

Early evening, Jo went for a walk with the dogs and, on the way back, heard gales of laughter coming from Ladymead. Wondering who on earth was there when the house was empty and the workers finished for the day, she walked through the arched gate and into the front garden. There she was disconcerted to find Sybil, Trixie and Fiona Myles seated at the stone garden table with glasses and a couple of empty wine bottles discarded on the grass beside them.

'We're waiting for a taxi,' Sybil announced with very careful diction.

Trixie tried to say something and then caught her sister's eyes and just giggled like a schoolgirl.

'Fiona called in and we brought her over to see the house,' Sybil volunteered as a horn honked in the drive and the older woman stood up. 'That'll be us,' she said and grabbed Trixie's hand to urge her upright. 'Time to go home, Trix.'

Fiona beamed at Jo. 'I'm sure you're surprised to see me here, but Gianni told me where your family lived and I dropped in to see them.'

'It's good that you've met all of us now.'

'Would you like a drink?' Fiona asked.

Jo walked towards the house. 'A glass of water will do me. Alcohol would send me to sleep.' Not to mention her conviction that drinking with the client's family was as unprofessional as visiting the property without the owner present. Tact, she reminded herself, *tact*. She had to switch the water on and then run off the first discoloured gush for several minutes before she could risk satisfying her thirst and by then Fiona had joined her.

'I've got so many ideas for this kitchen,' the brunette told her, leaning back against the table and continuing to drink her wine.

'My grandmother will have her own ideas, too,' Jo warned her.

'Oh, don't you cook?'

'Not if I can help it.' Jo laughed. 'And I'm not living here at present.'

'Fliss was a fabulous cook.'

'We all have our different talents,' Jo responded evenly. 'I wasn't taught to cook. When I was home from school, my grandfather was too busy teaching me how to keep the accounts and how to nurse along our very basic plumbing system in winter.'

'Excuse me, I've got something to get out of the car.' Fiona turned on her high heels and staggered ever so slightly. 'When I come back, I'll tell you my ideas for the Great Hall. Get rid of those moth-eaten screens and the space will be transformed. More space…more light!'

Jo rolled her eyes, because the medieval hand-carved screens were a special feature of the house.

'Let's go back outside. It's gloomy and dusty in here,' Fiona complained, a large photo album in one hand and another bottle of wine in the other. 'Where's the cork-screw gone?'

'It's outside on the table.' Jo was thinking that, by the uncoordinated way Fiona was moving, she had already had more than enough to drink.

Outside again, Fiona pressed the photo album across the table. 'I brought this for you to have a look at…it's from when Gianni and my sister were together.'

'Thanks, but no. I would feel like I was prying,' Jo said truthfully, sipping her lukewarm water while Fiona poured herself a fresh glass of wine and frowned when Jo shook her head. 'And we can't move the screens.'

'I'll talk to Gianni about it,' Fiona cut in, her mouth tight as she pushed the photo album aside, annoyed that Jo had refused to look at it.

'No point talking to him about it.'

'Gianni is very open to my ideas.'

'But the local authorities wouldn't be. The screens are protected by law. They're listed. We're not allowed to remove them,' Jo explained gently.

Fiona grimaced. 'But they're ugly. I'm sure Gianni would agree with me.'

'It really doesn't matter if he does or not. It's *my* house, Fiona.'

'Surely, it's your grandmother's house?'

'No, my grandfather left it to me because I'm the last Hamilton in the family. My grandmother, naturally, has the right to live here as long as she likes,' Jo explained. 'I'm your client.'

'*Gianni's* my client.' Fiona's hostility was no longer hidden. 'He hired me, he pays me, *he* has the last word!' she asserted sharply.

'I'm afraid that I have the last word when it comes to Ladymead,' Jo countered as gently as she could because she didn't want to make the other woman even angrier.

'I wouldn't take that for granted,' Fiona responded in an acid tone. 'You do your five years with Gianni and, in return, he fixes up this house. It's a business arrangement and he's only married to you in the first place because of that stupid scandal in the newspapers!'

Jo went white and literally stopped breathing for several timeless seconds. The private information that Fiona was flinging in her face was only known to a handful of people: Gianni, the lawyers involved and Jo. Even Sybil didn't know about that five-year clause. That Fiona was aware of that fact cut Jo to the bone with angry chagrin because she knew that the most likely explanation was that Gianni had told Fiona the exact circumstances of his marriage. And why on earth would he do that? Didn't he understand the concept of discretion?

'Perhaps you should lay off the wine,' Jo murmured tautly. 'My marriage is none of your business. I'm your client, not your target. I think you should return to the lodge now and have a good night's sleep.'

'Gianni would be much better off with someone like me!' Fiona flung at her, the words slurring. 'He should've been with Fliss but that wasn't to be, and he and I are very close friends indeed.'

'I'm sure you are.' Jo was determined not to get into an argument as she stood up. 'Goodnight, Fiona. Do you still want to do that tour of the house tomorrow morning?'

'Of course not!' the brunette snapped brittlely. 'I won't stand for you treating me like this!'

Jo made no response but inside herself she felt like glass that had been trodden on and smashed to pieces. She did not want to accept that Gianni had put her in a position where she could be humiliated. Their marital agreement was supposed to be private, not something he shared with a woman like Fiona, who only wanted to put her down. As the brunette stalked away, Jo turned back. 'Tell me…do you resent my existence on your sister's behalf? Or on your own?'

'Gianni said he'd never marry after Fliss died!' Fiona slung at her accusingly, but Jo recognised Fiona's jealousy. It was personal. Maybe Fiona had hoped that Gianni would turn to her after her sister died. It hadn't happened, but Fiona had still cherished hope as long as he was single. His marriage, business arrangement or not, had seriously rattled the brunette.

'People change.' Jo didn't say it, but Gianni had matured from the heartbroken young man he had once been. Her heart was hammering with stress inside her chest and she found it impossible to swallow as she walked back towards Belvedere.

Fiona was half in love with Gianni. It took one to know one, Jo acknowledged heavily. She was so hurt now because she was no longer detached from Gianni in *any* way. Not only was she pregnant, but also in love with him. When had that happened? Or had that development been inevitable? He was the boy she had craved as a teenager, the young man she had fallen passionately in love with. Her restive fingers touched the bouquet pendant at her throat. Gianni knew how to touch her heart. He knew what to say, what to do to entrance a woman. Jo had been a pushover, a complete pushover from the evening she had put on her wedding dress again for his benefit and when he had inched off each lace glove with deft fingers her heart had been hammering so hard she had been scared it would burst.

'I will never forget how beautiful you looked on our wedding day,' he had told her on the yacht with one of his flashing smiles. 'Everyone always says that a bride is beautiful, but you looked spectacular.'

And he had meant it, every word of it. She had practically flung herself at him afterwards, but she did not regret the wedding night that they had spent apart. She honestly believed that Gianni would not have appreciated her in the same way had she got into bed with him that first night.

In a pensive mood, she walked back home, wondering wearily if there would be repercussions for her decision to stand up to Fiona Myles. Gianni's friend and honorary sister. Well, what was done was done and she wasn't about to beat herself up for defending her own corner, and Gianni had questions to answer as well, she reflected ruefully.

A long lazy bath relaxed her. She dried her damp hair and picked an elegant wrap and a short silk pyjama set from her packed drawers. When she told Gianni about

the baby, she wanted to look good. She was on the stairs
when she heard the helicopter overhead and she smiled.

Gianni's fast, impatient stride carried him indoors before he even saw Jo at the foot of the stairs, wearing
something fluttery, feminine and blue that bared her
perfect legs. With supreme effort, he mastered the immediate surge of hunger that made his heart race and
the fit of his trousers tight. He strode forward, smouldering dark golden eyes glittering below the thick canopy of his lashes.

'What on earth did you say or do to Fiona?' he demanded hoarsely.

CHAPTER TEN

Jo FROZE, WARM COLOUR washing up her throat into her cheeks as she tried to think how to answer that leading question.

Gianni released his breath in a hiss of annoyance and said levelly, 'Fiona was in hysterics when she phoned me, and I had a hell of a job getting her off the phone again. I'm just asking what happened to set her off in drama-queen mode.'

Jo was in no mood to discuss Fiona Myles. 'Well, possibly *I* got annoyed.'

'You don't get annoyed...not the way I do and other less controlled people do,' Gianni rebutted with confidence.

Jo leant back against the carved pillar that adorned the foot of the stairs, unaware that that position pushed her bare breasts against the silk top she wore and showed a tantalising few inches of her smooth inner thigh. 'In this case, I got annoyed,' she confided.

'Why?' Gianni was attempting to look directly at her without being distracted by that very sensual pose that affected him in all sorts of inappropriate ways. The timing was all wrong, he thought regretfully.

'You see,' Jo continued, 'Fiona quoted the exact terms of our marriage contract to me—'

His ebony brows drew together. 'That's impossible!' he insisted. 'Only you and I and the lawyers are aware of that agreement.'

'Naturally, I assumed that *you* had told her,' Jo replied, but she was impressed by his air of incredulous surprise.

'*Madonna mia*, I'm not on those kinds of terms with her. I would only have discussed that with someone I was intimate with—I don't just mean sexually when I use that word, I mean someone to whom I speak without reservation,' he clarified. 'And you are the only person in my world who has *ever* known me on such intimate terms.'

Jo laughed, startling him, startling herself. 'I was just fixing to have the most massive row with you,' she explained unevenly. 'And you've cut the ground from under my feet.'

Gianni was still frowning. 'Fiona could only have found out from a leak at the lawyer's office. It'll have to be investigated. I expect the strictest confidentiality in my private business,' he declared with a grimace, digging out his phone.

'Phone them tomorrow…it's almost one in the morning!' Jo pointed out. 'So, can I take it from that that you have never been intimate in any way with Fiona?'

'Of course not,' Gianni asserted very drily. 'Surely she didn't give you that impression?'

Jo shrugged a slight shoulder. 'To be honest, I didn't know what to make of her. I think she feels more than friendly towards you and certainly not sisterly. Possessive, jealous. She had had too much to drink and it loosened her tongue. I can't be sorry for that. I couldn't have worked with her. She has no respect for boundaries and she likes to make sarky remarks.' She sighed. 'She even produced a photo album that contained pictures of you and her sister together. I mean, *why* would she do something like that to me?'

'That's weird. Did you look at the album?'

'No, I did not. I know it's all in the past but I didn't want to see you with another woman...' Not looking all loving and caring, as she was sure he did in such photos with his lost love. It would only have underlined what *she* didn't have with Gianni.

'I would have felt the same about seeing photos of you with another man,' Gianni told her, looking thoughtful.

'"Speak low if you speak love,"' Duffy quoted, perching on a plant pedestal.

'It's bedtime, Duffy,' Jo told him, extending her shoulder for him to clamber on board. She put him in his giant cage and covered it. 'Night, night.'

'"Love looks not with the eyes, but with the mind,"' the parrot recited.

'Spot on, Duffy,' Gianni remarked. 'Do we have to give him back? I like him.'

'We'll see,' Jo said as they returned to the hall. 'Abigail left supper for you. I'll put on the kettle.'

'I'm not hungry...well, not for food,' Gianni admitted rather abruptly. 'You look ravishing, *cara*.'

'I thought we were about to argue about Fiona.'

'No. I'm embarrassed that I trusted her and she behaved so badly. She lied about what you had said to her. Fortunately, I know you well enough to know that she was lying,' Gianni murmured, his mouth twisting.

'She's a drama queen and she likes to be the centre of attention and, of course, there was no chance of her taking pole position with you here.'

'I'm not a drama queen. I don't even like being the centre of attention,' Jo began defensively.

'No, but you are the indisputable queen of Ladymead *and* Belvedere,' Gianni informed her with a charismatic smile. 'Queen of my heart as well, if there is such an expression...'

Jo lowered her lashes, wondering what he meant by that. 'Not something I ever expected you to say.'

'Not something that I ever thought I would say,' Gianni confided, bending slightly to lift her up into his arms. 'If I have to put you down before we get up both flights, at least give me points for trying,' he urged.

Airborne without warning, Jo gazed up at him in astonishment. They reached the first landing. Gianni grinned and carried her up the second flight with a perceptible look of achievement. 'Let's forget about Fiona and the lawyers' office leak and all the other stuff that clutters up our days,' he suggested. 'I rushed home instead of staying in London tonight because I wanted to be with you.'

Jo's bright smile illuminated her flushed features. 'Truly?'

'Yes. I am truly hooked on you,' Gianni told her without hesitation.

'I like the sound of that.' Jo slid off her wrap and lay down on the bed.

'Sadly, I only realised what was amiss with me this morning. I'd just been ignoring my feelings. I've always done that and then those feelings just knocked me flat when I looked at you,' Gianni confessed ruefully. 'I don't know when I started loving you. I only know it happened and I can't picture my life without you now. You crept up on me. It started with desire and ended with me wanting to keep you for life. For ever and ever and all that jazz...'

'Done,' Jo murmured. 'It's a new deal. You don't ever get to look at another woman again. You only get to look at me. You only get to love me. And it'll be the exact same for me because I'm very possessive of you and I will not share you with anyone except our children. And this is where I have news to share with you.'

'You love me too?' Gianni cast his jacket and tie aside and came up on the bed to join her, ignoring the reference to her news. 'How did that happen when I put my feet in it every chance I got?'

'Well, it started with a crush when you were a teenager.'

'Are you serious?' Raw amusement danced in Gianni's dark eyes.

'Do you remember sending me a signed photo of you playing polo?'

He nodded slowly.

'I stuck it on the inside of the door on my school locker and never shared it with anyone, which was really mean of me because you had a lot of admirers when I was in sixth form,' Jo confided.

'I was such a flirt,' Gianni admitted.

Jo nodded agreement. 'But you'll practise not being flirtatious now that you're married,' she pointed out.

'So there will be rules. I expected that,' Gianni volunteered with a grin, gazing down at her with a new tenderness in his gaze. '*Madonna mia*... I love you so much. I couldn't wait to get here tonight, *cara*.'

'That five-year clause in our agreement. What was that all about?' Jo asked. 'Just you wanting to get value for money?'

'No, even at the beginning I wanted to be sure that I kept you that long. A year down the road, otherwise, you could have decided to ditch me,' Gianni pointed out.

Her smooth brow furrowed as she struggled to accept that explanation. 'I was never going to ditch you...well, not unless you did something dreadful like murdering someone!' she extended. 'And even then, it would depend on the circumstances... Gosh, I've got it bad for you.'

'I feel so lucky.' Gianni had a huge smile on his lean dark features and a rare look of relaxation.

'That news I mentioned a few minutes ago,' Jo said abruptly. 'I'm pregnant.'

'Pregnant?' Gianni sat up to exclaim in shock.

'I hate to be the one to be telling you this,' Jo teased in a whisper, 'but what we've been doing tends to lead to conception.'

'I know that!' Gianni laughed, his eyes glinting with pleasure, and then he stretched out a hand to rest his fingers gently across her stomach. 'You feel the same.'

'You'll have to wait a while for anything to show.'

'It's magical. Everything I want all at once. A wife, a family, a child. You're amazing,' Gianni told her with fierce conviction. 'You love me and you're pregnant.'

'A child is likely to mean a lot of changes in our lives,' she warned.

'I'm good with change now,' Gianni declared.

Jo began to unbutton his shirt, revealing his glorious muscular chest inch by inch. She felt so happy that she was vaguely surprised that she wasn't floating.

'Do you think you'll stay in love?' she heard herself ask and almost winced at that need for reassurance grabbing her.

'I do. I'm a lot older and wiser than I was the first time around. But I was hurt after my mother passed and then Fliss...as well,' he framed wryly. 'I honestly believed that I could protect myself from falling in love again but then the right woman appears, the one who keeps on catching your eye and surprising you, and, all of a sudden, falling in love is the most wonderful thing in the world.'

'Fliss couldn't have been similar to Fiona,' Jo guessed.

'No, Fliss was quiet and a little shy and very kind, but I'm bright enough to accept now that if she hadn't been ill, we wouldn't have stayed together so long. She never disagreed with me. She thought everything I did was fantastic.'

'I'm not like that.'

'We were too young, and university isn't the real world.' He sighed. 'I wasn't ready for such a major commitment, but I did love her.'

'I'm sure you did.' Jo removed his cufflinks and tugged down the sleeves of his shirt. 'But I know I've grown up a lot since I was a student.'

Gianni kicked off his shoes and peeled off his socks. 'I'm so comfortable with you. I've never had that with a woman.'

'Comfortable like an old armchair that's been worn in?' Jo scoffed.

'No...' Gianni tugged her down to him. 'I can just be myself and if I'm grouchy, you'll complain.'

'Darned right I will,' Jo interposed, running an appreciative hand down over his ridged abdomen, skimming his waistband, tracing the zip. 'I'm feeling much more confident now.'

'Will I survive the night?' Highly amused, Gianni lay back with a flourish. 'I'm all yours.'

'Always,' she muttered, the upswell of emotion threatening to overwhelm her. 'I love you. I need you.'

'I love and need you too, Jojo,' he groaned with pleasure.

EPILOGUE

Jo stood outside Ladymead and simply savoured the view of the old Tudor house with the glow of lights behind the mullioned windows. It had taken five years and there had been many problems along the way but the house was finally finished. Temporary repairs had ultimately given way to a full restoration once the various permissions were granted and finally it was finished. The fantastic skyline of the house with its parade of elaborate chimneys and little turrets made her smile fondly. Repointed, the ornamental brickwork looked fabulous.

'Was it worth marrying you-know-who for?' her great-aunt Sybil whispered from behind her.

'So worth it, I'm dizzy thinking about it!' Jo laughed, turning round to see the older woman clad in a long emerald-green gown.

'Your costume is spectacular,' Sybil commented at the sight of the younger woman garbed like a Tudor queen.

'You look amazing, Sybil.'

'You don't think it's a bit mutton dressed as lamb?' Sybil asked with a grimace.

'Not a bit of it. You've got the looks and the figure

and, for goodness' sake,' Jo chided, 'you're not so old that you have to be thinking that way!'

Sybil grinned. 'I knew you'd sort me out.'

'Is he planning to ask you tonight?'

Sybil went pink. 'I think so. He's been going on so much about what a special night this is and I can't think why our celebration party for Ladymead should be special for him in the same way it is for us.'

'Federico is a law unto himself.' Jo sighed, confident that Sybil's hopes would be met with a marriage proposal.

The changes through the last five years paraded at speed through Jo's brain. She had become a mother twice over, or maybe three times over since the first set had been twins, non-identical, a boy and a girl called Lorenzo and Alice, now lively four-year-olds. Trixie had been unbearable over her accurate prediction until Sybil pointed out that the twins weren't that surprising an arrival when Jo's mother and her uncle had been twins. Their toddler, Gabriele, had been more unexpected. Not a planned pregnancy, that last one, although Gabriele was such an adorable little boy nobody wanted to hand him back. The twins were dark of hair and eye, like Gianni, but Gabriele was blond like his mother, with big brown eyes, a mixture of both parents.

Fiona never had come back to work at Ladymead. Gianni continued to have a business connection with her firm but little personal contact. Sybil had taken over supervision of the work with Federico showing great interest and proffering advice.

'He's weaselling his way into her affections,' Gianni had said uncharitably when, near the end of that first year, Sybil finally agreed to a dinner date with his father.

Two years later, Gianni's tune had changed. 'He's totally gone on her. I hope she doesn't hurt him. He's surprisingly sensitive.'

Jo counted the transformation of her husband's relationship with his father her biggest success. It had taken a long time and an abundance of tact for Gianni to accept that his mother might not have been as honest as she could have been about her marriage. But once he had realised how the marriage had functioned from his father's point of view he had been gutted when he had to look back at his mother through the lens of an adult. Ever since that evening when the two men had talked in depth, Gianni had dropped his guard with his father, invited him into their lives and begun talking to him as the parent Federico was. Federico had been too strict a parent and he was well aware of the mistakes he had made.

'Let's go in...' Sybil tucked a hand in the crook of Jo's arm. 'This is so exciting! Parties at both houses and Ladymead finally alive again!'

'Where's Gianni?' Sybil asked.

'He'll be back in time. He promised,' Jo said confidently, because Gianni always kept his promises.

'That jewellery is breathtaking.' Sybil sighed enviously, touching a finger to the ruby and diamond necklace and drop earrings her great-niece wore. 'Isabella's collection...right?'

'Yes, no need to buy much with that collection in the safe,' Jo quipped. 'You can borrow it for special occasions. Gianni wouldn't mind.'

'But Federico wouldn't like me wearing anything

that belonged to her,' Sybil replied wryly. 'Thanks, but no, thanks.'

They strolled into the great hall with its medieval screens and minstrels' gallery. Jo peered up at the decorative hammerbeam open timber roof, which had been freshly picked out in the original Elizabethan colours. Tapestries she had forgotten once hung at Ladymead now adorned the walls again. Subtle light glowed in corners as catering staff hovered to offer them drinks. Everyone local as well as their friends and Gianni's business acquaintances had been invited. Belvedere offered a rather different level of hospitality with the ballroom and a buffet and loads of seating for a crowd. Ladymead was still primarily a family house, a beautiful one but not a grand one, Jo reflected fondly, wandering through the restored rooms with growing pleasure.

Her biggest surprise in the five years of her marriage had been Gianni telling her that he had a temperature-controlled warehouse storing every valuable article that had ever been sold from Ladymead. Apparently, the Renzettis had begun buying those items when his grandfather was a young man and his father had continued the purchases, as had Gianni. Thus, the priceless original oak trestle table and benches and the tapestries and the family portraits were now in place again. There was a valuable Chinese vase restored to the tiny, wainscoted library and a few precious old books, as well as a couple of oak four-poster beds now returned to the main bedrooms. The warehouse had proved to be an Aladdin's cave and none of the articles had ever crossed the threshold of Belvedere, not being deemed suitable for the grandeur of the Edwardian mansion.

'The Renzettis had a plan to take over your family home for many, many years,' Gianni had explained with a grimace. 'And just think, all I had to do was marry you!'

'Smartass,' she had teased back. 'But I'm really grateful that all these items can come back where they belong. If your family hadn't bought them, they would have been lost for ever.'

Her grandmother was sitting in the library. Never keen on large gatherings, she was relying on her sisters and her granddaughter to do the honours. None of them minded because the older woman had had a heart attack the year before and only surgery and a very strict diet in the aftermath had returned her to health. These days, she promised to take it easy but was regularly to be found cooking at Belvedere because she was great friends with their housekeeper and very fond of Gianni and his father.

McTavish was no longer at Jo's heel. Age had given him arthritis and he only left his basket at home if tempted by food. Fairy was older too but no less graceful and quiet. A labradoodle had also come into Sybil's rescue barn. Ace was the twins' dog because Lorenzo and Alice had fallen madly in love with the fluffy puppy of indeterminate parentage. Duffy had stayed with them, loving a household where there was an almost constant audience. Lorenzo was trying to teach him rap and make him less of an 'oldie' because Duffy's biblical and Shakespearean quotes were meaningless to a four-year-old.

Gianni and Federico, clad in smart dinner jackets, walked through the arched front entrance together and Jo grinned while her heart leapt at the sight of her husband. She hadn't lost an atom of her susceptibility to those spectacular dark good looks of his.

He accepted the glass offered to him and did a double take at his wife, garbed in her very elaborate Elizabethan silk and brocade embroidered costume. 'You take my breath away, *cara*.'

'The kids are all in bed,' she warned him.

'I thought you'd surrender and let them come.'

'No, there's too many strangers about *and* the lake. They're too young and adventurous to be trusted.' She sighed with regret.

Gianni groaned. 'Their nanny's bringing them. It's a big night. I thought you'd want them to enjoy the experience.'

He was the fun parent and she was the stricter one. It had never occurred to her that that was how they would turn out as parents. Lorenzo hurtled across the room. 'Mum…where's the fireworks?' he demanded.

'The fireworks won't be happening until ten, which is two hours away,' Gianni told his disappointed son.

'Fireworks.' Alice ground out the word with disdain. 'I want to see everybody admiring our house.'

'She's so like you it's ridiculous,' Gianni whispered fondly, closing his free hand over Jo's and even that small connection sent a quiver of awareness through her.

Gabriele left their nanny, Janessa, to seek out his mother. He grabbed a handful of her gown to keep her within reach and sucked his thumb happily, almost tottering with the exhaustion he was fighting off.

Sybil whispered in her ear, 'We'll keep the kiddoes here tonight with the nanny. He still doesn't think far ahead. It's your wedding anniversary. You deserve a child-free night.'

Jo turned round but her great-aunt had already moved away.

'Happy anniversary,' Gianni breathed tautly. 'Guess I blew it again with the kids. Sybil doesn't whisper as quietly as she thinks she does.'

'The twins will be fine here for the night with Trixie and Gran.' Jo gave him a serene smile. 'Has it occurred to you that I've now done my five-year sentence in marriage?'

His hand jerked on hers and he turned her round to face him. 'If I thought you meant that, I'd lock you up sooner than lose you.'

Jo leant dangerously close and feathered her lips across his cheek. 'I hope you're planning to lock yourself up with me.'

Fire smouldered in his very intent gaze, black lashes like fans low. 'Anything you want, you get.'

'I like it when you're…ruthless,' she selected softly.

Lorenzo yanked at her gown. 'Mum! What's Grandad doing? He's being weird!'

'*Madonna mia…*' Gianni groaned half under his breath. 'How could he embarrass himself like that?'

Jo looked past him and saw her father-in-law down on one knee extending a ring box while Sybil stood there frozen between pleasure and terror. 'He's asking Auntie Sybil to marry him and I think it's very romantic. He even brought a photographer to record the moment,' she explained calmly.

'You *knew* about this?' Gianni demanded.

'He needed my help to choose the ring.'

'And you didn't let me in on the secret?'

'No. He trusted me to keep it quiet.'

She watched Sybil slide the ring onto her finger as a champagne toast was offered to the happy couple.

'At least she didn't say no.' Gianni sighed in relief. 'Because with Sybil you never quite know. You share that trait for the unexpected.'

'I think we need to take Gabriele home and tuck him into bed,' Jo told her husband gently, not wishing to sound critical. 'And greet our guests at Belvedere while we're there.'

Gianni stooped to pick up Gabriele, who was already half asleep. 'I thought he would have more staying power.'

'He's still a baby.'

'If we're going home, while we're upstairs,' Gianni began thickly, 'we—'

'No, you'll have to wait until after the fireworks,' Jo told him with some satisfaction.

As they drove back to the house, the original gate having developed into a proper roadway to the rear of Ladymead, connecting the two houses, Jo thought blissfully of how happy she was with just her family. She still helped out Sybil, Trixie and her grandmother and took a continued interest in the community but she had bags of time to spend with Gianni. They often went horse riding on the estate. He had bought her a splendid Arab mare for their anniversary. They travelled together and often took weekends away at his other properties.

'You promised me for ever and ever,' Gianni reminded her as she tucked Gabriele into bed.

Jo laughed. 'You couldn't get rid of me even if you tried!'

His stunning dark golden eyes glittered over her

lovely face with intense appreciation. 'I'm crazy about you too, *cara*.'

As he caught her to him and kissed her breathless before she could even protest, her body went liquid in his embrace, the sexual heat that only he could awaken sending an arrow of hunger through her. 'Stop it...we have to go down,' she scolded him.

'If I have to wait until after the fireworks, I'll be expecting quite an experience,' he warned her with a slow-burning smile of sensual intent.

Jo tilted her head to one side and skimmed a playful forefinger across one high cheekbone. 'Well, I don't like to boast—'

He grabbed her at the top of the stairs and held her tight, which was quite an achievement with the voluminous skirts of her costume. 'I love you so much, Jojo...'

'And you show me that love every day, which is why I'm insanely, deeply in love with you too,' she declared with a luminous smile before they went downstairs hand in hand to greet their guests.

* * * * *

RULES OF
THEIR ROYAL
WEDDING NIGHT

MICHELLE SMART

MILLS & BOON

CHAPTER ONE

ELSBETH FERNANDEZ STEPPED into Ceres Cathedral, her arm held by her cousin, Dominic. Why he gripped it so tightly was beyond her. She'd been nothing but compliant with his wishes that she marry Prince Amadeo. She was always compliant. King of her home principality, Monte Cleure, Dominic's word was law, especially for the female members of his family.

Her handsome prince, who she'd met only once at their pre-wedding party, stood far in the distance. Their marriage had been agreed, like everything else in her life, without Elsbeth's input, but when the man tasked with negotiating the marriage had privately asked if she was willing, she hadn't hesitated to say yes. In all honesty, her prince could be the ugliest man in the world and she would still have agreed to marry him, so it was her good fortune that he was the handsomest prince in Europe.

He was so tall! She'd marvelled at the height difference between them and secretly delighted that he stood a foot taller than Dominic. He didn't look to have an ounce of fat on him either, unlike her obese cousin and the majority of the male members of the House of Fernandez, who liked to gorge. Her prince—and Elsbeth had taken to privately, gleefully, referring to him as *her* prince since the order had come for her to marry him—had a body that was indisputably hard. Sculpted. His face had a sculpted quality to it too with its chiselled jawline, accentuated bow of the top lip and long, straight nose.

She hoped he would be a kind husband. Or at least as kind as a royal prince used to his word being law could be. Elsbeth knew her duty as a future king's wife was to follow her husband's lead in all matters, speak only when spoken to, never give an opinion on anything weightier than flower arrangements, never disagree with her husband in public or in private and, most importantly, breed as many children as her husband desired. She prayed she was fertile. She would hate to disappoint him on any matter but a failure to breed would be classed as unforgivable and could see her divorced and sent back to Monte Cleure. It had happened to her aunt. Three years of a childless marriage and she'd been set aside and replaced with a new model.

Please let me give my prince children. Don't give him an excuse to send me back to Monte Cleure.

Since their pre-wedding party, she'd prayed nightly that God grant her prince children, and then she'd closed her eyes and drifted into sleep, happily conjuring his clear green eyes and the black lashes surrounding them, and imagining what those firm but full lips would feel like pressed against her own and what his thick black hair would feel like threaded through her fingers.

The urge to run down the aisle to her prince was strong but Elsbeth maintained her steady pace by reminding herself that when she left this cathedral she would no longer be under Dominic's subjugation.

While she knew much about the public image of the Berruti royal family and the workings of its reigning queen to ensure their relevance in the twenty-first century, she knew little about its private workings or the kind of man her prince was behind closed doors. Whatever the future held for her, it couldn't be worse than her lot in the House of Fernandez. God wouldn't be so cruel. Would He…?

Amadeo watched his bride make her way sedately down the aisle towards him, her arm linked with the man he despised most in the world, and made sure to keep his revulsion at both of them far from his face. The only positive he could take from this union was that Elsbeth was pretty. Very pretty, he grudgingly admitted. Her silky blonde hair had been elegantly swept off her oval face and as she walked closer to him the excitement was evident in her big blue eyes and the smile of her wide, plump mouth.

She'd displayed the same excitement at their pre-wedding party, the one and only time he'd met her. And yet, for all her smiles, which had quickly become grating, she'd hardly said a word. Not once had she started a conversation. She'd answered direct questions with a smile that didn't falter but seemed not to have a single opinion or idea in her head.

Already sickened at being stuck with a Fernandez for the rest of his life and becoming a relation by law to the tyrannical, narcissistic, megalomaniac Dominic, his bride being a wilting wallflower only added to his antipathy at the situation. There had been no alternative though, not with their two nations on the brink of a full-blown trade and diplomatic war. Amadeo's brother had lit the fire. Then, just as it was brought under control, his sister had thrown a can of petrol on it. This marriage was the only way to extinguish the fire in its entirety. For the sake of his nation, the monarchy he would one day head and his family, Amadeo was prepared to marry his enemy's cousin. His whole life had been spent doing what was best for the monarchy, his human inclinations and desires stifled into submission.

If his siblings had stifled their desires and inclinations more effectively, he wouldn't be standing here now.

His bride reached him.

As heir to the throne, Amadeo had always known the priority when he came to choose a bride would be suitability. After all, his wife would one day be Queen Consort and a figurehead for his great nation. Elsbeth's breeding made her highly suitable for the role. He had though, expected to marry someone he could like and respect and whose company he enjoyed. Of those three traits, Elsbeth ticked the box of none.

Conscious that this most magnificent of occasions was being broadcast into the home of every Ceresian not lining the streets and into the homes of many Italians and other Europeans, he reached for her small hand and bestowed her with a practised smile. Baby blue eyes sparkling as brightly as the diamonds on her tiara, she returned his smile with an eagerness that made his stomach turn. With over a hundred million eyes watching his reaction though, he hid it, playing up for the cameras by mouthing, truthfully, 'You look beautiful.'

She blushed at the compliment in a manner the cameras would adore. No doubt the cameras already adored her. He could already imagine the comments from the gushing reporters about the fairy-tale wedding dress the bride was wearing, all white lace and silk, emphasising but not displaying her generous bust—not a hint of cleavage was on display—and enhancing her slender waist before the skirt splayed out in the shape of a flamenco fan.

Hands clasped together, they turned their backs on the packed congregation and faced the bishop.

Elsbeth had never known cheers and applause like it. The streets lined with well-wishers had been loud on her entrance to the cathedral but when they came back out the sound would have taken any roof off.

A row of horse-drawn carriages awaited them. Her romantic husband assisted her into the first one and then, once seated beside her, took her hand in his.

The journey back to the castle seemed to go on for ever, and so did the applause. These people were genuinely happy for them, she realised with amazement as she blew a kiss to a frantically waving child being carried on her father's shoulders. Her husband's people cheered them all the way to the castle gates, and by the time they reached it her cheeks hurt from smiling and her wrist ached from all the waving.

Feeling as if she were in the most fantastical dream, she stood beside Amadeo to greet their guests, from the important to the not-so-important. There were so many heads of state and A-list celebrities that the castle's roofs were thronged with snipers and the surrounding grounds thick with heavily armed security. Inside the castle though, the banqueting room their twelve-course meal was being held in was a mass of glittering gold and silver, and any security was unobtrusive enough to melt into the background.

She tried so hard to take everything in so future Elsbeth could dip into her memory bank whenever she wanted, but her dreamlike state was such that the only thing she could focus on with anything like clarity was her new husband. He was just so charming! Having lived her life in a royal palace infested with charming snakes, she wasn't naive enough to think the charm was anything but a public act but he was being attentive to her, constantly checking that she liked the food and that she had enough to drink. Not only was he a prince but a gentleman!

Her mother's watchful gaze though, was a reminder that, gentleman or not, her husband, a future king, had expectations and standards he expected her to adhere to, and that Elsbeth must abide by them from the start. She wasn't foolish enough to do anything less.

Hours later, their meal over, it was time to move to a stateroom for the wedding reception party. Glad to have Amadeo holding her hand, she let him lead her to a table and tried not to overtly marvel at how exquisitely the room had been adorned. The colour scheme followed on from the banqueting room and yet managed to be even glitzier.

She caught the eye of her new brother-in-law's wife, Clara, who gave her such a beaming smile it made Elsbeth's belly warm with pleasure. Dominic had kidnapped Clara some months back and would have forced her to marry him if Amadeo's brother, Marcelo, hadn't rescued her and married her himself. Elsbeth had been terrified of meeting her at the pre-wedding party but her fears had been unfounded, Clara welcoming her generously and with no hint she blamed Elsbeth for Dominic's cruel, unconscionable actions.

Her new sister-in-law, Alessia, had been very welcoming at the pre-wedding party too, although Elsbeth thought she looked a little distracted today. It warmed her belly even more to think these nice women were her new family. Maybe one day they would be her friends too. She could hope. She hoped for lots of things.

Elsbeth's prince leaned into her and murmured, 'It is time for us to dance.'

A frisson raced up her spine and, her heart bolting into a canter, she rose to her feet. With her hand enveloped in Amadeo's, and catcalls and whistles from the increasingly raucous crowd, who'd been guzzling champagne as if it were going out of fashion, she walked to the centre of the dance floor.

One hand held in his, she put the other lightly on his shoulder. Another, deeper frisson careered through her when his hand slipped around her waist to rest on her lower back.

Her heart thumping too hard and too fast for anything more than the underlying beat of the romantic song they danced to to register, Elsbeth could hardly draw breath. The first time she'd danced with Amadeo she'd been too excited at the thought of escaping Monte Cleure to think of anything other than not screwing it up by making a bad impression on him. This time she'd had a month since their first dance and had done little but dream of him. To be in his arms, her breasts pressed lightly into his hard stomach, her senses filling with his scent, was enough to send her into overdrive.

Amadeo danced with his new wife until the dance floor was so crowded their bodies were crushed together. She didn't utter a single word, simply kept the fixed smile on her face that had been ever-present since she'd arrived at the cathedral. Did she even have thoughts in that pretty head or was it only air?

'Shall we get a drink?' he suggested, dipping his head to speak into her ear over the growing noise. He caught a light, delicate scent that perfectly suited his insipid bride. It turned his stomach.

'If you like,' she replied brightly.

Mentally gritting his teeth, he led her—she didn't make the first move to leave the dance floor, just as she hadn't made the first move on anything at all that day, always waiting for him to take the lead—back to their table. She'd finished her glass of wine during the wedding breakfast by the end of the fourth course, but had made no effort to call any of the waiting staff over to refill it for her. He was certain the glass would have remained empty if he hadn't asked if she would like some more. She'd responded with a bright smile and a 'Yes, please.'

What had he married? A walking, talking, wind-up doll like his sister used to play with when she was a child?

When they reached their table and fresh drinks had been brought to them, his brother, Marcelo, caught his eye and nodded to the dance floor. Following his gaze, Amadeo saw the tall figure of their new brother-in-law, Gabriel. A gap in the crowd gave him a glimpse of their tiny sister wrapped tightly in Gabriel's arms.

A small breath of relief escaped his lungs. Gabriel had negotiated the wedding contract between Amadeo and Elsbeth. He'd also had a one-night stand with Alessia that had resulted in a baby-sized consequence.

Amadeo and their parents had emotionally blackmailed Alessia into marrying him. It had ended in disaster a week ago when Alessia had kicked Gabriel out of the castle and told him to never come back. Normally, Amadeo would have taken it on himself to bring them back together for the good of the monarchy but his sister had been so distraught over the collapse of her short marriage that, for once, he'd held off from interfering. The way they held each other told him his instinct to hold back had been right as they'd obviously found their way back together without his assistance.

Taking a large gulp of his champagne, he watched Marcelo take a cheeky grab of Clara's bottom, and saw Clara's response, a mock slap of the hand followed by a passionate kiss on the lips. Theirs was a marriage Amadeo had emotionally blackmailed them into making too. As with Alessia and Gabriel, love had found them. And happiness. What Marcelo and Clara shared was a happiness he sometimes envied.

Sometimes too, his envy tasted bitter.

Marcelo had been allowed to escape the confines of royal life for a decade, joining the Ceres army and thriving amidst all the adventures that life had brought. It would have been out of the question for Amadeo to do the same. He was the heir. Every step he took and every word he spoke and every action he made was done with the dignity of his role at the forefront of his mind. It was beyond the realms of credulity that he would have swooped in to rescue a kidnapped woman from a palace window via a helicopter, as Marcelo had done. Both his siblings thought him rigid and stuck up. If he was, it was because he had to be. The path of his life had been laid out from his conception and he'd always known that to deviate from it could bring danger to his whole family. His siblings had not been so conscientious with their own recent behaviour. The pair of them had, in their differing ways, allowed their emotions to rule their heads and the repercussions had come close to threatening their family's existence. It had been left to him to clear up the mess of their making.

Marcelo's rumble of laughter at something his wife said echoed in Amadeo's ears as his gaze locked onto his sister stealing a kiss with her husband on the dance floor.

Draining his glass, he looked again at his blank-faced bride and his chest tightened. He would never be susceptible to the kind of adolescent emotions that had seen his siblings lose their heads but he'd hoped for more than this. More than a blank face from the despicable House of Fernandez.

Once the party had finished and her prince had thanked their guests, Elsbeth walked through the maze of wide corridors to their quarters. She'd been hugely looking forward to seeing the private space she and her husband would make their home. Tucked in an L on the ground floor of the castle, the size and proportions didn't disappoint. She followed Amadeo through a large reception room and into an even larger living area with high ceilings and an abundance of bay windows. Richly decorated in dusky pinks and gold, it surprised her how feminine their quarters were. The faint scent of paint told her it had been recently decorated.

'What do you think?' Amadeo asked her.

Knowing better than to tell the truth, she replied, 'It's beautiful.' She wouldn't dream of telling him she preferred bold colours and less kitschy furnishings, even if she didn't have the feeling it had been redecorated with her in mind.

He inclined his head and opened another door into a corridor. Instinct told her where this led and her heartbeat accelerated.

'The master bedroom,' he said blandly, opening the door at the far end.

What greeted her made Elsbeth, the cousin of a king, someone who'd lived her entire life in one of Europe's finest palaces, gasp.

Vast and high-ceilinged, most of the oakwood flooring was covered in a prettily patterned rug of pale blue threaded with gold. The four-poster bed was a work of art, the drapes pale blue damask, the headboard pale blue velvet topped with an elaborate gold moulded frieze of cherubs at play, at its foot a pale blue velvet chaise longue. The panelled walls were cream, the huge chandelier, along with all the other lighting, gold and crystal. This was a room fit for a queen, never mind a princess. Catching another trace of paint, she thought Amadeo must have stifled his own preferences to create a room with her in mind and, though he was wide of the mark with her taste, her heart swelled with gratitude that he'd gone to so much effort to make their home something he thought she would like and be comfortable in. It was a gesture that proved him a better man than the men in her family.

He indicated the two unobtrusive maids who'd followed them and said to Elsbeth, 'I shall take a shower in one of the guest bathrooms while you prepare for bed. I will join you when you are ready.'

She arranged her features into a smile, making sure

to hide the relief that he wasn't going to remove the wedding dress himself. Another sign he was a gentleman! She knew perfectly well that Dominic had used her virginity as one of his selling points in the marriage negotiations. Men, Elsbeth had been assured, prized virginity in their brides.

Once the dress had been removed and carefully wrapped in tissue paper and boxed away, she sat at her antique dressing table having her hair brushed by a maid. There was something incredibly romantic about preparing herself for bed for the first time as a bride, she decided. The nightdress her mother had chosen for her, if not to Elsbeth's taste, was romantic too. White silk with thin straps, it was modestly cut, square beneath her collarbones and falling to mid-calf. Remembering the sage-green negligee she'd been drawn to, dismissed by her mother as being too 'slutty', she reminded herself of what her mother had said about this one being the perfect nightdress for a virgin giving herself to her husband. The virginal nightdress was very becoming and felt wonderful against her skin so she shouldn't complain, even if only to herself.

With her body and teeth clean, her face scrubbed of make-up and moisturised, her hair gleaming, the pretty virginal nightdress on and the bedsheets turned down, she was ready.

Swallowing the lump of fear that had suddenly formed in her throat, she smiled at the maids. 'You can leave me now. Please tell...' She swallowed again. 'Please tell the prince that he can join me.'

'Would you like the curtains of the bed to be drawn?' one of the maids asked.

Imagining with another clutch of fear how it would

feel to be cocooned on the bed and only able to hear Amadeo's approach, she shook her head.

Alone, she took a deep breath and got under the bed-sheets. After trying a number of positions, she ended up propping herself against the headboard, folded her hands loosely on her lap and, her heart thumping louder than ever, waited for her groom.

The wait seemed to take for ever. The longer it went on, the louder her mother's stern advice rang in her ears. *Wait for him to make the first move. Be compliant. Do whatever he tells you to do. Do not complain if it hurts.*

Give him a baby.

There was a knock on the door.

Taking one more deep breath, Elsbeth fixed a smile on her face and brightly called out, 'Come in.'

CHAPTER TWO

AMADEO'S GUTS CLENCHED as he crossed the threshold.

As he'd expected, his wind-up doll was waiting in the bed for him, expecting him to do his duty with that irritating vacuous smile on her face.

'Have I taken the right side of the bed?' she asked. 'I will move over if I've taken your side.'

It was the first time she'd instigated a conversation between them.

He shrugged his robe off and placed it on an antique armchair. 'It doesn't matter.'

Noticing the flush of colour on her cheeks at his nakedness, even though she avoided dipping her eyes any lower than his face, he climbed onto the bed and covered his lap with the bedsheets to spare her further blushes. Why Dominic had assumed the bride being a virgin made her a prized asset was beyond him. It just proved the sickness in Dominic's own head. Amadeo would be the first to agree that many traditions needed to be preserved to maintain royal mystique but the concept of the virgin royal bride was something he'd long believed consigned to the scrapbooks of history.

He'd have preferred someone experienced. Someone with a hint of nous and personality. But Elsbeth had been offered, and Elsbeth had been a willing pawn in the drive for peace between their two nations.

They were both willing pawns, he thought grimly. His own willingness stemmed only from his desire to kill the existential threat to the Ceres monarchy that a trade and diplomatic war with Monte Cleure would bring. Elsbeth's willingness came from her desire to be Queen.

God help him.

'Have you enjoyed our day?' he politely asked to cut through the tension.

'Very much, thank you.'

'Anything you would have changed?'

'It was all perfect.'

'Even the coffee profiteroles?'

'They were delicious.'

'You ate little of yours.'

The vacuous smile dimmed a fraction. 'I'm sorry.'

'Why?'

She blinked as if she didn't understand the question.

Amadeo hid the fresh swell of irritation. 'You have no need to apologise for disliking something.'

'I did like it,' she assured him, the smile firmly back in place.

Unsure why he wanted to argue this point, he let it go. He sensed Elsbeth would only agree with everything he said, so arguing would be fruitless.

It infuriated him that he even wanted to argue with her. A wedding night should not begin with the groom despising the bride and wanting to shout at her.

He had a job to do. Time to get on with it.

He turned his bedside light off and lay down.

'Would you like me to turn my light off too?' she asked.

'Unless you prefer to do it with the lights on?'

Her glimmer of uncertainty gave him a stab of guilt. His attempted humour had come out sounding more sarcastic than intended. Whatever his personal feelings towards her, Elsbeth was a virgin and likely to be nervous.

'You will probably feel more comfortable with the lights off,' he said in a gentler tone.

She turned her light off and copied him in lying down. The castle's ground lights were still on for their departing wedding guests, enough illumination filtering through the tiny gap in the heavy curtains for him to see she'd positioned herself on her back with her hands neatly folded on her belly.

Turning her face to him, she gave another smile.

It was the lack of emotion behind that smile that sent another wave of revulsion kicking through him. Sitting upright, he ran his fingers through his hair. 'I'm aware this is your first time.'

She didn't answer, just looked at him, her expression that of someone waiting for him to continue.

'You and I are strangers,' he said tersely. 'If you would rather we wait until we know each other better before we do this then all you have to do is say.' When she still didn't respond, he added in a tone he fought valiantly not to sound rough, 'Is this something you want to do?'

This time she spoke, and without any hesitation. 'Yes.'

Amadeo looked at her a moment longer. As pretty—as *beautiful*—as Elsbeth was, *he* didn't want to do this. Somehow he had to get this over and done with as quickly as he could, being as considerate and gentle as he could. Perfunctory sex. Close his eyes and think of Ceres.

Elsbeth's heart was beating so hard she could feel its impact against her ribs. She didn't know if it was anticipation of what was to come or fear that Amadeo might not go through with it.

If they didn't consummate their marriage, how could they make a baby? That terrified her far more than Amadeo's growing coldness towards her. Coldness and indifference she could deal with. Not having a baby and therefore always having the threat of being sent back to Monte Cleure hanging over her head… No. She didn't think she could handle that.

Should she hitch her nightdress up to her thighs and spread her legs to encourage him? Or would that be too wanton?

Too wanton, she decided. Her mother had been emphatic about it. Amadeo had to make the first move. Elsbeth was to be nothing but compliant putty in his hands.

And so she waited for him to make his move, doing nothing more than smile encouragement.

Her heart almost smashed through her ribs when he finally made his move and pulled the bedsheets off her.

His gaze drifted over her. If he liked what he saw, he gave no sign, but when he put his hands to hers and unfolded them from their position on her stomach there was a tenderness to his actions that loosened the knots in her belly she'd not even been aware had formed. Hovering over her, one hand splayed on the bed by her waist, his chiselled jaw tight, his chest rose before he lowered his face and kissed her.

In all Elsbeth's fantasies about their first kiss—the

one at the cathedral didn't count as it had been only a dutiful peck on the lips—she'd imagined how it would feel. She'd imagined it would be warm and that it would feel nice. She'd certainly *hoped* it would feel nice if she was going to have to kiss him for the rest of her life. The last thing she'd expected was the crackle of electricity that shot through her.

This was more than *nice*…

Closing her eyes, she thrilled as the pressure of his mouth deepened and his hands began to roam over her body. Yes, this felt far, far more than nice, especially when he cupped her breast, and she squeezed her eyes tighter and reminded herself of her mother's words that she was only to be compliant. She must resist touching him back. If he wanted her to touch him, he would tell her. Amadeo was heir to a throne and, like all spouses of future kings, Elsbeth was his to command, nothing more.

For all her mother's words though, it was hard to stop herself shivering at the pleasure that came when he gathered the hem of her nightdress and tugged it up to her hips, his hand skimming the flesh of her inner thigh. Every brush of his skin against hers felt like fire. Delicious fire.

Amadeo had had enough. From his bride's unwillingness to touch him or respond properly to his kisses, he could believe that she too, was simply lying back and thinking of Ceres. Or, in her case, Monte Cleure. The only sign that she wasn't simply going through the motions came from the puckering of her nipples beneath the silk of her nightdress, but that could be easily explained by her being cold-blooded. Even when he traced his fingers up her thigh and over her soft, flat belly, she gave no reaction. It seemed his wind-up doll had run out of charge.

Ready to put an end to this travesty, he went to right himself and as he moved his hand away from the top of her thigh his fingers accidentally glanced between her legs. To his shock, he heard a faint mewing, the only sound of life since he'd kissed her.

He stared at Elsbeth for the longest time. Her chest was rising and falling rapidly, the finger and thumb of her left hand pinching and rubbing at the bedsheet.

Unsure if he was imagining this most silent display of desire, he tiptoed his fingers up her inner thigh and gently cupped her sex.

The last thing he expected to find there was heat.

The faint mew sounded again.

A bolt of lust suddenly crashed through him, as strong as he'd ever experienced, almost as if Elsbeth's heat had transfused through his skin and straight into his blood. Shocked at the strength of what he'd just experienced, it took a good few beats for Amadeo's head to clear.

His mouth now filled with moisture, his heart pumping hard, he gently ran his finger along the hot stickiness and was rewarded with a jerk of her body so subtle that, if he hadn't been paying such avid attention, it would have been imperceptible.

Slowly rubbing his finger over her swollen nub, he took in the closed eyes and trembling plump lips, the slight arching of her back and the tiny tremors shivering across her body.

Mio dio, she was as ripe for him as the juiciest plum.

All thoughts of climbing off the bed and leaving the room had gone. The erection that had gone from nothing to full bloom in less than a second throbbed, and he gripped it tightly to control the deepening ache.

Still keeping the pressure on her nub, he released his excitement and put his hand to her thigh. Gently, he spread it to one side. There was no resistance. All her fingers were now rubbing against the bedsheets.

Fascinated at her reactions, he pressed his knee to her other thigh but this time, her breaths now coming in short hitches, she parted it herself.

Not taking his eyes off her face, he carefully positioned himself between her legs, took back hold of his arousal and pressed it against her opening. Her eyes flickered but didn't open. The only sound was the scratching of her fingers against the mattress.

Moving slowly, he inched himself inside her. When he clenched his jaw, it wasn't through irritation but for control because, *dio*, he'd never, in his whole life, felt such welcoming heat. So exquisite did it feel that he had to grit his teeth and remind himself that Elsbeth was a virgin. With infinite care, he slowly buried himself all the way inside her.

And then he felt the lightest of touches as finally… *finally*…she touched him. Her hand on his back was so light he probably would not have noticed had his skin not burned beneath it.

Gripping tightly to the sides of the pillow her beautiful head rested on, Amadeo closed his eyes and began to move. *Mio Dio…*

Elsbeth had never in her wildest dreams imagined it could be like this. Could feel like this. She'd expected pain at worst, discomfort at best. She hadn't expected pleasure. Pleasure was something she'd hoped for once she'd become accustomed to sex. But *this*…oh, it was incredible. She'd never known anything like it, and as Amadeo's strong body moved over hers, steadily increasing the tempo of his thrusts, little grunts of pleasure vibrated from his throat and something deep in the heart of her began to pulse strongly and thicken.

Never had Amadeo fought to hold back his release as he did in that moment. The exquisite pain of this self-torture was more than he'd thought himself capable of enduring but still he fought, refusing to let go and fall into the indulgence of the ultimate pleasure, not until…

And then he sensed it happening. It was there in the shortening of her quiet breaths and the tightening around his arousal. Overcome by the sudden urgent need to look at her, he raised himself onto his elbows at the same moment Elsbeth's eyes flew wide open in glazed shock and locked onto his, and her lips parted in a silent O.

He could hold on no more. Burying himself as deep inside her as was humanly possible, Amadeo let go.

Elsbeth tried valiantly to pull herself back to earth and knit herself back together. It felt as if she'd been shattered into stardust. She could hardly breathe through the heavy beats of her heart.

That had been…

Nothing came to her. No single word could describe what she'd just experienced. She'd had no idea. No idea it could feel like that. Not for her.

Her mother had been wrong.

Amadeo's cheek, pressed so tightly against hers, turned aside. He pulled away from her and rolled onto his back.

Feeling the cold of his loss, she swallowed to stop herself crying out a protest.

Had he liked what they'd done as much as she had? She wished she could ask. As with so many things in her life, this was a wish she dared not grant herself.

Amadeo had never known silence could be so loud. The thrills of his climax still laced his blood but the whooshing in his head had finally lessened enough for him to think. His thoughts though, gave no comfort.

The last thing he'd expected was to enjoy sex with his new wife, although 'enjoy' was the wrong word. It didn't fit at all. But then, neither did any other word.

He supposed he should take solace that his weekly duty wouldn't be the chore he'd envisaged.

Closing his eyes first to brace himself, he turned his stare back to her.

Her eyes were open.

'Elsbeth?' he said quietly.

He watched as she summoned the vacuous smile as she turned to face him.

'Are you okay?' he asked.

'Yes.'

Unable to read anything other than emptiness behind the returning stare, he breathed deeply and nodded. 'That's good.' He climbed off the bed and strode over to his discarded robe. 'Do you know how to contact the domestic staff if you need them?'

'Yes.'

He inclined his head again as he put his arms in his robe. 'Good. Then I will leave you to get some sleep.'

Her head lifted sharply. 'You're…?' But she snapped her mouth shut before she'd finished uttering her first word.

'You're?' he prompted.

The smile returned. She shook her head. 'Nothing.'

Staring at her, he tried to decipher the flash of emotion he'd detected when she'd opened her mouth. 'Tell me what you were going to say.'

Her throat moved and her lips pulled in together before she answered. 'I was just going to ask where you'll be sleeping.'

Still watching her closely, he tightened the belt of his robe. 'I thought you were aware of our living arrangements. They were agreed during the negotiations.' When she only continued staring at him, he smothered a sigh. 'Were you told about the arrangements?'

There was a slight hesitation before she shook her head. 'No.'

'You should have been. I was told you were in agreement with them.'

'I will abide with whatever has been agreed between you and my cousin,' she intoned.

Was she for real? She couldn't be. If he couldn't still feel the imprint of her body on his skin, he would question if she was even human.

'These are your quarters. I have separate ones on the floor above.' At her blank expression, he only just stopped himself from adding, *Nod if you understand what I just said.* Instead, he continued with, 'We will see a great deal of each other during our shared engagements but our private lives will be separate. I've been told you are keen to be a mother—is that correct?'

Her nod was emphatic. 'Yes.'

'Good. Then I suggest we share a bed together each Saturday until a child is conceived. Do you agree?'

The vacuous smile this time came complete with

pretty, white, even teeth. 'I will abide with whatever you think best.'

'I do think that is best.'

'Then I abide.'

Needing to get out of this room and far away from the woman he'd married before he said something he'd live to regret, Amadeo bowed his head. 'Then I wish you a goodnight.'

'Goodnight,' she replied.

After closing the bedroom door behind him, Amadeo took what felt like the deepest breath of his life.

He really had married a wind-up doll. Beneath the beautiful veneer, there was nothing. Only emptiness.

Elsbeth pulled the bedsheets up to her neck, closed her eyes and swallowed to get air into her lungs.

Why had her mother not warned her that she would be living alone in this castle? She must have known. Her mother knew everything. She had a way of listening at doors. Elsbeth had tried it herself once but had been caught. The beating she'd received from her father had stopped her ever trying the same again. Mercifully, it was the only beating she'd ever suffered, but it was a lesson she'd never forgotten and never wished to have repeated.

It was inconceivable that her mother hadn't known. It wouldn't have changed her mind about marrying Amadeo. Nothing could have changed her mind. The opportunity to escape Monte Cleure had been too great.

A royal woman's role was as an adornment, her function to breed and obey. Elsbeth knew that. She'd seen it and lived it every day of her life, and she knew she should be grateful that living separately from Amadeo made it much less likely that she could disappoint him. Much less likely that she'd find herself on the receiving end of his displeasure. Much less likely she would find out what form of chastisement his displeasure took. Her gut told her he would not be a man to use his hands as weapons for punishment, but powerful men didn't need to use their hands to punish women. There were a myriad of ways they could punish them, and she had no idea what form Amadeo's punishments would take.

Whatever form his punishments ended up taking—and it was a near certainty, whatever their living arrangements, that one day she *would* do something to displease him—what kind of fool would she be to listen to her gut? Hadn't it tantalised her with the possibility of happiness in her new country with her new husband?

The solitary tear rolling down her cheek told her happiness was as far away as it had ever been.

CHAPTER THREE

ELSBETH LAY UNDER Amadeo's weight, his breathing heavy in her ear.

Their second copulation. She wouldn't call it making love. Couldn't call it that. It was humiliating that she'd enjoyed it so much. More humiliating that she longed to wrap her arms tightly around him and press her mouth and nose into his strong neck and breathe him in. She supposed it was the euphoria of good sex bringing those longings out in her. It certainly wasn't him.

Their 'honeymoon week' had been spent apart. Elsbeth had spent it with only her domestic staff for company. She'd dined alone. She'd had no visitors. Her husband's absence had been stark.

Amadeo shifted his weight off her. Immediately she conjured her smile. She doubted he'd see it but she was taking no chances. A royal woman must always be agreeable. Or face the consequences.

No, she didn't think he'd notice whether she smiled or not because the room was in complete darkness. There had been a slight gap in the curtains of the window nearest the bed but he'd closed it himself before getting into bed beside her, turning off the lights and getting down to business. From the moment he'd entered her room that evening and made some stilted effort at small talk, his eyes had rested on her face for barely seconds at a time.

Despite all her best efforts to please him and be agreeable, Amadeo did not want to be married to her. She knew it in her heart.

When he wished her a goodnight a short while later, it took everything she had to wish him the same in her usual bright tone.

Please, please let me conceive soon.

Another lonely week passed, ending with Elsbeth sitting at her dressing table while the castle's beauty team transformed her appearance for her first Saturday evening engagement, which was being held at the Italian embassy, in her honour no less.

She'd undertaken only four engagements that week with Amadeo. They had been select daytime engagements with Ceresian industry, chosen to ease her into her new role as princess. Having often acted as Dominic's consort since he'd inherited the throne, she'd found the familiar routine soothing and a welcome distraction from her loneliness.

For the first time, she felt an unexpected pang of homesickness. At least she'd had friends in Monte Cleure, cousins and second cousins she'd been raised and educated with. She knew exactly where in the palace she was permitted, knew who to trust—no one—and who to be extra wary of. She'd had her mother to guide her. She missed her wise counsel. She missed having a goodnight kiss brushed against her cheek each evening. Her new family in Ceres, she feared, had already forgotten her existence.

She felt guilt that, despite all her mother's coaching and advice, Elsbeth had turned her husband away from her. All their engagements were shared but they had been as lonely as if she'd conducted them alone. Amadeo's Prince Charming persona did not extend to her. In public he was courteous and gentlemanly and stayed close to her side like a good prince should, and yet somehow he managed to avoid ever touching her. All journeys to and from their engagements were spent in the back of their car with their private secretaries and security, all conversation conducted in rapid Italian. Elsbeth understood Italian but not at the speed in which they spoke it. It only served to exacerbate her sense of isolation.

With the time rapidly approaching for their latest engagement, one that would end with Amadeo sharing her bed for a short while, Elsbeth tried to cheer herself up. Loneliness was making her wear rose-coloured glasses about Monte Cleure. Here, in Ceres, she had more freedom than she'd ever enjoyed. If her staff were spying on her, they hid it well. She was allowed to choose the food she ate and the clothes she wore. She'd not once inwardly cowered under menaces or threats…

But, as she thought the latter, she became aware of a dull ache deep in her abdomen that quickly turned into a painful cramp. As a beautician was, at that moment, sweeping her eyelashes with mascara, Elsbeth fought the instinct to double over, instead clenching her teeth and gripping tightly to the arms of the chair she was sitting in, and rode out the pain.

Amadeo, having just had a scotch poured for him and bracing himself for the evening ahead, was surprised at his brother's appearance in his quarters. 'I'm about to leave for the embassy,' he told him.

'I know. I wanted to catch you before you left.'

'Is something wrong?' Their quarters were reasonably close together but generally they found it easier to message or call when they wanted something from the other.

Marcelo helped himself to a scotch. 'Clara's been badgering me to arrange a night for you and Elsbeth to have dinner with us.'

'For what purpose?'

His brother leaned back against the mahogany bar. Where Elsbeth's quarters had been turned into a princess's paradise, Amadeo's own identically sized quarters had a dark gothic vibe. His mean-spirited misanthrope grandmother had lived in the quarters before him, and most of the dark wood furnishings and intense chiaroscuro paintings from artists such as Caravaggio had been there since her time. As the only thing he required from his quarters was privacy, he'd seen no need to make many changes to it.

'For the purpose that she's the newest member of our family and we've seen nothing of her since the wedding,' Marcelo replied. 'Clara's been itching to spend time with her and I'm afraid I can't restrain her any more—she says two weeks is long enough for the two of you to spend alone getting to know each other, so unless you agree and set a date you'll have Clara to deal with.'

This was the most effective threat Marcelo could have hit him with. Knowing better than to roll his eyes—Marcelo was extremely protective of his wife and Amadeo had no wish for another punch in the stomach—he inclined his head. 'I'm sure something can be arranged.'

And something arranged could be unarranged. He had no desire to suffer Elsbeth's perma-vacuous smile aimed at him over a dinner table unnecessarily for a whole evening. It was always there. Always. His wife must have the strongest cheek muscles in the universe.

'Where is she?' Marcelo craned his neck as if he expected her to emerge from the walls.

'Either in her quarters or waiting for me in our joint reception room, so unless you want me to be late meeting her and then late for our engagement I—'

'Why isn't she here with you?'

'She has her own quarters.'

The silence that followed this wouldn't normally bother him but, coming from Marcelo, it was unusual. 'What?'

His brother narrowed his eyes. 'How much time have you spent with her since the wedding?'

'Enough.' More than enough.

'How much? Clara overheard one of the domestic staff saying you and Elsbeth are leading completely separate lives.'

'I hope she reprimanded the staff member for spreading gossip,' Amadeo said sharply.

His brother grunted a laugh. 'Clara reprimand anyone?'

He grunted a laugh back. As soon as he'd realised how unsuited Clara was to being a royal princess, Amadeo had done a U-turn and worked to prevent Marcelo's marriage to her, believing the damage she could do with her unfiltered, unthinking ways was too great to risk. He'd been proved wrong—the public loved her and, if he was being truthful with himself, he was growing to love her too—but not *that* wrong as it had been his idea and insistence that they marry in the first place. All the same, he often found himself biting his tongue when she was overfamiliar with the staff or shared indiscreet stories that had no place at a royal dinner table. He could easily imagine her overhearing talk and gleefully demanding to know more.

Now he understood why Marcelo had come to his quarters rather than just call him.

'I had to tell her this was just a spiteful rumour and that you wouldn't be so callous as to treat your new wife so shabbily,' Marcelo added.

'What is shabby about it?' he asked tightly. 'She is living in quarters that have been made fit for a queen, with everything she could want or need at her disposal. She wants for nothing.'

'So it is true?'

'It is no more and no less than was agreed in the terms of our marriage.' Terms he'd been upfront about with his family and with the King of Monte Cleure. That Dominic and his advisors hadn't seen fit to tell Elsbeth about it was regrettable but, once he'd advised her of their living arrangements himself, she'd been perfectly agreeable—when *wasn't* she agreeable?—to it. *Dio*, if she was any more sweet and agreeable she'd come coated in fondant icing.

Marcelo's face darkened. 'You see nothing of her?'

'We conduct our engagements together.'

'And that is it?' He shook his head in blatant disbelief. 'Clara and Alessia are desperate to get to know her and invite her out with them but Gabriel and I told them to give you a few weeks to get to know each other and settle into your marriage, and all this time she's been alone in her quarters? How can you treat her in this way?'

'Need I remind you that I married a Fernandez to save our country and our monarchy from a situation *you* ignited? A *Fernandez*.' He practically spat the word out. 'I do my duty by her and I do and say nothing disrespectful to her. Elsbeth wants for nothing.'

'We all hate her family,' Marcelo snapped. 'Her cousin kidnapped my wife. If anyone should hate her for her blood it's Clara, but she wants to give her a chance and befriend her. Elsbeth is a young woman alone in a strange country. You're her husband. Whatever reason you took those vows, you did take them, and you owe it to her to give her a chance. I'm not saying you have to live with her, but she deserves *something*. She might one day be the mother of your children…if the rumours are right that you have graced her with your royal presence in the bedroom on two separate occasions?'

'Your wife certainly knows how to extract idle gossip,' he snapped back. It infuriated him that his brother, whose undignified bout of rule-breaking had cast the stone creating ripples that had led to Amadeo having to marry Elsbeth, should cast judgement on him. 'For your information, Elsbeth is perfectly happy with our living arrangements. I do not interfere with your marriage and I will not tolerate you interfering with mine, so let us regard your lecture as over. You can see yourself out—I have an engagement to attend.'

Downing the last of his scotch, he slammed the crystal glass on top of his three-hundred-year-old piano and stalked out of his quarters.

Amadeo usually enjoyed his time at the Italian embassy. Sharing a language and much of the same culture made the two nations natural allies, and time spent with the gregarious ambassador was rarely a chore. This evening's engagement was far different to normal, as all his engagements that week had been. Used to working a crowd and meeting dignitaries on his own, having a companion who wasn't a blood member of his family put a different flavour on events.

The few engagements he'd shared with his wife that week had been designed to ease her into her new role. She'd handled them with aplomb. In truth, it would have been impossible for her to put a foot wrong considering she stuck to his side like glue, smiled vacuously and let him do all the talking.

But those had been business engagements. Tonight's embassy gathering was a social event in Elsbeth's honour and, as their first course was being cleared away, she was still to open her mouth for anything other than food.

Biting back his irritation, he leaned into her and whispered, 'I think the ambassador's husband is feeling overwhelmed to be sitting next to you. Why don't you talk to him and put him at ease?'

She blinked slowly, widened her smile and turned to the man in question. Her voice was too low for him to hear what she said but the ambassador's husband responded. Soon the two of them were deep in conversation…or, rather, the husband was deep in conversation, Elsbeth deep in listening. When the ambassador excused herself for a few minutes, Amadeo turned his full attention to them. Elsbeth's head was turned away from him but she must have sensed he wished to join in for she adjusted her stance so the conversation could include him too. The husband, it transpired, was telling Elsbeth all about the school his children went to.

'What subjects do they find the most interesting?' she asked when he came up for air, which immediately set him off again.

When the ambassador returned to her seat, it struck Amadeo that Elsbeth had so skilfully woven the conversation so that it was all about him, and given him the full weight of her attention, that the ambassador's husband had hardly registered Amadeo's presence.

Unsure why this should irk him, Amadeo threw himself back into conversation with the ambassador but when, much later, their coffee cups were being cleared away and everyone in attendance had followed his lead and risen to their feet, he found he still had one ear on Elsbeth and the husband, paying enough attention that both ears strained when he heard the husband say, 'Are you okay, Your Highness?'

He had to strain even harder to hear her reply and, as she spoke, he realised Elsbeth always pitched her voice so that it was just audible. 'I'm fine, thank you.'

'Are you sure? You've gone very pale.'

Turning sharply to look at his wife, he saw what the other man meant. The subtle blush on Elsbeth's pretty cheekbones visibly contrasted with the paleness of her usually golden complexion.

'I thank you for caring, but I promise you I am well and would very much like to see Livia's painting.'

The ambassador caught Amadeo's eye and murmured with an indulgent eye-roll, 'Giuseppe thinks our eldest daughter is going to be the next Frida Kahlo.'

As the CEO of Italy's biggest car manufacturer was

heading towards him, Amadeo was forced to stay where he was and not follow his wife.

It disturbed him that he wanted to follow her at all.

Amadeo's private secretary and head of security kept up the usual flow of chatter on the drive home. Amadeo joined in as he always did but Elsbeth was aware of him glancing across at her face far more than he usually did, and didn't dare let her smile drop for a second.

Rather than scare herself by imagining his reaction to what she needed to tell him when they reached her quarters, Elsbeth thought longingly of a hot bath and a large glass of port to help ease her cramping stomach.

Nothing was said between them from the car all the way to her quarters. Every step though, increased the rate of her heart.

All evening she'd been worrying about the news she'd have to share with him, so much so that Amadeo had felt the need to tell her to make conversation with Giuseppe because her head had been too full of worry to engage with him. Poor Giuseppe. And he was such a nice man too. She hoped she'd made up for her initial rudeness.

Her two evening maids appeared moments after they entered her quarters.

'The princess won't be needing your assistance this evening.' Amadeo's smoothly delivered words made her stomach plunge. 'Feel free to return to your rooms—she will call if she needs you.'

Instead of obeying, they both looked at Elsbeth. To her horror, she realised they were waiting for her to give *her* assent.

Locking eyes with Amadeo, she caught what could

only be described as annoyance as his look quite clearly said, *Go on then, dismiss them.*

'I'll call you if I need anything,' she said with a smile which hurt her cheeks.

They both nodded. 'Goodnight, Your Highness.'

'Goodnight.'

She couldn't help closing her eyes when the door closed and, for the first time in a week, she was alone with her husband.

Panic clutched at her chest.

Why had he dismissed the maids? Was he angry with her about something? She thought quickly, frantically, wondering what faux pas she could have made that evening. The only thing she could think of was his having to tell her to make conversation with Giuseppe. Would something that innocuous be enough to aggravate him? She wished she knew. Two weeks into their marriage and her husband was still a stranger to her.

'Would you like a drink?' he surprised her by asking.

She took a deep breath to stem the panic and get a grip of herself. The following conversation was not going to be easy and working herself into a lather about an unknown quantity would not help. That she had to admit to failure in their quest for conception was enough to worry about. She'd take whatever else he wanted to throw at her as it came. 'Yes, please.'

Amadeo rifled through her bar. Not knowing what Elsbeth liked to drink, he'd ordered it to be stocked with every kind of alcoholic and soft drink. It didn't surprise him to find not a single bottle had been touched.

Helping himself to a fifteen-year-old scotch, he poured a liberal amount, took a gulp of it then turned back to her and raised the bottle in a question.

She shook her head. Her smile didn't seem as wide as she usually fixed it, he noted.

'What would you prefer? Wine? Champagne? Something stronger?'

'Is there any port?'

Anyone would think it was his bar and not hers. 'There is everything.'

'Then I would like a glass of port. Please.'

He found the bottle easily enough, poured her a hefty measure, then topped up his scotch. From the corner of his eye he noticed her press a hand low into her abdomen and her shoulders rise as if she were sucking in a breath.

Carrying the glasses over to her, he held her port out.

'Sit down, Elsbeth,' he said as she took her drink from him with quiet thanks.

Just as he knew she would, she obeyed, sitting primly on an armchair with dusky pink upholstery.

Choosing the Chesterfield for himself, he took another sip of his scotch before saying, 'You don't look well. What's wrong with you?'

She closed her eyes and breathed in as if bracing herself, then whispered, 'Menstrual pains.'

'Have you been in pain all evening?'

Her gaze fixed on floor, she nodded.

'I thought something was wrong when Giuseppe commented that you looked unwell. Why didn't you tell me before we left?'

'I was embarrassed to tell you in front of other people.' She breathed in deeply again. 'I'm sorry.'

'Sorry for what?' he asked, faintly bemused.

'That I've failed to conceive.'

What on *earth*...?

'Elsbeth, look at me.'

She raised her head slowly. For the first time he saw real human emotion on the usually empty expression. The expression was one of fear.

CHAPTER FOUR

ELSBETH CLASPED HER trembling hands tightly around the glass, her mind awhirl. Was this the reason Amadeo had dismissed her maids? Because he'd realised she was feeling unwell? That suggested a degree of empathy, didn't it? Which was a good thing. Even so, would that empathy extend to her failing at the first attempt to conceive a child? Amidst these thoughts her mother's voice echoed, stressing the importance of conceiving as soon as possible, stressing that royal men would not take the failure to conceive as their own failure, stressing that menstruation itself disgusted them.

She tried not to flinch when Amadeo leaned forwards and rested his elbows on his lap.

Swirling the amber liquid in his glass, his narrowed eyes didn't leave her face. And then he tipped his drink down his throat, wiped the residue off his lips with his thumb and said, 'What are you frightened of?'

Elsbeth took a sip of her port. The almost sweet liquid slid down her throat and injected her with strength. 'Disappointing you.'

'And you think I'm disappointed that you're not pregnant even though we've only been married for two weeks?'

'I would not want to disappoint you in any way.' She forced herself to ask, 'Are you disappointed with me?'

He grimaced and closed his eyes. 'Not in the way you think.'

Her heart sank heavily and she breathed out a sigh. 'Oh.'

He fixed his stare back on her. 'My disappointment is not your fault, Elsbeth.'

She could only gaze at him, trying to read the expression in his clear green eyes, grateful that for once she didn't see irritation in them.

And then he opened his mouth and she wished for the irritation to come back.

'You're not the kind of woman I envisaged making my queen.'

Her throat caught at the starkly delivered admission.

'Given a choice, I would never have married a Fernandez.' His thumb played on the rim of his glass. 'I despise your family. But that is not your fault,' he reiterated, and Elsbeth wondered if he could hear how grudging that reiteration sounded. She realised with a stab of despair that he wanted it to be her fault. He *wanted* to hate her.

She summoned all her skills to stop the hurt showing on her face. Amadeo's attitude to her family shouldn't come as a surprise; she despised them too, and she had to fight equally hard to smother the urge to shout that she was nothing like the others, that she couldn't help the blood that ran in her veins and that he should judge her for *her* and not be influenced by his preconceived notions about her.

She would never say any of it, of course. She wouldn't argue with him even if she hadn't spent her life witnessing the consequences for royal women who dared argue with their husbands or fathers: the thickly applied concealer that didn't quite hide the bruised skin beneath, the stiffness in their stride.

While she still believed Amadeo was not a man to use his hands to instil obedience in his wife, her position as his wife was so precarious that she didn't need to give him more ammunition with which to hate her.

The simple truth that trumped everything else was that she'd rather be married to a man who hated her than return to Monte Cleure.

And at least she knew. She wouldn't have to spend the rest of her life, or however long her marriage lasted, wondering why she felt such coldness from her husband. Her very existence made him cold.

For as long as she remained childless, her position as his wife would never be safe. But she'd known that already.

'I want to assure you that my personal feelings towards your family do not mean I will treat you with anything other than respect,' he said into the silence. 'I know it will take time but I want us to have a good relationship. It will make life easier for us both.'

She conjured her smile back into place. 'I feel the same.'

'Good.' He drained his scotch. 'Are you happy with our living arrangements?'

'Yes.' That was only a partial lie. Despite the loneliness, she'd come to quite like having a home to call her own and being able to relax in it. These quarters were hers in a way nothing had ever belonged to her before.

'My brother thinks I've effectively abandoned you. Do you agree with him?'

'Our living arrangements were agreed before our marriage.'

'That's not an answer.' Rubbing the back of his neck, his shoulders rose. 'If there's anything that makes you unhappy, you must tell me. I cannot read minds, and my sister would be the first person to tell you that I cannot read women.'

Amadeo's effort at humour brought no response. 'Are you unhappy?' he pressed.

'No.'

Truth or lie? He didn't know her well enough to be sure. He didn't know her at all. The brief flare of emotion—*had* it been fear?—he'd seen in her eyes had been shuttered behind the usual vacuity with such speed that he wondered if he'd imagined it. If his honesty had affected her, she'd done a wonderful job in hiding it, holding his stare without looking away, movement in those baby blue eyes but nothing to read in them.

'Are you happy with your quarters?'

'Yes.' The emphasis she put in this affirmation rang true.

'And are you content with your life here?'

She was equally emphatic. 'Yes.'

Damn Marcelo for planting ideas in his head. His brother had palpitations when he spent more than five minutes apart from Clara, but that was because his brother was 'in love' and ruled by hormones and emotion. Marcelo couldn't appreciate just how different Amadeo and Elsbeth's marriage was, that in essence it was one of convenience. Even if Amadeo had married a woman he actually liked, his marriage would still have been in a similar vein. It was usual for royalty to have separate bedrooms if not separate quarters. His siblings were the anomaly in that.

All the same, Amadeo could appreciate that his brother might have a point about Elsbeth being lonely.

'We have a full schedule of engagements this week.' Elsbeth's easing-in period was over. From now on their itineraries meant their weekdays and a couple of evenings each week would be spent together. Chances were Elsbeth would be as sick of the sight of him as he would be of her and relish the evenings and weekend days spent apart. 'Are you going to be well enough to do them?'

Dark colour stained her previously pale cheeks. 'I'll be fine by Monday. The pains normally only last a day.'

'Have you taken anything for it?'

She raised her glass and gave a wry smile. It was the first smile from her that didn't revolt him.

He rubbed his neck again. 'If I'd known you were unwell, I would have cancelled our engagement.'

'It's just cramps,' she said quickly. 'I was fine. There is no need to cancel anything on my behalf.'

'Have you seen a doctor about it?'

Her cheeks turned so dark he had the impression she was on the verge of spontaneously combusting with embarrassment. 'It's only menstrual cramps.'

'I'll get Dr Jessop to see you. He's my mother and sister's gynaecologist.' Pulling his phone out of his inside pocket, he called his private secretary.

When he was done, Elsbeth was staring at him in wary shock. 'Are you getting the doctor to see me *now*?'

'It would be rather pointless having him see you when you are well,' he riposted drily, then nodded at the glass in her hand. 'Another drink while we wait?'

He caught a flash of gratitude in her eyes, her smile soft. 'Yes, please. And thank you. It's very kind of you to bring the doctor to me.'

His chest tightened in a way he'd never felt before. After a beat, he said, 'Don't ever feel you have to suffer in silence.'

Two days later, Elsbeth hit the ground running with her first full week of engagements. Their teams—hers and Amadeo's—had arranged timings for maximum efficiency, the royal couple and their entourage moving from one engagement to the next with fluid precision. Her first proper evening engagement came on her first day too, an award ceremony for Ceres' most successful and innovative young entrepreneurs. She was given an exact two-hour window at the castle to prepare herself. Her beauty team were waiting for her and sprang straight into action. As a result, she and Amadeo arrived at the awards venue at the exact appointed time.

After posing for the press photographers, they were taken straight to their table for the preceding four-course meal.

Now knowing what was expected of her, Elsbeth turned to the gentleman on her right, the event organiser, who also happened to be Ceres' youngest billionaire, and struck up a conversation.

As fascinating as the man was on paper though, she found herself having to concentrate hard on their talk, every inch of her painfully attuned to the man sitting on her right. Amadeo.

Had she imagined that he'd made an effort to include her more that day in the conversations that flowed with their private secretaries? That he'd slowed his speech so she could keep up more easily? It was hard to be certain, it could have just been a necessity for him because of the sheer size of their workload. It didn't help that she was so *aware* of him, of his languid movements, the bronzed flesh of his throat above his starched white collar and tie, the surprising elegance of his huge hands… And now she was having to contend with all that awareness of him while he was wrapped in a tuxedo. Was it any wonder she was in danger of her brain scrambling?

What was it about the wearing of a tuxedo that magnified a man's masculinity? On the drive to the event she'd had to fight harder than normal not to stare at him.

Their first course was cleared away. Having come to a natural pause in her chat with the organiser, Elsbeth had a sip of her wine, then found herself holding her breath as Amadeo leaned his body a little closer to hers—not close enough that he brushed against her but close enough for her awareness to rocket—and said in an undertone for her ears only, 'How are you feeling now? Have your pains gone?'

The barest whisper of his breath caught in her hair. A frisson raced up her spine…and down too, into the apex of her thighs. Stunned at such an instantaneous reaction, Elsbeth had to force her body into stillness. Arranging a smile on her face, she met his stare. 'Much better, thank you.'

'I thought you looked better.' A fleeting wry smile played on his lips. 'But I am aware of the tricks women can use with make-up to make themselves appear healthier than they are. Alessia is an expert at it.'

It was the sensuality in the firm lips as he spoke that finally scrambled Elsbeth's brain. For too long a moment, all she could do was keep her smile fixed in place while she strove desperately for a response. 'Thank you again for calling the doctor to me.'

He inclined his head. 'I'm glad he was able to help you. You stored his number in your phone so you can call him directly if you need him?'

'Yes. Thank you.'

His green eyes continued to bore into hers as if he was searching for something or waiting for something, but then the evening's servers swarmed to their table with their second course and whatever Amadeo was searching for or waiting for was forgotten.

Elsbeth arranged herself on the bed and tried to breathe through the tightness in her lungs, her ears straining for the sound of Amadeo's arrival in her quarters.

The effort she'd sensed him making on Monday had continued throughout the week. There had been a definite shift in his attitude towards her. He included her more, especially during conversations when they were being ferried backwards and forwards to engagements. She tried hard to reciprocate, working harder than ever to maintain her agreeable persona and be the most perfect adornment a future king could wish for.

But he still made sure to never touch her, still wished her a goodnight from the reception room that connected their individual quarters and then disappeared up his private stairs without so much as the suggestion of a drink together. She still hadn't been invited into his quarters. She had no idea what he got up to in the privacy of his own domain, but the shift in his attitude made her hopeful that one day soon she would be invited into it. Maybe one night she would be invited to share *his* bed.

A pulse burned between her legs and she squeezed her eyes tightly shut, trying to tamp down the thrills of anticipation spreading along her veins.

And then she heard movement and her heart set off into a canter.

Amadeo assumed that going without sex for two weeks was the reason he didn't dread joining Elsbeth that night, and the reason he descended the stairs to her quarters with his heart and loins thrumming.

But they'd thrummed since he'd woken.

Anticipation was understandable, he reasoned. The three weeks of his marriage had resulted in the least amount of sex that he'd had since his teenage years... Not quite true, he reminded himself. He'd called off the casual relationship he'd been in as soon as his marriage to Elsbeth had been agreed. The six weeks of celibacy from then until the wedding had been perfectly manageable. Amadeo had a high sex drive but his position meant it was something he'd always had to manage. In his adult life a series of discreet affairs with like-minded rich women—rich women had no need to sell stories about him—had sated his appetites as much as they could. There had been occasions when he'd wondered if he'd be fortunate enough to find a suitable wife with a matching drive for sex but, with all the other attributes that had to come above it, had not held his breath. Self-denial was nothing new to him, had been an underlying factor of his whole life. He'd known since he could form thoughts that he was heir to the throne of a great and noble country and that his behaviour and the choices he made must always reflect that. Personal desires were an unwanted inconvenience, something his siblings would have done well to remember.

Elsbeth's head of housekeeping let him in. The other domestic staff had already been dismissed for the night.

His veins thickening, he walked along the corridor to her bedroom.

As expected, she was waiting in bed for him, propped upright against the velvet headboard wearing another variation of sacrificial virgin nightdress. The vacuous smile that turned his stomach was firmly in place.

He'd left her quarters a week ago thinking they'd reached an *entente cordiale*. He would make more of an effort with her, he'd vowed, but *dio*, it was hard, especially as Elsbeth had slipped back into her wind-up doll ways. He'd noticed though, that when they were on engagements she'd become more engaged with the people they met, more willing to share a few words and show her interest. She'd positively charmed the event organiser on Monday evening, had him eating out of her hand. It was just when it came to Amadeo alone that she reverted to being vacuously smiley. Elsbeth still answered his questions in few words and never volunteered anything about herself. If he didn't make the effort of conversation there would be no conversation at all. He supposed the constant smiles stopped her talking much. Getting cheek muscles and lips to multitask was a difficult ask. Or maybe he was being too generous and his initial impression had been right—there wasn't enough going on in her head for her to hold a conversation.

'How has your day been?' he asked as he removed his robe.

A blush stained her cheeks and she averted her eyes

from his body without losing the brightness of her expression. 'Fine, thank you.'

'What have you done with yourself?'

'I went for a walk with Clara and her dogs.'

At least that had saved his almost monosyllabic wife from having to talk. Clara could talk for the whole of Europe.

He slid under the covers. 'Do you like her company?'

'Very much.'

Effusive praise indeed, coming from his wife.

'And you?' she asked after a small hesitation. 'Have you had a good day?'

'I spent it at the Ceres National Racetrack. I'm an investor in a racing team who were testing there. Sébastien, the team principal, is an old friend of mine. I went along to watch and had dinner with him and one of the drivers.'

Elsbeth, struggling to breathe as the heat from Amadeo's body and the scent emanating from him seeped into her senses, scrambled for something else to say. She settled on, 'You are a fan of motor racing?' and then inwardly cringed at how gauche she must sound. But this was what Amadeo did to her. Overwhelmed her.

Life had taught her to be cautious and always think before she did or said anything, but it was a trait that amplified around him. When he was this close to her, her brain turned to mush. That he was naked and close enough that all she needed to do was move her foot a few inches and it would brush against his skin, made every cell in her body stand on end and every nerve strain towards him. The anticipation of Amadeo making his move and twisting his body to lean into her was almost unbearable.

'Obviously or I wouldn't invest in it,' he said.

Amidst the inward cringing and thrumming awareness sparked a tiny thread of anger, and she had to fight hard to keep her expression amiable and her tone bright. 'That's good.'

She didn't even know what she meant by that. *That's good.* What was good? That he had an interest in something outside the royal family? That he'd escaped the castle for the day?

She widened her smile, not making any motion that could betray her accelerating bitterness at his failure to mention in all the time they'd spent together that week that he was going off on a private jaunt.

He hadn't mentioned it because then he might have felt compelled to ask her along too.

Lying alone in her bed an hour later, Elsbeth stared up at the tester. Despite the lingering tingles racing through her body, only emptiness lay in the place where her heart should be, and she placed a hand to her chest to check it was still beating. It pulsed strongly against her palm and with it came a swell of tears to know that sex with her was nothing but a chore for him. Amadeo knew exactly what to do to make it good for her but never went beyond that. He made no attempt to see her naked and never kissed her anywhere but her mouth. He didn't invite her to touch or kiss him anywhere.

Maybe it was for the best that he always left straight after they were done. That he always made her climax…

that was the problem. It softened her, weakened her limbs and lowered her emotional defences.

Made her ache for a tenderness that could never be hers.

Elsbeth added a sweep of mascara to her eyelashes.

Another week had passed.

Her life had turned into Groundhog Week. Monday to Friday engagements, weekends and non-engagement evenings spent apart from her husband…

Apart from Duty Night. She'd taken to calling it that because she knew that was how Amadeo viewed it. She hated that she'd spent the week anticipating it.

She was coming to hate Saturdays. Allocated time for having sex.

She'd been married for four weeks and she'd had sex only three times.

It made her burn with humiliation to know that while he went through the motions with her, she came apart at his touch. But while she physically enjoyed every minute of their coming-together, emotionally she hated having to fight so hard to keep her passion contained and lie there passively beneath him. Hated that such passion had to be contained because he clearly felt none for her.

And she hated that she felt such excitement to be going out with him for a dinner date at Marcelo and Clara's quarters. She had a strong feeling this was at Clara's instigation and that the Englishwoman had refused to take no for an answer. It certainly wouldn't have come from Amadeo. He was still making an effort with her but the problem for Elsbeth now was that she could actually *see* what an effort it was. She didn't know what more she could do to win him over, and as she opened one of her cleverly fitted wardrobes disguised in her room's panelling, she rifled through the racks of beautiful clothes with his opinion in mind.

Oh, why had she decided to get herself ready? Usually she trusted the judgement of the beauty team she shared with her mother-in-law and sister-in-law, and wore whatever they picked out for her, but as this was a private meal and not an official engagement she'd given them all the evening off. After all, Alessia was in Madrid and Queen Isabella in Muscat so the team could actually go out and enjoy their Saturday evening.

The personal designer and seamstresses she also shared with her in-laws had collaborated on a swathe of beautiful dresses for her and the latest finished pieces had been added. A flash of vivid red caught her eye and when she pulled it off the rack her heart rose to her throat at how bold and daring, and *sexy,* the dress was.

Had the designer peered into her mind and seen the kind of dress Elsbeth so longed to wear?

Her heart sinking back down, she replaced it on the rack. This was a dress she would never wear. She couldn't. She was the future queen and it was imperative she dress with modesty at all times.

Sighing, she selected another, perfectly modest, dress with a side zip she could fasten herself.

She'd no sooner fastened the zip and checked her hair was in place when she heard the doorbell chime and her heart thumped into her ribs.

Amadeo was here.

CHAPTER FIVE

AMADEO ENTERED ELSBETH'S quarters and took a seat in her dayroom while he waited for her. It was the first time he'd been here since their evening at the Italian embassy and he was still unsure what had prompted him to suggest he come into her quarters rather than wait in their joint reception room as he usually did

His critical eye noticed a couple of changes to the room, the most obvious being an acrylic painting of a woman wearing a headdress of vivid flowers. It was good but, to his practised eye, naively painted and un-original. That it was displayed over the ornate five-hundred-year-old fireplace made him scratch his head as he was quite sure there had been a Renaissance painting there before.

His attention was drawn from the painting by movement and he turned his head to find Elsbeth entering the room, her motions so graceful she made no sound.

Wearing a high-necked, long-sleeved, form-fitting blue dress, so dark it could be mistaken for black, with what appeared to be silver stars patterned over it and falling to her feet, her hair was twisted back into her usual elegant chignon and her face subtly adorned with make-up. There was nothing special or unusual about her appearance. Nothing that could account for his throat catching and his intended polite greeting refusing to form.

'My apologies for making you wait,' she said in that soft, quiet voice he was slowly becoming accustomed to.

He cleared his throat and rose to his feet. 'You haven't. I was a few minutes early.' He'd been ready over an hour ago and had ended up watching the last half of an Italian football game to pass the time. He didn't even like football but he'd run out of distractions from the tingles that had plagued his body the entire day. What he wouldn't have given to be able to jump behind the wheel of a racing car and thrash it around Ceres National Racetrack and feel the machine bending to his will. Too dangerous, of course. He had done many laps of his country's racetrack, but those had been in ordinary cars in which he'd been obliged to resist the compulsion to put his foot flat on the accelerator and take them to their limits, and push himself to the limit too.

She stood before him. A waft of her perfume coiled into his senses. It was the same perfume she'd worn on their wedding day and every day since. He must have become accustomed to it for his dislike had vanished without him noticing. Probably familiarity, he supposed, even as he resisted the temptation to dip his face into the graceful curve of her neck and breathe it in more deeply.

Yes. Familiarity. It could do that. He'd always thought familiarity bred contempt or indifference but was learning it could have the opposite effect too. The opposite effect on him when it came to his wife in any case.

It had to be all those working hours they spent together causing it, he reasoned. No wonder his senses were attuning themselves to her. She'd arrived at his castle like a long-forgotten ghost, bland and insignificant, barely seen or noticed, but slowly her form was taking shape and solidifying, and now he was always wholly aware of her presence. And her absence. Slowly but surely, she was coming to dominate his thoughts in the weeknights and private days they spent apart. This would have been as disconcerting as his awareness of her if he didn't have an answer for that too, which was that Elsbeth was a conundrum to be worked out. *That* was why she invaded his thoughts. Amadeo had always insisted on knowing how things worked, from car engines to the pendulum of a grandfather clock.

Elsbeth's insipidness was an act, he was certain of it, the smiley face a mask. Every day his conviction grew that there was more between her ears than a little grey matter and a lot of hot air. Sometimes his fingers itched to rip the mask off her face and insist the real Elsbeth show herself.

'Where did you get that?' he asked, nodding at the painting above the fireplace.

'It was a gift from the Italian ambassador's daughter. Giuseppe told her how much I liked it so she sent it to me.'

'That's the danger of always having to be complimentary,' he observed. 'People take our compliments at face value. You didn't have to hang it—we have a room the size of the Blue Stateroom filled with gifts from the public where it can be stored. Your team should have told you that.' Noticing her gaze dart to the floor, he narrowed his eyes. '*Did* they tell you about the storeroom?'

A blush covering her cheeks, she nodded.

'Then why did you hang it?'

'Because I like it.' She chewed on her bottom lip before adding, 'But if you don't think it should be hung there I will have the old painting put back.'

'You *like* it?' He wouldn't have been more surprised if she'd actually pulled the vacuous smiley mask off her face with her nails.

She nodded again.

'Why?'

'I just do.'

'More than the original painting?'

Another nod.

His incredulity rocketing, he shook his head. 'Elsbeth, this is your home so what you hang on the walls is entirely up to you, but I'm curious why you would prefer the work of a fifteen-year-old schoolgirl over a Renaissance masterpiece.'

She raised her head and stared at the painting. 'I like the colour of the flowers.'

He recalled the waterlilies of the original painting. There had been something insipid about them he'd believed perfectly matched his wife.

'They're so bright and bold. And honest.' Was that a wistful note in her voice? 'And I like the expression in the woman's eyes. It's like she's saying, "Yes, I know, I'm wearing a headdress of flowers but aren't they wonderful?"' Her shoulders rose and she gave him a smile that contained no vacuity at all. 'Seeing it there makes me feel warm.'

Looking more closely at the painting, Amadeo began to see what she meant. There *was* something playful and knowing in the sitter's eyes.

And then he looked back into his wife's eyes and his throat caught again.

For an instant, her baby blue eyes were soft and warm, and in that instant he saw that behind them *was* a real woman of flesh and blood, with thoughts and opinions and dreams all of her own, and when the instant passed and the vacuous smile began to set itself back into place, his heart thumped and he snapped, *'Don't.'*

Elsbeth's smile froze on her lips.

What had she done to make him raise his voice at her like that?

Holding her breath, the individual beats of her heart pounded loudly in her ears while she watched Amadeo's shoulders and chest rise, and his head lift as he cast his gaze to the ceiling before his stare locked back on her.

'Only smile if you mean it.'

She stared at him, not knowing what he meant.

His eyes closed briefly again, the rise and fall of his shoulders and chest less pronounced. 'Elsbeth...' He grimaced and shook his head. 'I do not say this with the intention of hurting you, but all your smiles... they're too much. It seems to me that you hide behind them. They have their place when we're out on engagements, but when it's just you and me they're unnecessary. That painting makes you feel warm... Well, your smiles make me feel cold. Because they're not real. It's like being married to a blank canvas. I don't want a wife who hides behind a fake smile and agrees with everything I say. I want to know the real Elsbeth, the Elsbeth I just caught a glimpse of. I don't want to spend the rest of my life married to a stranger.'

The good Lord help her, she felt like a deer caught in the headlights. As hard as she tried to think, her thoughts were too many and too jumbled for any coherence. Panic swelling, she couldn't even think of something to say in response and, from the expression on his face, he was waiting for her to say something, but she didn't know what to say and, even if she could, she didn't know how to say it, not when she'd spent her whole life having it drilled into her that the best decorative adornment to a man's arm was a silent one.

After far too long of this excruciating silence he rubbed his knuckles to his forehead and sighed. 'We should go or we'll be late.'

Her cheeks automatically tried to pull her lips into a smile, but she stopped them by the skin of her teeth. 'I'm sorry.'

'And no more apologies,' he said roughly.

'Sorry,' she whispered. Like her smiles, apologies were an automatic response.

His grimace looked more rueful this time, the shake of his head less one of exasperation. 'Elsbeth…just be you. Okay?'

'What happens if you don't like the real me?' she surprised herself by saying.

She caught a glimmer of something like sympathy in his eyes. 'Then there will be no real change, will there?'

Surprisingly, the blunt honesty and directness of his answer didn't puncture her as deeply as it should.

Elsbeth liked Marcelo and Clara's quarters from the moment she stepped inside. As regal and chintzy as the rest of the castle, it had warm undertones she thought perfectly suited the couple who lived there, especially when Clara threw her arms around her.

Unprepared for such a gregarious welcome when

the most she was used to was air kisses, she froze in Clara's tight embrace.

Laughing, Clara let her go, but only so far as to take Elsbeth's hand and drag her through to the bar at the far end of the dining room, speaking at a hundred miles an hour as she'd done during their walk together. As Elsbeth's English was minimal, she couldn't understand a word of it, but Clara's body language was enough for her to know how happy the Englishwoman was to host her, just as her body language on their walk had told her how happy she was in Elsbeth's company. It had been a lovely warming feeling and she'd been sorry when their walk had come to an end. When a glass of champagne was thrust into her hand and Clara held hers aloft with a beaming, 'Cheers,' she knew exactly what was meant and chinked her glass to it.

Somehow, with two native Italian speakers, an English speaker and herself a native French speaker, communication was no issue at all throughout the meal. Amadeo and Marcelo were both fluent in English and French and able to make any translations when Clara spoke too fast for Elsbeth to keep up or when Elsbeth's English failed her. By the time their main course was cleared away she found she'd relaxed so much that she was practically slouching in her chair!

But how could anyone fail to relax in such generous company? Generous in the sense that they made her feel she'd completed their year simply by being there. She'd never heard such laughter before. Not real laughter. Clara had a ready smile that Elsbeth studied, wondering how it differed to her own smile that left Amadeo cold. And then she saw for herself what the difference was—Clara's smiles came naturally. There was nothing practised in them, nor in her infectious laughter.

'You have had happy life?' she asked in tentative English. How else could it be possible for someone to be so free within their own skin?

Clara pulled a face that made Elsbeth giggle. She caught the sharp turn of Amadeo's face to her from the corner of her eye but then Clara answered, saying, 'Gosh, no, before I met Marcelo my life was hard. My mum died when I was a little girl, my father died when I wasn't much older and left me in the care of my brother, who hated me and packed me straight off to boarding school, and then I got expelled from that horrible school, which was excellent because I hated it there and, quite frankly, it hated me, and then my brother sold me to your cousin, King Pig and...'

Even with Amadeo translating as quickly as Clara spoke, Elsbeth struggled to keep up, and when it came to her cousin she could listen no more. 'I am very sorry for what he did to you.'

'It wasn't your fault,' Clara dismissed cheerfully. 'I'm just glad you weren't one of the women he sent to guard me and stop me escaping. I'd probably have to hate you then!'

Even Elsbeth laughed at that. 'I couldn't have,' she said when the laughter had died away. 'I would never have.'

'I know,' Clara said with a smile. 'And that's why I don't hate you. I imagine you suffered at his hands too?'

'I...' Elsbeth shrugged helplessly and strove for the correct English. 'All women suffer under Dominic.' It was the reason she'd been too cowardly to do anything to help Clara. The whole palace knew, despite Dominic's assertion that the Englishwoman he'd locked away was there willingly, that she was being held against her will and forced into marriage.

'Then I'm glad I only had to put up with him for a couple of weeks before Marcelo saved me.' She looked adoringly at her husband and was rewarded with a look so loving that Elsbeth felt a huge pang of envy and had to stop herself from glancing at Amadeo.

The sun would expire before he looked at her like that. Or consistently lean his body into hers the way Marcelo did with Clara. Or follow her every move with his eyes. This was a couple madly in love and lust, and it was almost painful to witness their constant need to touch each other. Were they afraid the other would disappear if they didn't have that anchoring contact?

She knew with instinctive clarity that the moment she and Amadeo left them they would be ripping each other's clothes off in the way she had seen couples behave in movies. Their lovemaking would be exuberant. Filthy. Loving. Everything her own couplings with Amadeo were not.

When this evening was over, Amadeo would come to her bed and they would do their duty and attempt to create the next heir to the Ceres throne. He would be naked but she would be wearing her nightdress. There would be no effort to remove it. She would climax. He would climax. And then he would wish her a goodnight and leave, and she would lie in her bed alone, her skin and pelvis still thrumming but her heart a gaping wound.

Lemon tarts were placed before them and, once demolished, coffee was brought out. Even two sugars and a thick swirling of cream couldn't disguise the underlying bitterness, but she sipped politely at it, unaware how sharp Clara's eyes really were until she said, for once at a speed Elsbeth could keep up with without translation, 'Don't drink it if you don't like it. What would you prefer?'

Amadeo twisted his stare back to his wife. Her cheeks had caught fire. The image of the coffee profiteroles at their wedding floated into his mind. 'You don't like coffee?'

She looked trapped, fearful blue gaze stark on his, white teeth slicing into her bottom lip. Instantly, he understood. To admit to disliking coffee—and, of course, she did dislike it or she wouldn't be looking so panicky—would be to admit to lying to him.

The usual irritation he felt when Elsbeth became all tongue-tied refused to form. He couldn't even summon irritation that she'd proven herself a liar, and about something as petty as coffee no less. Instead there was a weird compulsion to palm her scarlet cheeks and swear on his life that no harm would ever come to her.

Shaking the strange compulsion off, now aware that a tension had formed, that it wasn't only Elsbeth holding her breath but also his brother and sister-in-law, who likely had no idea why they were holding their breaths or any notion of where the tension had come from.

Placing his elbow on the table, he propped his chin on his hand and murmured in French, 'You know, Elsbeth, confession is good for the soul?'

Her stare remained stark on him.

'Is there something you wish to confess?' he continued. 'Something, say, about marrying into a family of coffee fiends, in a country of coffee connoisseurs, and feeling obliged to hide your aversion to the glorious black stuff so as not to be drowned in a vat of it?

Because, let me assure you, we haven't drowned non-coffee-drinkers here for at least two hundred years.'

A few beats later, having had to wait for the punch-line while Marcelo translated for her, Clara gave a bark of laughter. The sound of it seemed to snap Elsbeth out of her panic. In an instant, her features were transformed. Her lips curved into a smile that tugged at her eyes, her whole face lighting up into something so beautiful that Amadeo's heart skipped a beat. A giggle flew out of her mouth, sounding like music to his ears—he *hadn't* imagined her earlier one—and then her hand flew to cover it.

Her shoulders shook a few times before she removed her hand and looked him squarely in the eye. 'Okay. I confess. I hate coffee.'

'And coffee profiteroles?'

Her cheeks caught fire again but she nodded. 'Coffee in all its forms.'

It was on the tip of his tongue to tell her she should have spoken up before, that approving items she disliked on her own wedding menu was masochistic, but he held it back. She would take it as criticism and slip back into her vacuous shell.

How he could be so certain of this, he didn't know, and nor did he know what it was about criticism that affected her so much, but he did know this was not something he could draw out of her with an audience.

In his mind flashed an unbidden image of stripping Elsbeth of all the shields and masks she hid behind. It was an image that sent a short but potent stab of lust burning through him.

CHAPTER SIX

AMADEO SHIFTED HIS weight off Elsbeth and rolled onto his back. It was a struggle to catch his breath.

Doing his duty was incrementally feeling less like duty. Less like a chore.

As she always did after they'd come together, Elsbeth lay silently beside him. He knew she'd climaxed, was becoming attuned to the signs, the shortening breaths, the barely perceptible mewing, was learning the motions that tipped her over the edge and made her thicken around him and her fingers press into his back. Afterwards, she would lay her hands neatly by her sides, the only sign that she'd enjoyed what they'd just shared the rapid beats of her heart pounding through their joined chests until he rolled off her and she folded her hands neatly over her abdomen and lay in silence until he wished her a goodnight.

Her hands were neatly folded over her abdomen now.

What was she thinking? Her mind wasn't the blank canvas he'd believed. The wind-up doll persona was only a persona. So what was she thinking as she lay silently beside him, waiting for him to leave? Was she imagining how she would spend the next day? Thinking of her family? Formulating maths equations that had the potential to change the world?

Or was she thinking of him, as he was thinking of her? Was she silently encouraging him to go and leave her in peace so she could sleep? Was she wondering why he hadn't left already? She wouldn't ask him to leave. His wife might be an enigma to him but he knew that much.

'How did you suffer under Dominic?' he asked. The question had swirled in his mind since their earlier conversation at dinner.

She took a long time to answer. 'I didn't say I'd suffered. I said women suffer under him. I spoke out of turn.'

'So you didn't suffer under him?'

'It depends on your definition of suffering.'

'Why are you prevaricating?'

She fell silent again.

Trying to keep the frustration from his voice, he said, 'Elsbeth, I am trying to understand you. I *want* to understand you. But you don't make it easy. Stories have circulated about the House of Fernandez for a long time.'

'What kind of stories?'

'That Dominic rules with an iron fist—not his people but those within his sphere: his family and the courtiers and staff who work for him. That his sister Catalina fled Monte Cleure and refuses to return while he is alive because he used to beat her. That he's paid off a number of lovers to gag them from sharing tales of his depravity. I've known the man all my life and none of the stories about him come as a surprise. His reputation alone was enough for me and my parents to refuse talks of him marrying my sister, and that was before he kidnapped Clara.'

'You refused permission for Alessia to marry him?'

'I wouldn't marry my worst enemy to him. Clara calls him King Pig which is, I think, far too generous a title. He would have forced her to marry him and forced himself on her if Marcelo hadn't rescued her. And now I have told you what I think, I would like to hear your thoughts about him.'

She shifted slightly, half turning her body towards him. 'Why do you want my thoughts?'

'Why would I not?' He took a deep breath to quell his frustration.

'I am coming to see that things are different here.'

'What do you mean?'

'The way you treat your women. Here, they are allowed opinions, yes?'

'So are women in Monte Cleure,' he countered. 'There is complete equality, written in law.'

Through the darkness, he could feel her gaze searching his. 'Not quite.'

'There are no barriers to your women doing whatever they want.'

'Not ordinary women, no,' she agreed softly. 'But royal women aren't ordinary women. Dominic loosened many of the old laws when he took the throne and fully emancipated the women of Monte Cleure so that all discrimination was outlawed, and he was feted by the European press and governments for it, but he tightened the laws regarding the royal family itself. Any member of the royal family closer than a third cousin is not allowed to marry, leave the country or hold a bank account without his written permission. Fathers and husbands of the Fernandez family have effectively been granted ownership of their wives and daughters but Dominic has absolute power over us all, so you must forgive me when I say that the opinions I have of him can never be spoken. If he heard about them he would kill me.'

It was the longest speech she'd ever made to him and, as she'd spoken, an intelligent, eloquent woman had emerged, so intelligent and eloquent that the words themselves took a few moments to penetrate.

'Are you being serious?' He'd known Dominic was a tyrant but what Elsbeth described was medieval, there was no other word for it, a system of governance and power that hadn't existed in his own country in that form for centuries.

Her eyes rang. 'If he can kidnap a British citizen, what do you think he would do to one of his own subjects?'

'But you're no longer one of his subjects. You're a Ceresian Princess now, and future Queen Consort.'

'For now,' she said wistfully.

'For always. You're my wife.' For the first time, acknowledging Elsbeth as his wife didn't make him shudder internally. Was it acceptance evoking this softening towards her?

'Amadeo, I am not a fool. You don't like me. If I don't give you children then in a year, two years, three years at most, you will see that things have settled between your country and Monte Cleure, and that sending me back home will not result in the trade and diplomatic war you married me to avoid. You will have done your bit for your country and there will be no good reason for you to keep me.'

Astounded, Amadeo sat up and turned the bedside light on so he could look at her properly.

Elsbeth clasped the bedsheet covering her and tried to breathe naturally through the thudding of her heart. Speaking her thoughts out loud was a new thing for her. She could never have uttered such things at home, and while she knew there would be no punishment from Amadeo, she didn't know what kind of reaction she was about to receive for speaking her mind.

Closing his eyes, he breathed deep and hard, his smooth olive chest rising, the defined pectoral muscles tightening. Quickly, she averted her gaze from his body, not wanting to be caught staring at him improperly. Safer not to look for her own sake too. It did strange things to her, made her feel liquid inside, much the same way his touch did. Made the wound in her heart throb with something that felt very much like a pang of yearning, and there was already too much yearning at this moment in her.

Amadeo would normally have left her bed by now. Nothing inside her felt right when he was naked beside her. Before the event, her body would thrill with anticipation. Afterwards, a cold desolation would form in her chest when he moved off her that ran counter to the tingles from her climax which would last for hours. Pleasure and pain in one Amadeo-sized dose. At least alone she could hold his pillow to her chest and curl into it, a sorry substitute for the warm hunk of man she craved to cuddle into in those hours after sex but better than nothing. Better than feeling the tingles and desolation with him still lying beside her without a single part of his body touching hers. One minute as intimate as a man and a woman could be, the next, the connection severed.

The longer their marriage went on, the more grateful she was that she slept alone. She didn't know how she'd endure sleeping night after night beside a man who only touched her to make a baby. Better the way things were: get the job done then sleep apart. No false promises. No false affection. Less time for her heart and body to crave more. Less chance of further hurt.

She wished he would leave so she could cuddle into his pillow and self-soothe.

Instead, his clear green gaze locked back on hers. 'I don't know how things are done in the House of Fernandez, but in my family we take our wedding vows seriously. Till death us do part. That's what we both promised.'

She took a long breath before summoning the courage to voice her deepest fear. 'What if I don't conceive?'

'You are twenty-four. I'm thirty-two,' he said dismissively. 'We are both fit and healthy. There is nothing to suggest we will have trouble conceiving.'

'But what if we do?'

'Then we cross that bridge when we come to it.'

'You might choose a path that doesn't include me when we've crossed it. There is no affection or shared history to bind you to me.'

His eyes penetrating, he shook his head. 'But that works both ways.'

'How?'

'If you choose to end our marriage there will be nothing I can do about it.'

The idea was so preposterous that she gave a short laugh. 'And where would I go? What would I do? I own nothing but my name.' Elsbeth had a team of domestic staff who catered to her every whim, a team of clerical staff to manage every minute of her working life, a personal designer and seamstresses to create bespoke clothing for her, an unlimited credit card for everything else, but she didn't have a cent in her own name. Not one cent. The credit card could be turned off in an instant.

'That would be up to you.' He climbed off the bed and reached for his robe. 'This is Ceres, not Monte Cleure. I have committed my life to you as your husband, not your ruler. We have obligations to each other and the monarchy, rules we must both abide by, but no rights over the other. I hope you will abide by those obligations but I cannot force you to do so. You are your own autonomous woman.'

Was it wishful thinking on her part that he sounded sincere?

Or was it the dim light turning Amadeo's chiselled features into plains and shadows that made the gape in her heart yearn even harder for something she could never have?

Something she must train her heart into believing she no longer wanted.

A week later, dressed in an old pair of black shorts, Amadeo carried his coffee out onto his bedroom's balcony. The early morning sun was rising in the warming sky, the castle sleeping. He'd woken to duskiness with a strange fluttering in his stomach. Unable to fall back asleep and unwilling to break this rare moment of solitude by calling in his staff, he'd made his own coffee…okay, *made* was a loose term seeing as a pot with fresh beans was prepared for him each night so only a button needed to be pressed to get it working, but the intention was there.

The balcony overlooked his sprawling private garden. Standing at the stone balustrade, he gazed out at the immaculate lawn surrounded by orderly hedges and symmetrically arranged flower beds, and waited for this momentary peace to settle the fluttering.

When a figure appeared on the lawn his heart thumped as he blinked to clear the mirage. But the figure remained and the flutters became heavier. Denser.

It was Elsbeth.

Amadeo's quarters being set over hers, the garden was the one space they shared. He'd debated before their wedding whether or not to partition it but dismissed it as unnecessary as he so rarely used it.

Cradling a mug between her hands, she stepped barefoot over thick grass damp with early morning dew, her dishevelled blonde hair hanging down to her shoulders. Unlike the variant of modest virginal white nightdress she always wore when he joined her in bed, that morning she was wearing a pair of short, red and white checked pyjamas, the bottoms loosely wrapped around supple golden thighs.

His own bare feet had descended the iron stairs from his balcony before he could stop them.

She must have sensed him for she whipped around, and any chance of turning back was gone. Even with the distance between them he could see the colour rise up her cheeks.

As he strode lazily towards her, the beats of his heart accelerating with every step, he soaked in every inch of the body usually hidden beneath modest clothing, the swell of unhindered breasts pushing against the simple cotton of the pyjama T-shirt in a way he'd never noticed beneath her virgin nightdresses.

The urge to greet her with a kiss was strong enough to make him grind to a halt two paces before her.

They never kissed outside of the bed, not even the polite air-kisses of acquaintances. By unspoken agreement, physical contact between them was strictly limited to their Saturday night sex window, and that in itself was limited too. Did Elsbeth ever wish for more…?

He breathed in deeply through his nose and summoned a half-smile. 'You're up early.'

She returned the smile shyly. 'I'm an early riser.'

He'd be an early riser too, in more ways than one, if he woke up next to this ravishing, tousle-haired, sexy creature…

Sexy? Elsbeth?

Staring into those baby blue eyes with a tightening chest and thickening loins, it came to him with something akin to shock that the stirrings of arousal he suffered with increasing frequency around her were proof that, on some level, he already found her sexy.

In her own unique, quiet way, Elsbeth was truly ravishing and, as all these thoughts built in his head, the eyes he found himself unable to break the lock of his gaze from darkened and Elsbeth's slender throat extended, and suddenly he knew, in that long, charged beat of silence, that his steadily growing attraction was reciprocated…right until she blinked her stare away from him and drank from her mug.

When she met his stare again a moment later, whatever he'd seen in the baby blue eyes had gone.

Amadeo searched hard but no, it had vanished with no trace of it ever having existed.

He swore loudly in his head. He was getting the hots for his wife, and she was standing there sipping her drink with her usual calm demeanour, waiting for him to speak—she still only rarely instigated conversations—and with no hint whatsoever of what was going on in her head.

Elsbeth was fast becoming the most infuriating, intriguing, exasperating woman he'd ever known. When he'd been busy being irritated by her fake smiles he'd failed to notice the sheer stillness with which she held herself. Having always prided himself on his self-control, he had to accept that Elsbeth was a master of composure who made him look and, more importantly, feel like an amateur.

Determined to take back control of himself, he nodded at the mug in her hand and idly said, 'Coffee?'

Sheepish mischief flashed in her eyes. 'Tea.'

Mio Dio, that hint of mischief was as unexpected as if she'd suddenly started doing cartwheels across the lawn and, damn it, as sexy as hell.

'I thought only the Brits drank tea?' he teased, refusing to allow this fresh hit of arousal derail his determination for control.

She gave a delicate one-shouldered shrug. 'I always wanted to be British.'

'Really? Why?'

'I love their gardens.'

That amused him. 'Really? You wanted to be British because of their gardens?' He'd never met a woman under the age of thirty who had any interest in gardens whatsoever.

'The British love their gardens and make such an effort with their flower beds, and their seasons are so much more pronounced than in Monte Cleure so you can watch them unfold like a living calendar. They have the barren wasteland of winter, but then the first appearance of shoots appear in early spring and then, by the time summer comes, their gardens just bloom with colour. Even their autumns are beautiful, when the leaves change and everywhere's all russet and gold.'

Although delivered as quietly as she always spoke, there was an animation in her voice and a light in her eyes he'd never heard or seen before.

'What do you think of my—our—garden?' Seeing her eyes widen fractionally before her lips started pulling into the fake smile that had rarely made an appearance all that week, he stopped it fully forming by shaking his head and giving a short laugh. 'Don't try and lie. You don't like it. I can tell.'

Her mouth dropped open. 'How?'

Now he was the one to shrug. 'It is something I have noticed. When you're afraid you're going to say something you believe could be incriminating, you put your mask on so you can hide your real thoughts behind it.' Strangely, the mask she used to hide behind was the only time he was able to read her. Stripped of it, her composure was too strong for him to read anything she didn't want to give away. 'It's okay,' he added nonchalantly. 'I understand it will take time before you trust that you can speak freely with me.'

Their talk the last time they'd shared her bed had opened Amadeo's eyes to the factors that had made his wife the way she was. He assumed it was the knowledge of those factors that had seen him spend a full week of engagements with her without once getting irritated by her in those few times her mask had slipped back on. A telephone conversation with Dominic's estranged sister, the Princess Catalina, had revealed Elsbeth had spoken the truth about the power Dominic had extended to himself over his family. Things were worse there than even he'd suspected.

Dominic was playing a clever game, he grudgingly admitted: principality-wide reform to keep the investment flowing in—Monte Cleure was a billionaires' playground—but behind the scenes turning the House of Fernandez back into a medieval court where he reigned supreme. Centuries ago, Amadeo's ancestors had had the same uncontested power over their people...until the people had risen and toppled them. He doubted such a toppling would happen to Dominic, not while his people enjoyed the highest incomes and lowest taxes in the western world. Only an internal coup would oust him.

Elsbeth's father was Dominic's uncle, the most senior royal courtier in the House of Fernandez. Any coup would need his backing, but when he'd said this to Catalina she'd laughed. 'Your father-in-law is Dominic's biggest supporter. It will never happen.'

The uncle of a tyrannical monster would be grandfather to any children Amadeo and Elsbeth had. It was a thought that sickened him and he was trying hard not to let his reaction further colour his feelings for the man's daughter. Although his growing attraction to her was undeniable, attraction was a chemical thing that sooner or later would burn itself out. His marriage, however, would last until death. Amadeo would never forget that Elsbeth was a Fernandez by blood, contaminated to her soul, but he had to believe he could come to accept her as a Berruti. As his wife.

Trying to loosen the sudden tightness in his chest with a long inhale, he gave a quick encouraging smile. 'Go on, tell me. What would you change about our garden?'

Her face screwed up a fraction before she blurted out, 'All of it.'

'It's that bad?'

'It's not bad at all. It's very ordered and pretty.'

'But you say it as if ordered and pretty were a bad thing,' he countered, catching her out with the tone of her own words.

'They're not if you like that kind of thing,' she protested, half laughing. 'It's just that I like the English country cottage style where there's much less order and different varieties, sizes and colours of flowers are clustered together all higgledy-piggledy.'

He couldn't help but smile at her turn of phrase. Higgledy-piggledy. He would never have imagined his neat, ultra-composed wife would consider higgledy-piggledy to be a good thing. 'Have you spent much time in England?'

She shook her head ruefully. 'None at all. But I watch all their gardening shows. You went to boarding school there, didn't you?'

He nodded.

'And are their gardens as beautiful as in the television shows?'

'I didn't take any notice of them.'

'Why not?'

'Because I was a teenage boy and flowers and gardens were not my thing,' he answered drily.

He caught a sudden knowing flash in her eyes. 'No, I don't suppose they were,' she said, and in that instant Amadeo was taken back to his adolescent boarding school years, where he'd experienced a degree of freedom away from his country and castle walls that had never been repeated. Images flashed in his mind of lazy weekends spent in the local town with friends, catching the eye of pretty girls with knowing smiles, gropes and fumbles by riverbanks, illicit cigarettes and smuggled alcohol.

Those had been halcyon days of rampant hormones, the constant prickles of awareness capable of turning into full arousal at the sight of a short skirt rolled up a few extra inches, and as Amadeo gazed into his wife's eyes he realised there was something similar in the thrill of awareness that so often zipped through him for her as he'd felt in his teenage years. It had to be the thrill of forbidden fruit, because was anything more thrilling than when it was forbidden? Would he still desire to speed full throttle around the Ceres National Racetrack if it wasn't against the rules and so forbidden?

And would he still desire Elsbeth as much as he was growing to if he hadn't made her forbidden to himself?

Amadeo was so locked in his memories and thoughts that he only realised silence had elapsed between them again when Elsbeth smoothed her hair and delicately cleared her throat. 'I should take a shower and get some breakfast,' she murmured.

He snapped himself back to the present.

Walking in step, they reached the bottom of his stairs, beneath which lay the short path to Elsbeth's French doors.

Their eyes met at the point where they went their separate ways.

'Well...' she said with another of those graceful shrugs. 'I will see you later.'

He gazed again at the elegant swan of her neck. His mouth watered to imagine tracing his tongue over it.

Amadeo was halfway up the iron steps when he looked down to where Elsbeth was about to step into her quarters. 'Elsbeth,' he called.

She looked up at him.

It was on the tip of his tongue to invite her to join him for breakfast. 'Enjoy your day.'

A soft smile played on her lips. 'And you.'

And then she vanished from his sight.

CHAPTER SEVEN

ELSBETH'S LEGS WERE still shaking when she stepped out of the shower and wrapped a large fluffy towel around herself. They'd started shaking the moment she'd closed her French doors and finally escaped her half-naked, rampantly masculine husband.

Since their wedding, she'd taken an early morning walk around her garden every day and not once had she been disturbed by anyone. The garden was the only place in the castle where she could be alone without feeling lonely. As the weeks had passed, she'd redesigned it in her mind, imagining it as a riot of colour with quirky statues and hammocks, occasionally allowing herself to dare to dream about the children who might one day play in it. She'd become so used to being alone with only her thoughts and early morning birdsong that when she'd sensed another human presence and spun around to find Amadeo walking down the iron steps, she'd been completely unable to control the contraction in her body that had felt much too much like joy to be healthy.

She'd barely held it together from that point.

When he'd strode over the lawn to her, she'd inwardly cringed at being caught wearing pyjamas more suited to a teenage girl than a princess, had been unable to stop her mother's stern voice repeating in her ear the warning given *ad nauseam* in the weeks before the wedding. 'A prince expects his wife to be a princess at all times.'

He hadn't looked disapprovingly at her though. In fact…

If she didn't know better, she'd think the hooded glimmer in his eyes had been desire. She must have imagined it. How could he desire her when being civil was an effort for him?

For the first time though, she hadn't sensed the effort. It had been a strangely intimate encounter, filled with a weird, indefinable tension that had only added weight to the heavy wings of the butterflies loose in her belly. It hadn't helped that Amadeo had been practically naked, only a pair of low-slung black shorts covering him. It had taken every fibre of her being to stop herself openly staring at him, hardly daring to allow her eyes to skim over the deeply tanned broad, hard chest and flat brown nipples, or the washboard abdomen where dark hair gathered beneath his navel and thickened as it lowered to the waistband of his shorts. Lord, just to think of him like that was enough to send heat flushing her skin again, and she sank onto the bathroom chair and gripped her hair.

She needed to banish the butterflies and train her body better. She was married to a man who disliked her, despised her family and had admitted he'd never wanted to marry her. To have all these feelings for a man like that was dangerous. Especially when he was her husband.

'Out!'

Amadeo glared at his sister-in-law, who was sitting in the umpire's chair casting judgement on his serve. 'It was not.'

'Yes, it was. Second serve.'

Taking his place back on the line, he lobbed the tennis ball into the air and thwacked it.

'Out. Game to Marcelo.'

'You don't know how to umpire,' Amadeo seethed.

'And you don't know how to serve,' she retorted chirpily.

He resisted the furious urge to hurl his racket at the clay court by the skin of his teeth and readied himself for his brother's serve.

In less than an hour Marcelo had thrashed him three sets to nil, the worst defeat Amadeo had ever suffered.

He blamed Elsbeth. Or tried to. Damn it, she was getting under his skin. He'd spent the morning with the concentration span of a goldfish, official paperwork shoved to one side unread, the image of her, all sexy and dishevelled in those sexy little pyjamas a memory he could not rid himself of. The knowledge that she was doing whatever she was doing in the quarters below his had only added to the infuriating distraction.

Reasonably telling himself that exercise would help his mindset, he'd bribed his brother out of his marital bed for a game of tennis, but instead of the usual outcome where a five match set between them would go down to the wire...

Damn it! He couldn't even blame it on Clara's blatantly biased umpiring. He'd been useless.

Amadeo hated losing, but not as much as he hated losing when it was his own damn fault.

Elsbeth's jitters were regaining strength. The clock was ticking to Duty Night hour. Amadeo would be here in three hours.

She hadn't stopped thinking about him all day, and it was much worse than his usual crowding of her head. A long walk in the castle's woods hadn't helped and nor had a swim in the family's private indoor pool. Thank the Lord they had a week free from engagements coming up. No being stuck in a car with him for hours each day and glued to his side for hours more.

Fed up with pacing her quarters and resisting the urge to go back outside and loiter in the garden—she didn't want to look as if she was hoping for his company—she decided to take another shower before her dinner was brought to her from the castle kitchen, but that didn't help either. Lathering her naked body only brought home how badly her skin craved Amadeo's touch.

Oh, this was madness!

Stomping to her wardrobe, she yanked a green maxi dress off the rack—no point putting on a virgin nightdress this early—and had just slipped it over her head when there was a tap on her bedroom door.

'Come in,' she called.

One of her domestic staff entered. 'His Highness is here.'

Her heart slammed against her ribs. 'Amadeo?'

'Yes.'

'What does he want?'

The maid gave her a look that clearly said it was not her job to question him.

Panic clutched her like a vice and she immediately began to pace.

He was two and a half hours early! She wasn't ready! How could she receive him like this, with her hair all wet and not even any moisturiser on her face? *Look* at her face! It was all red from the heat of the shower!

It was catching sight of the sweet maid waiting patiently at the door that calmed her.

She couldn't help that she wasn't ready for him, and she could at least take consolation that her dress was perfectly modest, if a little more colourful than the clothing she endured on their engagements.

With the butterflies all loose again in her belly and her heart beating like a hummingbird's wings, she found Amadeo in the dayroom looking at the latest picture she'd had hung there.

Her hummingbird heart rose up her throat. She didn't know if she would ever get used to the thrill that shivered through her whenever she set eyes on him, her internal reaction the same whatever his state of dress. That evening, he was wearing his usual attire of shirt, this one a pale blue, and trousers, but had abandoned the tie and jacket he would usually match with it. His thick black hair was tousled and swept to the side, and...

Oh, was it any wonder she couldn't control her pulse around him? Just *look* at the man. She defied any woman not to get all hot and flustered around him.

For the first time in her life, Elsbeth was grateful for her upbringing. At least she'd long ago had to master the art of self-control, and she channelled everything her mother and the other senior ladies of the House of Fernandez had taught her to contain the turbulence and keep it hidden from her face and outer body.

He turned his head, a lazy half-smile forming. 'Nice painting.'

'You like it?' It occurred to her that she'd not had the slightest concern whether he would or would not.

It wasn't just words from him, she realised with a jolt. Amadeo *didn't* try to control her.

'I'm sure I'll like it once you've explained why *you* like it. You can explain while we eat.'

Eat? *We*? Was he saying…?

'I thought I would join you for dinner. Unless you have other plans?' he added with a knowing smile and a raised brow.

Her hummingbird heart expanded and rose so quickly that she almost threw it up.

Elsbeth took a moment to compose herself before attempting to mimic his nonchalance, but as her only plans had been to eat her dinner then probably have another shower to calm her nerves and get herself ready for his appearance in her bedroom, the only word that came out of her mouth was, 'Okay.'

Amadeo nearly laughed out loud, but not with humour. *Okay?* Was that it?

While finally admitting to himself that his wife was sexy had flicked a switch in his brain that had meant Elsbeth was all he could think about, she'd continued with her day, blithe and oblivious. After his disastrous tennis match, he'd sat on his balcony with a cold beer in a futile attempt to calm the explosive feelings shooting through him. Only when an hour had passed did he realise he hadn't wrenched his eyes from the garden and that the reason his stomach lurched at every sound and movement was because he was waiting for her to appear.

And that had been the moment he'd said, *To hell with it*. This thing he had for his wife clearly wasn't going to disappear just because he commanded it. It was time to do something about it. And so he'd strode back inside, giving orders to his butler, and hit the shower. He could share a meal with his wife before sex. That wasn't breaking any rule.

'Is this a new dinner set?' he asked once their first course had been served. It was nothing like the fine china the family ate from, a variant of which had been given to Elsbeth for her personal use. He wondered if she'd ransacked the storeroom.

'It's from the art college we went to a couple of weeks ago.'

His brows drew together. At one of their engagements they had awarded prizes to graduating students at Ceres' top art school. 'This won an award?'

'No, but it was on display.'

'I don't remember seeing it.' As far as he remembered, it had been the usual paintings and ceramics exhibited. He had no recollection of crockery displayed that had comedic cactuses painted on them.

'It's all still a novelty for me,' she said kindly. 'I imagine you've been undertaking engagements for so many years it's become monotonous.'

'Undoubtedly,' he agreed. Their coming engagement-free week would be a welcome break from the monotony. The summer months, August in particular, were always exceptionally busy with engagements, the Ceresian tourist sites organising events to entice visitors, businesses and the charities the Berrutis patroned opening their doors and gardens to the public. Amadeo, his siblings and their parents, highly aware their positions were dependent on the Ceresian public's goodwill, tried to attend as many of the different events as time would allow. Now that September had arrived, the children had returned to school and tourist numbers reduced, the number of engagements would significantly reduce, allowing them to concentrate more on their specific charities and the non-public-facing part of royal life.

He looked closely at his side plate before looking back at Elsbeth, a burn in his loins as he imagined stripping her naked and examining her with the same close scrutiny. *Dio*, that sleeveless dress she was wearing… Like all the other clothes she wore, it showed not the slightest hint of breast or cleavage, only her arms and shoulders exposed, but what little flesh was on display was enough to make his fingers itch to dip into the shallow where her graceful neck met her collarbone.

Swallowing the moisture that had filled his throat, the knowledge they would soon retreat to her bedroom a pulse that throbbed in every part of him, he forced his attention to stay on the conversation in hand. 'Did the student offer it to you?'

'No, I got in touch and asked if it was for sale.' At his raised brow of surprise, Elsbeth felt a pang of anxiety. 'Is that not the done thing? No one said I shouldn't.' She meant Lia, her private secretary, who reported to Amadeo's private secretary. Lia hadn't batted an eyelid when Elsbeth asked about the possibility of buying the set. Lia had sorted it all out for her, including arranging for the talented student to dine with Elsbeth two nights ago so Elsbeth could get an insight into her quirky, creative mind. She didn't want to get Lia into trouble for any of this.

He gave a bemused shake of his head before reaching for his red wine. 'You are not answerable to me. How you spend your money and furnish your quarters and instruct your staff is up to you.'

She blew out the breath she'd been holding. This

was the first purchase she'd ever made for herself with her own taste in mind. She'd taken a leap of faith that Amadeo had meant it when he told her she was an autonomous woman.

She had to admit that buying the dinner set had felt amazing. She'd actually *felt* autonomous. Inviting the student to dine with her had been a new experience too. In the palace, she'd shared her parents' quarters, every minute of her day controlled and decided for her.

What felt even more amazing though, were the thrills racing through her to have Amadeo's full, sole attention. Dangerous though. She knew that. Her head, at least, was clear, and knew not to read anything into the looks from him that made her bones melt. She was projecting her own desire for him onto him. To imagine anything more was to set herself up for a fall. That he was here, spending time with her outside work duties... She mustn't read anything into it. He'd probably been bored.

He speared a tiny tomato. 'The things you have added and replaced to your quarters—the ones I've seen—are all striking and modern. You seem to have...eclectic taste,' he added drily before casting his gaze around the pastel pink dining room. 'Tell me honestly, what do you think of your quarters' furnishings and decorations?'

'Do I have to?'

He grinned. 'You should blame Alessia. I put her in charge. I thought that, as a young woman, she'd have a better idea of what you'd like than I would. Maybe it would have been better to put Clara in charge.'

A tiny giggle escaped from her mouth before she even knew it was coming. 'I would have liked to see the results of that.'

'I wouldn't.'

That did make her laugh, and as her eyes met Amadeo's clear green gaze, a rumble of laughter spilled from his lips and hit her veins like a pulse of energy.

How could she possibly *feel* laughter? It didn't make any sense but it felt as real as if it were a living entity. Everything about him did, from his voice to his slow smiles to the glimmer in his eyes. She didn't just see them, she felt them through the buzz in her veins and the pulses of heat that came close to sucker-punching her.

She'd never imagined a person could be so in tune with another and so alive in their company, but she knew she wouldn't betray herself so long as she concentrated on their conversation. What she mustn't do was think about what would happen once their meal finished, but then telling herself not to do that immediately made her think of it and, as she gazed into his eyes, heat coiled its way from deep in her pelvis and into her veins as a sudden image flashed through her mind of Amadeo following her down the corridor, closing the bedroom door and taking her into his arms...

'Are you okay?'

Her heart thumped and she blinked sharply to pull her brain back into focus but that pulled Amadeo's dreamily handsome face back into focus too and sent her pulses soaring all over again. Grabbing her glass of wine, she smiled brightly. 'Of course.'

'You're sure?' His probing stare bored into her. 'You look flushed.'

'It's a little warm in here, that's all.' She drained her wine in one swallow.

She was lying. Amadeo knew it. The vacuous smile was the giveaway. And the faint tremor in her hand as she put her empty glass on the table and reached for the bottle to top it up. Another improvement, he noted. A month ago, she would have gone thirsty.

He knew she was lying but didn't care, because at the same moment her cheeks had turned the same colour as the tomatoes his lobster had been served with, her wide eyes had held his, darkening and pulsing with the same heat that had plagued him since he'd spotted her from his balcony that morning.

His euphoria lasted seconds, the time it took for her to have a sip of her replenished wine and fix her eyes back on him.

The only thing to read in them was friendliness.

Damn it, whatever he'd seen had gone *again*.

He watched her even more closely over their next course, looking for even a flicker of the desire he now thought he'd seen twice that day. But there was nothing. She answered his questions about what she liked so much about the latest painting she'd hung on the wall with the same animation as when she'd explained her love for the ambassador daughter's painting, but there was no intimacy in her body language. She didn't subconsciously lean forward to be closer to him or play with her hair. When he deliberately rested his hand at the mid-point between them on the table, she didn't inch her fingers closer to it. Her eyes didn't linger on him with anything approaching seduction.

This was driving him crazy! He could be sharing a meal with his sister for all the attraction Elsbeth was displaying towards him.

Had those glimmers of desire been conjured by his overinflated ego being unable to accept that a woman could share his bed and keep her feelings compartmentalised? He could laugh at the irony that his intention at the outset of his marriage to a Fernandez was for the whole thing to be kept compartmentalised. It bruised his ego that Elsbeth was perfectly content with the separation he'd imposed while he was the one suffering.

Draining his wine, he determined that his suffering wouldn't last for long. Whatever else she might feel, he knew Elsbeth had a basic desire for him. It had been there, just like his own initial basic desire, from the night they'd consummated their marriage. That was simple chemistry. Put two willing, sexually compatible people in a bed together and their bodies would do what needed to be done. All he needed to do was draw that basic desire out of her into the flame currently consuming him, because doing what needed to be done wasn't enough any more. He wanted more. Much more. He just needed to gorge himself on her and then he would be satisfied and this strange fever for her would cool back to its original apathy.

CHAPTER EIGHT

THIS WAS HORRENDOUS.

Elsbeth had never in her entire life worked so hard at maintaining outward composure. It wasn't just dining alone with Amadeo causing it, it was all the signals her needy brain was interpreting. His stare didn't leave her face, his green eyes seemed to drink her in with an appreciation she *must* be imagining.

When he put his first mouthful of their divine dessert into his mouth and slowly sucked the dark chocolate off his spoon, the motion was so sensual she came close to spontaneously combusting.

How on earth was she supposed to keep control over herself when he joined her in bed for their Duty later, when just watching him eat was turning her on so much that she could feel arousal over every inch of her skin?

Stop looking at me!

Quickly eating her chocolate torte in the hope he'd follow her lead as if by osmosis, she was ready to scream when she noticed he still had over half his portion left.

Was he doing it deliberately?

She pushed her empty bowl to one side and determined to distract herself from the eroticism of watching

Amadeo eat. 'Now you know I like bold and quirky art and furnishings and English gardens, it is only fair you tell me of the things you like. I assume motor racing is one. I mean as a sport and not just as an investment.'

He pulled the spoon out of his mouth. 'You assume correctly.'

'Cars or bikes?'

'Both, but cars are my preference. I've attended nearly every Grand Prix held on Ceres National Race-track since I was a small child. One of my earliest memories is watching a race with my father and being jealous that he was allowed to present the trophy and champagne to the winner on the podium while I was forced to stay in my seat.'

'I bet it was a good seat.'

The spoon sliced back through the torte that still wasn't disappearing quickly enough for Elsbeth's sanity. 'The best in the stadium. We were so close to the track I was made to wear ear defenders.'

The divine lips closed over the chocolate-filled spoon. All she could do was cross her legs tightly and take another drink of her wine and hope it cooled her down. 'Have you ever driven a racing car?' she asked.

Remembering the school project in which he'd taken the lead in building a go-cart and then made the mistake of telling his parents and being instantly forbidden from driving it, Amadeo shook his head. 'It's considered too dangerous an activity for the heir to the Ceres throne.'

The point had been drilled into him that being heir meant he must not do anything that could endanger him. He'd had to watch from the stands while the go-cart he'd designed and engineered in his sixth form years was driven over the finish line in second place by his second-in-command. If he'd been driving it, he would have won. That wasn't arrogance talking—and Amadeo would be the first to admit he had as much arrogance as testosterone in him—just cold fact. Before he'd been banned, he'd test-driven it around the track. His lap times had averaged four seconds quicker than the winning go-cart.

It had been as humiliating as being excused from playing rugby. He'd had to watch in envy from the sidelines while Marcelo, the younger brother and therefore expendable, had barged his way through opposing players, sending them flying like bowling pins. But he'd swallowed that humiliation, lifted his chin proudly and cheered his brother on, just as he'd cheered on Sébastien, his number two.

'Dominic was guest of honour at a Grand Prix in France a few years ago,' she told him. Amadeo couldn't stop the curl of his lip at this nugget of information but strove not to let his revulsion at Dominic's name show on his face. 'He ignored his advisors and talked one of the teams into letting him drive their test car when the race was over. He crashed it.'

That brought a smile back to his face. 'Was he hurt?'

'Unfortunately, no.'

The deadpan way she'd said it made him laugh.

She giggled, but then the amusement died away and a softness came into her eyes. 'It is difficult, always having to go through life limited in what you can and can't do.'

'It is not something I should complain about,' he said dismissively. 'I have a very privileged life.' The strictures of his life were chains he had the freedom to break. No one would or could have physically stopped him from stepping onto the rugby pitch or getting into the go-cart, or prevented him following his dream into motor-racing. The only person who'd forced him to obey his parents' commands had been himself because he wanted what was best for the monarchy every bit as much as they did.

Amadeo had never been susceptible to emotions that would steer him away from his predestined path. Emotions had never controlled him, not even when he'd been a hormonal adolescent. Duty came first. Always.

It was duty that had led him to this point. Married to a woman he'd despised on sight. But he'd spent the entire meal alternating between fantasising about taking her on this dining table and searching for a sign that his growing desire for her was reciprocated.

Dio, how had he been so blind to how sexy she was? The way she ate was sexy. The tilt of her head. Even her composure was sexy. The thought of breaking that composure down until she lost complete control...

'You're still human,' she said.

If she could read his thoughts she'd discover just how human he was.

Dio, he wanted to lean across the table, gather the material of that sleeveless dress into a fist and pull her to him and kiss her so thoroughly she'd be unable to stand.

'Human, but not like other men.'

'If you were like other men you wouldn't be married to me,' she observed. 'And if I'd been born into a different family I wouldn't be married to you.'

Over a month of marriage and he'd never felt her tongue in his mouth. Never seen her naked.

'Who would you be married to if you were a different man of a different family and hadn't been obliged to make this marriage with me?' she asked, breaking into his erotic thoughts.

His mind went blank. The only face he could conjure was the woman swirling her wine glass opposite him. Her hair had dried during their meal. Ungroomed, it was wavier than he'd thought, cute flyaway curls springing out around her temples.

'I'm talking about your ideal woman if you could have chosen anyone,' she persisted. 'The fantasy of your imagination. Who would she be?'

'I don't have one.'

There was a slight narrowing of her eyes before a wry smile played on her plump lips. 'I think that might be the first lie you've told me.'

He scraped the last of the chocolate torte onto his spoon and hit her with a meaningful stare. 'A woman should only ask a man to reveal his fantasies if she's fully prepared for the answer.'

The stain that covered her cheeks reminded him that, until their marriage, Elsbeth had been a virgin. If she knew of all the erotic thoughts that had played through his head during their meal she would probably run out of the room screaming.

Or would she?

Was that a blush of embarrassment or indicative of something else?

Dio, he needed to strip that composure away and get her to open herself to him.

As tempting as it was to challenge her, ask her if she *really* wanted to know the female fantasy of his imagination, Elsbeth wasn't ready for his answer. She was too inexperienced.

Dabbing his mouth with his napkin, Amadeo rose to his feet. 'Time for bed.'

Elsbeth kept her chin up and her back straight as she walked the corridor to her bedroom. The twenty steps to reach the door took an eternity, as if she were in one of those crazy dreams where your destination was right in front of you but time itself had slowed down so much you couldn't reach it, every step the same step.

But she did reach it. And so did Amadeo. He'd walked silently beside her with an ease to his gait she had to fake to match.

Lord help her, she thought she really might throw up. She hadn't been this nervous on her wedding night. Nowhere near.

It was the deliberate way he'd thrown his napkin down and the decisive way he'd then stood. As if he'd come to a snap decision. Now was the time for sex!

She longed to believe the hunger she'd seen in his eyes throughout their meal had been real and not a figment of her needy imagination. She also longed for it not to be real, because if it was real then it was a false reality. How could a man with such an intense dislike of her and her family possibly want her?

But maybe she hadn't imagined it. Maybe he did want her, maybe he was having one of those days her mother had warned her about when a man's testosterone levels rose and he became amorous. But Amadeo would never want *her*. She would always be the wife he'd been forced to marry, not the wife of his choosing. Not the wife of his fantasies, whoever that woman was. Whoever that woman was, she wasn't a Fernandez.

At their pre-wedding party she'd convinced herself

Amadeo was the husband of her dreams. Those dreams had been ripped apart on their wedding night and she must not allow the craving her body felt for him dupe her into believing the impossible.

He was coming to her room for sex. Normal Duty sex. In an hour he'd be gone and everything would be as it should be.

The door closed.

She couldn't hear the silence through the blood drumming loudly in her head.

Now they were well and truly alone. Her maids wouldn't enter the room with Amadeo in it. They wouldn't even knock on the door to see if she needed them for anything.

They were well and truly alone and she didn't have a clue what she was supposed to do. The clock had turned back a month to their wedding night, when all she could do was wait for Amadeo to make his move.

His smooth voice broke through the whooshing in her head.

'Would you mind if I used your shower?'

Surprised, she shook her head and forced herself to meet his stare. 'Go ahead.'

His eyes glimmered and then, to her complete and utter shock, he brushed his lips against hers and murmured, 'I won't be long.'

Her mouth had barely registered the fleeting pressure and warmth before he nonchalantly strode away.

Feet rooted to the floor, lips tingling, heart pounding, Elsbeth watched him disappear into her bathroom. She pressed her trembling fingers to her mouth.

She was still standing there, feet rooted, fingers on lips, when the shower started up. That snapped her out of her trance, and she hurried to her wardrobe and grabbed the first nightdress on the pile. In seconds she'd yanked the maxi-dress and her knickers to the floor and shrugged the nightdress over her head. As her laundry basket was in the bathroom, she chucked her discarded clothes in the wardrobe, closed the door, then threw herself onto her dressing table seat.

Her naked face reflected back at her. Lord help her, her eyes look fevered, her skin flushed.

Elsbeth took ten deep breaths then reached for her cleanser.

She must stop reading too much into things. So what if Amadeo was using her shower? It was more convenient than using her guest room like he'd done on their wedding night, which she was certain he'd only done so she could get ready in privacy. In that respect, he *had* been a gentleman. It was on her that she'd taken his consideration for her virgin nerves as a sign of romance.

The handle turned on the bathroom door.

The butterflies in her belly expanded their wings and became electrified.

Amadeo appeared with only a small towel around his waist.

One glance and inhalation was enough for her senses to be engulfed.

If the good Lord really had created Man in his own perfect image then that image would be Amadeo standing in the bathroom doorway in a cloud of steam, black hair damp, broad, tanned chest gleaming, as solid an example of the beauty of rampant masculinity as she'd ever witnessed.

How many times could a woman come close to spontaneously combusting in one evening?

Glimmering gaze on her, he padded to the bed. 'I hope you don't mind but I used the spare toothbrush in your vanity unit.'

She shook her head and rose to her feet. 'I don't mind at all. Excuse me a moment.'

Somehow she managed to force her feet to walk, not run, to the bathroom.

Amadeo watched Elsbeth slip gracefully into the bathroom with narrowed eyes. Did he detect signs of fluster in her speech and movements? Or was he back in the realm of wishful thinking?

Sliding under the bedsheets, he propped himself against the velvet headboard.

There was a weight to his heartbeats he'd never felt before. He could only assume anticipation was the cause. It had been many years since excitement had reached its tentacles all the way to his core. His long-ago teenage years to be precise.

His decision to take a shower had been impulsively made when the bedroom door had closed behind them. Elsbeth wasn't used to preparing for bed with him around and, much as he'd fantasised about stripping her naked, he needed to keep his ardour in check if he wasn't going to frighten her.

He thought back to their first night together and how clinically satisfying it had been. Satisfying was no longer enough for him. He wanted fulfilling, and he wanted Elsbeth to be fulfilled and not merely satisfied too.

If he knew his wife, she'd go along with whatever he wanted. Yes, she'd go along with it but whether she'd take any enjoyment from it was unknown. He knew her, knew she had it in her head that her role in their marriage was to please him—probably the basest of all male fantasies but the most stomach-turning when applied to real life—but he couldn't read her.

How infuriating that the first woman he'd been unable to read properly in his thirty-two years on this earth should be his wife.

There was movement behind the bathroom door.

Amadeo took a deep breath, stretched his neck and rolled his shoulders.

Elsbeth took one last deep breath for luck and opened the bathroom door.

Her heart slammed against her ribs to see Amadeo in bed waiting for her, a complete reversal of all the other nights they'd shared together. A half smile played on his sensual lips and he lifted the bedsheets off her side of the bed in invitation.

The short walk from bathroom to bed was the most excruciating taken in her life. With Amadeo's gaze openly on her, she didn't think she'd ever been so self-conscious, so aware of her naked breasts moving beneath the silk of the white nightdress.

She climbed onto the bed with all the elegance she could muster. No longer feeling she needed permission to turn her own bedside light off, she pressed the switch so only the dim light on Amadeo's side illuminated the room, lowered herself under the sheets and held her breath.

Now Amadeo would turn his light off. He would climb on top of her. He would kiss her. His hands would roam her body. His fingers would slide up her nightdress, discover she was ready for him—her body was her brain's ultimate betrayer—and then he would take her. He would hold his climax off until she'd had her climax—no one could say he wasn't a gentleman—and then, when they were both done, he would roll off her. If she was lucky, he would leave immediately and let her get on with self-soothing the gap their tender-less coupling left in her heart with his still-warm pillow.

She knew she was being unfair and making it seem as if they were two robots following a script when, during the act itself, she felt so much, but she needed to be unfair otherwise her growing need for more would grow *too* big and the rejection that underlay everything would bring her spiralling down.

Her brain accepted that Amadeo would never be her true lover. Their couplings had the sole purpose of making a baby. Now she just needed her body to accept it and stop responding to things that weren't there.

Amadeo stretched himself out next to her and settled onto his side. Propping himself on an elbow, he gazed down at Elsbeth's face. She was just so incredibly beautiful, from her big baby blue eyes to the snub nose and those lips that felt like marshmallow against his. He pressed a finger lightly to the centre of those lips and was rewarded with a widening of her eyes.

Gently, slowly, he trailed his finger to the edge of her mouth and then brushed it against the soft skin of her cheek. Not taking his eyes from hers, he brushed his fingers down the graceful neck to the shallow at the base he'd fantasised about touching earlier.

'Why do you wear these nightdresses for me when you wear shorts and T-shirt for yourself?' he murmured, now fingering the neck of her virgin nightdress, which skimmed across her collarbone.

Her eyes had darkened. Her breaths, when they came, were faint hitches he had to strain to hear. Her lips parted then pressed back together before she whispered, 'To please you.'

He skimmed over the swell of her breasts and encircled a tip that had hardened and strained against the white silk. 'Why would you think dressing like a sacrificial virgin would please me?'

She swallowed. 'My mother.'

His finger drifted over her flat belly, feeling almost imperceptible quivers. 'She told you that?'

She nodded. Colour flared across her delectable cheekbones.

Across her abdomen he drew to her hip, and down her thigh. 'What else did she tell you?'

Her always quiet voice was barely audible. 'Many things.'

He clasped the silk of her nightdress. 'Things to do with pleasing me?'

Another nod.

He gathered more material, sliding it up her legs to the top of her thighs, stopping short of exposing her to him. 'Do you want to know what would please me now?'

A nod so small it was hardly there.

'What would please me most is if you took it off.'

CHAPTER NINE

ELSBETH'S HEART STOPPED beating at the impact of Amadeo's lazily delivered words.

Eyes hooded, he lowered his face closer to hers and her heart kick-started back to life, the beats so loud and fast they were nothing but a deafening burr.

'Will you let me see you the way I let you see me?' he whispered before dipping his face lower still so the tip of his nose brushed against her cheek and his warm breath melted into her skin. Her nightdress was now bunched at the top of her hips.

She was helpless to stop the quiver that rippled through the whole of her body, and groped desperately for coherent thought.

The palm of his hand slipped under the ruched silk and flattened against her back. Slowly he eased them both upright until Elsbeth sat facing him, trembling, the whooshing in her head a hot roar.

Fingers dragged through her hair, hooded green eyes seeming to drink her in. He leaned in closer. Her breath caught in her throat and her eyes closed as his lips pressed against hers, as fleeting as the touch of a feather, his hands slowly moving down from the back of her head to her shoulders and down her sides to where her nightdress was gathered.

Pulling his face back, his eyes locked back onto hers and then, bit by bit, her nightdress was pushed over her belly and breasts. She lifted her arms. Silk fleetingly caressed her neck and face and then, for the first time in her life, Elsbeth was naked in front of a man, shaking, her heart beating so hard he must be able to see its ripples through her chest.

A finger gently lifted her chin.

She'd never been so scared of what she would find in Amadeo's gaze, terrified too of what she was feeling, how deeply her desire for him ran, trapped in every cell in every part of her body.

She forced herself to look at him. The dim glow of the bedside light cast his face in the shadows and plains that turned his features from mere drop-dead handsome to heart-breaking, and Elsbeth fought even harder to keep the essence of herself intact and not fall into the heady promise of the lie in his eyes, however desperately she wanted to believe the hunger she was reading in them was for her.

This was what her mother had warned her about, the day when a man's ardour was stronger than normal.

When it was over, she would still sleep alone.

He palmed the flat of her back again and, with the same care as when he'd pulled her upright, lowered her back down so her head rested on her pillow. Then, with infinite care, he laid himself between her legs, elbows resting either side of her head, cocooning her with his body and the sheets he'd pulled up to his shoulders.

It was the romantic scene she'd longed for on her wedding night.

The weight of his erection brushed against the top of her thigh. The tips of her sensitised breasts brushed against his chest. Heaven help her, she had to make fists with her hands to temper herself against the craving to crush herself tightly against him.

For the longest time he said nothing, just gazed at her, his fingers smoothing her forehead. Desire was there, but something else too, as if he was trying to bore into the hidden caverns of her brain. It was a look that made her heart want to punch out of her chest and fly into his.

Don't fall, she begged herself, even as her body trembled at the tenderness of his touch. *It isn't real. Don't fall*.

His mouth closed in on hers. A feather-light kiss. Light, but with the power to send more thrills racing through her than all the other kisses they'd shared.

Another feather-light brush of his mouth.

Don't. Fall.

His lips fused against hers in the way they'd only ever done in her dreams, hard, demanding and yet so very sensual and, at the first flicker of his tongue against hers, the stray thoughts Elsbeth had managed to recapture and all the frantic warnings in her head flew away as heat and electricity crackled through to her core.

With a sigh of pleasure, she cupped the nape of his neck and melted into his mouth.

Amadeo shuddered at the scorch Elsbeth's light touch branded on his neck, and deepened the fusion of their mouths. Never had mere *kissing* been so potent, the clash of lips and tongues so erotic. What had he imagined? That to delve into a Fernandez's mouth would poison him? If there was poison it was soaked in nectar, an addictively sweet toxin that fed into his bloodstream and fed the hunger for her that had taken on a life of its own.

Her skin was laced with the same sweetness and, *Dio*, it was so soft, softer than brushed velvet, and he trailed his mouth and tongue down her brushed velvet neck into the shallow at the base that had so caught his fantasies.

He shifted lower, using his hands and mouth to explore her body. Even his wildest imagination couldn't have adequately conjured its beauty. Above her left breast sat a small mole he'd never seen before...he'd hardly seen *any* of her before. He kissed it before kissing lower still, over the swell of breasts so much fuller than he'd appreciated. Reverently, he took a hardened peak into his mouth, an electric thrill racing through him to finally hear the soft mew of Elsbeth's pleasure.

Forcing himself to keep his ardour in check, he lavished attention on each breast in turn, revelling in the subtle responses of her passion. It was all there, in the arch of her back, the delicate hitching of her breath, the familiar clenching of the bedsheets and the grazing of her right foot against the mattress.

More than that, he could *feel* it, the fevered heat consuming her, could feel it as deeply as the burn consuming him.

Flames were licking Elsbeth's skin. Every touch of Amadeo's hands, every brush of his body against hers, every lick of his tongue, every mark of his mouth burned through her flesh, melting her bones until she was nothing but a mass of pulsating need.

Who knew a tongue trailed in a circle around her

navel could be so arousing, could send the flame burning even deeper? Nothing could have prepared her for such pleasure. She could lie there for ever, putty in the hands of this most hedonistic assault to her senses.

Putty in Amadeo's hands.

Those same hands were now holding her hips, his lips trailing down her abdomen. So lost in the sensations was she that when his mouth drew down her pubis she didn't realise what he intended until his tongue brushed against the place where her pleasure was always the most intense and sent a deep thrill rushing through her.

Reflexively, her heart thundering at both the unexpected action and the charge that rocketed through her, she pressed her thighs together.

Instinct told her this was a line of intimacy it was far too dangerous to cross.

But how could she say no to him? How many times had her mother told her that she must never say no to him about anything, that in the bedroom she was to take whatever he gave and give whatever he demanded?

She only realised Amadeo had stilled when his fingers suddenly bit deeper into the flesh of her hips and he kissed his way back up.

Had he guessed that she didn't want…?

He took a breast back into his mouth and her thoughts fragmented into dust.

One taste of heaven, that was all she'd allowed before clamping her thighs together. Just one little taste of a musky heat that had to be heaven-sent. The judder of her body at the first touch of his tongue… *Dio*, Amadeo had never known a reaction like it.

But she wasn't ready for it. As much as he longed to bury his face in her bliss and bring her to orgasm with his tongue, the freezing of her body told him it was too soon for her.

That was okay. He had the rest of his life to open her mind and her body to the hedonistic pleasures of the flesh.

Covering her with the entirety of his body, thrilling at the sensation of her naked breasts crushed against his chest, he gazed down, drinking in the shallowness of breaths through the parted lips swollen from his kisses, the flushed cheeks...

And then her eyes opened and locked onto his. What he found in them made the arousal he'd been containing through sheer will in his pursuit of her pleasure throb painfully.

It was a mirror of his own craving.

Dio, she was beautiful.

He kissed her. She moaned softly into his mouth and then he felt it, the light, almost tentative drag of her fingers over his back.

Breaking the kiss, the tip of his nose pressed to hers, Amadeo guided his arousal to the damp heat of her opening and almost lost his mind when she raised her thighs and pressed against him in, what was for his wife, a wanton invitation. In one long, slow thrust, he buried himself deep inside her, groaning loudly at the sheer heavenliness of it.

So this is what making love feels like...

Elsbeth cut the thought off. Whatever was happening to her, whatever ecstasy had been elicited under Amadeo's tender sensual assault, she must not fall into the trap of believing it had anything to do with love.

This, here, now, the *feelings*...

It was how she'd dreamed their wedding night would be.

Too late for that.

If this had been her wedding night she would have fallen in love with him.

Just hold onto yourself. Don't fall.

But it was so hard to hold on when their bodies were fused so tightly, Amadeo's muscles bunching beneath her touch, the taste of his mouth playing on her tongue and his groans of pleasure sinking into her ears.

All of her senses were filled with him.

She was slipping away from herself. The pleasure was just too intense to hold on. Wrapping her legs around his waist to deepen the penetration, she closed her eyes and submitted herself entirely to the heaven only Amadeo could take her to.

A strong hand clasped her bottom, lifting her only a touch, but a touch enough to tip her over the edge into ecstasy. Raising her head, she pressed her mouth into his neck and tightened her arms around him, breathing in the musky scent of his skin and tasting the salt on her tongue as the winding coil inside her shattered in an explosion of flickering light.

For the first time in his life, Amadeo didn't want to let go. This was just too good. Too…

Dio, he'd never felt anything like it. Ecstasy in every thrust. Ecstasy in every touch of her hand on his skin, in every kiss.

He didn't want to let go but he couldn't hold on any longer, not with Elsbeth's mouth so hot against his neck and the tight throbs of her climax dragging him so deep inside her he didn't know where she began and he ended, and the cries of her own ecstasy echoed in his ears.

Thrusting into her one last time, Amadeo submitted himself to the euphoria.

Elsbeth tried to breathe. Tried to gather her fragmented thoughts. Tried to stop her romantic heart attaching itself to the heart beating rapidly through the chest pressed so tightly against hers that they could be one.

How long had they lain there, her cheek in his neck, his ragged breaths hot in her hair?

She didn't know if she wanted to laugh or cry.

It had been beautiful. Everything she'd wished for on their wedding night.

For the first time in her life she'd felt cherished, but it was all a lie and at any moment Amadeo would roll off her, swing his legs off her bed and leave.

Even if she felt that she could ask him to stay, she wouldn't. She wouldn't be able to endure the rejection that would surely come.

And then it happened. His weight shifted off her and he rolled onto his back. Her heart shrivelled, opening up the hollow that always formed in the aftermath of their couplings.

Oh, why had he made it so *good*? Why had he acted as if he was making love to her when they both knew he despised her?

She tugged the sheets up over her breasts and folded her hands across her belly. It took a huge effort but she managed to drag air into her lungs, somehow breathing in a huge dose of Amadeo's scent and the scent of their lovemaking with it.

Stop thinking of it like that. It was only sex. Tender, beautiful sex.

Hot tears stabbed the back of her eyes and she squeezed them shut to stop them leaking. He'd be gone soon.

Amadeo, still trying to catch his breath, turned his face to Elsbeth. As usual, she was lying there placidly. It never ceased to amaze him how well she played dead after they came together. It was as if she switched a part of her brain off and disengaged with him entirely. Other than her shock on their first night when he'd told her about their living arrangements—and only then because she hadn't been expecting it—she gave the distinct impression that, his duty to procreation done, his presence in her bed was no longer required. Of course, she would never say it in words. Not the woman who'd been trained from birth to believe a wife's duty was to obey her husband. She never objected to anything.

How much of that playing dead was a mask, like the vacuous wind-up doll she'd portrayed? And if it was a mask, what was it hiding?

He couldn't understand why it plagued him to know what went on in the privacy of Elsbeth's head. It wasn't as if he actually *cared* what went on in there… Okay, he admitted, he did care, but only so far as he wanted to be satisfied that she wasn't unhappy. Any man would be the same. As his father had often said, an unhappy wife led to an unhappy life. He doubted he would ever be happy to have married her but, as he constantly had to remind himself, that wasn't her fault. Elsbeth's life before their marriage had been less than happy. He didn't want her misery within their marriage on his conscience, and that was the most infuriating thing because he couldn't read her mind or expressions to know when, if ever, she was unhappy about something. She was just too good at masking her true feelings.

Strictly, by the agreed rules and precedents already set between them, he should return to his quarters now, but there was something he needed to say before he could leave.

'What you said earlier about the nightdress and your mother... Elsbeth, I don't know what advice she gave you before we married but I need you to believe—and I cannot stress this enough—that I am not your overlord. Your purpose in life is *not* to please me. I understand life here is different to what you're used to and that it's taking time for you to adjust, but I meant it when I said you don't owe me anything more than the obligations we have to each other and the monarchy. We both have a duty to present ourselves to the world in a manner that is fitting as members of the Berruti royal family...'

Something his adrenaline-fuelled, impetuous brother had spectacularly failed in when being photographed dangling from a helicopter tied to his rescued damsel in distress, his now-wife, Clara.

'...and behave in a manner that doesn't bring disgrace to our country, but what we do and how we behave within the privacy of the castle walls is down to personal choice, and that counts for both of us.'

That all said, Amadeo shifted over to the side of the bed and sat up. He was about to climb off the bed when Elsbeth quietly said, 'Amadeo, until I came here I was never given a choice. Not about anything. I was raised in a palace where men have complete control over women, and my father had complete control over me. The only time my permission was needed for something affecting me was for our marriage, and that was only because Gabriel insisted on it.'

Gabriel, Alessia's husband, the man who'd been

tasked with negotiating the marriage. He'd refused to negotiate without Elsbeth's explicit consent.

'I didn't know how badly I wanted to leave until the opportunity came,' she added after a short silence. 'I would have agreed to marry anyone to get out of that palace. It's awful there, and things have got so much worse since Dominic took the throne. He's a bully and a narcissist. Everything has to revolve around him, and because he's cruel, others follow his lead and now there's a culture of cruelty and humiliation. He gets as much of a kick out of seeing others being cruel as he does being cruel himself.'

Amadeo, absorbing all this with a violent churning in his guts, twisted round to face her. 'How was he cruel to you?'

She shook her head. 'He wasn't. Not in the way he is to others. Dominic likes me. Or, should I say, he likes my silence and compliance. My father is his uncle and his closest advisor and confidant. I'm like a pet to him.' She gave a short bitter laugh. 'A cowering pet terrified it's going to be the next creature to get a kick. He chose me as your wife because, of all the eligible women in the House of Fernandez, I was considered the most meek and pliable and I was a virgin. Believe me, with my father, I never had the freedom to be anything *but* a virgin. In Dominic's eyes—and my father's—women are either whores or Madonnas, and all men want to marry the Madonnas. He assumed that's what you would want too, and assumed you would be grateful to be given such a highly prized asset.'

He felt sick.

But hadn't he known much of this? Hadn't Elsbeth's

virginity been dangled before him with the same smug aplomb as if he'd been offered a mythical unicorn?

He'd known it but it hadn't struck him properly until now, with Elsbeth spelling it out to him.

Her chest rose and she breathed out slowly. 'My first memory is of my father slapping my mother's face for answering him back. I remember watching Dominic walk past Catalina and pinch her for fun. He was always hurting her. I dread to think what she would have suffered if she'd still lived in Monte Cleure when he took the throne.' The silk sheets twisted around her body rustled gently as she turned onto her side so that her whole body faced him. There was an intensity to her stare he'd never seen before. 'Please understand, the men have *all* the power there, and I always knew that, to survive, I needed to keep my mouth shut and obey. I've never been brave like my mother. She's strong and she's always protected me, and while I know now that many of the things she taught me are wrong for our marriage, she taught me them for the best of reasons. She had no reason to believe you would be any different to the royal men of Monte Cleure and I hardly dared hope for more either.'

Dio, his heart had expanded so much it was a struggle to open his throat to speak. 'But you do believe it now?' he whispered hoarsely. 'That I'm nothing like them?'

After the longest of pauses in which his whole body became suspended in dread, she nodded. 'I do believe it. It's just that old habits die hard, and I've spent twenty-four years thinking twice about every word I say and everything I do.'

Amadeo's relief was indescribable.

He wasn't perfect by any means. He could be impatient. Arrogant. Manipulative. Demanding. He was too aware of his royal dignity and became aggravated when not given proper deference. He was all those things and more, but he wasn't a bully. For sure, he'd demanded his brother and sister marry for the sake of the monarchy, but their marriages had both been a success so he'd been right to demand it of them, and he'd also done the same thing himself in marrying Elsbeth. Amadeo would never ask anyone to do anything he wasn't prepared to do himself. He wasn't a bully and he wasn't corrupt and he would sooner be burned at the stake than lay a finger on a woman.

She gave another laugh, this time with a more genuine, if melancholic, ring to it. 'If Dominic or my father knew the attributes they prized the most in me were the things you hate most about me...' She laughed again, shaking her head.

'I don't hate you.' He didn't know what he felt for her, but hate it was not. Reaching for her hand, he brought it to his lips. 'Always remember, you have no obligation or duty to please or obey me. In the privacy of the castle walls, live how you want to live, dress how you want to dress, be free to say no to me and disagree with me and voice opinions and share your thoughts without fear of the consequences. I might not always like what you have to say but you might not always like what I have to say, and you shouldn't be afraid to say so.'

Elsbeth was helpless to stop her interlocked fingers from squeezing his or from searching the green eyes swirling with an emotion that terrified her, knowing if she stared long enough she could trick herself into believing that he cared. For her. When she knew it was impossible.

He wasn't heartless, but she already knew that. The truth about her life in the House of Fernandez had disturbed him, she'd seen it in the contortions of his face. His disgust at the situation there would be the same whoever had told it to him.

It came to her that she'd only confided the full truth because she trusted he wouldn't use it as a weapon to subjugate her, a threat like the bogeyman: *If you don't behave, you'll be sent back to Monte Cleure.*

What she couldn't do though, was trust her heart to him. Not when his heart was frozen to her.

'Thank you,' she whispered.

He shook his head, leaning in closer and matching the whisper of her voice. 'You have nothing to thank me for.'

Don't do this, she silently begged. *If you're going to leave then leave. Don't drag it out. Don't make it even harder for me.*

But her lips tingled at the whisper of his breath on them. The sigh of her heart had expanded into the hollow gap and, with it, lit the switch inside her so flickers of awareness zipped through cells still luxuriating in the sensations from just a short while ago, and deep inside her pelvis the flame reignited.

Hunger flared in the eyes gazing so intently into hers.

He was going to kiss her again.

Elsbeth swallowed the moisture that had filled her mouth. As badly as she ached to be gathered back into Amadeo's arms and experience all those glorious sensations again, at that moment her heart was too full and vulnerable to dare risk opening it even more to him. She needed to assert the freedom he'd just spelled out belonged to her and ask him to leave.

But then came the gentle fusion of his lips with hers and any thought of making him leave her bed flew away as she surrendered to the magic of his touch.

CHAPTER TEN

AMADEO WOKE WITH a start.

From the faint light seeping into the room, it was the cusp of morning.

He didn't remember turning his bedside light out.

Technically, it wasn't his bedside light. It was Elsbeth's. Because this was Elsbeth's bed in Elsbeth's room in Elsbeth's quarters. It was her warm body lying so close, her hip his hand was splayed on. Her rhythmic breathing the only sound in his ears.

There was a tightening in his guts as strong as the arousal in his loins. He didn't know where the tightening came from.

Making love to her a second time…

That hadn't been in the plan but he'd been caught in the moment.

The tightness eased as rationality returned. The rules set out before they had married and agreed with Elsbeth on their wedding night, had been separate quarters and separate personal lives. The other part of the agreement, spoken of and agreed privately between the two of them, had been to share her bed each Saturday until a child was conceived. Only by his own precedent had this been interpreted as him leaving straight after sex. Until the sun rose, it could still be interpreted as Saturday night rather than Sunday morning. But not for much longer.

It was time to return to his quarters.

Dio, extricating his body from hers felt like the hardest task in the world.

Careful not to wake her, he got out of bed and pulled his trousers on. Gathering the rest of his clothing, he took one last look at her before leaving the room.

Only when she heard the sound of the bedroom door closing did Elsbeth dare open her tear-filled eyes.

Oh, you silly fool. Why didn't you tell him to leave when you had the chance?

Swallowing back more tears, she reached for Amadeo's pillow and held it tightly to her chest.

Sébastien was explaining how his racing team had managed to achieve an average pitstop of two seconds. Usually, there was nothing Amadeo loved more than listening to his old school friend wax lyrical about his team's feats of engineering. As the motor racing calendar was on a two-week break, Sébastien's team were back in Ceres, testing and working hard to bring about all the incremental advantages that were the difference between first place and second.

Motor racing was a rules-based sport. Teams who flouted those rules could expect sanctions, and rightly so. Rules were the structure within which Amadeo lived his life. Without rules, systems were dismantled and anarchy given space to flourish. He'd obeyed the rule of not endangering his own life when he'd stepped aside all those years ago and let his number two take the wheel of the go-cart he'd taken the lead on engineering. Sébastien had been his number two.

It was possible he would have resented his friend if he'd used that race and the go-cart they'd created as a springboard to becoming a racing driver, but Sébastien was as clear-minded as Amadeo. He didn't have the talent to make it as a racing driver but he had the drive to create his own team. Amadeo had used some of his personal fortune to back that team and it had given him great satisfaction over the years watching them climb the ladder of success. Through his old friend and the team Sébastien commanded, Amadeo could live vicariously the path he would have taken had he not been born a prince.

Today though, Sébastien's words floated around him. They didn't penetrate. Amadeo's head was too full of the woman he'd left sleeping early that morning to allow anything else in. His veins were too full too, a lingering thrum of sensation a physical reminder of what they'd shared.

But what had they shared? he mockingly asked himself. Great sex? That was no reason to turn into a zombie. It had to be the things she'd confided in him about her life in Monte Cleure because, along with the constant image of Elsbeth's beautiful face in the throes of ecstasy, came fantasies of smacking his fist over and over into the King of Monte Cleure's nose.

It was just as well his family were only constitutional monarchs with no real power over their island, he reflected grimly. If power still resided in their hands, he would be tempted to call up the Ceres special forces and plot a way to topple the bastard.

King Dominic Fernandez was a monster with unlimited power.

But hadn't he already known the man was a monster, and known it long before he'd kidnapped Clara?

He'd known it but he'd been detached from it. The stories about Dominic had only been words. His loathing of the man had come from his own interactions with him over the years.

He didn't feel detached from it any more. Now his loathing felt personal.

He'd never had violent fantasies before. They were as disturbing as the frequent urge to cut his day short and return straight to Elsbeth's bed.

Monday morning, and Amadeo stood at the stone balustrade of his balcony, coffee in hand, watching the sun rise.

The hairs on the nape of his neck rose before she appeared in the garden. Throat closing, he straightened, drinking in the sleep-tousled blonde hair and the short silk emerald robe covering whatever form of nightwear she had on. His loins thickened as he considered the possibility she wore nothing beneath it...

Did she sense his stare or had she come outside hopeful of seeing him? Whatever her reason, she'd barely trodden ten steps barefoot over the lawn when she turned her head.

Dio, the thump of his heart as their eyes clashed.

Was this why he'd come out onto his balcony so early? Was this why he'd woken even earlier than was usual for him? Had a part of him hoped to see her?

This was getting ridiculous. He hadn't thought making love on Saturday would rid him of the desire he felt for her but had assumed it would go some way to assuaging it. It wasn't supposed to have made things worse. He was acting like a lust-fuelled adolescent.

That lightened his mood. When he'd been a lust-fuelled adolescent, it hadn't taken long for his infatuations to pass, the objects of his desire nice and shiny for weeks at a time then the lustre fading until nothing was left and it was time to move on. He'd never allowed those temporary infatuations to control him even at their height.

His current infatuation with Elsbeth would fade too. It certainly wouldn't last. He supposed a certain limited affection that came from being so closely wound in other's orbit was to be expected. Sleeping in her bed hadn't broken any rules, only set a new precedent. His obsession was certainly no reason to break the rules of their marriage and invite her up to his quarters and into his bed on a non-agreed day. That only had the potential to complicate a situation that didn't need complicating.

Settled in his mind, he raised a hand in greeting.

Too much time passed before she raised a hand in return. More time stretched before he watched her slim shoulders rise and then she started walking back towards him.

Despite everything he'd just settled in his mind, his breath caught in his lungs. The closer she walked to the iron steps that would lead her up to his balcony, the harder his heart thumped.

But she didn't reach the steps. Instead, she disappeared from view into her own quarters.

It wasn't her mother's voice sternly telling her that a princess never made the first move—she knew it was futile to expect the shackles of her past to be thrown off overnight—that had stopped Elsbeth climbing the iron steps to Amadeo, and nor was it the agreement, made at Amadeo's instigation, of them leading separate lives within the castle walls. It wasn't even that after well over a month of marriage he hadn't invited her into his quarters that stopped her. It was the explosion in her heart at the mere sight of him.

The intensity of that explosion terrified her. These were feelings that had no place in their marriage and she needed to get a handle on them quickly. One night of beautiful sex, confidences and falling asleep in each other's arms did not change the fundamentals of her marriage. Just because Amadeo wanted her did not mean he wanted more from her. He'd proven that by creeping out of her bed without a whisper of goodbye and then spending Sunday at the racetrack. He hadn't even mentioned he was going, which only proved the fundamentals of their marriage hadn't changed.

It shouldn't hurt. But it did. Badly. And it was all her own fault for not asking him to leave her quarters when she'd known how vulnerable her heart had been to him at that time.

The meeting in the Queen's private offices that Wednesday to discuss the royal itinerary was the first family meeting Elsbeth had been invited to.

Her nerves at what, for her, was a momentous occasion, were quickly soothed by her mother-in-law's gracious welcome and her father-in-law's affectionate embrace. She'd seen little of them since the wedding and they were both keen to satisfy themselves that she'd settled into their family and that there was nothing she was unhappy about. Reassurances given, an invitation for a family meal the following week accepted, Elsbeth took her seat next to Amadeo at the huge oval table, and arranged her face. She could only pray he hadn't sensed the huge thump of her heart at the sight of him, and pray he couldn't hear its staccato beat, the tempo rising even higher as the cologne she so adored seeped into the air around her.

They led separate lives. They would always lead separate lives. Her brain accepted that. The sooner her heart accepted it too, the less vulnerable it would be to him.

'How have you enjoyed our break from engagements?' he asked while the others sat themselves down.

'Very well, thank you.' That was good. Her voice sounded normal. To her own ears, at least. She'd spent much of Monday with the castle's head gardener, brainstorming how to transform her and Amadeo's private garden into something resembling an English country garden, and then spent Tuesday reading books on the history of the castle. She'd found it fascinating. Unlike the palace she'd grown up in, which had been built entirely in King Albert's reign centuries before and then considered a masterpiece needing nothing more to be added, the Berrutis predominantly Gothic castle had evolved over a millennia, but especially in the centuries of the early medieval period, by a succession of monarchs determined to put their own individual stamp on it. She'd wondered briefly if Amadeo would want to put his own stamp on it too when he became King but then, because she was absolutely determined not to think about him on her few precious days without his company, wondered no more.

'And you?' she added. 'Did you enjoy your day at the racetrack on Sunday?'

If he was surprised that she knew where he'd spent the day, he didn't show it. As she was coming to learn, nothing stayed secret for long in the castle. Gossip seeped through the draughts in the old stone walls or, in her case, through the mouths of her staff.

'I did, thank you.'

Queen Isabella's private secretary, who outranked all the other private secretaries, called for order, and the meeting got underway.

Since when had he come to like Elsbeth's perfume? Amadeo wondered. From the moment she'd taken the seat beside his, her delicate scent had swirled gently around him, and he was having to stop himself from greedily inhaling it deep into his lungs. To make things worse, he was wholly aware of the closeness of her body next to his too, and couldn't seem to stop his stare dipping down to the pretty hands folded neatly on the table and willing them to place themselves onto his lap.

It was one thing having lazy fantasies about her when they were being transported to and from engagements, quite another to fight flickers of arousal in the middle of an important family conference. How many times had he reproached his siblings for not contributing enough to these meetings over the years? And how often in the short time Clara had been in their lives had he bitten back words of censure over her tendency to get visibly bored and fidget her way through them?

Leaning his body away from Elsbeth, he gritted his teeth and forced his concentration onto the topic of planned state visits for the following year, and joined in the arguments with his family over who should and should not take each one. Unsurprisingly, everyone thought they were best placed to do the week-long visit to the Caribbean island of Bandhi, which would be celebrating its two-hundredth year of independence. Marcelo and Alessia, having worn their parents down, were on the verge of tossing a coin for it when his eyes, unbidden by his brain, glanced at Elsbeth.

His heart throbbed at the concentration on her face. How silently she sat there, trying her best to keep up with their language. They weren't making it easy for her, he acknowledged, not with them all talking over each other, all efforts to speak slowly so the non-native speakers could keep up forgotten.

If anyone deserved a week in the Caribbean, it was Elsbeth. That thought was all he needed to pull rank and nab that state visit for himself.

Ignoring his brother and sister's outraged faces, he quickly filled Elsbeth in and was gratified at the spark of excitement that flashed in her eyes before she turned her attention back to concentrating on the next argument. This one involved who didn't want to travel to a country renowned for its year-round atrocious weather.

Another hour passed before the meeting wound up but, before they could rise from their seats, his mother removed her reading glasses and looked at her three children in turn. 'There is one more item of business to discuss before everyone leaves. The King of Monte Cleure has announced his plans to attend next month's Grand Prix—'

'Here in Ceres?' Amadeo interrupted sharply.

Her eyes met his with equal sharpness. 'Yes. As

we're all aware, protocol dictates that we should offer him our hospitality.'

Both Amadeo and Marcelo snapped, 'No,' in unison.

Their mother was tiny, barely touching four foot ten, a good foot and a half shorter than her two sons, but what she lacked in height, she made up for in stature. Fixing them both with a glare, she said, 'I appreciate that feelings concerning that man run high but need I remind you both that you each married to prevent a trade and diplomatic war between our two countries? Failure to give due hospitality could be seen as provocation by him and then we could find ourselves back to where we were and our country and monarchy threatened.'

'I don't want that animal within a hundred kilometres of Clara,' Marcelo said flatly. 'We hosted him for Amadeo's wedding and that ridiculous pre-wedding party. We've done our bit.'

With steel in her voice, their mother said, 'I've already had my team invite him to stay here at the castle. He will fly in on the Sunday morning and go directly to the racetrack. After the race he will return to the castle as our honoured guest and attend the banquet we're hosting, and then fly home the next morning. We will only have to suffer his presence for the one night.' Then she looked directly at Clara, who Marcelo had been furiously translating for, and said in slow English, 'I am sorry. I know it is hard for you.'

Clara shrugged. 'I understand.' Then she grinned. 'I'll try not to accidentally stab him.'

'I'll try not to stab him too,' Alessia chirped up.

'What about you, Elsbeth?' Clara asked with a cackle of laughter. 'Are you going to try not to stab him too?'

As soon as the meeting was over, Elsbeth's arm was taken by Amadeo and she was steered into an empty office.

He looked frazzled. As impeccably groomed as he always was, there was a wildness in his eyes she'd never seen before. 'Did you understand all that?'

'About Dominic coming to Ceres?' she guessed.

He nodded tersely. 'The plan is for him to come for the Grand Prix and then attend the banquet we host each year for the race teams and their families, and stay for the night as our honoured guest.'

He practically spat the last three words out.

'I thought that's what you were all saying.'

'Say the word and I'll put a stop to it.'

Touched, she smiled. 'You don't have to do that. Not for me. If Clara can cope with him being here then I can too. After all, isn't harmony between our two nations the whole reason you married me?' She needed to say that more to remind herself than him because the way he was looking at her...

There was something about the wildness of his stare that made her think of dragon-slaying heroes of old.

It was on the tip of Amadeo's tongue to say it was the whole reason she'd married him too, but his conscience stepped in and stopped him. His conscience knew it would be a lie.

Elsbeth had married him because she'd had no choice. Not any real choice. Was it any wonder she dressed for bed as a sacrificial virgin when, in essence, that was exactly what she'd been? How free a choice was it to marry someone when the alternative was more subjugation?

Dominic and her father had sold her to the highest bidder. And that bidder had been him.

It was his conscience's good fortune that she held a genuine attraction to him and that she was happy here in her new life. God knew she'd not had much in the way of happiness before she'd come here.

'I will keep him away from you,' he vowed.

Taking his hand in hers, she squeezed it and said softly, 'Truly, there's no need. Dominic's never hurt me before, not like the others, and, even if he had, he's not stupid enough to try anything with an audience of hundreds. Don't ruin everything you and Marcelo and Alessia have achieved through your marriages out of anger. He's not worth it.'

And then her gaze lowered to their joined hands and, a hint of colour staining her cheeks, she let go and took a step back, her fingers grabbing at the skirt of her long, pretty, modest dress.

His fingers still burned from her touch.

Her eyes lifted back to his. Her chest made the tiniest, almost imperceptible hitch.

The strangest, tensest silence swirled and grew. The urge to push her against the nearest wall and work off the anger infecting him in the sweetness of her kisses grew with it. *Dio*, look at those lips. Did anything on this earth taste as sweet?

He closed the space she'd made.

Her chest hitched again, her graceful neck elongating then moving as if she were swallowing. Her eyes darkened, the colour on her cheeks deepening.

He leaned in, unable to look at anything now but

those divine lips, moisture filling his mouth in anticipation of his hunger being sated…

The office door opened and a press secretary walked in. 'My apologies,' he said, clearly startled at who he'd found hiding there.

Amadeo took a step back and resisted the urge to throw the man out of his own office. 'No need for apologies,' he said with all the smoothness he could muster.

Holding the door open for Elsbeth, she walked past him, causing another waft of her beautiful perfume to envelop him like a cloud.

The urge to snatch her hand into his and drag her straight to the nearest bed was strong. Too strong.

Everything he was feeling at that moment was too strong.

'I'm going to the gym,' he told her in as even a voice as he could manage when they reached their shared reception room.

There were agreed rules about their marriage. Good rules. Sensible rules. He should know—he'd imposed them. He would not break them for something as fleeting as lust. Their marriage was working perfectly well. Better than he could have hoped. They had achieved a cordiality he'd never believed he would find with a Fernandez.

But the dazed sheen he found in her eyes when she looked back at him made him come within a whisker of saying to hell with those rules and to hell with doing something as insipid as snatching her hand, and just throwing her over his shoulder, kicking her front door down and carrying her off to bed.

It was also that dazed sheen that stopped him following his baser instincts.

Elsbeth's heart was tender, that was becoming clearer the more time they spent together. He would do whatever he could to make her life here a happy one, and the state trip to the Caribbean was only the start. But what he would not do was let her believe their marriage could be anything more than what came within the bounds of the rules they'd agreed.

CHAPTER ELEVEN

ELSBETH HAD NEVER known time to pass as slowly as it did over the next few days.

Two days of engagements crawled at the rate of a lethargic snail. All she could think of was Amadeo. Spending hours with him, much of that time in a car, didn't help. It didn't matter how hard she tried to maintain her composure and indifference, the burn of his eyes on her skin was too much. And the burn was constant. Every time she caught his stare, he stripped her naked with his eyes. Every time she caught his stare, her bones melted.

Amadeo had lit something within her during their last night together, stoked it in those mad moments in the secretary's office when she'd been so *certain* he was going to kiss her, and she didn't have a clue how to extinguish it or control it.

Who cared about protecting her heart when she could barely walk for desire? She wished he had kissed her and whisked her off somewhere to make love to her again. Maybe then the heat that had bubbled incessantly since would have been sated instead of being allowed to simmer. And it had simmered every second of every minute of every hour.

Now it was two a.m. and she was wide awake, her heart still refusing to settle and her pelvis feeling as if it was on fire.

Saturday had finally come.

Tonight he would make love to her again.

She willed time to speed up.

By the time Saturday finally dawned, Amadeo felt like a tinderbox with a lit taper slowly crawling towards it.

As soon as he woke, he pulled on a pair of jeans and headed out to his balcony. Ten minutes of waiting and no sign of Elsbeth in the garden.

Where was she? Every morning that week he'd stood at the French doors of his balcony and watched her walk across the lawn of their garden. A warning voice had told him to stay hidden, take a little private fix of her beauty and then get on with his day.

Since that moment in the press secretary's office, getting on with his day had become a titanic battle with himself. He *burned* with unfulfilled desire. Burned. That perfume he'd so detested…now he couldn't get enough of it. Now, when they travelled to and from their engagements, every inhalation came with a dose of it, and it shot straight to his loins. *Dio*, it had been bad enough before, sitting in an enclosed space with the object of his infatuation there, close enough to touch, but now…

He could not believe the strength of his craving for her.

And she wanted him too. It had been written all over her face in that mad moment. As still as she held herself and as indifferent her outward body language during the hours they'd spent on engagements the last two days, she could no longer mask her eyes to him, or mask the desire they contained. That composure she wore like an iron cloak…slowly but surely it was slipping off her shoulders. He ached to rip it away and watch her lose the last of her control, and then bury himself in her.

Impulse took possession of him.

Not bothering to put a T-shirt on or anything on his feet, Amadeo bounded down the iron steps from his balcony and knocked loudly on her French doors.

He gave her ten seconds and knocked again. And again.

A shadow appeared through the glass before the door opened. Instead of Elsbeth, he was confronted with an armed palace guard, who took one look at him, turned bright red and set off with a profusion of apologies.

'It's okay,' Amadeo said, interrupting him impatiently once he'd got the gist that the guard had been stationed in his and Elsbeth's joint reception room and, when he'd heard unexpected banging on the French door at six in the morning, had done what he was trained to do. 'It's great that you're so alert and doing your job so well and keeping the Princess safe. Where is she?'

'In her room with Gregor.' Gregor was the other guard.

'Good man. You can return to your post. Radio Gregor and give him the all-clear.'

Striding through the day room—a deep red armchair had been added to it, replacing, he was sure, a dusky pink one—he then turned into the corridor at the same moment Gregor left Elsbeth's room, speaking into the walkie-talkie the guards used to communicate when stationed on duty. Behind him, Elsbeth appeared, wearing a short black nightdress that perfectly showed off the delectable golden legs he'd so admired from his balcony.

She came to a sudden halt.

Eyes puffy from sleep captured his, a light forming in them as her chest rose.

He stepped closer to her. *Dio*, in this sleepy tousle-haired state she really did look good enough to eat.

'I thought you were an early riser,' he murmured.

Her throat moved a number of times before she whispered, 'I had trouble falling asleep.'

Standing before her, he gazed deep into her eyes. 'And why is that?'

The colour staining her cheeks was a joy to witness, and he knew, without a solitary shadow of doubt, that what had kept her from sleeping was the same thing that had woken him before the sun.

Saturday. Their day.

She'd been waiting for it with the same heightened expectation as he had.

They had all day if they wanted. No rules would be broken.

A whole day to sate their hunger.

His arousal, finally freed from the mental chains he'd kept it clamped in for days, throbbed and burned.

He reached for her.

Elsbeth couldn't move. She was spent. Her limbs were jelly, her pelvis tingling, molten.

Amadeo was still inside her, his face buried in her hair, his breathing ragged.

She couldn't believe what had just happened. How it had felt to have her husband take her in his arms and practically throw her on the bed in his passion for her.

It had been like waking from the most wonderful dream, only to find the dream was real.

But now he raised his head and some instinct for self-preservation stirred within her, and she tried desperately to prepare herself for what came next and fought with equal desperation not to open her mouth and beg him to stay.

Instead of moving off her, he gazed down at her. He didn't say anything for the longest time, just stared at her before a half-smile formed on the lips that had kissed her with such fervour her mouth still buzzed. 'Breakfast in bed?'

Relief that he wasn't planning to leave straight away punched through her with such strength that she couldn't find the words to speak, could only nod.

'Good, I'm ravenous.' His eyes gleamed as he lifted his weight off her. 'Let's take a shower together while we wait.'

Her insides froze.

All their lovemaking took place under the protective cover of her bedsheets. She was exposed to him but the magical things he did to her overrode her shyness.

To shower with him? Her nudity on full display under the bright bathroom lights?

A week ago, she would have obeyed without question. She would have hidden her fear and gone along with it to please him.

You have no obligation or duty to please or obey me...

She had to swallow hard to loosen the constriction in her throat before she could speak. 'I don't think I'm ready for that.'

He stared at her with that look that always felt as if

he was trying to probe into her head, then smiled and gave a nonchalant shrug. 'No problem. Do you want to shower first or shall I?'

'I'm sorry.'

He captured her chin in his hand and brought his face to hers. 'Never apologise for saying no. You first or me?'

'You.'

'Then you can order the food. Tell the kitchen I'll have my usual.'

The relief this time was so overwhelming that her heart calmed. Palming his cheek, she whispered, 'Thank you.'

He kissed her palm and then kissed her mouth before jumping off the bed.

With the unashamed indifference to his own nudity she was coming to know so well, he strolled to the bathroom.

Shortly, the sound of running water started.

Elsbeth closed her eyes and placed the palm his lips had just kissed to her thrashing heart.

Breakfast was brought to Elsbeth's bedroom. Dressed only in her silk robe, Amadeo wearing only a towel around his waist, they sat on a wide chaise longue in the corner of the room, Amadeo peppering her with questions about her plans for their garden. It seemed surreal that it was still early morning. Surreal that she was sharing breakfast with her husband and that it felt so right.

She really was starting to think of him as her husband. To feel it too. What she was trying not to do was feel possessive about him, feel as though he was hers. He would never belong to her. Not where it mattered most, with his heart…

Or was she being too cynical? After all, there had been significant changes in his attitude towards her since their marriage. She no longer felt any kind of antipathy from him, no longer felt that she irritated him. Slowly but surely they were building an accord that didn't just include mind-blowing sex but also a form of friendship.

Was it possible that his heart could be opening to her as her heart was opening to him? She no longer sensed loathing from him, but it was foolish to even hope. Best to enjoy the time they shared together for what it was and what it gave her, and not leave her heart even more vulnerable by daring to dream for more.

'You know what we were talking about last week, about your mother?' Amadeo said when she'd finished enthusing about the plants and flowers she intended to grow and the huge greenhouse that was being built for her. The animation on her pretty face had been fascinating. He thought back to the frightened, shy stranger of six weeks ago—not that he'd recognised her fear and shyness for what they were back then—and was awed at her growing confidence. He remembered the first time he'd seen the animated side of her nature, that evening when she'd explained why she'd replaced a masterpiece with a schoolgirl's amateur painting. It had been the first time a hint of the real Elsbeth had shone through the wind-up doll persona she'd hidden herself behind.

But not all her barriers had been dismantled. The cloak hadn't slipped off in its entirety.

There was a passionate, sensual woman in there fighting to be released. He could feel that woman when he made love to her, ardent in her responses to him but always holding something back, frightened to take that last step and truly release the shackles her upbringing had placed around her and throw the cloak away. Embrace her sexuality.

Her cup of tea at her mouth, her pretty eyebrows drew together in question.

'About you pleasing me,' he reminded her. 'She told you to always please me in bed?'

Her cheeks coloured prettily and she nodded.

'What did she say?'

She lowered the cup from her mouth, the colour on her face darkening as she quietly said, 'That a prince's wife is a vessel for his pleasure.'

'Lie back, close your eyes, think of Monte Cleure and let me do what I want to you?'

He didn't think he'd ever seen such a flame cover her face, but she didn't drop her stare from his. 'Yes.'

'She never told you that you should expect pleasure too?'

'She said some women were lucky enough to receive pleasure from their husbands, but that I shouldn't expect it or ask for it.' She put her cup back on the saucer, her cheeks now scarlet as a contortion of expressions flittered over her face.

He removed the clattering cup and saucer from her, placed it on the antique coffee table the rest of their breakfast stuff was spread out on, and idly asked, 'Have you ever given yourself pleasure?'

Eyes widening in shock, her hands flew to her cheeks and she shook her head shakily.

'Don't be embarrassed,' he murmured, leaning into her. 'And do not be ashamed. Pleasure isn't shameful.' He captured the sash around her waist and untied it one-handed. 'Asking for pleasure isn't shameful...' He bent his head to capture a puckered nipple in his mouth, heard the short, soft mew. 'But to truly know what gives you the most pleasure you need to understand the basics of what works for you.' Loosening the towel around his waist, he kissed his way up to her mouth and stretched out on his side beside her.

Her eyes didn't leave his face, not even when he reached for a trembling hand and placed it on her pubis, nor when he took hold of his erection.

Slowly, he moved his hand up and down his arousal. Voice thickening, he leaned his face closer to hers. 'Do you see what I'm doing? There is nothing wrong with self-pleasure. It's how we learn best.'

Elsbeth felt almost drugged with arousal. It was the sensuality in Amadeo's voice…the heat in his eyes. She was almost afraid to look at what he was doing to himself.

Breathing raggedly, she lifted her head and…

Dear Lord…

He was masturbating. His gaze was fixed on her and he was masturbating.

'You don't have to touch yourself,' he whispered thickly. 'You don't have to do anything. If this makes you uncomfortable and you want me to stop then I will stop. Do you want me to stop?'

Her head shook itself.

His mouth hovered over hers. 'Does it excite you?'

Excite her? She'd never seen anything so erotic in her life as her giant, sexy husband pleasuring himself. She'd never *dreamed* she would find such a sight erotic.

Her heart thumping, skin inflamed, she tiptoed her fingers down to her slickness. Her index finger slipped over her swollen sex and she gasped at the shock of excitement.

He groaned. '*Mio dio*, you're so sexy.'

She touched the swollen spot that all her pleasure emanated from again, and this time she kept her hand there.

The pleasure…*heavens*. So different to how it felt when Amadeo was inside her and yet, with that hooded, burning look in his eyes, somehow even more intimate. She'd never imagined he would look at her the way he was now. As if he could stare at her for a thousand years and still want to look some more.

'*Dio*, you have no idea how badly I want to taste you,' he muttered.

'Then do it.'

Was that *her* voice? It didn't sound like her voice, but the words came from her mouth.

And that didn't feel like her quivering body his lips caressed as he snaked his way down it, but the sensation was everywhere, a heavy, dazzling cloud embracing her, making her head spin.

At the first press of his tongue to the place she most craved it, her thoughts dissolved into the cloud. When the lightning hit, its strength made her cry out as she shattered into a billion pieces.

Elsbeth opened her eyes and her heart twisted with sadness. At some point since they'd last made love, the room had darkened. Night was falling.

At some point soon, Amadeo would leave. The weight of his arm over her belly and the leg entwined with hers would leave with him. The mouth pressed into her hair. It would all be gone.

The most magical day of her life would come to an end.

But at least she'd experienced it. She'd had this day of utter, heady bliss, and that could never be taken from her. She would treasure it always.

She wished she could tell her mother how wrong she'd been, but that would be cruel. Unless something happened to Dominic, like an uprising or a personality transplant, her mother would never be allowed to leave her father. She would never know the delights that could be found in a man's touch. The joy. The hedonism. The effects more potent than the finest champagne and, she suspected, more addictive than any narcotic.

She had no idea how she could continue to protect her heart after the day they'd just shared. She didn't see how it was possible.

As all these thoughts played in her head, she became aware of a heaviness forming in her abdomen. Holding her breath, she concentrated hard on it but then let out a muted gasp as a cramp fisted in her.

Oh, no. No. Please, no.

The heaviness spread. Another cramp came. Not as sharp or as powerful as the ones she'd always had before the medication she'd been given to tame it, but unmistakable all the same.

She breathed in deeply and carefully disentangled herself from Amadeo's sleeping form.

In the bathroom, she took some painkillers then stepped into the shower.

As the hot water sprayed over her head and body, she let the tears fall. Only when the tears had turned themselves off did she turn the shower off.

Wrapping a towel around herself, she wiped the

steamed-up mirror. Her unhappiness reflected back at her.

The best day of her life given the worst possible finale.

Amadeo was awake and sitting up propped against the headboard when she walked back into the bedroom wearing clean pyjamas. The hungry, welcoming smile faded as he looked at her.

'I wondered what was taking you so long,' he said before giving a rueful smile. 'It is that time?'

She nodded, afraid she might start crying again. She didn't even know why she'd cried to begin with. When the doctor had seen her about her menstrual pains, she'd asked how long it would take to conceive. He'd told her it could take many months and that for some couples it took years.

He pulled the sheets back and patted the space beside him, and suddenly, with that gesture alone, her tears made perfect sense.

She'd been convinced the fact of her period would mean Amadeo had no reason to stay. She'd been afraid he would take it as his cue to leave.

She didn't want him to go.

Climbing onto the bed, she sank into the comfort of his arms and the strength of his masculine body and wished with all her heart that this didn't feel so right.

Leaving a bed had never been so difficult.

Amadeo hadn't planned to spend the whole night with her again. But then, he hadn't planned to spend a whole day making love to her. *Dio*, he couldn't get enough of her. Elsbeth was the most intoxicating aphrodisiac in the world.

He'd never had a day like it. An entire day devoted to nothing but pleasure. He could do it all again, starting right now. Press a kiss into that sensitive spot on her neck that he'd discovered and…

He took a deep breath and willed the surge of lust-driven adrenalin to abate. It wasn't just that it was the time of month when he couldn't make love to her that made him sever his amorous thoughts. The sun was rising. A new day was dawning. Their day and night together was over.

He placed a gentle kiss to her temple.

Her eyes flew open.

A weight lodged in his heart. 'I need to go now.'

She nodded.

'I…' It was on the tip of his tongue to invite her to share lunch with him. And dinner. 'I'll see you soon.'

Another nod.

Damn it. One swift, hard kiss to her mouth and then he left.

Climbing the stairs to his quarters, it felt as if the weight that had attached itself to his heart had a pendulum attached to it.

Elsbeth hugged his pillow tightly to her chest but there were no tears.

Amadeo had stayed the whole night with her. He'd kissed her goodbye. And she'd seen it in his eyes. He hadn't wanted to leave.

Dare she hope…dare she…that his feelings were changing in the same way that hers were?

CHAPTER TWELVE

ELSBETH DID NOT think she'd ever been as excited as she was when getting ready the following Saturday. She hadn't been this excited on her wedding day—there had been too much fear of the unknown mixed in with the excitement back then to compare.

They were going to a party. A proper party, not a royal engagement, hosted by a billionaire friend of Amadeo's who'd recently bought a street in one of the most affluent parts of Ceres' capital and knocked it into one big home for himself, and now wanted to show it off. A proper, social party. Even better, Clara and Marcelo, and Alessia and Gabriel were going too. It was rare for Amadeo's sister and brother-in-law to be in Ceres over weekends, preferring to spend their free time at Gabriel's Madrid home, but for this occasion they'd decided to stay at the castle and party with the rest of them.

Elsbeth knew Alessia and Clara had been friends for many years. Their history and closeness could easily make Elsbeth the spare wheel but the few times the three of them had spent time together, they'd gone out of their way to make her feel that she was one of them. That she belonged. It was a wonderful feeling. Acceptance. They'd been like that on Tuesday evening at the family dinner the King and Queen had hosted. Clara had downloaded an app that translated everything spoken into the phone and had insisted Elsbeth and Alessia do the same, then spent the rest of the evening narrating dirty jokes in English and cackling with glee as it was translated by monotone voices in their own languages. Elsbeth had laughed so hard that in the morning her ribs had felt bruised.

The best part about Tuesday evening though, had been Amadeo. She'd never seen her stiff-necked husband so relaxed, not outside the privacy of their bedroom. Her bedroom. When, after the meal, they'd returned to their shared reception room and they'd turned to each other to say goodnight…

To remember the look that had been in his eyes was enough to make her bones go weak.

To remember the groan of disappointment he hadn't been quick enough to stifle in its entirety when she'd had to tell him her period hadn't finished and the last, rueful look he'd given her as he'd trudged up the stairs to his quarters was enough to make her heart sing.

He'd been on the verge of breaking the rules. She knew it as clearly as she knew her own name.

The next morning, he'd casually asked if she would like to accompany him for a meal with the Italian ambassador and her husband on Friday evening. Equally casually, she'd said yes. They'd returned to the castle at midnight. They'd barely made it through the door before he'd started ripping her clothes off. She'd woken with the rising sun to the most beautiful climax then fallen back asleep in his arms. He'd left her bed two hours ago.

The beautician who'd now finished drying her hair

carefully gathered it together, a finger lightly touching Elsbeth's neck. She shivered, her mind racing ahead to their return from the party, when Amadeo would return to her bed.

God, she was starting to live for his lovemaking. She simply couldn't get enough of it.

She thought back to the shy bride who'd been so desperate to leave her home country she would have agreed to live in a pigsty. She remembered the naive virgin who'd believed she had to lie on her back and think of Monte Cleure. How apprehensive she'd been. How rigidly she'd held herself, believing her mother's advice not to touch him unless told. Believing that his pleasure was the only thing that counted, her own reactions to his touch and the climax he always brought her to a delightful bonus.

That shy, innocent bride would never have believed she would wake in the night aching so badly for him that she would bring herself to a climax with images of the time Amadeo had taught her *how* to bring herself pleasure behind her closed eyes. But as satisfactory as the solo climax had been, it hadn't been enough. It wasn't the same without him. Not even close.

That shy bride had gone. The rules her mother had drilled into her had no place here, and it was with this thought that she saw the dress she'd earmarked to wear that night hanging up, ready to be slipped over her head. A pretty, modest dress. As pretty and modest as everything she'd ever worn her entire life.

Not all the shackles of her past had been broken yet. Tonight it was time to smash another one.

Amadeo paced Elsbeth's day room, the glass in his hand filled with scotch from the bottle that had sat in her bar since the last time he'd drunk from it all those weeks ago. The night his loathing of his wife had first softened.

He would never have believed then that a time would come when he'd pace her quarters to stop himself marching down the corridor to her bedroom so he could throw her on the bed. If she were alone he wouldn't think twice, but she had an army of beauticians working on her—unnecessarily in his opinion. Elsbeth's beauty was innate. She didn't need any help. But, as he was a stickler for rules himself, he had to allow when others had rules they abided by, and for the women of the Berruti family that meant spending hours being pampered and beautified before an evening out. In this case though, he considered it a waste of valuable sex time.

Pouring himself another drink, he thought moodily back to Tuesday evening, when he'd come within a whisker of sweeping her into his arms. All that had stopped him was her rueful explanation that her period hadn't finished. Unlike that day in the press secretary's office, he knew he wouldn't have stopped himself.

That was what came of spending an evening sitting next to his wife with the scent of her perfume arousing his senses and the heat from her hot body so close to his, arousing his loins. It got to the stage where a man would throw aside every rule invented just for one taste of his wife's sweetness.

Mother Nature had had other ideas though. A cold shower had done nothing to ease his ardour and so he'd resorted to masturbation, Elsbeth's face as she climaxed and the soft mews she made vivid in his memories as he'd brought himself to orgasm. But it hadn't been enough. As satisfactory as masturbation was, it didn't compare. Nothing could compare with the rapture of climaxing buried deep in Elsbeth's velvet tightness.

Dio, when would this fever for her be spent?

Maybe he should arrange a week away for them. That wouldn't be against the rules. The rules of their sleeping arrangements only applied in the castle. He could whisk her away to the Berrutis' villa in the Seychelles and make love until neither of them could walk and the fever had broken.

There were no spaces in his schedule for a week away until the New Year.

This fever had to be spent by then. It had to.

He'd just tipped half his refilled glass into his mouth when there was movement at the door. His heart thumped so hard its kicking beat rippled into every part of him.

Unable to speak, he could only stare and strive for breath.

Gone were the muted colours and modest cut Elsbeth usually wore, her dress a strapless deep red with gold embroidery lacing through the tight bodice and through the flared skirt that became pure lace from mid-thigh to ankle. Her bare slender legs shimmered through it, on her feet high black criss-cross sandals that elongated her shapely body. Her light blonde hair was twisted into an elegant bun at the nape of her neck, her only jewellery her wedding ring and gold hooped earrings, leaving nothing between the curve of her neck and the creamy hint of cleavage. Minimal make-up adorned the face that needed no embellishment…apart from her mouth. Elsbeth's plump lips, usually painted a soft pink, were painted red to match her dress. Dragging his gaze down her a second time, he noted dimly her finger and toe-nails were painted the same hue.

The whole effect was electrifying.

A strong buzz thrummed through his veins, visions of pressing her back through the door and backing her to the nearest wall, yanking that dress up to her waist and—

Still fighting for breath, he scoured the image from his mind. Tried to scour it.

Mio dio.

This was his wife?

A warm glow fired in Elsbeth's belly at Amadeo's reaction. Not that there was much in the way of a reaction, not in the physical sense. But it was there in the hooded glimmer of his eyes and the subtle flare of his nostrils, and it sent a thrill rushing through her.

She hadn't had the last-minute change of mind about her dress for Amadeo. She'd changed her mind for *her*, the dress having hung behind the panelling of her room in the hidden wardrobe since the designer had made it for her all those weeks ago. She'd fingered the delicate lace many times, wistfully thinking she would never find the courage to wear it, the image of her mother's disapproval too strong.

But she wasn't Lady Elsbeth Fernandez of the royal House of Fernandez of Monte Cleure any more. She was Princess Elsbeth Berruti of Ceres. A princess of Ceres could wear whatever she pleased. And this dress pleased her. It was the kind of dress she'd always secretly longed to wear.

And Amadeo's reaction to it only added to the secret pleasure. To witness his reaction only added to the sense of unchaining herself from the strictures of her old life and embracing the path of the new.

'*Dio*, I want you,' he muttered ardently.

She drifted over to him with a smile, drinking in *his* appearance. Elsbeth wasn't the only one who'd discarded their usual rigid attire for the evening. Amadeo's magnificent, supremely masculine physique was wrapped in tight black chinos with a white shirt and blazer…but the shirts he usually wore were business shirts, not silk, not opened far below his throat. His fitted blazer wasn't usually velvet. And he didn't usually wear a leather chain around his neck with a silver ball at the throat. He'd never looked more devilishly sexy.

Putting her hands on his shoulders, she rose to her tiptoes and whispered, 'When we get home, you can have me.'

Eyes glittering, he bared his teeth. She imagined them sinking into her flesh and shivered as a wave of unadulterated lust thrashed through her. So deep was her desire that she would have let him take her there and then if her bell hadn't chimed and a maid hurried into the room to tell them Amadeo's siblings were ready and waiting for them.

Elsbeth couldn't get over how amazing the party was, and when Amadeo leaned into her to ask over the pulsing music if she was enjoying herself she had no hesitation in saying, 'It's the best party I've ever been to.'

He raised a brow at this.

She giggled. 'I was too nervous to appreciate our prewedding party and our wedding reception.'

'What about parties at the palace?' He said this casually but she caught the spark of loathing that always flashed in his eyes whenever Dominic or anything to do with Monte Cleure was mentioned.

'They were awful. I was so conscious of being on my best behaviour and not putting a foot wrong that I might as well have been a mute mannequin. Believe me, I never drank three glasses of champagne in one sitting there!'

Yes, three glasses of champagne and she was feeling decidedly lightheaded. But in a good way. She'd eaten enough of the delicious canapés being passed around—not as many as Clara, who was devouring them as if she were afraid there was going to be an imminent world shortage—and nibbles to soak up much of the alcohol and stop her passing the point of tipsy into drunk.

Finally ungluing herself from Amadeo's side a short while later to use the bathroom, she again admired this ultra-modern abode, even if it did strike her as having more an art gallery feel to it than a homely one. Still, all the other guests were tremendously impressed, which she supposed was the whole point. Why spend tens of millions knocking walls down and installing white marble everywhere, floor-to-ceiling windows with a tint that adjusted depending on the strength of the sun and remote-controlled skylights if there was no one to admire it?

When she'd finished in the ladies, she was about to head back to Amadeo when Clara pounced, Alessia at her heels. 'Come with me,' she demanded.

Allowing herself to be dragged out onto the balcony, she quickly realised Alessia was as bemused as she was.

'I can't tell you, so you're going to have to guess,' Clara said the second she'd closed the sliding door behind them. She had possibly the widest smile on her face that Elsbeth had ever seen.

Alessia looked her up and down. A smile formed. 'You're pregnant?'

'Yes! Well guessed!'

Elsbeth looked at Clara's belly, unsure if she'd translated correctly.

Clara nodded, beaming.

Alessia, visibly pregnant herself, threw her arms around her. After they'd embraced, Clara opened her arms to Elsbeth.

Touched to be included in such a special moment—she wouldn't have blamed her for telling Alessia privately before her—she hugged her tightly, delighted that the woman who was fast becoming a friend was expecting a child.

'Sorry, I've been bursting to tell you,' Clara said when all the hugs and congratulations were done with. 'I've known for a week but Marcelo wanted us to keep it private a bit longer. I wasn't sure if he meant private from the public or private from you too, so I didn't ask him and that way he couldn't confirm it! I've been *itching* for one of you to ask me!'

At that moment the glass door slid open and the man in question appeared. He took one look at the three of them and shook his head indulgently at his wife. 'I knew you'd tell them.'

The mischief on Clara's face made both Elsbeth and Alessia laugh. 'But I'm excited!'

'I've noticed.' But the grin on his own handsome face told Elsbeth that the expectant father was every bit as excited as the expectant mother. 'I suppose I have to tell Amadeo now.'

'And Gabriel,' Alessia piped up, then dashed back into the thrumming party to seek them out and drag them onto the balcony so the good news could be shared with them too.

Much back-slapping and manly hugs ensued, another bottle of champagne was opened, toasts were raised, crystal tapped against crystal before Clara and Alessia handed their flutes to their husbands to drink for them, and then they headed back inside. Before Elsbeth could rejoin the throng, strong fingers wrapped around her hand and pulled her to a stop.

Thrilling at the heat of his skin against hers, all the more acute as their flesh hadn't made contact since they'd got out of the car, she gazed up into Amadeo's handsome face.

'Are you okay?' he asked, his eyes searching hers.

Understanding his question, recognising the signs of his concern, her heart swelled. Smiling, she nodded and said truthfully, 'I'm thrilled for them.'

'It will happen for us one day.'

'I know.'

The concern turned into the gleam of a smile. Pressing his cheek against hers, he murmured huskily, 'Maybe we should look at making a minor alteration to the rules and adding Wednesdays to our conjugal nights.'

A thrill of joy and wantonness took hold of her and, without even thinking about what she was doing, she clasped hold of his hip and then slid her hand around to clasp a tight buttock. 'I could agree to that.'

Amadeo pulled his head back so he could look at her flushed face again. 'Just to help the conception process.' And the breaking of the fever. If he couldn't take her away for a week to screw this fever out of them, then he would amend the rules.

'Of course.'

'Original rules applying after conception.' By the time she conceived, the fever would be spent. It was not possible it could continue like this much longer.

Pupils dilated, her fingers squeezed tightly into his buttock. 'Naturally.'

Now he was the one to grab her bottom, pulling her to him and grinding his groin into her. Baring his teeth, he growled, 'Just you wait until I get you home.'

The next hour that passed was, for Amadeo, torture. He'd been so good up to that point on the balcony, ensuring no skin on skin contact with Elsbeth, keeping her by his side but not letting their flesh touch. Now, it was all he could do to keep his loins behaving. The way he was feeling, he was going to have to pour liquid ice down the front of his trousers.

He could hardly believe he'd behaved in such a debauched manner, grinding himself into her like that. Never before had he behaved like that outside the privacy of his own home. When he left the castle's gates, he never forgot who he was, not even in a private setting such as this amongst good friends.

Now it was all he could do not to check his watch every five seconds to see if it was a reasonable time to whisk his wife home.

A large group had formed around them, conversation flowing as freely as the champagne, but the moment it turned eleven he caught Elsbeth's eye. He didn't say anything, just indicated the door.

A knowing sparkle came into her eyes and she gave the subtlest of nods.

Fifteen minutes was all it took to escape the party and then finally they were in the underground garage with their bodyguards, his driver, parked next to Amadeo's siblings' cars and the vehicles used by their individual security details, already opening the back door for them.

Only ten paces away, Elsbeth tugged at his hand and whispered, 'Do our bodyguards *have* to sit in the back with us?'

The fever in his blood was alive in her eyes.

His vocal cords suddenly too thick to reply, he shook his head, then cleared his throat and told his head protection officer to sit up front with the driver. The other guards could arrange themselves in the convoy that always accompanied them.

Enclosed in the back of the car, the only sound was the heaviness of their individual breaths. Elsbeth stared straight ahead, her hands folded neatly on her lap, the rise and fall of her chest rapid.

He couldn't just sense her desire. He could see it. He could *smell* it.

The driver set off.

'Is this cab soundproofed?' she asked huskily.

'Yes. It is completely private...' His assurances had barely left his mouth when she pounced.

In seconds she was straddling his lap, hands clutching his cheeks, her hot mouth devouring him.

Amadeo had long reached an age where he believed nothing could surprise him any more, but the unleashing of Elsbeth's passion took his breath away and the arousal he'd striven to keep abated since their moment on the balcony roared into life.

'I want you inside me,' she muttered before plunging her tongue back into his mouth and scraping her fingers down his chest to the button of his chinos.

And, just like that, the need to be inside her was all-consuming. Thrills like he'd never known in his life ravaged him, Elsbeth's greedy hunger for him feeding his hunger for her. Dragging the lace of her dress to her hips, he grabbed at her lace knickers while she worked on his chinos and, using all his strength, ripped it.

Her mouth still feeding on his, she finally freed the button and unzipped him.

Certain he would combust if he didn't get inside her, Amadeo raised his hips and helped her tug his chinos and boxers low enough to free his raging erection.

There wasn't a moment of hesitation. She sank down on his length, taking him in his entirety in one long motion.

She threw her head back to look at him.

Dio, it felt as if he was seeing her for the first time. The cloak had gone. This was Elsbeth in all her uninhibited beauty. She was shaking with desire.

And so was he.

Cheeks flushed, pulsing eyes dark and heavy-lidded, she rested her hands on his shoulders and began to ride him.

Mio dio… This was incredible.

She was incredible. Exquisite.

Grabbing the bodice of her dress, he yanked it down to expose her naked breasts. Immediately, he took one in his mouth. Immediately, she clasped the back of his head to keep him there. Her moans deepened, her movements increasing in tempo until her head was thrashing, her nails digging into his skull and she was grinding down on him, crying out his name, the thickening force of her climax pulling him into his own exultant release.

Elsbeth, her cheek pressed tightly against Amadeo's, did nothing to stop the bubble of laughter from escaping.

For the first time in her life she'd let herself lose control and it had been unbelievable. Shy Elsbeth Fernandez would never have believed that hidden in her frightened heart had been a wanton, sensual woman capable of and, more importantly, willing to follow her basest desires.

She hadn't planned it. Not in the slightest. She couldn't have done it if she'd planned it! It had been hard keeping her composure after their scene on the balcony but she'd managed it, managed the heat simmering beneath her skin and the tingles of awareness that danced on it to act the part of gracious guest. Then they'd left the party together and that awareness had accelerated, knowing they were on the verge of being alone together and all the glorious things they would do…and in an instant the hot spot between her legs had become a pulsating mass of need.

What had followed…

She pressed herself even tighter against him, the man who had brought her out of her shy shell, the man who'd encouraged the dropping of the protective mask she wore, the man who'd encouraged her to be *her*.

Without Amadeo, the wanton, sensual woman would still be hiding in her frightened heart.

Another bubble of laughter rose up her throat. She wasn't frightened any more!

He moved his face to kiss her. 'You're incredible,' he breathed.

She sighed with a dreamy smile and gazed into his clear green eyes. 'I love you.'

CHAPTER THIRTEEN

As soon as the words escaped Elsbeth's lips they both froze. The shock in Amadeo's eyes mirrored the cold shock in her chest.

Where on earth had that come from?

Nowhere.

Recovering herself, she laughed. 'Well, that was one slip of the tongue—I meant that I love *sex* with you.'

That was the absolute truth, even if she hadn't actually meant to say anything at all. Amadeo had drawn out the woman in her and taught her not only of the joy in uninhibited, mutually fulfilling sex but that there was nothing shameful in embracing pleasure.

It wasn't possible she had meant more than that. It had been the heat of the moment, all those feelings fizzing through her—*still* fizzing through her—that had made her tongue run away with itself.

A beat passed; a tiny moment in time that seemed to stretch to the moon and back before Amadeo laughed too and kissed her. 'Sexy woman,' he growled, then kissed her again.

Relief that she'd covered her unwitting faux pas and hadn't caused any damage blew out the cold shock.

Uncoupling themselves, they straightened their clothing and held hands until they arrived back at the castle.

I love you.

Amadeo closed his eyes to the accounts printed off in preparation for his quarterly meeting with the team who ran the Berrutis' vast art collection, and kneaded his temples.

I love you.

His heart had come to an abrupt halt at those dreamily delivered words three nights ago. His lungs had closed. Time had hung suspended.

And then Elsbeth had laughed and made her quip about loving sex with him, and then he'd laughed and the moment had passed as if it had never been said.

The more time that had passed since then though, the louder those three words echoed in his ears. He'd spent their engagements the day before surreptitiously observing her, looking for any changes in behaviour or demeanour, but she was the same as she always was, gently wry, softly cool, calmly collected.

He wished he could say the same for himself. It felt like he had something acrid living in his guts, churning and coiling.

She *couldn't* have meant it. That was what he kept telling himself. It was a misfiring of words as she'd so quickly explained. She'd been as shocked at them as he had. No, she definitely hadn't meant it. Elsbeth was no fool. She knew their marriage would never be like the marriages of his siblings and had never even hinted at deviating from the rules laid out before they'd exchanged their vows.

James, his private secretary, who'd he'd poached

from the British royal family with the lure of Ceres' fantastic climate, entered his office. What he said pulled Amadeo sharply out of his thoughts.

'Dominic wants me to do *what*?' he asked, astounded.

'Have an informal race once the Grand Prix's finished,' James repeated. 'It's his understanding that one of the racing teams has agreed to lend their cars to you for the event.'

As tempting a proposition as it was to get behind the wheel of a racing car and publicly thrash the monster, there was no way he could accept. James knew that perfectly well.

'I assume you've already declined for me?'

'Yes, Your Highness, but as the request came from a monarch, I thought it best to inform you of it in case it came up in conversation between you.'

The thought of even talking to Dominic Fernandez made his already roiling guts churn harder.

He knew why King Pig—it was astounding how quickly Clara's nickname for him had stuck in his head; he'd have to be careful not to utter it publicly—wanted to race him. King Pig, for all his ego, was an insecure monster. Thick-skinned enough to try and force a woman who viscerally hated him into marriage, he was also thick-skinned enough to think he could cultivate a close relationship with his cousin's husband. And that was because King Pig, for all his thick skin, was also an insecure toad who craved acceptance by his peers. Turning Monte Cleure into a billionaires' tax haven and basking in the caviar-stuffed fools' so-called friendship wasn't enough for him. He wanted to bask in the approval and acceptance of his fellow royals. It must drive him insane that Europe's royal families disdained him, only inviting him to the events that protocol dictated they should.

King Pig had assumed Amadeo's marriage to his cousin would mean closer ties between the two men. King Pig was likely smarting that Amadeo and the rest of the Berrutis had maintained the distance they'd always kept between them. King Pig likely knew of Amadeo's financial involvement in Sébastien's team and his great interest in the sport. King Pig likely assumed a race between the two men would forge a bond between them. King Pig also likely assumed that the experience he had behind a racing wheel—his crash notwithstanding—meant he would easily beat the heir to the Ceres throne and thus earn himself the kudos money and status just could not buy.

King Pig was too thick-skinned to get it into his thick head that Amadeo would sooner spit on the man than play his games, even if he wasn't in a position to accept the offer of a race.

'Anything else?' he asked, noticing that James was still hovering.

'Princess Elsbeth came to your offices.'

Just the mention of her name made his heart judder and a coldness seep through his veins, and in that instant it came to him why those three little unwittingly delivered words were plaguing him: Elsbeth *never* spoke without thinking. She never made a slip of the tongue, and that she'd made this one straight after the height of passion…

He forced himself to concentrate on the rest of what James had to say.

'She asked you to call her if you have free time before your meeting, but said that it's not important.'

Amadeo inhaled sharply and nodded. 'Thank you.'

Once alone again, he rubbed his pounding forehead.

This couldn't continue. If he wasn't careful, he was going to waste the time needed to prepare for his imminent meeting thinking about Elsbeth. He'd wasted enough time as it was.

This was the kind of behaviour he'd been infuriated at his brother for displaying, the lapses of concentration when he'd known damn well Marcelo was thinking about Clara instead of the important work at hand.

It was the kind of behaviour he'd never been susceptible to before and he wasn't going to start now.

He forced his entire focus onto the pages before him. Elsbeth could wait.

Late afternoon and Elsbeth stood at the edge of the garden watching as a team of landscapers, supervised by head gardener Pep, excavated sections of the lawn to the design she and Pep had agreed between them. This was the manual part of the landscaping project that she couldn't be physically involved in, but it brought her joy to watch the slow transformation, and she took frequent photos on the professional camera she'd bought for herself to document it.

She sensed Amadeo's approach before he stood beside her, and turned her face to smile at him. 'Good day?'

'Long day. I'm sorry, I didn't get a chance to call you back.'

She shrugged. 'That's okay. I knew you were busy. I

was just going to see if I could tempt you into sharing lunch with me before your meeting started.'

'Sorry. Another time.'

'I'll hold you to that,' she said softly.

The pause that followed passed just a fraction too long before he nodded at the landscape team. 'Looks like they're making good progress. Are you pleased with what they've done so far?'

'Very much, although I think they're less pleased that I've spent most of the day openly spying on them. They'll be glad I'll be out of their hair tomorrow.' They had a full day of engagements scheduled.

He gave a quick smile. 'Let us hope the presence of a beautiful princess isn't too distracting for them.'

'They do seem very keen to work without tops on,' she mused. 'But as they haven't yet invited me to take my own top off, I'm sure they're managing the distraction just fine.'

His next smile was fractionally warmer and almost met his eyes. Then he looked at his watch. 'I need to go back in. Oh, and before I forget, I'm going to have to cancel our plans for tomorrow night—I need to do an overnight in Milan. There's a couple of issues the art team have brought to my attention that need to be resolved in person. I'll fly there straight from our last engagement and return Friday morning.'

Elsbeth, determined to keep her composure, arranged her face before saying, 'Am I not invited too?' Now that the frequency of their engagements had lessened, their schedule until the end of the year consisted of the majority being condensed into two days a week. Her diary for the next day was empty.

He shook his head and grimaced. 'It's purely work.

You'd be bored…' a glimmer suddenly flashed in his eyes '…*and* a distraction.' He looked at his watch again. 'I really do need to go. My mother's expecting me. Enjoy your spying.'

Elsbeth waited until he'd disappeared from view, then sedately made her way back into her quarters.

Alone, she sat on her new red armchair and breathed in slowly ten times.

After they'd laughed off her 'I love you', they'd returned to the castle, where Amadeo had promptly made love to her in the shower and stayed until the sun had come up. When he'd left, it had been with the promise of dinner in his quarters on that Wednesday evening, a promise that had *thrilled* her. Increasing the times they were together privately *and* being admitted into her husband's private sanctuary after all this time and making love in his bed…?

Slowly but surely, the rules he'd laid down on their wedding night, those said and those unsaid, were being dismantled. For the first time she'd allowed herself to dream of a future where they lived together as husband and wife, not separately as two individuals who just happened to be married and were trying to make a baby together. It was a dream that made her heart sing and her veins fizz, and made her confront a truth—that though her unbidden declaration of love had been a slip of the tongue, she could no longer deny that it contained more than a grain of truth. She was falling for him.

It was a truth she wished had kept itself hidden.

Her first real inkling that something was wrong had come yesterday during their engagements. They never showed any affection in work time. They didn't touch each other. That was normal. Amadeo was heir to the throne and she would be his queen consort. Standards needed to be maintained and that meant a dignified front befitting their status.

It was his eyes that had changed. The way he looked at her. She'd caught a few hungry looks from him but there had been no stripping her naked with his stare. The only thing it had felt like he was trying to strip was her skull so he could bore into her head. Conversation between them had been as easy as it had grown to be in recent weeks but there had been no hint of intimacy in his tone. Just little things that had made her feel that something was off and that he was pulling away from her, but small enough to make her uncertain whether or not she was being paranoid.

And now he'd cancelled their date.

But he'd looked stressed, she argued with herself. Maybe those issues identified with the art collection were more serious than she'd supposed. As the Berrutis did not accept a single cent from the public purse, amongst many other sources of income they monetised their highly prized art collection. Amadeo had taken control of the billion-euro collection on the family's behalf when he turned twenty-one, and it was a lot of work, even with a team running it on his behalf.

Or, even better, maybe he was stressed because he had to cancel their date. After all, he *had* called her a distraction. And promised they would do it another time.

Having successfully cheered herself up, she pulled her phone out of her pocket, called Clara and arranged to spend Thursday at a master sculptor's workshop as inspiration for her garden... And as a distraction to stop herself mooning and talking herself into making mountains out of molehills.

Late Saturday night, Amadeo lay on his back, Elsbeth using his chest like a pillow, her leg hooked around his thigh, an arm draped across his stomach. Her fingers were making idle circular sweeping motions over his skin.

'Who would you be married to, if you were born into a different family and hadn't married me to escape Dominic?' he asked into the peaceful silence.

Only the silence was peaceful. A week ago, Elsbeth had told him she loved him. The churning in his guts had got even stronger as the week had gone on. Knots had formed too, little tendrils in his chest knitting together and slowly tightening.

She tilted her head to look at him. 'I don't know. Why do you ask?'

'It's a question you once asked me.'

'Yes, but you never answered.'

'You answer me and I'll answer you.'

'You told me a woman shouldn't ask about a man's fantasies unless she was prepared for the answer. Or something like that.'

'That was then.' And this was now. Love had been mentioned when she should have known it was a forbidden word. She couldn't love him. She mustn't love him. He didn't want her heart. He'd never wanted it.

Lust was the most he could give Elsbeth. Lust would burn itself out and, when it did, Elsbeth would be his princess and then, one day, his queen consort. Together they would be the figureheads of his great nation, dignified assets his countrymen could look up to with pride, leading his family and the children he hoped to have by example. Messy emotions such as love, the kind his siblings enjoyed, were just that. Messy. They infected thinking. They turned perfectly reasonable people into hormonal adolescent-like creatures.

Just look at his sister. He couldn't use Marcelo as an example as he'd always had problems with his impulse control, but Alessia had never been afflicted, not until she'd stupidly let her hormones get the better of her and had an unprotected one-night stand. His dutiful sister hadn't been the same since, falling in love with her husband and often prioritising him and their growing child over her duties, recently announcing that from now on she'd only be undertaking one weekend evening engagement a month. He couldn't even begrudge her for it, though he wanted to. Love and emotions became so deeply entangled in people that their priorities changed and clear thinking went out of the window. It was beyond the realms of credulity that Amadeo would ever succumb to such nonsense. Elsbeth should know that.

It had been lust, and only lust, that had driven him to tweak the rules of his marriage, tweaks he now strongly suspected had made Elsbeth believe would lead to further tweaks until, bit by bit, everything agreed was dismantled and they became the couple they could never be.

He hoped his suspicions were wrong and that he was putting thoughts in her head that weren't there but, right or wrong, he needed to take them a step back and disabuse her of this thinking. He didn't really think she was in love with him...did he?...but, whether she was or wasn't, he didn't want to hurt her. Not his sweet Elsbeth. She'd suffered enough hurt in her life. Better lead her away from thoughts of a romantic love subtly and then, by the time their fever was finally spent, she would be as content as him to live separate lives as originally agreed, and everything would work out perfectly for both of them.

'Go on, tell me,' he coaxed. 'Given free choice, what kind of man would you have married? Who would have been your ideal husband?'

Dragging herself so her breasts were crushed against his chest and she could look at him properly, she said, 'I never had a specific fantasy man in my head. My dreams were always of an English cottage with a colourful, rambling garden and someone kind to live in it with me.'

For some reason, this answer made his sharp, knotted chest tighten into a point. 'You would have had to learn the language to live in England,' he pointed out, running his fingers up and down the soft skin of her back.

'I'd have used the translation app Clara made me download.'

'I'm sure your faceless husband would have helped you learn.'

She brushed her thumb over his mouth and smiled. 'He might not have had your patience.'

'Your improvement in my language has nothing to do with me.'

'Of course it does. You always translate for me when I need it, and you get people to speak slowly to make it easier for me to understand.'

'A husband who married you for love would have helped you far more, but that is the nature of ordinary people's marriages; they become couples in a way you and I can never be. But I don't suppose it is worth comparing the marriage we have with the ones we could have had if we'd been free to choose. All we had were pipe dreams we both knew could never come true. Take me, if I'd had free choice, if I'd been born plain Amadeo and not Prince Amadeo, I would have been a racing driver.'

Elsbeth's heart thudded heavily, the euphoria of their lovemaking dissolving. She didn't know if she was making another mountain out of a molehill but this all sounded like a veiled warning to her sensitive ears. If she was prone to paranoia, she could believe Amadeo had started the whole conversation just to compare their marriage to a marriage built on love.

She hesitated before asking, 'And your wife? Who would she be?'

'I've never had a particular physical type but, given the choice, I would have chosen someone fun and out-going with a zest for life, but I don't know if that's in response to the discreet women I've always been obliged to date, the allure of forbidden fruit. An ordinary man isn't bound to discretion like a prince. But then, I don't think I would have married at all had I been an ordinary man. I've never been susceptible to the kinds of emotion that leads an ordinary man into committing his life to someone.'

'Fun and outgoing.' Three words that pierced like an icy knife in Elsbeth's chest. As casually as Amadeo had explained it, they sounded pointed to her, a reiteration of the time he'd baldly stated he would never have chosen her for his wife. No one had ever used 'fun and outgoing' to describe Elsbeth. Shy and sweet were the usual descriptors.

And as for him not being susceptible to emotions

like an ordinary man… How could that be interpreted as anything but a warning?

Before she could make proper sense of any of this, he rolled her onto her back and gazed into her eyes with that hooded, lascivious stare that always made her pelvis melt.

'Whoever I would or would not have married given a choice, I guarantee that woman wouldn't be as sexy as you.' And then his mouth closed on hers, and all her thoughts and fears dissolved under the heat consuming her.

Elsbeth's sense of paranoia grew the next Wednesday when Amadeo joined her in her quarters. They shared a meal. They spent the night making love. He was as worshipful of her body and as adventurous a lover as the one she'd come to adore. They slept wrapped in each other's arms. He left when the sun rose.

But there had been something missing. It was in the way he'd held her after making love. A subtle mental detachment, as if his mind was far away from her. She sensed it was deliberate.

There had been no more talk of her being invited into his quarters.

Another week passed, Groundhog Week repeated. Engagements. Supervision of the garden. Saturday and Wednesday night: fantastic sex with her husband. And then the following weekend arrived.

Instead of dining with her on the Friday night like she'd become accustomed to him doing, Amadeo announced he was going for a night out with his friend Sébastien, who was on the island for a flying visit before that weekend's race in Belgium. There had been no suggestion that Elsbeth join them.

By the time Amadeo finally joined her on Saturday morning, nausea had settled so heavily in her stomach that even him pouncing on her the moment he walked in the door had hardly soothed it.

Later that night, long after he'd fallen asleep, she forced herself to look the facts in the face.

His words about ordinary marriages and emotions *had* been a warning.

All progress between them had stopped.

They were going backwards.

He was pulling away from her, and there was no point in burying her head in the sand about it any longer.

While they took each other to the heights of pleasure—she had no inhibitions with him at all now—a growing humiliation burned that she was essentially a slave for the touch of a man who only wanted her in the bedroom. She had to face the facts Amadeo had practically spelled out to her that, as far as he was concerned, they would never have a real marriage. Their lives would always be separate, and he wasn't going to include her in his any more than was necessary.

It was no coincidence that he'd spelled it out to her a week after she'd slipped up and told him she loved him and only days after his last-minute trip to Milan that she'd been deliberately excluded from.

He shifted in his sleep, throwing his leg over hers, the top of his dark head nudging against hers, and she squeezed her eyes shut as a wave of painful affection surged through her. Rolling onto her side, she wrapped her arms around him and held him tightly, trying to think of the situation in a more positive light. Was their marriage not a million times better than she'd dared hope when she'd first arrived in this country? Were they not perfectly matched in the bedroom? Did she not instigate their lovemaking as much as he did?

But these positive thoughts lasted less time than a climax. Because the painful gape that always used to form around her shrivelling heart after a climax had returned, and now it was a wound that ached unbearably.

It was the agonising ache that came from falling head over heels in love with a man who could never return that love.

She screwed up her eyes even tighter, trying desperately to stop the hot tears from leaking. She mustn't cry, not when the tears would fall onto him.

When she finally had her emotions under control, she relaxed her hold and opened her eyes. The room was lightening. The sun was rising. Soon, Amadeo would wake and leave her to spend his Sunday without her...

Elsbeth's heart made a sudden leap.

Sunday?

It was Sunday?

Placing a hand to her pounding chest, she quickly told herself not to get her hopes up. Just because her period was as regular as clockwork and for the first time in a decade hadn't started on a Saturday didn't have to mean anything.

CHAPTER FOURTEEN

WHEN AMADEO WAS admitted into Elsbeth's quarters that Wednesday evening, the anticipation was every bit as strong as always, its strength a relief that he hadn't thought of a way to get out of seeing her for an extra evening each week.

Dragging himself out of her bed got harder each time but the demons that had plagued him after her declaration of love were now well under control and he felt lighter in himself than he had in a long time. This fever for his wife would break soon. He'd already proved it, imposing himself on Sébastien on Friday night just to assure himself that he wasn't addicted to his scheduled time with her. It had been a fantastic night, with excellent food, the best wine and talk that was all things motor sport. He didn't deny that Elsbeth had accompanied him to Sébastien's in her own way, a spectre in the corner of his eye that floated into his vision whenever he wasn't actively thinking of her, but that didn't prove his addiction to her. When the fever broke, she would stop haunting his dreams as well as filling his thoughts. Everything would be as it should.

She was waiting for him in her day room. By now, there were so many changes to the furniture and furnishings that it was hardly the same room that had been created for her. The changes made it as warm and bright as the woman who'd chosen them. They suited her. They would suit him too...

Where the actual hell had that thought come from?

One look at her and the random thought, along with his intention of carrying her off to bed before their dinner was served, was forgotten. She was as pale as he'd ever seen her, her usually bright eyes sunken.

She hesitated before rising from her armchair.

He strode over so he could look more closely at her. 'Are you not feeling well?' She'd been looking a bit peaky these last few days but he'd assumed that was her period which, even with the medication, was never easy for her.

'I've not been sleeping well.'

Alarmed, he reached for his phone. 'I'll call Dr Jessop...'

She put a hand on his arm. 'I've already seen him.'

'When?'

'After our morning engagement. I'm pregnant.'

His brain froze. His mouth opened. Nothing came out.

A small smile formed on her lips. 'Why don't you sit down?'

Unable to tear his gaze from her, he absently ran his fingers through his hair. 'You're pregnant?'

The small smile still there, she nodded. 'Dr Jessop brought a test with him and confirmed it.'

Realisation began to dawn. They were going to have a baby. He was going to be a father. Elsbeth was going to be a mother.

A spasm of pure, unadulterated joy shot through him

and he pulled her to him, wrapping his arms tightly around her, breathing in Elsbeth's wonderful perfume and the honey scent of her shampoo. Until that moment, he hadn't realised how deep his own longing for a child was. 'That is just the best news you could have given me.' Pulling back a little so he could plant an enormous kiss to her mouth, he then cupped her cheeks and rained more kisses over every millimetre of her face.

'Why didn't you tell me your period was late?' he asked when he'd finished kissing her and wrapped his arms back around her.

'We haven't been alone for me to tell you.'

'You could have said you had something to tell me in private or come to my quarters.'

'I'm not allowed in your quarters and, in any case, I was trying not to build my hopes up.'

'What do you mean, you're not *allowed* in my quarters? Of course you're allowed.'

'I've never been invited into them. Can you let me go now, please? I can't breathe.'

He loosened his hold and swung her into his arms. 'Let's go to bed and celebrate.' A nice gentle bout of lovemaking would put some colour back in her cheeks.

But instead of throwing her arms around his neck and devouring his mouth like she normally did when he carried her, she wriggled against him. 'Please put me down.'

Immediately concerned, he placed her on the nearest sofa and sat himself beside her. 'Are you feeling unwell? Are you suffering from sickness? Is it the pregnancy causing it?'

How Elsbeth wished he wasn't displaying such solicitousness. She'd known he'd be pleased about the pregnancy but hadn't imagined he'd be this delighted. It only made what she needed to say harder.

Straightening, she tugged her hand out of his then linked her fingers together and rested them on her lap. 'No, I'm not ill and it's too soon for pregnancy sickness.'

'Then what is it?'

She took a deep breath and arranged her face. 'We agreed on our wedding night that once a baby was conceived, we would no longer share a bed.'

The way his handsome head reared back and his mouth opened and closed was almost comical. She assumed his excitement about the pregnancy had made him temporarily forget about the rules. It made her glad that she was the one to remind him and enforce them. She didn't think she'd be able to keep her composure if he'd been the one to say the closeness they'd found had to be severed with immediate effect. It would have come after he'd taken her to bed again. After he'd sated his lust.

At least this way she got to salvage a little of her dignity. Amadeo didn't want a real marriage with her. His heart was frozen to her. He would never love her.

She doubted he could love anyone.

He bowed his head, his composure regained, and then locked his eyes on hers. 'We both know we're not ready to stop being intimate with each other.'

'I am.'

'You're what?'

'Ready.'

Amadeo leaned in closer, eyes narrowing as they bored deep into hers, searching, searching. 'You're lying.'

'No.' One syllable, delivered so curtly it would be believable if her plump lips and chin weren't trembling.

He dropped his voice into a caress. 'You expect me to believe the desire you feel for me has ended overnight?'

She lifted her trembling chin with a hint of defiance. 'I didn't say that. I said I was ready to stop acting on it, as per the rules we agreed on our wedding night. Rules *you* imposed.'

Ah. *Now* he understood where this was coming from. Elsbeth was afraid he was going to enforce the rules himself and end the intimacy between them. If she only knew how hard he'd already tried to wean himself off her, her fears would evaporate.

He palmed her cheek, marvelling as he always did at how soft it felt against his skin. He inched his face closer still and whispered, 'Rules that can be tweaked if we are both in agreement.'

They'd tweaked the rules already, to their mutual satisfaction. Why not carry on as they were when things were so good between them?

'But I'm not in agreement.' Oh, God, Elsbeth hadn't meant to sound so tremulous but it was so hard holding onto her resolve when her body thrummed so madly from being held in his arms. And Amadeo heard it too. She saw it in the way his eyes gleamed.

His lips brushed against hers. The hand caressing her cheek gently drifted down her neck. She shivered at the tingles it set off.

'You are really willing to give up such pleasure?' he murmured sensually. 'To never feel our naked skin as one again…'

Lower his fingers dragged, over the swell of her

breast, his thumb encircling her puckered nipple, sending a strong bolt of need straight into her pelvis.

Stop it, she begged with her eyes. *Don't do this to me. This needs to end now.*

'To never feel my tongue where you like it the most…'

His fingers drifted down and over her abdomen. His breaths, hot against her mouth, were getting heavier. Elsbeth's breaths were getting heavier too. The sensations he was evoking…

His fingers tiptoed to the band of her skirt. God help her, she was trembling with desire. 'To never ride me the way that makes you lose yourself so…'

A finger slid beneath the band and pressed into the skin of her belly. The shock of electricity from his touch was strong enough to bring her to her senses by injecting a huge dose of humiliated rage to the fire in her veins.

Grabbing his hand, she shoved it away from her with a, 'Get *off*,' and clumsily jumped to her feet.

For the second time in as many minutes, he looked as if she'd punched him.

'How *dare* you try to seduce me when I've just told you I don't want your seduction any more?' she cried. 'Which part of *I'm not in agreement* did you think you could just ignore?'

Amadeo stood, palms raised, staring at her like a zoo keeper whose placid charge has just turned rabid. He'd wanted to see colour back in her cheeks but not this angry stain.

'This isn't you talking, Elsbeth,' he said steadily. 'This is the hormones from the pregnancy.' Hadn't he seen how pregnancy hormones affected his sister in the early stages, making her cry easily when she'd so rarely cried before?

'Don't you patronise me!' she snapped. 'The only thing the pregnancy has to do with my decision is that it's forced me to think clearly. I'm your wife but I'm not your partner, and you've made it perfectly obvious that what we have now is as far as you're prepared to go. You've reached your limit and now I've reached *my* limit. I'd rather spend the rest of my life celibate than share a bed with a man who only wants me to slake his lust. You're the one who made me see that I'm not on this earth to be a vessel for your pleasure and that I have the freedom to live my life within these castle walls however I choose. Well, I've made that choice and I choose to live it without you.'

Her words sliced through him, landing in his chest with icy, jagged barbs. 'I have never treated you like a *vessel*.'

'That's exactly how you've treated me. It's how you've treated me from the moment we married. I could have been anyone lying there beneath you.'

'You can't tell me you didn't get pleasure and satisfaction from it,' he retorted, breathing heavily.

'Physical pleasure but no emotional pleasure. No affection. Nothing to make me feel you saw me as a human being with feelings. And I notice you don't deny it.'

'What is there to deny? I've never hidden that I married you for the sake of my nation and the monarchy. I did my best to be gentle with you and leave you satisfied and I know damn well I achieved both those things, but you know too how I felt about you back then. How could I fake affection for a woman whose very name left me cold?'

'I was a stranger in a new home and you left me alone!' she cried, her voice rising. 'That wasn't cold, that was cruel, but I was so terrified of being sent back to the man whose name is responsible for your coldness towards me that, even if I had recognised your cruelty for what it was, I would never have spoken out. Not then.'

'I was never intentionally cruel,' he raged, furious at this character assassination. 'I did everything I could to give you a home you would feel happy and comfortable in, and you know damn well too how much more of an effort I made once I was aware of your loneliness. I've given you every support in everything you've done or wanted to do.'

'Give yourself a pat on the back then and tell yourself what a great man you are. And in many ways you *are* a great man and I know it's unfair of me to throw things in your face that are in the past, but they're things that still affect us today. They affect *me*. I know you made an effort with me because I could see it. I know you hated your desire for me because I sensed you fighting it. Things have been so good between us this last month but still I sense you fighting and trying to pull away and dropping hints to push me away. Whether it's because you will never accept the blood in my veins or because you're so used to thinking you're right about everything that you can't admit to yourself that you were wrong about me, or because you really do think yourself so damn superior to human emotion… I don't know! The only thing I *am* sure of is that you've never given us a chance. You will never give us a chance. You've fought your feelings for me every inch of the way and now I'm sick of the fight.'

The vein in his temple was jumping, the only sign

of life on features that had turned to granite. Elsbeth refused to let it sway her from what needed to be said.

'Nearly three months we've been married, Amadeo,' she said, 'and I've never slept in your bed. You're never going to let me in and be a real wife to you and you will never let yourself be a real husband to me, and sooner or later I'm going to start hating you for it. I don't want to hate you, especially not when I'm carrying your child, so this ends now. I will not share a bed with you again and unless you want me to assert my freedom and independence even further and move out of the castle altogether, respect my decision and autonomy, just as I have respected every decision you've made, even the ones I didn't like or agree with. As of now, our marriage reverts to our original agreement.'

The cold roar in Amadeo's head was deafening. The slicing of Elsbeth's words had spread, tearing at his throat and shredding his guts, his lungs…but not his heart. No, that particular organ had incrementally hardened at her twisting of everything they'd shared, and solidified into something impenetrable as her threats landed.

The vein in his temple was still jumping madly, his expression one Elsbeth could no longer read. Slowly, his body came back to life. His neck lifted, his nostrils flared as his chest and shoulders rose. He gave a short incline of his head and a terse, 'As you wish.'

And then he turned on his heel and walked out of her quarters for the last time.

Amadeo prepared himself for the next day's engagement in his usual fashion. Shower. Shave. Brush his teeth. Dress himself in the outfit he'd previously selected and which a member of his domestic team had laid out for him. Style his hair. Splash cologne to his cheeks. Head down the stairs to their shared reception area.

Elsbeth appeared moments later.

'Good morning,' she said politely.

'Good morning.'

And then they were whisked out to their waiting car by their teams.

On the drive, the usual chatter, led by his private secretary, filled the cabin of the car, a refresher of the imminent engagement and pertinent points to remember. When they arrived, the usual crowd awaited them. The usual tour was given, the usual speeches and further walkabout made. Then it was back in the car for the return journey.

Their week's engagements now over, James moved talk on to the weekend's Grand Prix, the banquet they were hosting and the King of Monte Cleure's overnight stay at the castle.

It was only when the King's name was mentioned that Amadeo flicked his gaze to Elsbeth. Up to that point he'd successfully tuned her out as Elsbeth, forging her in his mind as his faceless consort for the day. It was best to keep her faceless in his own mind until his fury with her abated, because, of course, he could not let it out. In public and amongst staff, a prince was dignified and regal at all times. He couldn't let it out in private either. In one swift move, Elsbeth had severed their relationship and made it impossible for him to have a voice in the severing. He had no doubt her threat to move out of the castle had been real. If he set foot in her quarters uninvited she would leave. If she left, scandal would ensue.

Where will you go? he longed to spit at her. *You have nothing without me.*

But that wasn't strictly true. She had money. Her own money. A bank account he'd had opened for her so she never felt trapped and helpless as she'd been in her old life.

He'd given her all the tools to live her life as an autonomous woman, given her all the encouragement to embrace her freedom, and look how she repaid him. With threats. Threats that were not empty.

So, to keep his loathing suppressed, he'd imagined her faceless, but the mention of Dominic's name instantly turned her back into flesh and blood, and as her beautiful face came back into focus, with it came a reminder of the torrid, fearful life she'd lived before she came to Ceres.

Before he could drag his stare away, her eyes suddenly darted to his.

One heart-stopping look passed between them, and then she blinked and the mask she'd always worn so well slipped back on.

He hardened his heart.

Amadeo stood on his balcony looking out over the garden. It had changed beyond all recognition. The neat and orderly space had turned into a wonder of shapes and colours, with snaking pathways, a large pond with a bench, a pagoda, quirky artistic statues, fruit trees, giant olive trees, cherry blossoms and an abundance of vividly coloured plants and flowers. And still it wasn't finished. Patches of soil indicated the spaces Elsbeth was still to fill with yet more colour. No doubt she'd be out there that afternoon while Amadeo and a good chunk of his countrymen were at the racetrack for Ceres' most popular Grand Prix.

He'd watched her work at it many times from behind his French doors. Never showing his face. Hiding away. Admiring the care she took over each and every plant. Heart tightening at the contentment on her face.

He concentrated on breathing. Since Elsbeth had severed the personal side of their marriage, there had been a bitter coiling in his guts. Every day that passed, the coil tightened, his body filled with something so malignant that no workout in his gym could even start to expel it from him. The only relief came when he looked out onto her garden.

Would their child inherit her love of gardening? Or his love of fast cars? Two polar opposite pastimes, one designed to soothe, the other to thrill.

Elsbeth did both. To watch her garden, to just be in her presence and listen to her quiet voice was to soothe him. To look at her, to get naked under the sheets with her was to thrill him.

His heart thumped hard against his ribs, almost winding him.

Elsbeth was like the flowers she'd planted. She'd arrived at his castle like an under-watered, wilting wallflower and slowly but surely blossomed into a passionate, colourful, highly scented frangipani.

Another even harder thump slammed into him and he bent over, gasping.

Why hadn't he defended himself? Her words had enraged him but he'd done little to stop them and nothing at the end to try and change her mind. He'd walked away from her without defending himself, without fighting for her. And why? Because nearly everything she'd said was true.

The only thing she'd been wrong about was her blood. He'd long ago stopped looking at her as anything but Elsbeth. His wife.

Everything else…

He *had* seduced her for his own pleasure. He'd revelled in the unravelling of her sexuality because he was the lucky recipient of it. He'd done all that while pushing her back and back every time she got too close, clinging stubbornly to those damned rules, believing himself immune to human emotion—no, call it true as Elsbeth had done: believing himself *superior* to it.

The agony suffocating him meant he could deny it no more.

He wasn't superior to or immune to emotion.

The woman whose defences he'd been so intent on breaking down had silently seeped under the defences of his own skin and embedded herself into his heart.

CHAPTER FIFTEEN

'HOW ARE YOU finding marriage to my cousin?' King Pig asked, having just squeezed his obese body to the front of the barrier to stand beside Amadeo. Loath though Amadeo had been to offer Dominic a seat in the royal enclosure of the Ceres National Racetrack, protocol—and his mother—demanded it. He'd filled the enclosure with dignitaries and trustees of a number of the charities he patronised, partly in the hope of diluting his presence, but Dominic had stuck close to him like a bad smell until Amadeo had excused himself on a made-up pretext. Now he'd been hunted down again.

He gripped the top of the barrier. The race was almost over. Only two more laps. 'Very well,' he lied.

'She is a good wife to you?'

'Yes.'

King Pig leaned in closer and dropped his voice. 'My sources tell me she's pregnant.'

Gritting his teeth both at the question and the foulness of Dominic's breath, Amadeo gave a tight nod and received a hearty slap on the back.

'My congratulations. A new Berruti heir. You must be relieved your virility has proved itself. You are hoping for a boy?'

Glad he was wearing shades against the autumn sun, Amadeo kept his tone neutral. 'A healthy child is all I hope for.'

'Sure, sure.' He dropped his voice again. 'That's what we all have to say in this age of equality, eh? I take it the pregnancy means my cousin is to your liking.' His eyebrows waggled leeringly.

'Elsbeth is a credit to your nation.'

'She is a real lady, the jewel of my nation.' He waggled his eyebrows again, his expression somehow managing to become even more lecherous. 'There's something about virgins, isn't there? You can break them in and mould them into what you want them to be.' He leaned in even closer, his mouth practically touching Amadeo's ear to whisper, 'When the baby comes and she can't service you any more, let me know. I can arrange another virgin to warm your bed.'

Something inside him snapped. The malignant, bitter coil suddenly unleashed in a ricochet of disgust and loathing. Turning abruptly to face him, Amadeo looked Dominic up and down with a sneer. 'I've changed my mind. I will race you. Three laps.'

Dominic's piggy eyes gleamed. 'Ah, so you *are* man enough.'

Now Amadeo was the one to lean into the shorter man and savagely whisper, 'Man enough not to abuse virgins for my own pleasure, you sick bastard.'

Even though Dominic's face turned puce, it didn't give even a modicum of satisfaction.

'Three laps. I will see you on the start line in one hour…that's if you can fit in the seat. I'll make sure they have a vat of grease to help you in.'

The first driver crossed the finish line and the crowd

erupted, shouts and cheers ringing so loudly that any retort Dominic might have found would have been drowned out.

Leaving him gawping like an outraged goldfish, Amadeo turned his back on King Pig and, his body-guards making the heaving crowd part for him, found his father and informed him that he would be making the trophy presentation instead. Not explaining himself, he left the enclosure to find Sébastien and demanded the use of his test car. He wouldn't be able to refuse, not when Amadeo owned sixty percent of the team.

He would race Dominic. Race him, beat him and humiliate him. And then he would put all his energy, and all his money if necessary, into bringing this vile monster down.

Elsbeth was planting climbing roses in the garden when Clara came flying out through her patio door, shouting her name.

Abandoning her plants, she hurried over to her. 'What's wrong?'

But the run Clara had made from her quarters to Elsbeth's had winded her and she bent over, gasping, 'Amadeo.'

A prickle of ice nudged at her heart. Trying to swallow it away, Elsbeth rubbed Clara's back. 'What about him?'

She lifted her pale face. 'He's going to race King Pig.'

'Don't do this,' Sébastien begged for the tenth time since he'd finally comprehended that Amadeo was se-rious. Hovering behind him stood Amadeo's father, his stricken face ashen.

But Amadeo was beyond caring. Some things were more important than the monarchy. 'I've told you already, I'm familiar with the car and I know the track like the back of my hand.'

'You've not driven this car on it, or *any* racing car!'

'I've used the simulator.'

'It's not the same thing!'

The test car, which an army of mechanics had been busy doing last-minute safety checks on, was ready. Lowering himself into it, his body wrapped in a spare racing suit, he listened carefully to the chief mechanic's instructions then rammed the helmet on his head.

He switched the engine on and slowly drove it out of the team's garage to the start line.

The news must have spread that the King of Monte Cleure and the heir to the Ceres throne were to race, for the crowd that would usually have dispersed by this point were still in their seats. The television crews had kept their spots too. Let them broadcast it. The more people who witnessed Dominic's humiliation, the better.

Moments later, Dominic appeared from a neighbouring garage in a car with yellow livery, his huge bulk squeezed into a race suit of similar colour.

The red light went on.

Amadeo turned his face to his rival. Even with his helmet on, he could feel Dominic's enmity.

He smiled grimly. King Pig's malevolence had nothing on the revulsion and contempt Amadeo felt for him, an excuse of a man at the forefront of a culture of cruelty, violence and misogyny that had made his wife's life a misery from birth.

Elsbeth's left hand was crushed in Clara's, her right in her mother-in-law's. The eyes of all three were glued to the Queen's television screen before them and the two racing cars, one white, one yellow, waiting side by side for the light to turn green. Marcelo paced the room on his phone, trying to calm Alessia, who was in Madrid with Gabriel.

The light turned green.

Amadeo streaked away, leaving Dominic for dust. Elsbeth knew next to nothing about motor racing but even she could see he was a natural at it, seeming to know when to take it easy and when to put his foot down, reaching speeds so fast her heart accelerated in fright.

She breathed a little easier and imagined the thrills he must be experiencing in this moment, his lifelong dream finally being realised.

What had made him abandon all the rules and protocol about his safety and behaviour to race like this?

'He's bloody amazing,' Marcelo observed in awe as Amadeo finished the first lap fifteen seconds ahead.

All three women nodded without taking their gazes from the screen.

Halfway through the second lap though, and his lead started to slip. The radio communication between Amadeo and the team crackled into life and Amadeo's smooth, irritated voice was broadcast to the world. 'There's something wrong with the accelerator. It's not responding to me.'

Another voice came through but the only words Elsbeth made out were '…pit lane'. The blood was pumping too loudly in her head to hear anything else.

Dominic was fast catching him.

Amadeo moved to the right-hand side of the track as they approached the final bend before the pit lane. Dominic was now right on his tail.

It happened without warning. Right at the bend,

Dominic accelerated past him…but he didn't pass. He swerved and rammed into the side of him.

The noise was ear-piercing.

A cloud of smoke filled the screen, through which a car could be seen flipping in the air and landing vertically, front down, before flopping forwards like a domino.

Elsbeth stared in frozen horror, the shrill yet roaring noise deafening her.

It was only when she felt a tap on her cheek and blinked to find Clara kneeling before her with tears streaming down her face that she realised the deafening sound was her own screams.

There was a banging in Amadeo's head, as if a dozen hammers were smashing into his brain. There was a metallic taste in his mouth too. What the hell had he been drinking? *When* had he been drinking? And why could he smell fire? And where was that whooshing noise coming from?

He tried to lift his head but couldn't move his neck. His legs wouldn't move either.

'Don't move.' The calm voice sounded distant.

He fought to open his eyes. Fought harder. Opened them.

There was pressure on his hand. The voice sounded again. 'Keep still and we'll have you out of here soon. You're going to be fine. Just don't move.'

He tried to focus on the face that the voice and hand belonged to but his vision was blurred. A growing awareness was stealing over him. Not alcohol. An accident.

He couldn't feel his legs.

Fear almost throttled him.

He licked his dry lips and fought for speech. The only word that came was a croaked, 'Elsbeth.'

The world went black.

Amadeo opened his eyes to dazzling bright light.

He must be dead.

He closed his eyes and gave a mental sigh. Strangely, the knowledge he was dead came peacefully to him. Probably because he'd been trained on earth to accept things for the way they were rather than the way he wanted them to be. He hoped the brightness meant that he'd gone up rather than down.

A door opened. He must be in a waiting room.

Soft voices spoke. One of them sounded like Elsbeth.

A fresh wave of peace flooded him. Definitely in a waiting room for heaven. He hoped the angel who sounded like Elsbeth looked like her too. It would be wonderful to see her face one more time. Wonderful to think the angel might move onto the next stage with him as his guide.

There was more peace to know his family would look after her and their baby, but with it sadness to know he would have to wait a long time to meet his child. But maybe up here time moved in a different way than on earth.

The Elsbeth voice spoke again. He slowly turned his face in the direction it came from and opened his eyes again. Joy filled him from his toes to his scalp. The angel sitting beside him looked just like her. Funny though, he'd never thought angels would have blotchy faces from crying.

He cleared his throat. 'How...?'

Angel Elsbeth leaned forwards and placed a gentle finger to his lips. 'Three days. Shh. Try not to speak.

The tube hasn't long been taken out of your throat. You'll be sore.'

Now that she mentioned it, his throat *did* hurt.

It was remarkable how alike angel Elsbeth was to real Elsbeth. Identical. Even the shade of blue and expression in her eyes. A tear rolled down the identical cheek and snaked over the identical plump lips. Those same plump lips formed a tremulous smile. 'I thought I'd lost you.' Her hand was laid on his and squeezed. 'But you're going to be okay. You've a broken leg and a shattered hip, three broken ribs, internal injuries and a bruised brain but the doctors are now confident you're going to make a full recovery.'

Forbidden from speaking, incapable of moving, Amadeo could only gaze intently at the woman he was no longer certain was an angel. Well, not an angel from heaven. If this was the real Elsbeth then she was his angel on earth, and if she was an earth angel then did that mean he wasn't dead after all?

'Dominic's dead.'

He blinked. In his joy of Elsbeth's presence and the pressure of her hand on his, he'd forgotten all about his nemesis.

'They say he died instantly. They put screens around you while they worked to save you.' More tears spilled. 'We didn't know if you were dead or alive for a long time.' She bent over in her chair to lean closer to his face and whisper, 'If you ever do that to me again, I'll kill you myself.'

He turned his hand over in hers and returned the loving pressure.

'I'm not going to let you push me away any more. If you're fearless enough to hurl yourself around a racetrack at over two hundred miles an hour then I can find the courage to fight for us.' The soft, dreamy smile he loved so much curved her cheeks. 'They said that in a moment of consciousness you called my name. You do love me, Amadeo. You love me and I love you, and when we get you out of this place we're going to live together and raise our family together, and every time you try to push me away I will push back, because we belong together and to live without you is to live with a gaping hole in my heart.'

'I'm sorry,' he rasped through his burning throat, using all his strength to squeeze her hand, willing her to believe him.

Her eyes, as soft as her smile, told him she did believe him. Believed him and understood him.

He closed his eyes as the bride who'd walked the aisle towards him all that time ago came into his vision. His heart swelled. Closer she inched, radiating a glow of bliss like the earthly angel she was.

He took his bride's hand and gazed deep into her shining baby blue eyes…

When he next opened his eyes, Elsbeth was curled in her chair asleep, as close to his bed as she could be.

It took three attempts to clear his throat enough to call her name. 'Elsbeth.'

Her eyes snapped open. Met his.

He opened his hand for her. She leaned forward and took it, threading her fingers into his.

He found the strength to raise his other hand and stroke her cheek. 'I love you.' And then his hand dropped and he fell back asleep.

The last of the wounded gap around Elsbeth's heart closed seamlessly, and as she watched the man she loved sleep a dizzying wave of happiness crashed and tumbled through her.

It was a happiness that was to be hers—theirs—for the rest of their lives.

EPILOGUE

AMADEO PUSHED HIS wife's dressing room door open. The hairdresser had plaited Elsbeth's hair and wound it into a coil at the base of her neck and was sliding diamond grips into it.

'Nearly done?' he asked, smiling indulgently at Elsbeth through her reflection at the dressing table mirror. She was still in her silk robe.

'Nearly,' she agreed with an answering smile.

He leaned against the door and watched. To his eyes, his wife needed no beauty tricks but tonight was a state banquet for Elsbeth's cousin, Queen Catalina of Monte Cleure, so all the Berruti women had had their beauty teams dispatched to them.

He still found it strange to remember how this dressing room had once been one of his guest rooms. When he'd been released from hospital and faced months of recovery before he could start undertaking engagements again, he and Elsbeth had sat together with an architect. Within months, their separate quarters had been transformed into a sprawling home with enough bedrooms to fill with half a dozen children. He'd given Elsbeth free rein on the design side. Often he walked through their sunny yellow day room with its bold furniture and quirky artwork and shook his head at the sheer pleasure the sight gave him.

The hairdresser slid another grip into the coil and stepped back. 'That was the last one. Shall I get Jenna for you?'

'I can help the princess into her dress,' Amadeo cut in smoothly. 'Tell Jenna she isn't needed.'

'Yes, sir.'

He waited until they were quite alone before putting his hands on his wife's shoulders.

She arched a brow. 'You're going to help me dress?'

'I'm going to help you undress first,' he murmured, then dropped a kiss into her neck. 'You look beautiful.'

She shivered as she always did when he kissed her there.

He dragged his hands down her arms and slid them over the swelling of her belly and down to her pubis. 'Good enough to eat.'

Her mirrored eyes glowed. 'We haven't got time.' But she did nothing to stop his hands pulling her robe apart and cupping her swollen breasts.

Five years of marriage and still the fever hadn't broken.

He twisted the swivel chair around so she faced him and dropped to his knees.

Dio, she was ravishing. How he loved to see her pregnant. Loved her. Worshipped the ground she walked on.

He took a breast into his mouth.

She moaned softly and clasped the back of his head. 'We'll be late.'

'So we'll be late. The world will still turn.'

'The children?' she whispered.

His attention went to the other breast. 'Gio's still sleeping, Bella's reading stories with the nanny.'

Then he dragged his mouth down lower and she stopped asking questions.

The stateroom was pulsing with life and music. Elsbeth, heavily pregnant and needing a short breather, had managed to find a place to sit unobserved so she could people-watch. She loved state banquets, especially when a party broke out from them, and tonight's was extra special. It filled her with joy to see so many of the people she loved together, and she gazed at her mother talking animatedly with her stepfather with a happy heart. As soon as her cousin Catalina had taken the Monte Cleure throne, she'd repealed all the cruel and misogynistic laws pertaining to the royal family. Days later, Elsbeth's mother, along with two aunts and three female cousins, had applied for divorce.

Rubbing her belly, she scanned the room for her husband and found him deep in conversation with his brother and brother-in-law. Alessia and Clara were on the dance floor with Bella, Elsbeth's four-year-old treasure, and their children of the same age, Alessia's son Diego and Clara's daughter Sophie, plus Clara's middle daughter, three-year-old Anna. The four children, along with everyone watching, were squealing with laughter as the two princesses taught them the funky chicken dance. From the corner of her eye, Elsbeth spotted her father-in-law mimicking their movements too, and giggled.

Amadeo broke away from the other two men and headed over to her, only the slight limp in his gait evidence of the accident that had almost cost him his life.

Her heart swelled, as it always did when he locked eyes with her. How she loved this man, the father of her children, her lover, her best friend.

'You look happy,' he murmured, sliding into the chair next to her and taking hold of her hand.

Leaning into him, she sighed contentedly. 'Happier than I ever dreamed I could be.'

* * * * *

COMING SOON!

We really hope you enjoyed reading this book.
If you're looking for more romance, be sure to
head to the shops when new books are
available on

Thursday 5th January

To see which titles are coming soon, please visit

millsandboon.co.uk/nextmonth

MILLS & BOON®

Coming next month

INNOCENT MAID FOR THE GREEK
Sharon Kendrick

His throat constricted. "Obviously, this changes everything," he said tightly. "I'm not having sex with a virgin," he snapped.

She was shaking her head, the glossy spill of copper curls tumbling down over her shoulders and he wondered if she had any idea how lovely she looked right then.

"I still don't understand," she whispered. "You want sex with me and I definitely want sex with you. A piece of paper says we're legally married – so what's the problem? Please explain it to me."

He chose his words carefully. "The fact that you haven't been intimate with anyone else is significant."

"How?

He shrugged. "It suggests you still care for me and will read too much into it," he continued repressively. "And I really don't want that to happen."

Mia stared back, her heart slamming hard against her ribcage as she took in what he'd just said. "Of all the arrogant things you've ever said to me, Theo Aeton – and there have been plenty of those," she breathed. "That one really tops the lots."

Continue reading
INNOCENT MAID FOR THE GREEK
Sharon Kendrick

Available next month
www.millsandboon.co.uk

MILLS & BOON

THE HEART OF ROMANCE

A ROMANCE FOR EVERY READER

MODERN

Prepare to be swept off your feet by sophisticated, sexy and seductive heroes, in some of the world's most glamourous and romantic locations, where power and passion collide.

HISTORICAL

Escape with historical heroes from time gone by. Whether your passion is for wicked Regency Rakes, muscled Vikings or rugged Highlanders, awaken the romance of the past.

MEDICAL

Set your pulse racing with dedicated, delectable doctors in the high-pressure world of medicine, where emotions run high and passion, comfort and love are the best medicine.

True Love

Celebrate true love with tender stories of heartfelt romance, from the rush of falling in love to the joy a new baby can bring, and a focus on the emotional heart of a relationship.

Desire

Indulge in secrets and scandal, intense drama and plenty of sizzling hot action with powerful and passionate heroes who have it all: wealth, status, good looks…everything but the right woman.

HEROES

Experience all the excitement of a gripping thriller, with an intense romance at its heart. Resourceful, true-to-life women and strong, fearless men face danger and desire - a killer combination!

To see which titles are coming soon, please visit
millsandboon.co.uk/nextmonth